Discover the series you can't put down . . .

'A high level of realism . . . the action scenes come thick and fast. Like the father of the modern thriller, Frederick Forsyth, Mariani has a knack for embedding his plots in the fears and preoccupations of their time'

Shots Magazine

'The plot was thrilling . . . but what is all the more thrilling is the fantastic way Mariani moulds historical events into his story'

Guardian

'Scott Mariani is an ebook powerhouse'

The Bookseller

'Hums with energy and pace . . . If you like your conspiracies twisty, your action bone-jarring, and your heroes impossibly dashing, then look no further. The Ben Hope series is exactly what you need'

Mark Dawson

'Slick, serpentine, sharp, and very, very entertaining. If you've got a pulse, you'll love Scott Mariani; if you haven't, then maybe you crossed Ben Hope'

Simon Toyne

'Hits thrilling, suspenseful notes . . . a rollickingly good way to spend some time in an easy chair'

USA Today

'Mariani constructs the thriller with skill and intelligence, staging some good action scenes, and Hope is an appealing protagonist'
Kirkus Reviews

'If you haven't read any Mariani before but love fast-paced action with a historical reference, maybe this one won't be your last'

LibraryThing

'A breathtaking ride through England and Europe'
Suspense Magazine

'This is my first Scott Mariani book . . . and I totally loved it. It goes on at a good pace, and for me Ben Hope was brilliant, the ultimate decent good guy that you are rooting for'
AlwaysReading.net

'Scott Mariani writes fantastic thrillers. His series of Ben Hope books shows no sign of slowing down'
Ben Peyton, actor (*Bridget Jones's Diary, Band of Brothers, Nine Lives*)

'A really excellent series of books, and would make a wonderful television series as well!'
Breakaway Reviews

'Scott Mariani seamlessly weaves the history and action together. His descriptive passages are highly visual, and no word is superfluous. The storyline flows from beginning to end; I couldn't put it down'
Off the Shelf Books

THE GOLDEN LIBRARY

Scott Mariani is the author of the worldwide-acclaimed action-adventure thriller series featuring ex-SAS hero Ben Hope, which has sold millions of copies in Scott's native UK alone. His books have been described as 'James Bond meets Jason Bourne, with a historical twist'. The first Ben Hope book, *The Alchemist's Secret*, spent six straight weeks at number one on Amazon's Kindle chart, and all the others have been *Sunday Times* bestsellers, most recently with *The Tudor Deception* being an instant number one. Scott was born in Scotland, studied in Oxford and now lives and writes in a remote setting in rural west Wales. You can find out more about Scott and his work on his official website: www.scottmariani.com

By the same author:

Ben Hope series
The Alchemist's Secret
The Mozart Conspiracy
The Doomsday Prophecy
The Heretic's Treasure
The Shadow Project
The Lost Relic
The Sacred Sword
The Armada Legacy
The Nemesis Program
The Forgotten Holocaust
The Martyr's Curse
The Cassandra Sanction
Star of Africa
The Devil's Kingdom
The Babylon Idol
The Bach Manuscript
The Moscow Cipher
The Rebel's Revenge
Valley of Death
House of War
The Pretender's Gold
The Demon Club
The Pandemic Plot
The Crusader's Cross
The Silver Serpent
Graveyard of Empires
The White Knight
The Tudor Deception

To find out more visit **www.scottmariani.com**

SCOTT MARIANI

THE
GOLDEN
LIBRARY

Harper
North

HarperNorth
Windmill Green
24 Mount Street
Manchester M2 3NX

A division of
HarperCollins*Publishers*
1 London Bridge Street
London SE1 9GF

www.harpercollins.co.uk

HarperCollins*Publishers*
Macken House, 39/40 Mayor Street Upper
Dublin 1, D01 C9W8, Ireland

First published by HarperNorth in 2024

3 5 7 9 10 8 6 4 2

ISBN: 978-0-00-860115-7
Printed and bound in the UK using 100% renewable electricity at
CPI Group (UK) Ltd, Croydon

This novel is entirely a work of fiction.
The names, characters and incidents portrayed in it are the work
of the author's imagination. Any resemblance to actual persons,
living or dead, events or localities is entirely coincidental.

MIX
Paper | Supporting
responsible forestry
FSC
www.fsc.org
FSC™ C007454

This book contains FSC™ certified paper and other controlled
sources to ensure responsible forest management.

For more information visit: www.harpercollins.co.uk/green

For Susan

'A state that uses the good to rule the wicked
will always suffer from disorder...

A state that uses the wicked to rule the good
will always enjoy order.'

From The Book of Lord Shang, *early
3rd century BC*

PROLOGUE

Imperial China
217 BC

Of all the fabulous wealth and splendour of the emperor's domains, there were few more magnificent places to work. To be called upon to do so should have been the most exalted duty, the highest honour. And yet, these men who spent their every hour of every day in these grand surroundings, their entire lives engaged in this task so dear to the heart of their Divine Ruler the god-king of Qin, were little more than slaves.

At this time the great library housed over forty Confucian scholars, though their numbers often fluctuated as the older ones died of illness, exhaustion or other less natural causes, and new recruits were pressed into service to replace them. Yen Wan-sun with his long white beard was over eighty and had worked here for several years now, almost from the time when the library had first been created. The much younger man working at his side that day was one of those recent arrivals, a seventeen-year-old novice by the name of Liu Hsuan. Both wore the plain robes of their lowly station and neither spoke, conversation being forbidden, as they sat at the long table under the flicker of the lanterns with their heads bowed over their work.

Some men went blind as a result of their duty, eyes worn out by the sheer amount of time spent reading and studying in the dim light. For those who could endure it, their daily task was a constant grind of repetition. Hour after hour, day after day of intensely poring over the endless trove of parchments and manuscripts, many of them dating back to the most ancient eras of their country's history, long, long before the great kingdom had become an empire under its current all-powerful ruler. Somewhere among this vast collection of philosophical and scientific knowledge amassed over so many generations was the mysterious secret that their emperor so craved to learn. The search for that hitherto elusive gem of wisdom was the scholars' one and only goal, to which the library itself owed its very being. And as driven as they were to find it, there wasn't a man among them who didn't dread the day when their task was accomplished at last and their usefulness to the emperor was at an end. Nobody on the outside knew about this place, which was kept hidden from the eyes of the world. Those few men whose duty had obliged them to become aware of its existence would, once obsolete, certainly be eliminated in order to ensure things stayed that way.

Certainly little better than slaves, if at all. None of them would ever be permitted to leave here. Their living quarters were harsh and uncomfortable, far below ground beneath the great gilded subterranean chamber in which they worked. Rest and sleep were luxuries kept to a bare minimum and their diet of rice and thin vegetable gruel was barely enough to subsist on. In general, though, the scholars could at least console themselves that for all its hardship their lot was far preferable to that of the countless poor serfs who lived out their short, worthless and miserable lives labouring in the mines and in the fields, treated worse than animals by their brutal masters.

Except that now and then, they were given a reminder of their emperor's limitless power over them. Today was going to be one of those days. The scholars had been silently absorbed in their work for many hours when the library doors swung unexpectedly open and a unit of imperial guards entered. Yen Wan-sun and the young novice exchanged anxious looks, knowing this couldn't be good news.

It wasn't. The guards came marching through the library and picked out a dozen of the scholars at random. They were told to stop what they were doing and made to file out into the high, broad stone passage beyond the doors, where more armed guards were gathered with horses and a wagon with iron bars like a cage. Yen Wan-sun and Liu Hsuan, among the chosen, found themselves being herded like cattle into the rolling cage. 'Where are we being taken?' Yen Wan-sun dared to ask one of the guards. Because he was so old and frail-looking, his questioning was tolerated without the usual severe reprimand. 'Before his Divine Majesty the Emperor,' the guard replied.

As the military convoy set off on its long journey the library workers were all convinced they were being taken away to their deaths. It had happened before, when the emperor became frustrated by previous teams of scholars' lack of progress in finding the secret. It was said that the last contingent who had failed to satisfy his demands had been thrown into a pit and buried under tons of hot coals.

For the rest of that day and into the next, the convoy made its way through the lantern-lit tunnels, just part of the vast subterranean network that the emperor had had constructed to connect all two hundred of his palaces. His Divine Excellency never travelled above ground, as this made him vulnerable to evil spirits that might prey on him for his greatness.

Then at last the convoy reached the great palace where the terrified scholars were to learn their fate. They were used to the splendour of the library, but the even greater opulence of their unfamiliar new surroundings made them gape as they were released from the cage and marched through corridor after corridor, each more wondrous than the last, until they arrived at the throne room that was the most breathtaking of all. And there he sat surrounded by his courtiers, high on his golden perch, clad in all the magnificence to be expected of the greatest ruler in the universe. Yen Wan-sun had expected him to be taller and more impressive, somehow.

The scholars were made to grovel before him. After a long silence the emperor addressed them, in a voice that was high and reedy and quivering with rage.

'Where is the knowledge with whose discovery you were tasked? Why has it not yet been brought to me? You there. Stand up and reply to your Emperor.'

It was old Yen Wan-sun who had been chosen to speak on the scholars' behalf. Bowing his head in humble deference he said, 'Your Divine Excellency, we are still searching for it. The undertaking is so great, our numbers so few—'

'Silence!' barked the emperor. 'You are lazy and worthless. And such failure will be met with the appropriate chastisement.'

The hearts of the scholars went cold and they trembled with fear at his words, but nobody dared to make a sound. Nothing could change their fate now. Next the guards seized them and marched them to the windowless stone tower where the sentence was to be carried out. Once they had been stripped naked of their robes and bound up in chains the emperor appeared again, come to enjoy the spectacle.

'Let the punishments begin,' he announced with a smile.

Then one by one, to the thundering beat of drums that only partly drowned out their screams, the scholars met their grisly end. Some were blinded with hot irons before being disembowelled. Others were flayed alive and their raw flesh doused with salt until those who hadn't died of shock and agony were beheaded. Some, including the poor young man Liu Hsuan, suffered the slow and deliberate amputation of all four limbs, along with ears and noses sliced off, tongues removed, eyes put out.

Yen Wan-sun was the last in the line. He was on his knees, broken and weeping at the terrible scene he'd been made to witness, and now knowing he couldn't live with the memory of such inhuman suffering he closed his eyes and prayed for death. The image of his young friend Liu Hsuan being dragged away screaming in terror by the ankles, soon to join the heap of mutilated bodies whose combined blood pooled an inch deep on the floor, was more than he could stand.

But as the guards stepped towards Yen Wan-sun with their bloodied torture implements ready, the emperor signalled for them to halt.

'I have decided to let this one live,' he announced. 'If he has survived to such an age, then it is to be presumed he must be the wisest among them, and therefore worth preserving as an example to his peers. Now, old man, you will return to the library and let the others understand that what you have seen happen here today is nothing compared to the pain I will inflict on the rest of you if you continue to fail in your task. Do you understand?'

Unable to speak, tears pouring from his eyes, Yen Wan-sun only nodded.

'Good. Now get back to work.'

Chapter 1

It was nearly three a.m. and the team had been at it nonstop since their hurried dinner of steamed chicken and rice that evening. The night was warm and sticky and the air conditioning was working full blast to cool the interior of the building.

The large room in which Dan Chen and his four colleagues were feverishly trying to complete their work task was in a part of the museum complex not accessible to the public. Exhausted, the others – Mei, the only female of the group, Hao, Bai and Zimo – had finally taken a break from their long hours of hard work for a well-earned cup of tea, leaving their team leader Dan on his own. But he didn't feel alone in there, surrounded by a crowd of tall warriors so lifelike and well preserved despite their considerable age that he half expected them to start moving about and talking to him at any moment.

The complex's official name was The Museum of Qin Terracotta Warriors and Horses, and it was situated a short drive from the Mausoleum of the first ruler of imperial China, Qin Shi Huang, near the city of Xi'an. Its primary attraction, drawing countless visitors each year from China and the rest of the world, was the famous terracotta army itself. Discovered in the mid-1970s, it had been without a doubt the single most significant archaeological find of the twentieth century, anywhere in the world. Like so many astounding discoveries, it had come about purely by chance: some peasant farmers had been digging a well in a remote spot some miles east of the ancient Qin capital of Xianyang, near modern Xi'an in China's Shaanxi Province, when they came across a vast underground vault. Putting down their tools to explore, to their amazement they realised that they'd uncovered a buried vault containing a treasure nobody could have imagined: an entire army of terracotta statues – thousands of them – that had been hidden since the reign of China's first emperor more than two millennia ago. Each of these fired-clay warrior figures stood more than six feet tall, and all bore individual features as though they'd been modelled after living men. The vast majority remained incredibly well preserved after all these centuries, their only real sign of age the fading of the colours in which they had once been vividly painted to make them even more lifelike.

That initial discovery had been only the beginning. Archaeologists excavating the site had soon uncovered an extensive and elaborate tomb complex, a vast necropolis that the emperor had started building for himself the moment he'd taken power at the age of only thirteen. More and more terracotta figures were uncovered, until the army grew to seven thousand strong with many others believed to be still buried. Among their massed ranks were infantrymen, archers, cavalrymen mounted on horses, charioteers, and even musicians and an entire circus troupe whose purpose, it was believed, was to entertain the emperor in the afterlife.

Today the stunning display was contained in three sections designated Number One Pit, Number Two Pit and Number Three Pit, over which had been built a vast domed roof to protect them from the elements. The first section was the largest, but the second still contained over a thousand warriors and horses. It remained to be seen how many more would eventually be unearthed, but even as it stood it was a spectacular sight. On a normal day the museum complex attracted busloads of people to stare in wonder at the sheer awe-inspiring enormity of the display. For the last week, however, the place had been closed to the public while Dan and his team carried out their special task, sanctioned by government authority.

Since its discovery the terracotta army, or small samples of it, had been exhibited in many countries around the world where it had drawn enormous crowds of people. More recently, China's rulers had agreed to lend an unprecedented seventy-five figures of warriors and horses to be shown in the British Museum in London, the largest ever exhibition of the army outside China. Needless to say, the task of safely transporting such a large collection of priceless artefacts represented a huge logistical challenge. But it was one that Dan Chen was proud to undertake. At the age of only twenty-nine it was a great honour for him to have been put in charge of the team of expert conservationists whose job was to separately pack each and every item in its transit crate ready for their long journey.

And so, they'd got to work. The seventy-five pieces selected to represent the glory of the terracotta army had been removed to this private part of the museum complex, which Dan and his team called the packing room, for final inspection before they were crated. Like the vast majority of public spaces and working environments in urban China the room was heavily monitored by security cameras, under whose unblinking gaze the team had been working virtually nonstop to meet their deadline. The items must be ready to ship by late morning tomorrow, or there would be hell to pay.

Everything had been going smoothly enough until the final pre-packing inspection had revealed what looked to Dan's well-trained eye like an old repair to one of the warrior statues, leaving no more than a hairline crack that was barely visible. It seemed that, at some point in his ancient history, the warrior must have lost his head and had it carefully replaced. Fired-clay statues like these were hollow inside, due to the method of their manufacture, and notoriously prone to breakage. The conservation team were all agreed that the expert repair, barely visible, had likely been carried out by the same highly skilled artisans who'd created the clay figures back in around 200 BC. But its discovery had raised concerns over the possible risk of damage if this particular warrior should be moved.

'I say we play it safe and pick another to take his place,' had suggested Mei, Dan's female colleague. 'It's not as if we don't have plenty to choose from, after all.'

But Dan hadn't been so sure. Part of his job was to put together the most impressive possible collection of items to represent their country to the outside world, an international public relations exercise that the authorities took very seriously. This particular warrior had been chosen for his splendid looks and presence. If Dan chose to replace him now, at the eleventh hour, would the senior officials of the Ministry of Culture be displeased? In China, everything depended on gaining the approval of one's superiors. Dan was afraid that by making the wrong decision he might cause irreparable harm to his career.

The team's long debate over the matter was one of the reasons they'd had to work so late that night. And it was still far from settled. Dan was anxiously pondering the dilemma as the others wearily trudged off to the staff canteen for their much-needed cup of refreshing green tea.

'I don't know what's best for you, my friend,' he said to the warrior when they were alone. 'You tell me, are you in a fit state to travel, or should you stay at home?'

The terracotta warrior said nothing.

'What's the matter, can't you talk?' Dan joked. 'Then give me a sign.'

Almost the instant he said it, he felt the stone tiles give a judder under his feet. He barely had time to wonder what the hell was happening before the main shock of the earthquake hit. To a deep rumbling that shook the entire building and the ground beneath it, the floor tilted several degrees and threw Dan off balance. As he went sprawling to the floor the power lines were taken out and the room went black.

Dan felt a sharp pain as his brow connected with the hard floor tiles. Suppressing a cry of terror he huddled into a ball in the pitch darkness, covering his head with his arms. All around him he could feel the walls of the complex shaking violently. His whole body seemed to tremble with the vibrations and the deep rumble that sounded like a thousand thunderstorms resonating all around him. Every split second felt like drawn-out minutes. Dan was convinced that he was about to die – but even at a time like his, his greatest fear was for the safety of his precious terracotta warriors. Could the quake be severe enough to bring the building down on their heads, destroying them all? What about the structural integrity of the enormous domed steel-girder roof covering the rest of the exhibit? If that were to collapse . . . the damage would be beyond catastrophic.

Then, as suddenly as they'd begun, the tremors subsided, the rumbling stopped and the earthquake was over. He wasn't dead. It seemed that total devastation had been abated. Or had it?

Dan clambered to his knees. He could feel a cool wetness where the blood was leaking from his cut brow. He coughed from the dust and blinked his eyes, trying to adjust his vision to the darkness but at the same time terrified of what he might see. The hum of the air conditioning had stopped, and in the silence he could hear the eerie groans of the damaged building, the patter of plaster dust sprinkling from the ceiling – and the muffled voices of his colleagues yelling his name from outside in the corridor.

'Dan! Dan! We're all right! What about you? What happened?' They were thumping on the door, trying to force it open. Dan realised that it must have become jammed shut by the distortion of the walls and ceiling.

'I'm okay!' he yelled back, or tried to, but his throat was full of dust and all that came out was a croak nobody could have heard through the door. He was glad his colleagues were okay – but for how long would any of them stay that way? An aftershock could be worse than the first. The whole building, including the five floors above this one, could still come crashing down around them and bury anyone still inside under hundreds of tons of rubble.

Even so, at this moment Dan's own survival was the least of his concerns. Remembering his phone in his pocket, he dug it out and staggered to his feet on the strangely tilted floor, fumbling for the button to activate the device's inbuilt LED flashlight.

Dan was momentarily dazzled by the strong white light. He shone the torch around him, fearing the worst. And seeing it.

'Oh, no!' he croaked. 'No! NO!!'

Thump, thump, thump at the door. Mei's voice, sounding frightened. 'Dan! What's happening? Open the door! We have to evacuate the building!'

But Dan was too transfixed by the horror of the sight in front of him to reply. It would be several hours before he thanked his stars most of the terracotta statues had escaped being damaged.

All he could see right now was the figure of the magnificent warrior that had toppled over in the tremor, falling against the horse next to it. It was the same statue they'd been discussing just moments earlier, the one with the ancient repair that they'd feared might not withstand the stresses of travelling.

Now they'd never know, as the earthquake had got there first. The now headless warrior lay at an angle against the overturned horse that had broken his fall. The trembling light of Dan's phone torch picked out shards of smashed clay among the dust. The warrior's disembodied head had rolled away across the tilted floor and vanished in the shadows. With a gasp of despair Dan stumbled over to the fallen statue and tried to heave it upright, but it was too heavy to move on his own. When he strained with all his might to shift it, it only rolled off the horse and crashed horizontally to the floor, almost trapping his hand underneath.

The urgent hammering on the door continued. 'Dan! Dan!'

Dan no longer even registered his colleagues' frightened calls. Because at that moment he saw the thing that was about to change his life.

Where the warrior's head had been attached to his shoulders, now there was only a gaping empty neck socket, a round hole through which the bright LED of Dan's phone illuminated the inside of the warrior's hollow torso.

Hollow, but not empty. There was something inside. Something so strange and unexpected that Dan thought at first he was experiencing a hallucination.

Thump. Thump. 'Dan! Talk to us! Are you hurt?'

His fingers trembled as he reached his hand through the hole. The object felt smooth and cool to the touch. It didn't weigh much, just a few ounces. He drew it out and laid it on the floor because he was shaking so badly from shock and amazement that he was afraid he might drop it. He knelt there gently rocking in disbelief, examining the object under his light.

The thing that had been hidden inside the warrior's body was a slender, smooth cylinder, about three inches in diameter and about eight inches in length. It was made of some hard black material like ebony, lacquered to a gleaming mirror finish and ornamented with inlays of gold, pearl and jade, whose beauty and intricacy took Dan's breath away. He knew that it had to be at least as old as the soldiers themselves. In its own way, every bit as wondrous – and even more mystifying. Who could have hidden the cylinder inside the warrior statue? Why? Was this the reason for the ancient repair to the warrior's neck: because the head had once upon a time been deliberately removed to access the hollow space within?

With all these unanswerable questions swirling through his mind, Dan noticed that one end of the cylinder was capped with a lid. He wanted to run to the door and let his worried colleagues know that he was okay. Wanted to join them as they hurried out of the building to safety before anything worse happened. But he was so mesmerised by what he'd found that he couldn't resist finding out what might be inside. He grasped the smooth, cool cylinder with both hands, gently twisted, and with not much effort the end cap came away to reveal the mouth of the tube.

Dan could scarcely believe what was happening to him. This was how those peasant farmers must have felt when they discovered the underground vault containing the terracotta army.

He couldn't stop now. He had to know more. Holding the end of the tube towards the light he oh, so carefully inserted his fingers and felt around inside. Something was in there, something rolled up. A paper parchment of some kind? No, if his guess was right that the cylinder dated back to the time the statues were built, it couldn't be paper because that hadn't been invented until centuries later, during the Han Dynasty in 105 AD. Dan gently eased the scroll from the tube and realised what it was. A roll of silk, inked with ancient Chinese characters as vivid and sharp as the day the scribe had penned them more than two thousand years ago.

'Dan! Dan! Please open this door! We have to get out of here! Can you hear me, Dan?' This time it was Zimo's voice, hoarse with fear and anxiety. Zimo was a big, powerful guy and now he was hammering harder at the door, throwing his weight against it to try to crash it open.

Still Dan couldn't bring himself to respond. Hands shaking, heart thudding with the fear that it might disintegrate under his fingers, he unrolled more of the silk parchment. There was more marked on it than just characters. It was a map of some kind. And as he peered more closely he realised with a shock just exactly what it was.

The answer to a mystery so ancient that people had long ago given up even trying to solve it. It was a legend, almost a fable. And here he was, Dan Chen, eyes boggling as he held it right under his nose. Could it be true? Was he dreaming? No, he wasn't. This was real.

He knew he had to make a decision, and fast. Any moment now Zimo and the others would come bursting through that door. Dan would have to show his colleagues what he'd found. Then the Ministry of Culture officials would need to be notified, according to the protocol. Knowing the deeper significance of his discovery, Dan couldn't allow the silk parchment to fall into the hands of the authorities. It must be kept secret from them.

Dan had his particular reasons for making such a choice. It was a terrible risk, but what must be done must be done. He quickly replaced the roll inside the tube, pushed the end cap

14

back on and shoved the cylinder into the only place he could think of to hide it, down the back of his trousers so that it pressed against the hollow of his spine and was covered by his shirt. He scrambled to his feet and staggered towards the door, finding his voice and yelling, 'Hold on! I'm coming!' Just as the door finally crashed open with such force that Zimo and the others almost fell into the room. Dan blinked as their phone lights shone in his face.

'Where were you? We were so worried!'

'I . . . hit my head,' he muttered, pointing at the bleeding cut on his brow. 'Must have been knocked out for a moment. I'm all right.'

'Thank heaven,' Mei said urgently, grasping his arm. 'Come on, let's get out of here!'

'The statues . . .' protested Dan.

'Never mind the damn statues, boss. Hurry! This whole place is liable to come down on our heads!'

As he ran with his colleagues through the blacked-out corridors towards the exit, nobody noticed what Dan was hiding under his shirt.

None of them could have dreamed what he'd found. And none of them could have the faintest idea of his real motivation for wanting to preserve its ancient secret.

Chapter 2

The dawn had been and gone by the time Dan finally got home, having first been dragged to the hospital at Mei's insistence to be checked for signs of concussion. The museum complex had long since been taken over by a horde of emergency services personnel who secured the valuable exhibits and sealed off the damaged building pending a major structural safety survey. Whatever the investigators determined, the place would surely be closed for the foreseeable future as the extensive repairs got underway. There had been no aftershocks to the quake, but that single tremor had peaked at almost 5.8 on the Richter scale and many buildings in the surrounding area had come off a lot worse. Thankfully, there had been no fatalities.

The medical staff at the Shaanxi Lintong Kangfu Hospital put a couple of stitches into Dan's cut brow, gave him an otherwise clean bill of health, told him how lucky he'd been and sent him on his way. Meanwhile the precious scroll tube and its mind-blowing contents were hidden under the passenger seat of Mei's little BYD electric hatchback in the hospital car park, where he'd managed to slip it without her noticing. The whole time he was waiting to be seen to he was nervous and jumpy, and Mei kept asking him if he was okay. He insisted he was fine, but in reality he was tormented by the thought of someone stealing Mei's car with the precious scroll tube inside. While the crime rate was generally low in Chinese cities because of the heavy-handed justice system, vehicle theft was rife.

He needn't have worried. When they came out of the hospital Mei's car was still where she'd left it, untouched. She drove him back to his apartment building, asking him for the thousandth time if he was okay. Mei had always been a mother hen to him, even though she was only five years older.

As she pulled up at the kerb outside his building he went to retrieve the scroll tube from its hiding place beneath her passenger seat. His plan was to get it out the same way he'd slyly managed to slip it under there, using his jacket bundled on his knees to hide his movements from her. But as he reached down to retrieve the tube he found to his horror that it had rolled further under the seat and he had to bend right down to get at it, which he couldn't do without drawing her attention.

'What's up?' she asked, frowning as he struggled bent over double in his seat.

'Damn it, my wallet and my pens must have fallen out of my jacket pocket,' he said self-consciously and overacting the part horribly. His reaching fingers found the end of the tube and he managed to pull it towards him and cover it with his jacket. 'Got them. No worries.' From the strange look she was giving him, he could tell his little deception wasn't too convincing.

'Anyway, you take it easy and I'll see you soon,' Mei said. 'Take care, Dan.'

'You too,' he replied, grinning sheepishly. 'Thanks for looking after me.'

When he reached the relative privacy of his apartment on the thirteenth floor, Dan was so utterly spent that he could barely stay on his feet. But as desperately as he craved a warm shower and a soft bed, he had far more important matters to attend to. In his tiny living room he closed the drapes out of paranoia that someone could be spying on him, then reopened the scroll tube and once again carefully unrolled the silk manuscript on a coffee table to examine it more closely. If there'd been even the tiniest twinge of a doubt in his mind before about what this was, it was gone now. He could quite literally not believe his good fortune. It was such an incredible coincidence that the artefact could have fallen into his hands the way it did, that to Dan it felt like more than just serendipity. It had to be some kind of miracle. As though he'd been chosen, not just by the government authorities to be in charge of the team, but by some higher power to be there at that precise moment when the precious scroll was revealed from its hiding place. As though he'd been *meant* to be there. As though the earthquake had been *meant* to happen. Dan didn't consider himself a religious person per se, but he held deep spiritual beliefs that he kept to himself.

What none of his work colleagues or superiors, not even his parents or his girlfriend knew – indeed what only a tiny number of people were aware of – was that he belonged to an organisation, more a creed than a faith, that existed in almost total secret. Its reasons for doing so were born out of necessity, due to the fact that its adherents and their beliefs were cruelly and unjustly victimised by the Chinese government. Though Dan and his ilk had done nothing wrong, were deeply pacifist by nature and asked only for the freedom to quietly pursue their harmless practices unmolested, for the last twenty years or more the authorities had been committed to a relentless campaign of persecution. Many thousands of them had been imprisoned, and many had died. Murdered by the state.

And worse.

And the reason why Dan was so awed by what had just happened to him was that the silk scroll he'd found just so happened to have a particular significance to the followers of his spiritual creed. More than that, it was of prime importance to them. There was no way he'd have taken such a risk otherwise. To be caught stealing such a priceless historical relic would not only be the end of his promising career but, once the authorities had prised the truth out of him, would likely result in his spending the rest of his days in the most appalling conditions and suffering the same awful fate as so many others.

When you were labelled an enemy of the state you were compelled to behave like one, like it or not. The organisation operated like an underground network and they were very careful about contacting one another in such a heavily surveilled society as China. Communicating via social media was out of the question, because the eyes of the authorities' spies were everywhere. Phone calls were frequently monitored, and thanks to ubiquitous cameras and facial recognition technology even personal meetings could invite the risk of arrest and imprisonment. The government went so far as to employ members of the public to act as informants, whose job was to walk the streets on the lookout for anything suspicious.

But with a little ingenuity it was still possible to stay in touch with one's fellow members. Dan had a secret cellphone that wasn't registered to him personally and on which he could make limited calls without too much risk of getting caught. The phone was kept hidden under the floorboards beneath his bed, and he dug it out now and tapped in the number of one of his clandestine contacts.

'It's me,' he whispered. As a precaution, no names could be mentioned on the phone. 'Something's come up. Something incredibly important that I must show you. I can't say more, but you'll be amazed. We have to meet.'

'Damn. Sorry. I'm at a conference in Beijing for most of this week,' his contact told him, sotto voce. 'No way I can get away any sooner. The earliest I can make it would be Friday evening.'

That was a whole three days from now. Dan tried to mask the disappointment in his voice. 'The usual place?'

'I'll be there,' his contact said.

Dan ended the call and replaced his illegal phone in its hiding place, along with the scroll tube. Then he covered them over with the piece of floorboard, pulled the rug back and the bed on top. He took a deep breath. He was totally committed now, come what may.

Shaky and far too agitated to get any sleep, he walked into the kitchen and visited the fridge for something to eat, only to find it all but empty, bar a half carton of milk that had turned into lumps. The joys of living like a bachelor. Dan's girlfriend had her own place a few miles outside the city, and they hadn't been together long enough for him to develop much of an instinct for domesticity. Feeling suddenly ravenous, he decided to go out and do some grocery shopping.

His local store was just a five-minute walk away down the street. He filled a basket with a few simple and inexpensive items, queued quietly at the checkout without making eye contact or speaking to anyone, paid for his groceries by contact-less digital transaction like most Chinese citizens did nowadays, and stepped back out into the street with his plastic shopping bag.

Returning towards his building he noticed that the short, balding man in the black jacket who'd been standing behind him in the queue had emerged from the store and was following along behind him, keeping pace about twenty metres back. There should have been nothing unusual about that, but something about it felt strangely unsettling to Dan. He could sense the man's gaze on him, and it gave him the creeps. He quickened his step a little, and a discreet glance at a reflective window across the street told him that the man had quickened his too.

Dan walked faster still. Rather than head straight back home he took a detour in the opposite direction from where his building was. The man followed. Then Dan tried another trick, which was to pause outside a shop and pretend to be interested in the window display. Twenty metres away, the man halted and appeared to be checking something on his phone.

No question about it. Dan knew he was being followed, and the realisation sent a chill down his spine. But by whom, and why? He was suddenly gripped by the terrifying thought that it must have something to do with his discovery. Was it possible the authorities were already onto him? Had the security cameras inside the museum complex been working after all, and managed to spy on him stealing the scroll tube even after the power had gone down and the lights were out? Maybe using some kind of infra-red system with an independent power source? In that case, had the higher-ups in the Ministry of Culture already been informed of his crime?

If so, he was in awful trouble. Visions of steel bars, of dungeons and grisly torture chambers and men in masks and overalls, crowded his thoughts.

Dan had started walking so fast that he was almost running. His plastic shopping bag ruptured and canned vegetables and packets of dried noodles spilled onto the pavement, but he didn't stop to retrieve them. Only when he'd hurried on another three hundred metres did he dare to slow down and look back.

The man was gone.

Had Dan imagined it? He didn't think so. Now they knew he was onto the short balding man, they'd simply pull him off Dan's tail and send another of their agents in his place. They knew where he lived. They'd be watching him. When the moment was right they could pick him like an apple off a tree and he'd be made to disappear.

If that was the case, then Dan's own fate was sealed. So be it. But as horrifying as that thought might be, making his heart thump and his mouth go dry, his own fate had to matter less than that of the precious scroll.

What could he do? Dan racked his brain. One option was to pass the scroll to his secret associate. But that rendezvous wasn't until Friday, and he couldn't afford to wait that long in case they came for him sooner.

Then a thought came to him. Tomorrow, Wednesday, he was due to meet up with his girlfriend. What if there was some way he could pass it to her?

The subject of Dan's affections wasn't Chinese. Her name was Lara Hartmann and she was a twenty-three-year-old student at Zurich University, taking a year off in the middle of her degree course in Chinese Philosophy to immerse herself in the country's culture and learn the language. She and Dan had met quite by chance at a nightclub two months ago. Lara had been there with her flatmate Olivia, and Dan had allowed himself to be corralled into the night out by his work colleague, Hao. Neither of them was much into the nightclub scene, and when she'd suggested getting out of there he'd been eager to agree. The relationship had developed fairly quickly after that, although because of Dan's intense work schedule they weren't able to get together as often as either would have liked. On Wednesday afternoons she always had lectures at the college, and would catch the bus into the city from the village where she lived. After her lecture they would sometimes meet in a park near the college – assuming he was able to get off work a little early – and would spend a blissful evening together.

Nobody knew about Lara. The authorities couldn't connect her to him. If he could meet up with her tomorrow without being followed . . .

And so, that was what Dan did. His first action was to re-contact his secret associate, tell him there'd been a change in his circumstances and that he couldn't make their rendezvous after all. Next day, with his work now suspended in the aftermath of the earthquake, he stayed hidden inside his apartment all morning and early afternoon.

At 3.30 p.m. he sneaked from the building wearing a hoodie and one of the anti-pollution air filter masks that many Chinese city dwellers used to protect against the smog, though it was virtually nonexistent in Xi'an compared to the likes of Beijing. Hoping that his disguise would be enough to foil the watchers he boarded a bus and crossed the city. Hidden inside the hoodie's pocket was the ebony scroll tube, carefully wrapped in paper and packing tape.

As far as he could tell, nobody was shadowing him – but just to be safe he changed buses three times and took an auto rickshaw taxi the rest of the way to the park.

Lara was sitting on their usual bench in an avenue of trees and didn't notice Dan approaching, partly because she was so deeply immersed in one of her Chinese language study books and also partly because he was still wearing the air mask and had his hoodie pulled up over his head. She looked beautiful. His heart ached for what he was about to do.

He glanced nervously around him, walked quickly up to her and sat down on the far end of the bench, leaving a gap between them. Only then did she notice him, and turned to look at him in surprise and confusion.

'Dan? Why are you—?' English was a second language to her, but it was the one they spoke in together because her Chinese wasn't yet fluent.

'Don't talk to me,' he muttered, staring down at his feet. 'Don't look at me. Act like you don't know me.'

She stared at him as though he'd lost his mind. 'What?'

'Shhh. I'm serious. I'll explain later, okay? Just do what I say. They mustn't see us together.'

'Who mustn't see us? What are you on about? You're scaring me.'

Dan glanced up and down the pretty aisle of trees. It was a busy little park. Crowds of people were coming and going, enjoying the sunshine. In a nearby grassy area a group of Tai Chi practitioners were going through their slow-motion movements. He couldn't see any sign of the sinister man who'd followed him yesterday, or anyone else who might be a government agent. But who knew?

He quickly, discreetly slipped the paper-wrapped tube out of his pocket and laid it down on the park bench between them. Attached to the parcel was a sealed note he'd written her, in which he'd tried to explain his reasons for what he'd done. He'd agonised for hours over what to say, all the things he wanted to explain to her now but couldn't, for fear of being seen together. She had to understand how crucially important this was, not only to him but to a great many other people. And she needed to know just how dangerous that information could be, if it fell into the wrong hands.

Dan was racked with guilt at the thought of placing such a burden of responsibility on her. But what choice did he have? Until he could make contact with his fellow members again, she was the only one he could trust.

'What's that?' she asked.

'Take it. Keep it safe. Don't let anyone else know you have it.'

'Dan? What the heck—?'

'The letter will explain. Read it, and then burn it. Please, Lara, you have to trust me.'

'But—'

'I'll call you,' he said tersely. Then he stood up and hurried away. Before Lara could make a move to go after him he'd slipped off into the crowds of passersby, leaving her sitting there alone and frightened.

Then he was gone. And neither she, nor anyone else who knew him, would ever see Dan Chen alive again.

Chapter 3

Switzerland
Two days later

It felt like déjà vu, except this time it looked as if he'd actually make it.

Speeding along the twisting Alpine roads at the wheel of a fast car, a clear blue sky above him and a breathtaking vista of sparkling lakes and towering snow-capped mountains and green forests all around him, puffing on a Gauloise and listening to hard-driving modern jazz pumping through his stereo system, Ben Hope was reflecting on his last attempt to visit his sole surviving relative.

On that occasion, he'd got within two hours' drive of his destination before being called away to deal with yet another crisis. It seemed to be his fate always to have to put his own life on hold in order to rescue others. But this time around, on this glorious sunny summer's day, he'd managed to make the long drive from his base in rural Normandy, a place called Le Val from which he'd departed at the crack of dawn that morning, cutting diagonally eastwards all across France and through the mountain passes into Switzerland. No emergency calls had come through to divert him from his objective. No forced U-turns, no urgent cries for help, nobody finding themselves in sudden dire need of the skills and expertise he'd acquired in the course of his Special Forces career and his years of freelance operation since quitting the military. For once he was being left alone to do exactly what he wanted.

It was the strangest feeling, as though he was getting away with something.

And long may it last, he thought, with just a passing twinge of guilt for wanting to do his own thing for a change. Was he being selfish? Maybe a little, he admitted to himself, but then again he had good reason to be. Because this was a special occasion like no other, and he intended to honour it. After all, it wasn't every day that his little sister, who was especially dear to him and whom he'd thought he'd lost for many years, was celebrating her engagement to the man she planned on spending the rest of her life with.

Ben was no kind of a party animal, and though he was far from being antisocial or reclusive he generally preferred his own company and the solitude of nature's wide open spaces. Yet he was looking forward to the event, which promised to be a lavish affair attended by hundreds of guests. This would also be his first meeting with Ruth's new fiancé, a Swiss architect by the name of Stefan Hartmann.

He kept wondering what kind of guy this Stefan was. One worthy of his sister, hopefully. Someone who would step up to the mark and give her the undivided dedication and devotion she deserved. If it should happen to turn out otherwise, Stefan would have some serious problems to deal with when big brother came to kick his arse so hard he'd be wearing it as a hat.

Ben put that ugly thought away, knowing he was at risk of being unreasonably judgemental and overprotective. Showing his toxic masculinity, no doubt, the anachronistic product of a patriarchal society. That was how the snowflakes would have put it, according to his friend Jeff Dekker, who was an authority on these things and a pre-eminent critic of the modern age of 'woke'. In any case, if this guy Stefan was good enough for Ruth, then he was damn well good enough for Ben too. Ben decided he was going to like Herr Hartmann, instinctive brotherly protectiveness notwithstanding.

Being in good time and tired of travelling on an empty stomach, he stopped at a roadside auberge for a light meal, a traditional Swiss dish called Papet Vaudois that he washed down with a glass of Chasselas. He wasn't really a white wine person; for that matter he wasn't really all that much of a wine person generally, but he resisted the temptation of whisky, partly because he was trying to go a little easier on the hard stuff these days and partly because he didn't want to turn up at the Steiner estate reeking like a distillery.

Driving on, he thought about the strange turns of events that had brought his younger sister to become the adopted daughter of the Swiss billionaire couple Maximilian and Silvia Steiner. Her abduction from a Moroccan street market as a little girl had been the great defining trauma of Ben's teenage years and torn the Hope family apart at the seams, leading directly and indirectly to the demise of both their parents. All those years Ben had given her up for dead, unbeknownst to him or anyone she'd been growing up like a little princess on the Steiners' vast secluded estate in the Swiss Alps, brought up to believe that none of her blood relatives were still alive. It had been a long road for both of them, and even after he'd been reunited with her their relationship had been rocky at first. But that was years ago.

It had also been some years since Ben's last visit to the estate. What had brought him here initially, quite by chance, was a professional commitment – not the kind of job he'd have chosen to undertake, but one that had been foisted on him against his will when he'd been compelled to head up a close protection team to safeguard Maximilian Steiner after the billionaire had been targeted by kidnappers. How exactly the task had landed in Ben's lap on that occasion was a long story, involving Ben's having put the existing team leader in hospital. The fact that the individual in question had at that time been going out with Ben's longtime love, Brooke Marcel, had of course had little to do with it. That relationship, too, was a long time in the past.

So, it seemed, was the heavy security presence that had greeted him on that first visit to the Steiner estate. Gone were the closed iron gates and the double checkpoints at which forbidding guards in uniform had interrogated him and examined his ID as though he was a wanted terrorist. Gone, too, were all the security cameras that had watched his progress as he'd made his way up the private road towards the main residence. Having handed the running of his multi-billion-dollar global enterprise entirely over to the care of his adoptive daughter, old Maximilian must have mellowed in his retirement.

Ben rolled up the mile-long driveway, passing through acres of primly-tended woodland that were only a fraction of the estate's lands. He finally passed under the high stone archway where the trees parted and the big house came into view. Though, as he'd noted on that first memorable visit and couldn't help but be reminded on seeing it again, 'house' was hardly the right term for the palatial Swiss château. It was the kind of property that would make the average multimillionaire feel decidedly ordinary. Ben was no stranger to the homes of the ultra-wealthy, and he supposed that you could get used to pretty much any degree of luxury. But the Steiner residence was something to behold, more like a Disneyland castle than a home. You'd almost expect to see armoured knights riding their chargers in and out of the drawbridge, and fire-breathing dragons perched on the lofty battlements. The spectacle was still enough to make Ben puff his cheeks and shake his head in wonder as he continued up towards the main entrance with its gleaming white stone columns and a flight of steps wider than a motorway.

Some of the party guests had already starting showing up. Ben's dusty blue BMW Alpina looked very humble next to all the Rolls-Royces and Astons and Ferraris. He parked it near the line-up of caterers' vans, where it seemed less out of place. Stretching his legs he self-consciously flicked away his cigarette, smoothed his crumpled jeans and denim shirt and wondered if maybe he should have changed into the black tux he'd brought before getting here. Turn up looking like 007, maybe people would be less likely to notice the cheap car.

He was walking towards the steps when he heard a familiar voice call his name and turned to see his sister Ruth running towards him from the direction of the grounds. Her hair was longer than last time they'd met, golden in the light of the sun. She was dressed for riding, in a pair of rough old jodhpurs and a faded rugby top that instantly put him at ease about his own appearance. As if he'd really expected her to appear dressed in a sequined ballgown and festooned with emeralds and diamonds. She was a Hope, after all.

She flung herself at him, embracing him so excitedly that she nearly knocked him over. 'You smell like horses,' he said, hugging her tight. It was the kind of affectionate greeting he always kept in reserve for his only sibling.

'And you reek of those nasty French cigarettes you're always puffing on. What a fine pair we make. Let's go inside and stink the place up, just to shock everyone. Oh, Ben, I'm so glad you could make it! It's wonderful to see you. You haven't changed a bit.'

'Neither have you,' he replied. One thing was different about her, though. He'd never seen her looking so radiant and happy.

'Let me get you something to drink,' she bubbled, gripping his arm and steering him up the entrance steps and into the grand hallway of the château. The ring of her riding boots on the marble floor echoed up to the frescoed dome high above. 'Champagne? Oh, no, you prefer something a little stronger, don't you?'

'I could be tempted. But later.' *What amazing self-discipline,* he thought.

'Max and Silvia are dying to see you again. It's been so long! Oh, and here they are.'

The Steiners were still much the same as Ben remembered them, if a little older and greyer. The handsome, elegant Silvia Steiner was ageing somewhat better than her husband. Maximilian's hair and beard were now silvery-white and he'd taken to walking with a cane ever since getting shot some years back, but his iron constitution was still evident in his powerful grip as he warmly shook Ben's hand. 'What a sincere pleasure it is to see you again, Major Hope.'

Ruth tutted. 'Oh, Max, you know Ben hates being called that.'

'Just Ben,' Ben said.

Suddenly remembering, Ruth asked, 'How's Jude?'

Jude was the grown-up son Ben hadn't known about for the first twenty years of his life. 'He's doing well,' Ben replied. 'Living in New Zealand now. Or somewhere offshore, to be precise. Got himself a nice new boat and started a business taking rich executives on mini-cruises.'

'An enterprising young man,' Maximilian Steiner said approvingly. 'And clearly every bit as talented as his remarkable father.'

'What do you expect, Max?' his wife said with a beaming smile. 'They come from the very best stock.' All this flattery was more than Ben was used to.

'It'd have been lovely to meet him again,' said Ruth. 'I haven't seen him since—'

'Yeah, we don't need to talk about that,' Ben said quickly.

'Sorry. Oh, look, here's Stefan.' A tall, slim, dark-haired man in a well-tailored suit was coming down the sweep of stairs. Ruth ran over to him. 'Darling, someone I want you to meet.'

Ben had never imagined he'd ever hear his sister call anyone 'darling'. He met Stefan at the foot of the stairs with his hand extended. Ruth's fiancé was in his mid or late thirties, good-looking with intelligent brown eyes and an open smile. 'Stefan Hartmann,' he said rather formally, shaking Ben's hand.

'I'm very happy to meet you,' Ben said pleasantly. And he didn't add anything like 'But remember that if you ever mess my sister around I'll hunt you down and neuter you with a rusty chisel.' Strictly best behaviour.

'Stefan's family are here too,' Ruth told Ben. 'You'll get to meet them later, I'm sure. The only one who couldn't make it is Lara.'

'Lara?'

'I too have a younger sister,' Stefan explained. 'Sadly she's on the other side of the world at the moment, taking a break from her university studies to spend a year in China. This is her.'

Like everybody seemed to do these days, he whipped out a phone to show Ben a picture of her. The image had been taken at what appeared to be an ancient temple, surrounded in lush greenery with ornate columns and those turned-up roof corners that were so archetypically Oriental. In the foreground stood a pair of young dark-haired women, both in their early or mid twenties, both smiling, and remarkably similar to one another in build and facial features.

'Which one's your sister?' Ben asked, peering at the phone.

'Lara's the one on the left. That's Olivia with her, Olivia Keller. They were best friends at university and decided to travel to China together.'

'They could be twins.'

'It's true, even I have to look twice to tell them apart,' Stefan chuckled. 'Especially as the two of them have a habit of always swapping clothes, even earrings and hats. Anyway, Lara's having a wonderful time there.'

'I've never been there,' Ben said. 'I'd imagine it must be very fascinating.' Not that any of the countries he visited, covering most of the globe, had drawn him mainly for their cultural interest, and geographical differences apart they were all much of a muchness for him. Once you'd seen one wreckage-strewn butcher's shop of a battlefield you'd seen them all; and kidnappers' hideouts tended not to vary too widely either.

'*Liebling*,' Silvia Steiner said, tenderly taking Ruth's arm, 'I hate to interrupt your conversation, but you really should change out of those riding clothes. More guests are arriving.'

'I suppose I should,' Ruth replied with a grin. 'Before my carriage turns into a pumpkin.'

'She looks beautiful as she is,' Max Steiner said fondly. 'Would you not say so, Stefan?'

'Indeed I would,' Stefan answered, and Ben could see the love in his eyes.

'I'd better unpack my kit from the car,' Ben said. Consisting precisely of one suit carrier containing his tux and a pair of shiny shoes, and the battered, tattered old green military haversack he'd toted around on his adventures to many of those countries he *had* visited. He'd always believed in travelling light.

'Dorenkamp will show you to your guest accommodation,' Silvia said warmly. 'I hope it will be to your liking? I think you have stayed there before.'

Chapter 4

Ben had indeed stayed there before. In a rare nod to modernism, the Steiners had once commissioned the world-famous architect Peter Vetsch to create a radical-looking set of guest quarters nestling deep into one side of a hill, completely covered over on top with a wildflower meadow that at this time of year had come out in an explosion of colours. To get there, you had to cross kilometres of pristine grounds by golf buggy. For Ben it was another, not altogether welcome, reminder of his previous visit to the estate and that time of his life, bringing back memories of his troubled, ultimately failed, relationship with Brooke Marcel.

But nobody could have complained about the luxuriously-appointed accommodation itself, and at least on this occasion he didn't have to share it with a bunch of half-witted bodyguards. He dumped his kit in the bedroom, took a short cool shower and then, clad in just a towel around his waist, padded barefoot into the kitchen where the surprise discovery of a bottle of his favourite Laphroaig scotch whisky broke his resolve to lay off the hard stuff. Just a couple of fingers in a crystal tumbler, no ice, no water.

Carrying his drink into the sumptuous living area he was about to light another Gauloise when he remembered the Steiners' strict rules and looked up at the ceiling to check if the smoke alarm was still there – or its replacement, to be exact. Yes, there it was, the plaster around it still showing slight traces of damage from when he'd blasted the original alarm into pieces with a 9mm pistol. Why he couldn't simply have pulled out the battery, he didn't know. Maybe he'd been a little impetuous in those days. It had been a difficult time for him.

He wandered out onto a terrace to smoke his cigarette and savour his drink while he took in the spectacular Alpine view for a while. Inactivity wasn't his thing, but with nothing else to do he mooched idly around the guest quarters until it was time for him to put on his glad rags and wait for the Steiners' longtime and long-suffering PA, Heinrich Dorenkamp, to pick him up and take him back to the main residence for the start of the engagement party.

By now the rest of the guests had come flooding in and the courtyard in front of the house had become like an exclusive car park. The formal dress code was being strictly observed. Ben fell in with the procession of mostly short, paunchy men dressed like penguins and slinky women in long backless dresses, towering above their menfolk in their impossibly high heels and bunched-up hair, each of them apparently participating in some unofficial contest for who could cover themselves with the most spectacular display of high-end jewellery. Among them, the guests could probably have bought out the Bank of Switzerland several times over.

Ben felt acutely out of his element. He'd have liked to spend some time alone with Ruth, but as he entered the enormous ballroom where the party was already getting into full swing she was so completely surrounded by people he didn't know that he couldn't get close to her. Instead he stayed in the back-ground and quietly observed the goings on.

No question about it, the Steiners had gone all out for this special occasion. Neither effort nor expense had been spared to create the most lavish affair possible – and of course the most civilised. If anyone had come expecting blaring pop music, they were going to be mercifully disappointed. In one corner of the room stood a gleaming black concert-sized grand piano, near which a formally attired string quartet was playing something by Strauss. In the opposite corner, a stage had been erected for a jazz big band, complete with music stands, drum kit and Hammond organ. The band were over at the bar, tanking up with beer before they were due to come on stage. Meanwhile waiting staff in neat white uniforms circled among the crowd offering trays of drinks and tasty little canapés made of caviar and salmon mousse with capers and olives. The buzz of laughter and chatter echoed up to the high ceiling. In the middle of it all, Ruth and her future husband were the stars of the show, she in a splendid canary-yellow ballgown and he looking trim and elegant in his tuxedo. It was funny, Ben thought, how some men seemed to carry formal dress off so naturally. He personally felt stiff and restricted in his buttoned-up shirt collar and bow tie, and should've taken more time to break in his shiny black shoes, which pinched his feet.

Wrapping up their set to polite applause, the string quartet gave way to Silvia Steiner, who had been a concert pianist in her younger days and now sat down at the keyboard to play some very difficult-sounding pieces by Chopin and Liszt to the attentive audience. Then it was the turn of the jazz band to get up onstage, and the party finally started getting livelier as they launched into a rousing swing number.

Ben smiled to himself as he watched Ruth and Stefan spin around the dance floor, thinking with a little wry amusement about how much had changed. Not so many years had passed since his sister's wild, spiky-haired, fuck-you rebel phase, when she'd openly despised everything about her adoptive father and the evil capitalist ideology he represented in her eyes. Now here she was, the belle of the ball, fitting in perfectly with the rich and the beautiful, the sole heiress to Maximilian's empire and running the billion-dollar corporation as though she'd been born to it. The transformation was complete. But she was clearly very happy, and that was all that mattered to Ben.

Serving staff kept coming at him with more flutes of champagne, and he'd knocked back several by the time he was accosted by a very attractive but not particularly bright young twenty-something who seemed to have identified him as the most eligible single straight man at the party. Her name was Mila and she was a Capricorn (as she was quick to inform him), and actually used web-chat acronyms like 'LOL' and 'OMG' in speech, which was something he hadn't known existed. Maybe he was falling behind the times. He was contemplating a range of increasingly desperate ways of escaping from Mila's clutches when he was rescued by Ruth, who'd spotted him from across the room and filtered through the crowd to grab him on the pretence of wanting a dance. Ruth knew her brother well enough to know that wasn't an option.

'Whew,' he said as Ruth led him to safety. 'Thanks for saving me.'

'I could see you were in trouble,' she laughed. 'You missed your chance there, though. Mila's family happens to own the biggest confectionery company in Switzerland. She's quite a catch.'

'I never was much into chocolate,' he said.

'So what do you make of Stefan? Approve of my choice?'

What was there to say? Ben fell back on the standard response, 'He seems like a really nice guy. I like him a lot.'

'What a relief. That means I can marry him now.'

'I'm glad to be here, Ruth. Thanks for inviting me.'

'I know parties aren't your kind of scene. But I hope you appreciate the jazz band. I got it especially for you.'

'Can I take it home with me afterwards?'

They retreated to a quieter part of the ballroom, and helped themselves to some more of the limitless champagne. 'At last, a moment to ourselves,' she said. 'It's all been so hectic. We hardly ever seem to get the chance to meet up any more. And I know I don't get in touch as often as I should.'

'You've a busy life,' he replied. 'Don't worry about it.'

'I still find time to think about you a lot. And I worry about you, too.'

He smiled. 'Why should you worry? I'm just running a business, spending most of my life in a classroom.'

'Come on, Ben. What you call a classroom is a live firing range with bullets spraying everywhere and people being taught how to storm buildings and kill everyone inside them.'

'Taught how to respond in crisis situations where innocent people are in danger,' he corrected her.

'Call it what you like. It's nasty.'

'I won't disagree with that. But it also happens to be necessary, sometimes. When those calls come in, someone has to be there to answer them.'

She sighed. 'Yeah, I get it. Straight out of the recruitment manual. But there's more to it than that, isn't there? You say you're just a teacher, but I think you're only telling me that to reassure me. I know you get those calls, too. All the times I've tried to phone, and you weren't there because you were off on another mission somewhere. Getting yourself into more scrapes, barely surviving by the skin of your teeth. And for what?'

'I've always tried to help people who needed it,' he said. 'What was I supposed to do, leave them to their fate?'

'Sometimes I think you love the risk. Like you're not happy unless you're up to your neck in danger. Is normal life really that dull and boring, Ben?'

He was beginning to find this discussion a little uncomfortable, and wondered why they were having it. 'You make it all sound much worse than it really is.'

She cocked one eyebrow. 'Do I? I'm not so sure about that. I still haven't forgotten about what happened to my aeroplane.'

'Oh, please,' he said. 'You know I've always felt bad about that time. I wouldn't have borrowed it from you if I'd known I was going to run into those air force jets.'

'And ended up almost killing yourself ditching the aircraft in some Indonesian lake to avoid getting blown to bits, as I recall.'

'It didn't quite happen that way. As for the plane, I've always said I'd pay you back for it if I could.'

'Forget the damn plane. And I don't give a toss about the money. That's not what I'm talking about. I'm talking about *you*. My brother, who I'm terrified is one day, sooner or later, going to get himself into something he can't get out of.'

'It's never happened yet.'

'No, but every time you take that chance, you're raising the odds that this could be the one when you're not coming home. What if that happened? I can't afford to lose you twice, Ben.'

'Hey, I'm the one who lost you, remember?' he said, trying to make light of the subject. 'But I found you again in the end.'

'Don't make a joke of it. We lost each other, for years. It was the worst trauma I've ever experienced, thinking you were gone for ever. And I'm not going through it again.'

His smile fell away. 'Is this the real reason you invited me here to Switzerland, to give me a lecture about how I choose to live my life? I do what I do, Ruth. It's all I know.'

'Don't give me that crap,' she said, shaking her head and frowning.

'What crap?'

'That whole he-man "There's no other life for a guy like me" bullshit line.'

'Maybe there isn't,' he said in all earnestness. 'I've never done anything else.'

'Then learn some new skills. Diversify. Put your talents to some better use that isn't going to end up getting you killed.'

'Sounds as if you've already figured out what that better use might be.'

'I told you, I think about you a lot. And it occurred to me that, since, business appears to be booming at Le Val, maybe you should think about selling up your share. Seems to me the other guys can manage pretty well without you. Let's face it, you're hardly ever there anyway, because you're always shooting off around the world looking for more trouble.'

'Even if I was prepared to run out on my friends like that,' he said. 'Sell up my share and do what? Retire?'

'Not so much that. Maybe there are other avenues for you to pursue. Where you could still make use of your skills, but in a safer way.'

'Other avenues?' Maybe he sounded a little defensive.

Ruth shrugged, trying to look nonchalant and hide the fact that she'd actually planned this all in quite some detail. Ben could see straight through her as though she were made of glass. 'Well, for example,' she replied, 'it just so happens that there's going to be an opening here at Steiner Industries. Our international head of security is leaving us at the end of the year. I was thinking perhaps . . .'

'That it could be an opportunity for me?' he finished for her.

Ruth shrugged again. 'It's an idea, isn't it? I mean, look at this estate. There's so much room here for all of us, and I know how much you love the mountains and the wide open spaces. We could build you the most beautiful house, any style you wanted, designed by your very own architect who'll be part of the family. The job title sounds like a big deal and it comes with a great salary, but in reality you wouldn't have to work long hours, and most of it could be done from here. You've probably already noticed that we don't have half the security on the estate that we used to. Think of all the free time you'd have to spend doing the things you love doing.'

'A life of peace and tranquillity,' he said.

'That's what you're missing, Ben,' she said matter-of-factly. 'Admit it. You've been searching for it all these years and never found it. And who knows, maybe you might even meet a nice Swiss girl. Settle down.'

'Not the lovely Mila, God help me.'

'Seriously. It's not too late to start a family, even, if you wanted to.'

'Remember Winnie, our old housekeeper when you were a kid? She was always trying to matchmake and plan my future for me, too.'

'Please don't take it badly,' Ruth said, touching his hand. 'You're my brother, I love you and I truly want what's best for you. All I'm saying is, think about what I'm suggesting. There's no pressure on you to make a decision any time soon. But wouldn't it be wonderful for us to be able to see so much more of one another? I've been thinking that after the wedding I'll scale back my own workload as company CEO and spend a lot more time here, maybe even sell up the house in Zermatt and move back permanently. Heaven knows Max and Silvia have been on at me about it enough. They'd be so happy for you to be here, too.' She looked at him expectantly. 'So what do you say, Ben?'

There was a lot Ben felt like saying, but he said nothing. He finished his drink, whipped another one off a tray as a waiter walked by, and wished he could light up a Gauloise. Maybe if he did that, a bunch of seven-foot security guys would appear out of nowhere and ask him to leave. Then he could either let himself be peaceably escorted outside, or start a big fight. Either way he'd have an excuse to get out of this conversation.

He didn't need to resort to such extremes, though, because at that moment Stefan came pressing through the party crowd, a beaming smile on his face as he spotted Ruth. His cheeks were a little flushed from the champagne and the warmth of the ballroom. 'There you are! I've been looking for you. Ben, may I presume to steal my fiancée back from you for the next dance?'

'She's all yours,' Ben replied.

As Stefan led Ruth away towards the dance floor, she turned back towards Ben and called, 'Promise me you'll think about it.'

'Yeah, yeah, I'll think about it,' Ben muttered into his drink. Then, detecting incoming danger at three o'clock in the shape of the lovely Mila purposefully stalking over his way with a predatory gleam in her eye, he decided it was time to escape the party.

Chapter 5

In truth he hadn't intended to give it a single moment's consideration, but even so his sister's proposition lingered strangely in his mind for the rest of that evening. It was floating in the background of his thoughts as he went to bed that night, and still hovering there like the remnants of a dream when he woke up to the rays of dawn the following morning.

Since his earliest days in the military it had always been Ben's way to get up early and complete set after set of gruelling exercises before breakfast. When he'd finished, judging that the Steiner household would probably all have a lie-in after last night's excitement, he decided to wait a while before heading over to the château. After his usual quick, cool shower, a couple of mugs of fortifying black coffee and the first Gauloise of the day, he went for a stroll around the estate. The sky was the most perfect unbroken blue and the sun was already becoming warm.

As he walked, Ben observed that the diminished security presence wasn't the only change that had been made on the estate in recent years: for instance the nine-hole golf course that had once been the pride and joy of Maximilian and Silvia's nephew Otto had now disappeared and been replaced by a range of new equestrian paddocks and fancy stabling. That was because dear Otto, formerly the heir to the Steiner billions before Ruth, was no longer around to spend his days idly whacking those little white balls into those little holes. His demise, specifically the manner of his demise and the reason why Maximilian had pitched his nephew off the edge of a high stone balustrade, wasn't regarded as a fit subject for discussion within family circles. Ben had noticed yesterday that the ornamental fountain featuring the bronze statue of the sea god Neptune with his trident was now absent from the conservatory adjoining the house. Understandably so, since it had been the upward-pointing spikes of that trident that had arrested Otto's spectacular fall through the glass roof – and nobody really wanted to be reminded of that gruesome scene.

But in every other respect, the Steiners' sprawling great fairyland retreat was physically unchanged from Ben's last visit, and certainly no less beautiful an environment. What a fantastical place for a little lost girl to grow up in, he thought. It was no surprise that Ruth planned to come back here to live after her wedding. No doubt there would be fresh additions to the family before too long, a new generation of little Steiners running around who would call Ben 'Uncle' and one day inherit all this in their turn.

Uncle Ben. Like the rice. It felt strange to him.

As he walked, by chance Ben came across the old chapel that he remembered from before. With its stained-glass windows, ivied grey stone walls and studded oak door, it was a perfect reproduction of an eighteenth-century church. He nudged the door open, walked inside the cool, silent emptiness and sat on a pew nearest the altar.

Being inside a church always carried Ben back to his religious days, a part of his life that might have become his whole future if fate hadn't taken him in such a radically different direction. These days his faith might not be as resolute as it once had been, but even though he thought of himself as in many ways a lapsed Christian, that sense of reverence from being inside a holy place would always remain with him. The last time he'd sat in this same chapel, on this same pew, he'd bowed his head and prayed to the image of Christ on the cross to give him the strength to see through his temporary task of working for Maximilian Steiner. Back then he couldn't have imagined that one day the serious offer of permanent employment with the company would come along.

Is that something I'd ever really want to do? He asked himself now. The thought of leaving Le Val was a painful one, even just to toy with.

After a few minutes' silent reflection, he left the chapel and continued on his way. What had started as a leisurely stroll turned into a long, long walk, way past breakfast-time and deep into the morning as the warm sun rose steadily overhead and his path led him upward towards the foot of the mountains. The air was crisper and cooler at this higher altitude, and the snow-capped peaks loomed so brightly white against the vivid blue sky that he needed to put on his aviator shades to gaze at them. There was absolutely nobody around, but it was the kind of solitude that Ben deeply relished, so immersed in the stillness and beauty of this place that he might have been the last human being on earth, with the whole planet to himself.

On and on he walked, wondering how many hours, days, weeks, he could wander before he reached the edge of the estate. Presently he came to a building, what appeared to be a large wooden barn standing alone in the remoteness of the green hillside, and looking up he realised that it was a station for a private cable car that could travel far up the slope of the nearby mountain. Who ever used it was anybody's guess; but unable to resist, he boarded the empty car and found the control box for the electric motor. At the press of a button he found himself whooshing upwards with surprising speed, the wooden building and the landscape around it shrinking smaller and smaller and the view stretching for miles around.

The cable car glided to a halt at its docking station many hundreds of feet up. Ben stepped out onto the railed wooden deck and craned his neck to peer at the mountain peak still far above. A walking path led from the cable car station, winding its way up and up the slope until it disappeared from view. He followed it eagerly at a fast pace and kept going past the point where the path petered out and he had to scramble over rocks as the slope began to steepen dramatically. Without proper equipment he couldn't hope to reach all the way to the top, but looking down at the roof of the docking station, now a long way below, he realised how far he'd climbed.

Perched on a high ridge with the cool, fresh mountain wind whistling around him and ruffling his hair, he had a dominating view of the whole majestic panorama. But someone else had managed to gain a far greater altitude than he ever could. Hearing a high-pitched peal overhead, he looked up and thrilled at the sight of a solitary golden eagle wheeling above, effortlessly riding the thermals on long tawny wings.

For several minutes the magnificent predator soared round and round that vast bowl of a sky. To Ben, the eagle was the supreme incarnation of capability, independence and freedom. Lord of the air, master of his own destiny. He answered to no one. He knew exactly what his purpose in life was, and pursued it with single-minded keenness. And as Ben watched him, he couldn't help but search his own heart for the answer to the questions that had been troubling him for much of the night and since he'd got up that morning.

Was Ruth right? Had the time come for Ben, too, to spread his wings, soar to new heights and liberate himself from his old life? Should he draw a line and put his days of risk-taking and conflict behind him? Hadn't he done his part? Paid his dues? Didn't he deserve to spend the rest of his life in peace?

He stood there gazing at the sky long after the eagle had gone. As much as it hurt to admit it, he knew that all of these same doubts and misgivings had been nagging at his thoughts for a good while already – months, if not longer. That at a deep, deep level, something felt *wrong* somehow with his life. That he'd long been restless in his heart and soul, secretly searching for a new direction without any clear idea of what it could be.

So many questions. So few answers. Sometimes he didn't know what was in his own mind. Maybe he should listen instead to the wisdom of someone who loved him and cared about his future happiness. And maybe that voice of wisdom had already told him the right thing to do.

Slowly, thoughtfully, Ben made his way back down the mountain. Then he returned to the big house, and suddenly everything changed.

Chapter 6

The last of the party guests who had stayed overnight in the château's many bedrooms were leaving in their Rolls-Royces and Ferraris. As he entered the marble-floored coolness of the grand hallway and made his way through the passages, to begin with Ben wondered where Ruth and the others had disappeared to. They weren't gathered together in the salon, as he might have expected; and nor had they gone out to the gardens to enjoy the warm sunshine. Except for the usual comings and goings of the maids, who didn't seem to be able to tell him much either, the house seemed strangely deserted. Ben felt that prickly tingle of apprehension he knew so well, telling him something was amiss. Unfortunately, those kinds of instincts were all too often proven true.

He finally found everyone assembled in the Steiners' dining room, the smaller and homelier one used for less formal occasions like birthdays and fun family get-togethers. But there was nothing cheery or celebratory about the mood inside the room as he stepped through the door and saw them all gathered there still in their pyjamas and dressing gowns. That was when he knew his feeling had been right.

Ben had barely met Stefan's parents for more than a minute or two last night, on his way from the party. Conrad and his wife Leni were a little younger than Maximilian and Silvia, but evidently not in as good health – and at this moment they both appeared to be in an alarmingly bad way. For an instant Ben thought they must have been taken ill, but then he realised it was something else. Stefan was there with them, grimly trying to console his mother as she wept floods of tears. His father was slumped like a cadaver in a dining chair with his head hanging. Ruth stood near the window, dabbing her own reddened eyes with a tissue. The elder Steiners looked no less distraught, hovering in the background and too upset to even speak.

'What the hell's going on?' Ben asked, shocked.

Ruth turned to him with a look of relief. 'Oh Ben, thank God. I've been looking everywhere for you. Something's happened. Something awful.'

Before Ruth could say more, Leni Hartmann burst out in a wailing cry, '*Mein armes kleines Mädchen! Ermordet!*'

Ben understood German pretty well, even though it wasn't every day he heard a tragedy-stricken mother bewail the fact that her poor little girl had just been murdered. That could only be referring to Lara, the young woman in the photo he'd seen yesterday.

Stefan hugged his mother tightly, desperately trying to reassure her but struggling with his own tears. 'You mustn't think that,' he told her in German. 'We don't know that.'

'I do know! My Lara! She's dead!' Leni bawled. 'She should never have gone to that place! I never wanted her to! I told her—'

'Mother, please—'

'I'll go and fetch her a drink of water,' Silvia Steiner said anxiously.

'And some more sedatives, if you have them,' said Ruth. 'Before she gives herself a heart attack. Maybe we should call Dr Fischer.'

'I'll call him right now. We can send the chopper to collect him.'

As Silvia hurried from the room Ben asked, 'Will someone explain to me what this is about?'

Ruth waved him over to the far side of the room. In a low whisper tight with emotion she explained, 'Conrad woke up this morning to find a message on his phone. It was redirected from their home landline in Bern. The call was from Olivia, Lara's friend in China.'

Olivia. The other young woman in the picture, Ben remembered.

'We could tell Olivia was upset,' Ruth went on, 'but it was hard to make out why. We called her back this morning, first thing. And she told us what happened.'

This had all been going on while Ben was on his long walk, climbing mountains and gazing at eagles. He said, 'Told you *what* happened?'

Ruth blinked away tears and replied, 'Lara's gone missing, Ben.'

'How? When?'

Ruth just shook her head. Ben looked at Stefan for an answer, the only other person in the room who seemed fit to explain anything.

'I can't be going through it all right now,' Stefan snapped. 'I need to be with my mother.'

Ruth took Ben's arm and pointed at another door. 'Let's go in here where we can talk better.'

The adjoining room was a small, comfortable salon with a bay window overlooking the gardens. Ruth went over to a large wooden globe on a stand and hinged the top of the world open to reveal a drinks cabinet inside. She grabbed a bottle of scotch and two glasses, without needing to ask Ben if he'd join her in a drink. She sloshed out two large measures, handed one to him and downed half her own in one swallow. 'It's too early to be drinking, but Christ, I needed that. I'm shaking all over. It's a nightmare, Ben.'

He was beginning to glean the broad strokes of the situation. He'd been through this same unpleasant routine so often that he could switch back into detective mode as readily as an ex-cop. His voice was calm but hard. 'Talk to me, Ruth. Details. Times. Places. Exactly how it went down.'

They could hear Leni bawling again in the next room. Talking fast, Ruth explained, 'As far as we can tell, it happened early Friday evening. Lara and Olivia rent a small cottage in a village a few miles outside Xi'an. They've been living there since the spring. Before that, they were sharing a flat in the city. It's a quiet neighbourhood, out in the countryside, and nothing ever happens there. Nothing like this, anyway.'

'Keep it short and simple, Ruth.'

'Lara goes out jogging every evening around seven. She went out for her Friday run, telling Olivia she'd be back in half an hour, as usual, and she had her phone with her as always. The time she was due back came and went, then an hour passed, and no sign of her. Olivia was a little bit worried, and she tried calling Lara's phone but it was switched off, which she thought was odd.'

'Did she leave a message?'

'Two of them, and texted her too. Then she had to go out herself, because she'd been invited to something at the college where she's studying and she couldn't get out of it. By the time she got home it was late, and there'd been no reply to her phone messages or text. Still no sign of Lara.'

'And that's when she called the police?'

'It's what I would have done,' Ruth said. 'But I suppose some people are slower to press the panic button than others. Olivia thought maybe Lara had come home while she was out and then gone off to a party or something. They spend a lot of time together but it's not like they're joined at the hip. They have their own independent social lives and they respect each other's privacy. That's why she didn't raise the alarm at that point.'

'Okay,' Ben said. 'Go on.' He took a sip of the whisky.

'When Lara still hadn't appeared by Saturday morning, Olivia went into her room to find that the bed hadn't been slept in and all her stuff was still there. That's when she started to really worry and picked up the phone to report her missing.'

It was the old familiar story, with the typical lag of too many hours between the incident and the emergency call, during which time anything could have happened and the victim might have been saved. If indeed there was a victim in this case. These things weren't always what they appeared. 'What did the police say?' Ben asked.

'Nothing, to begin with, because they were so slow responding. In the meantime Olivia hunted through Lara's things because she remembered she keeps a diary and thought there might be something there to shed light on where she'd gone. By chance she found Lara had written her parents' phone number in Bern. She tried calling but it was the middle of the night here, so she left the message that Conrad found redirected to mobile this morning. In between her trying to call and us calling her back, the police had finally turned up and it looks as though they're treating the disappearance as suspicious.'

'Are there any witnesses?'

Ruth shook her head. 'Doesn't look that way. Nobody who might have seen anything suspicious. It's only a small village, but a lot of the residents know each other and two pretty western girls are kind of an unusual thing there so everyone's familiar with them.'

'Anyone locally we might suspect of being antagonistic towards them? The neighbourhood creepo? Someone with a grudge against westerners, or western women?'

'Nothing like that either. From what Stefan says, they've always got on great with everyone nearby, and are popular there. While she was waiting for the police Olivia went around some of the neighbours, asking if anyone had seen Lara. They buy a lot of their food in this little grocery store down the street and the lady there said she saw her jog past sometime just after seven-fifteen, and smile and wave hello. As far as we know that was the last sighting of her. And the police don't have any leads yet either. It's like she just vanished into thin air.'

The wheels were turning fast in Ben's mind, questions swarming like bees. 'Is she a good timekeeper? A sensible sort of person? Not someone who'd be in the habit of going off without telling anyone where she was?'

'Absolutely not. Stefan says she's totally responsible and level-headed. No way she'd be that thoughtless.'

'And what about Olivia?' Ben asked. 'The way she delayed calling the police makes me think maybe she's a little more on the scatty side than her friend. Can we trust that she's telling this right? That maybe Lara told her she was going somewhere and she's just forgotten or misunderstood?'

Ruth reflected for a moment, looking doubtful. 'I don't buy that, Ben. She sounds totally sincere and she was able to supply a lot of detail. I believe her.'

'All right. Now let's go back to this diary Olivia found in Lara's room. Apart from the phone number, it didn't reveal anything of value?'

'Only that Lara had met up with her boyfriend a couple of days earlier, and that he gave her something. But I don't think that's of any significance.'

But to Ben, it did mean something important, and the mention made his ears prick up. 'She has a boyfriend there in China? You never mentioned him before.'

'His name's Dan. I already knew about him, from Stefan. They've been going out together for about three months now. Seems like a very nice, very sweet guy.'

'You said he gave her something. What was that?'

'Her diary didn't say. Who knows? People give each other things, don't they? A romantic gift, a bunch of flowers, a silver neck chain, does it really matter?'

Maybe it didn't and maybe it did, Ben thought, but without that information there was no point speculating. 'Tell me more about this Dan. Does he have a second name?'

'Chen. Dan Chen. Except in China they traditionally put the surname first.'

'So this Dan Chen, Chen Dan or whatever you want to call him. Who is he? What does he do? How did they meet?'

'I don't know how they met. I think he works for the government, affiliated to the Ministry of Culture. An antiquities expert, conservation, restoration, that kind of thing. He's quite ambitious, according to Stefan.'

Ben asked, 'And do we know if the police have tried to contact him about Lara's disappearance?'

'I was coming to that part. Olivia told them about Dan, in case Lara might have gone there. But she says when they went to his apartment they found it empty.'

Ben frowned. 'What are we saying, that the boyfriend has disappeared too?'

'I have no idea, Ben. I'm as much in the dark about this as you are.'

'Well, hold on,' he said. 'Doesn't it strike you as a bit coincidental that both of them apparently dropped off the face of the earth at the same time? Isn't it possible that Lara hasn't gone missing at all, and we're just dealing with a couple of lovebirds who've gone off together?'

'Without telling anyone?'

'It's been known to happen before now. Young folks aren't always that considerate.'

'They're in their twenties. They're not children.'

'They're in love,' Ben said. 'That basically makes them about three years old, in terms of rational behaviour.'

'Cynic.'

'Just saying. Who hasn't been so besotted with someone or other that nothing else seemed to exist?'

She sighed. 'I hear you. But we're talking about China, Ben. Trust me, I've had a lot of dealings with people there since we opened our new offices in Beijing three years ago. They have a totally different work ethic to us, and they're very proud of that. They work extremely long hours and they don't go swanning about the place like everyone seems to feel entitled to do in the west nowadays. No flexi-time and four holidays a year for them. If Lara's boyfriend works for the Chinese government you can bet your boots he's employed six days a week, and I seriously doubt that his employers would allow one of their people to take time off to run around with his girlfriend anytime he felt like it.'

'Maybe not on a whim,' Ben said. 'But maybe they'd planned it in advance. That'd be something to try and check up on. Have his employers reported him absent from work? If not, then perhaps he's simply got some vacation time, and Lara's gone off with him.'

'But then Olivia would have known about that,' Ruth shot back, getting annoyed now. 'Aside from anything else, Lara wouldn't have just disappeared and left all her stuff behind. Even her toothbrush and personal items.'

'Fine. Here's another possibility. You say they've been going out for about three months?'

'Something like that. Not long. She's only there for a year.'

'But nonetheless, if it's a fairly serious relationship, perhaps they had a big argument or a split. Maybe she went off because she was upset.'

'Look, I don't know if it's the big love of her life. It probably isn't, Ben. But surely Olivia would have known about that too? If there'd been a major bust-up in their relationship then Lara would have needed a shoulder to cry on. Why didn't she even mention it?'

'That's how we get to the truth. By eliminating all the other possibilities.'

'Well the way I see it, there's only one that makes any sense, and that is that poor Lara has come to some kind of harm. Either she's had an accident, been hit by a car or something and is lying in a ditch somewhere, maybe not too badly hurt, waiting to be found . . .' Ruth was letting her imagination run wild here, hoping for the best. 'Or else,' she went on, a darker look coming into her eyes, 'someone's taken her while she was out running. Grabbed her, stuffed her in a car or a van, raped her, strangled her, or God knows what. Christ, I can't bear to even think it. Even if it's just a straightforward kidnapping.'

'Maybe so,' Ben agreed. 'Though if it was a snatch, I'm pretty sure the kidnappers would have been in contact by now, with the usual demands for money.'

'It's not always about extorting ransoms from the families, though, is it? She could be in the hands of people traffickers.' Ruth shuddered, probably imagining what her own fate could have been.

'Perhaps,' he said. 'But that's just more speculation.'

'What's the matter with you?' she demanded. 'It's as if you don't want to believe anything serious has happened here. Why do you keep asking all these sceptical questions?'

'Because this is something I have a lot of experience of,' he replied evenly. 'I've seen a lot of things, Ruth. This is a side of the world that I know a lot better than most people. And if I seem to be playing devil's advocate, that's only because I've learned you have to eliminate all the alternatives before you go crying "kidnap". Especially when you're dealing with a case that's halfway around the world from here. For all we know, as we're standing here thousands of miles away debating what might or might not have happened to her, she's about to turn up any minute, perfectly well and unharmed with a perfectly innocent explanation for why she went off and drove everyone crazy with worry.'

It was true. He could clearly remember three of his past cases where he'd been hired to find a kidnap victim and travelled long distance to where the incident was supposed to have taken place, only to discover that the alleged abductee had already popped up again in the meantime, safe and sound and wondering what all the fuss was about.

Ruth sighed, relenting. 'You're right, of course. And I realise it's important to look at all the angles. But bad things happen too, Ben. You of all people don't need me to tell you that. And I know it too, because it happened to me. I was just luckier than most.'

'We both know it,' Ben said.

'Then will you help Lara?' Ruth pleaded. 'For the family's sake. We have to do something.'

He looked at her.

'Please, Ben. You have to go there and try to find her, or at least find out what happened to her.' Ruth gave a grim laugh. 'Listen to me. The irony of it. There I was last night, giving you the big lecture about how you needed to change your ways and put your old life behind you. What was it I said? I can't even remember now. Too much champagne, and now all this happening so fast I can hardly think straight.'

'You said I needed to diversify,' he reminded her. 'Learn new skills.'

'What an idiot I was, saying that to you.' She took both his hands and held them tight, looking earnestly into his eyes. 'And now here I am begging you to help us. But I wouldn't know who else to turn to. Like you said, it's what you do. And I'm lucky to have you, because there isn't a living soul on this earth who could do it better. Please, Ben.'

He was silent for a long beat. Then he shook his head.

'You want my honest opinion? I think we'd be better off sitting tight and letting the local authorities handle this.'

She looked as shocked as if he'd slapped her. 'I can't believe you'd say that. Why? You've never trusted the police before. You told me that yourself. What changed?'

'What changed is that, this time around, I don't know how much use I can be to Lara, or to the rest of you,' he replied frankly. 'Look, Ruth, I've always worked within my own particular area of operations. France, Germany, Italy, Spain, the Americas, Arabic-speaking countries. Places where I knew the language at least reasonably well, and the general lie of the land. I often had safehouses in place, plus I had a whole network of connections that I could rely on for help if I needed it. But China, that's a whole different situation. I'd be alone in an alien territory where I couldn't speak a word of the language and with zero contacts. Where would I even begin? I'd be totally out of my element there, and even more out of my depth.'

'You're a fast learner,' Ruth said. 'Nobody's better than you at adapting to new situations and thinking on your feet. And anyway, lots of people speak English in China.'

'Maybe in the big cities and business centres they do,' he replied, 'but given where she vanished that's not where I'd be searching for her, at least not to begin with. And quite apart from anything else, it's not a country anyone can just zap halfway around the world to on the spur of the moment. I'd need a visa application, a letter from my host there, all kinds of red tape to clear first. It could take weeks. With that much of a delay, anything could happen.'

'Not if you have connections with Steiner Industries, it won't. I've got you into tricky places before. Like when you and Jeff needed to rush off to Australia in such a hurry that time, remember?'

'Of course I remember. But—'

'And this would be even easier. I told you, we've set up new company offices in Beijing. Our executives travel freely all over the world almost every day of the week, and the new head of international security wouldn't need much more than a rubber stamp to get into China, drop of a hat, no questions asked.'

'You're giving me the job, just like that?'

'I'm the top of the food chain,' she replied. 'The head honcho, the big cheese. I can do whatever I want. One phone call and it's done. I'll have a contract emailed across from head office. Nothing binding, just a provisional agreement between ourselves for the moment, subject to confirmation. Sign and you're on board.'

Ben was about to reply when he suddenly became aware of another presence in the room. He and Ruth both turned towards the doorway. They'd been so intensely focused on their conversation that neither had noticed the sounds of emotional distress from the other room die down as the sedatives took effect. Leaving his parents to rest a while, Stefan had slipped away and closed the door quietly behind him. How much of Ben and Ruth's conversation he'd heard was unclear, but he'd heard enough.

Stefan said tersely, 'If Ben is going to China, then I'm going with him.'

Ben shook his head. 'No, Stefan. If I do this, I do it my own way and I won't be taking passengers. What you need to do is stay here and take care of your family.'

But Stefan shook his head too, just as assertively. 'Lara *is* my family. What I need to do is find her.'

Ben looked at his future brother-in-law and could see the serious intention in his eyes. Then looked at Ruth and saw the thoughtful expression come over her face. As usual, Ruth was the pragmatic one. 'You said you'd be all alone there, Ben,' she said. 'But this way you wouldn't be. It makes perfect sense for Stefan to come along with you, being Lara's next of kin. *That's* how you open doors and get to speak to the right people.'

'Anyhow, you damn well try to stop me getting on that plane,' Stefan added. 'And please don't tell me you wouldn't do the same thing, in my shoes.'

Ben realised that they were both right. It was true: there wasn't a force of nature that could have prevented him from getting involved, if it had been his own sister's safety or life in the balance.

'All right then,' he said to them. 'Looks like we're headed for China.'

Chapter 7

Everything moved very quickly from that point on. Suddenly, Ben's two-day Swiss break was turning into a long-haul flight aboard the Steiner jet, with no idea how long he might be away for. Just like all those times before, he had to call Jeff Dekker at Le Val to tell him about the change of plans. And just as always, Jeff's response was a reassuring grunt and a 'We've got you covered, mate.' Jeff was like that, bless his cotton socks.

Meanwhile Ruth was a human whirlwind, pacing up and down making phone calls, tapping on laptop keys, all her anxiety for Stefan's sister channelled into getting the impromptu business trip to China organised in double time. It wasn't long before Ben's official employment contract pinged into her email inbox. If he accepted the provisional offer – and he didn't see that he had much choice, under the circumstances – it would be the first actual, proper job he'd had in all the years since quitting the military; and his first ever as a civilian. It was a strange feeling. The speed and ease of the process were strange to him, too. All he had to do was tap a tablet screen, and the digital signature Ruth had already prepared for him was magically entered into the contract. The wonders of modern technology.

'Welcome aboard,' she said with a smile.

'The salary's too much,' he replied. 'It's ridiculous.'

'You're worth it.'

'Let's hope so.'

By another stroke of her wand, Ruth had fixed things so that her fiancé could be squeezed through the same corporate loophole as her brother. The result was that, just as she'd anticipated, the two of them would be permitted to enter China on a business visa allowing them to bypass swathes of the usual red tape. By the time Ben and Stefan were ready to leave, the Steiner family physician, Dr Fischer, had finished his examination of Leni Hartmann, prescribed more sedatives and ordered that the patient have complete rest. Stefan shook hands with his father, himself so wrecked with stress and grief that he could barely speak except to croak, 'Get her back for us, son. Bring our little girl home.'

It was a hard scene to watch. Then minutes later, a shiny black company Lexus arrived at the château to whisk Ben and Stefan off to the nearby private airfield where the Steiner Industries Bombardier Global, too large to land on the little strip at the château, was now fuelled up and waiting.

Over the years Ben had become fairly used to being ferried around the world on private jets, but he'd seldom seen anything quite so organised as the Steiner machine going into hyperdrive for this kind of crisis. The Bombardier was capable of long-haul flights of over 7500 nautical miles, which allowed it to take the mere 5000-mile hop to Beijing easily in its stride without having to touch the ground once. It was the same ultra-luxurious plane that Ruth had provided on that previous occasion when he and Jeff Dekker had needed to make a rapid trip to Australia, to take care of some urgent family business of Jeff's. Ben had become fairly well acquainted with the chief pilot, Pierre, and the rest of the crew. The interior was all plush leather and wood, with the entire length of the vast passenger cabin at the disposal of its two occupants – not that either of them, especially Stefan, would be able to enjoy the luxury at this time of emergency when every passing hour was a nail-biting frustration.

Stefan wasn't in the mood to talk much, either on the fast drive to the airfield or once they'd boarded the jet. He slumped in a seat at the back and stared fixedly out of the window. Ben got the message. He could relate to how the guy felt. Respecting his desire for space and privacy, he took a place near the front of the passenger cabin, helped himself to a generous glass of single malt scotch from the well-stocked bar, and settled in for the long journey promising himself he'd try not to drink whisky all the way to China.

The plane was so smooth and silent that he barely even noticed the takeoff. Switzerland disappeared below the clouds and would soon be far, far behind them. Ben took his time over his drink, slowly ate some grilled chicken and potato salad that the flight attendant brought him; then somewhere over Slovakia or Hungary he closed his eyes and relaxed into a troubled kind of half-sleep.

When he opened them again, it was night outside his window and he guessed they must be overflying eastern Turkey. Still a long way to go before they'd even begin to discover what could have happened to Lara Hartmann. Her brother was still sitting motionless at the back of the dimly-lit cabin. Feeling a surge of sympathy for the guy, Ben left his seat and walked back there to join him.

'Thought you might want some company. Feel free to tell me to bugger off and leave you alone.'

'No, no, please. I'm sorry if I was being antisocial.'

'Don't worry about it,' Ben said with a smile. 'I've been there.'

Stefan sighed. 'I know what happened to your family. Ruth's told me the whole story so many times. I could never have imagined anything like that happening to someone in my own.'

'You have my sympathies,' Ben told him. 'We'll do everything we can.' He was being sincere, but privately couldn't help questioning that a young child being snatched from a North African street market by white slavers was necessarily quite the same thing as a grown woman happening to go AWOL at the same time as her boyfriend. Though he never would have said it, he was still harbouring a few doubts about this whole business. He was very willing to believe they'd be on their way home within a few short hours of landing in China, either leaving a shame-faced and very much alive Lara behind them or bringing her home to face the embarrassment of having caused a major family incident.

'Do you know where we are?' Stefan asked, glancing at his watch.

'Relax. We're not there yet.'

Stefan fell silent, looking nervous and biting his lip. 'I wanted to say—'

'What?'

'First, how grateful I am to you for helping us. You've no idea what it means to me, and to my parents.'

'No need,' Ben said. 'It's what I do.'

'I know. You've helped so many people. Saved so many lives.'

'Ruth told you everything, did she?'

'Everything she knows. All strictly in confidence, of course. Please be assured I'd never breathe a word to anyone. Not a living soul. I mean, I understand that you sometimes had to do things that were . . . were . . .'

'Not always strictly above board,' Ben said. 'Like hunting kidnappers down like sewer rats and leaving them dead where I found them. Whatever got the job done. Whatever was required to bring people's loved ones back home safe.'

Stefan turned a little paler under the dim glow of the cabin lights. He swallowed.

'It's okay, Stefan,' Ben said. 'You're family now. Or as good as. Soon you'll be my brother, and I trust you like one.'

'It's an honour for me,' said Stefan. 'I truly mean that.' He paused, biting his lip nervously. He obviously had something else to say, something that was eating him alive as he tried to find the words. 'Ben . . . I mean, as we're talking openly and frankly . . .'

Ben had a pretty good idea what was coming. 'You want to ask me what I think the chances are for Lara.'

Stefan nodded and looked as if he wanted to cry. 'I know it's impossible to say, and that it's unreasonable of me to even expect you to predict what the outcome of this could be.'

'But you need to hear it anyway,' Ben said. 'You're right, Stefan. It is impossible to say. But I'll tell you this. No matter what might have happened to your sister, no matter how bad this turns out to be, I swear to you that we will not give up until we find her. One way or another. Do you understand?'

Stefan nodded anxiously. 'Whether she's alive or whether—' He couldn't say the rest.

'One step at a time,' Ben said. 'Whatever comes our way, we'll deal with it. And you *will* bring your sister home. That I promise.'

Stefan grasped Ben's hand. Ben could feel Stefan's shaking. Stefan clenched his jaw and closed his eyes and slumped in his seat. 'Thank you,' he muttered.

'Now get some sleep,' Ben told him. 'You're going to need it.'

After he'd dimmed the cabin lights and returned to his seat he sat there for a long time in the darkness, feeling the soft thrumming vibration of the aircraft coming up from the floor and through his body, his head too full of thoughts he couldn't switch off.

Until this moment he hadn't fully known what to expect of the man Ruth had chosen to spend her life with. He'd been afraid he wouldn't like the guy. But the age-old saying that how a person deals with extreme adversity is the best reflection of their character couldn't have been more true. And now that this situation had arisen, the gentle yet stoical qualities Ben was seeing in Stefan made him warm to the man much more deeply that he might have otherwise, and to understand that Ruth had made a good choice.

Which was good enough for Ben, too. That last thought lingering in his mind, he fell asleep with a half-smile on his lips. Whatever it might bring, tomorrow was another day.

Chapter 8

China

Having been in the air for ten hours, plus the six-hour time zone difference, it was early morning as the aircraft finally came in to land. After the fresh clean air and immaculate blue skies of Switzerland, the world into which Ben and Stefan now found themselves arriving couldn't have been more different. From a distance the vast, sprawling suburbs of Beijing appeared wreathed in murky grey smog, and that impression had only diminished slightly by the time the Bombardier was on the ground and had finished its taxi run at the private jet terminal. Beijing's new Daxing International Airport was said to be the biggest in the world, looking from the air like a giant red star-fish spread out over a hazy landscape as flat as a chessboard. Just gone 7.30 a.m., and already the heat and humidity were so intense that Ben's shirt was sticking to his back just moments after he and Stefan emerged from the plane and started crossing the tarmac towards the private reception building where a gaggle of smartly-attired executives from Steiner Industries' China Division were assembled to greet them.

Ruth had insisted that Ben and Stefan should be dressed for the part, if they were to be convincing in their role of fellow company employees. It had been easy enough to provide Stefan with the appropriate freshly-pressed dark suit and tie, as he already had an entire wardrobe to hand at the estate. Ben had posed more of a dress code problem, since he'd brought only his tux with him from home and couldn't very well wear that. The dilemma was solved by the lucky coincidence that he and Stefan were about the same height and build, allowing him to borrow a spare suit. And so for the second time in two days he was feeling awkward and constricted in his buttoned collar and tight-fitting shoes, with his more characteristic and infinitely more comfortable outfit of black jeans, denim shirt, leather jacket and chunky boots all stuffed into his old green bag. He was itching for the moment when he'd be able to throw off the suit and tie and become Ben Hope again.

This was a vast country and Beijing was a long way from Shaanxi Province where Lara Hartmann had gone missing. It was only because Ben and Stefan were ostensibly here on company business that Ruth, obliged to keep to the narrative, had made the capital city their initial destination. 'You'll be met at the airport by the second-in-command of our China operations, Sammy Tsang,' she'd told Ben back in Switzerland. 'He'll make all the arrangements for you to travel on to Xi'an, and from there to Lara's village.'

Ben asked, 'And does Sammy Tsang know the real reason we'll be going there?'

'Someone in the company had to be told. But don't worry about him. He's someone we can trust.'

Sure enough, as Ben and Stefan walked into the slick FBO private jet terminal building, from the welcome committee of mostly middle-aged Steiner execs stepped a brightly energetic and surprisingly youthful man in a nicely-tailored light grey silk suit, who shook hands with the arrivals and, in the most perfect English without any trace of an accent, introduced himself as Samuel Tsang, Vice-CEO of the company's Beijing

Division. 'But please call me Sammy,' he said with a warm smile. 'Everyone does.' The distinctive quasi-Americanised tinge to his accent was down to his having been raised and partly educated in Hong Kong and California before moving back to his native China. Ben took a liking to Sammy right away and could see why Ruth trusted him so implicitly.

The arrivals process was as efficient and cursory as Ben had expected it to be, thanks to their useful new corporate connections. He was less thrilled with the digital face recognition scanner he and Stefan were required to pass through before they could access the main part of the building. At last they re-emerged outside into the unbreathable air, and their escorts ushered them courteously towards the three gleaming black Hongqi limousines that were to whisk them the forty-something kilometres to the company headquarters in Beijing's central business district, on the east side of the city. Both Ben and Stefan were anxious to waste as little time as possible in pressing on towards their next destination, but the game needed to be played for appearances' sake. 'We can discuss certain matters in my office,' Sammy told them with a discreet twinkle.

Ben didn't generally consider himself an urbanite, but he'd frequented most of the larger capitals of the world and was used to that environment. Even so, it was hard not to be boggled by the sheer titanic scale and ultra-modernity of the Chinese megacity. Even Stefan, as a professional architect, seemed quietly blown away. Though here and there the breathtaking futuristic panorama of glittering steel and glass was interspersed with architectural reminders of China's ancient past, there was no trace of the poverty and more primitive trappings of places like Delhi, where Ben had travelled some years ago on another emergency mission, that time to search for Amal Ray, the new man in Brooke Marcel's life. That was another story.

Even in the midst of such dense urban jungle the citizens of Beijing were well provided with green areas, and viewed from the road some of the parks were strikingly large and beautiful. In one of them Ben caught a fleeting glimpse of a crowd of people performing an odd kind of slow-motion dance ritual he'd never seen before, on a stretch of lawn in the shade of some cherry blossom trees. The dancers' movements were perfectly synchronised, almost balletic in their gracefulness. Their legs were bent in what reminded Ben of a martial arts fighting crouch while their arms rotated in sweeping circles and their upper bodies turned smoothly this way and that. They could have been working through a sequence of karate katas like some of the ones practised in unarmed combat classes at Le Val, but slowed right down with painstaking deliberation. From the blankly concentrated expressions on their faces it was obvious they took it extremely seriously. Then Ben lost sight of them as the car sped onwards.

'What were those people doing?' he asked Sammy, who was sitting up front.

'That?' Sammy replied nonchalantly. 'That was Tai Chi. Or perhaps it was Qi Gong. I'm not sure, but they're both very popular traditional practices here in China, for promoting mental and physical health and inner peace.'

'Sounds like something we could all do with,' Stefan commented dourly.

It took almost an hour for their small motorcade to carve its way through the intense early morning traffic to the Steiner HQ in the Chaoyang business district. The company offices were situated on two floors high up within the giant Beijing World Trade Center Tower III. In the plush ground-floor lobby the rest of the corporate welcome committee evaporated after a final round of handshakes and courtesies, leaving them alone with Sammy, who led the way to the penultimate floor of the building in a lift that was about the size of the average stateroom at Versailles palace and twice as sumptuous. 'It's quite a building,' observed Stefan, who'd been drinking in his surroundings with a trained eye.

'I'm glad you're impressed,' Sammy replied proudly. 'At 330 metres it was the country's tallest skyscraper until 2018, when it was beaten into second place by the Guangzhou International Finance Center tower. Still, we are one metre taller than World Trade Center 3 in New York. Not that we're in any way competitive,' he added with a grin.

Sammy's personal office occupied one whole end of the fiftieth floor and offered a sweeping view of the business district from its enormous plate-glass windows. He sat his guests down on a suite of Italian designer leather, had a secretary bring in a tray of dainty porcelain cups of the most excellent coffee, and pulled up a seat opposite them. Glad to have escaped all the formalities of the welcome committee, Ben slackened his tie and unbuttoned his shirt collar.

Sammy's cheery smile flattened out into a frown and his tone became serious as he began, 'Now, gentlemen, as you're no doubt aware, I have been informed of the real purpose of your visit. A very regrettable situation indeed; and, Mr Hartmann,'–bowing his head in Stefan's direction–'may I take this opportunity to extend to you my deepest sympathies. I can't imagine what your family must be going through at this moment, and I can only pray for the safe return of your loved one. From what I'm given to understand, you are in the best possible hands with Mr Hope here, whose skills in that department are second to none.'

Stefan thanked Sammy graciously. Ben said nothing, wishing that his blabbermouth of a sister hadn't taken it upon herself to tell Sammy so much about his background and expertise. The fewer people who knew, the better.

Sammy went on, 'I'm sorry we're not able to discuss this matter more openly with our associates, but this is China. The authorities would be most displeased at the idea of two western visitors involving themselves unofficially in an ongoing criminal investigation. At the very least, it would certainly be regarded as an abuse of the terms of your business visa – and at worst, could be taken as grounds for your immediate deportation from the country. Or even your arrest. Our government tends to behave rather defensively over such matters. Therefore, as I'm sure you understand, we have to proceed with the utmost discretion. But please rest assured that I will do everything in my power to assist you in this difficult situation.'

'We appreciate your help,' Ben replied. 'And likewise, you have our assurances that we'll be very careful not to draw attention to ourselves, and won't do anything to compromise Steiner Industries in the eyes of the authorities.'

Sammy smiled. 'Excellent. Then we understand one another.'

'Have there been any developments in the police investigation while we were in the air?' Stefan asked.

'None that I'm aware of,' Sammy replied sadly. 'But then I'm hardly privy to that kind of information.'

'We'll find out soon enough,' Ben said.

'I daresay we will,' Sammy said. 'Now, my friends, I am entirely at your disposal. How do you wish to proceed? I imagine that you must be anxious to get started immediately? Or would you perhaps prefer to rest a while after your journey? This building also comprises a five-star hotel with 278 rooms and some of the best restaurants in China, should you wish. Entirely at the company's expense, needless to say.'

'That won't be necessary,' Ben said, standing up. 'I'd like a shower and something quick and simple for breakfast, and then I think we'd prefer to move straight on. Right, Stefan?'

Stefan nodded. 'Absolutely.'

'I forgot to add,' Sammy said, 'that Steiner Industries will also be delighted to foot the bill for all accommodation and other expenses you might incur during your stay in Xi'an.'

'That's very kind,' Ben said. 'I'm sure we can manage ourselves, once we get there. All I'd ask is that we be provided with a company vehicle to use. That would save the time and trouble of arranging a rental.' He had a long and extremely chequered history with car hire firms, thanks to his habit of returning their property looking as though it had been used for target practice on a military firing range. He'd thought about hiring one in Stefan's name, but they'd be bound to want his details, too. It could be a problem.

Ben didn't think that requesting the use of a car was such a big ask of a company that owned fleets of private aircraft and offices in the second most prestigious skyscraper in China. But apparently it was, because to his surprise Sammy responded to it by just staring at him in confusion. Or perhaps Ben hadn't expressed himself clearly enough. He repeated, 'I asked if it would be possible to get a car. It doesn't have to be anything fancy or expensive and we're happy to pay something in return for borrowing it.'

'Pardon my hesitation,' Sammy said apologetically. 'Only the situation there is somewhat more complicated. We wouldn't dream of charging you for the use of a car, of which we have any number we might have been able to offer you. However, as I should have mentioned to you earlier, foreign visitors to this country aren't allowed to drive here, unless they have a Chinese driving licence.'

'Seriously?'

Sammy nodded. 'I'm afraid our country's laws are extremely strict. Miss Steiner' – he said Ruth's name with reverence, as though he was talking about an empress – 'asked me to make arrangements for you to be provided with a driver for the duration of your stay. Under the circumstances and considering the need for discretion, I have offered to take that duty on myself.'

'*You're* going to drive us?'

'It will be my privilege to act as your chauffeur,' Sammy said with a bow of his head. 'As a bachelor without any family ties I'm free to devote some spare time to my honoured guests. And I can assure you that the company will make available one of its most top-of-the-line executive vehicles for your convenience and comfort.'

'That's very kind of you,' Stefan said.

Ben was used to having the freedom to go his own way, and he wasn't entirely happy about the idea of being driven about by a corporate chaperone who would be sure to be breathing down their necks at every step. 'I hope you're a fast driver,' he said to Sammy. 'I gather it's about an eleven-hour road trip from Beijing to Xi'an. I would have aimed to make it in nine. There's no time to waste.'

Sammy smiled. 'I hope you won't be disappointed in my driving skills. However, I'm entirely in agreement that time is a main priority. And so I have taken the liberty of arranging a somewhat faster means of travelling to Xi'an. A car will be waiting for us at the other end.'

Chapter 9

Sammy's faster option began with a climb up to the helipad on the roof of the World Trade Center tower, where a shiny black AVIC chopper with the Steiner logo emblazoned on its sides was waiting to zip them back to the private terminal at Beijing Capital Airport. As he explained en route, Ruth had given him the green light to charter another jet, this one smaller and off the books for discretion's sake, to carry them the six hundred nautical miles to the city of Xi'an.

By this time Ben had jettisoned his borrowed suit for the more comfortable attire he much preferred to travel in, while Stefan had changed into jeans and a lightweight jacket over a polo shirt. They'd each wolfed down a rapid breakfast of a Beijing speciality called Baozi, consisting of steamed buns filled with vegetables and tender, spicy lamb, which the hotel restaurant kitchen upstairs had whipped up at a moment's notice and had delivered to Sammy's office with more strong black coffee. The vice-CEO had allowed them to freshen up in his personal ensuite bathroom, as well as providing them with a bag containing nearly twenty thousand yuan in crisp new banknotes.

'Almost nobody in China uses cash any more,' he explained. 'Even the street beggars nowadays have card readers for taking digital payments. But we thought it might be useful for you to carry a certain quantity of paper money, for expenses. And it's still untraceable, which is a rare commodity in these times.'

Their new private jet was a diminutive but sleek Eclipse 500, just 33 feet long with a single pilot and capacity for five passengers. It felt like being in a winged sports car, right down to its lack of a bathroom. After their long journey alone in the spacious Bombardier, it was strange to be joined by a new travelling companion aboard the much more cramped cabin of the Eclipse. As charming, well-spoken and courteous as Sammy might be, the prospect of having him along for the entire duration of their journey, both by air and road, wasn't helped by the fact that the man just wouldn't shut up. Stefan clearly wanted to be left alone to brood in peace and Ben had always preferred an atmosphere as serene as an undiscovered tomb.

But perhaps out of nervousness or else simply because he was naturally loquacious, Sammy talked all the way from leaving the ground in Beijing to the moment they touched down at Xi'an Xianyang International Airport an hour and forty-five minutes later. By the time they landed, Ben had become an involuntary authority on the culture and history of their destination. Back in ancient times the city had been known as Chang'an, which translated to 'place of eternal peace'. It marked the starting point of the famous Silk Road that had been one of the great trade routes for some thirteen centuries, as well as being the centre for many of China's great ruling dynasties: the Zhou, the Qin, the Han and the Tang. In modern times it was still regarded as one of the country's great capitals, though its population was dwarfed by Beijing's at a meagre nine million or so inhabitants.

Hardly more than a hamlet, then. Aside from being home to the legendary terracota army, the city was also famous for its ancient fortifications built in the reign of Hongwu Emperor Zhu Yuanzhang and its eighth-century great Mosque. Sammy babbled on like a tour guide while Stefan appeared to drift off

76

to sleep and Ben sat quietly craving a Gauloise and a scotch. But delicately steering the mostly one-sided conversation away from the wonders of the city itself, he was interested in learning more about the surrounding countryside, where he anticipated they might be conducting most of their search for Lara Hartmann.

'As it happens,' Sammy explained, 'I know the area quite well, or of it. A third cousin of mine, Mingze Shuang, works as a contractor and was hired to help build a six-lane motorway nearby, which was never completed because the project ran out of money. There's some tourism development in the region with some new parks and resorts being built, but my cousin told me that in general the area is still mostly unspoilt and quite traditional. Some of the villages date back to the Neolithic Age, and there are caves and ancient ruined temples that few people ever visit.'

Sammy glanced at Stefan to check he was still asleep, then went on in a lowered voice, 'The village where the girl disappeared is called Qingjiacun. When I discovered the name I called my cousin to ask if he knew of it, and he said he had passed through there a few times while he was working in that area. It's a small riverside community of only a few hundred inhabitants, about an hour's drive east from the city. It has a bicycle trail that some sightseers use, and one small hotel and restaurant, but otherwise it's the traditional rural kind of village where people live the same way they've lived for centuries.'

Ben said, 'What I've been wondering is why a couple of visiting students would want to rent a house there. Wouldn't it have been easier for them to live closer to the city?'

'My cousin said there's a bus service that comes and goes twice daily. And he also told me it's very scenic and quiet. That's what makes it all so shocking,' Sammy added, lowering his voice still further so as not to be heard by the dozing Stefan, 'that anything like this could happen in such a peaceful spot. Apart from the usual petty thefts and disturbances, there's no crime to speak of in Qingjiacun. Such a thing as a kidnapping is completely unheard of. It would come as a great shock to everyone in the community.'

'Except to whichever of them did it,' Ben said.

'You think it was someone from the village?'

'It's not a total impossibility. The appearance of two young, not unattractive western girls in the neighbourhood might have stirred things up a little, got tongues wagging and hearts beating, caused some jealousies among the local lads, who knows? That's if she really has gone missing.' They were talking almost in whispers now, just loud enough to be heard over the rumble of the plane.

'You don't believe it?' Sammy said, raising his eyebrows in surprise.

'Let's just say I'm keeping an open mind,' Ben replied.

The private jet terminal at Xi'an Xianyang International Airport was pretty much a carbon copy of the one in Beijing, except this time it was a gleaming black Mercedes V-Class seven-seater luxury people carrier that was waiting for them rather than a gaggle of Steiner Industries suits. The car was massive and boxy with an interior as opulent as the jet's, filled with the smell of new leather. True to his word, Sammy had arranged everything even down to the supply of bottled water and provisions for the drive from Xi'an to Qingjiacun. 'Chinese-made cars are far superior nowadays to anything in the west,' he declared as he climbed in the driver's door. 'But I thought you might prefer a European model.'

'Yup, makes me feel right at home,' Ben said, settling into the soft leather of the middle row of seats while Stefan got in the front. He reached for his pack of Gauloises, fished one out and clanged open his Zippo.

'Er, you're going to smoke in the car?' Sammy's face in the rear-view mirror had one eyebrow raised in disapproval.

'I appreciate all that you're doing for us, Sammy. But I never asked you to be our driver and tour guide. And I especially don't need a nursemaid. Let's go.'

Sammy seemed to take that blow to his dignity as his cue to demonstrate his skills behind the wheel. The big, plush Mercedes was fast and their chauffeur was determined to prove he was no slouch, either. Soon they were speeding away from Xi'an along a slick, smooth highway with Sammy recklessly overtaking everything in sight and the air conditioning pumping out an arctic blast. Stefan had called Olivia Keller before leaving Switzerland, to say they were en route and would call again when they reached Xi'an. Now he took out his phone to let her know they were on their way to Qingjiacun. 'Her English is good but it's easier if I speak German with her. Ben, I know you don't have a problem with that. Sammy, when we're with her I can translate for you.'

'That won't be necessary,' Sammy said. 'I speak German, as well as Japanese, Korean, Russian, French and Spanish.'

What's Japanese for smart arse? Ben thought, but he didn't say it out loud.

'Then I'll put her on speaker so we can all listen. She might have more news to tell us.' Stefan plugged his phone into the car's hands-free system and speed-dialled her number. Olivia picked up the call on the second ring and her voice came through the hi-fi speakers. She sounded as if she hadn't had a moment's sleep for days. 'Yes?'

'Fräulein Keller, this is Stefan Hartmann, Lara's brother. We're on our way to you from Xi'an and should be there within the hour. I wanted to check that you'd be at home.'

'Yes, yes, I'll be here,' she replied. 'I've been expecting you to call.'

'Has there been any more news?' He didn't need to specify what it might be about.

'There has. The police contacted me earlier this morning to say they've almost finished their search of the area.'

'And?' Stefan prompted her, sounding almost too afraid to ask.

'They've found nothing,' she replied.

It was a simple answer, but to Ben it conveyed a lot of information. More than just a lack of an identifiable body, it meant no trace of human remains, clothing or blood or anything else that could indicate she'd been raped or murdered anywhere in the vicinity. If they were doing their job even half properly the police would have covered a fairly large circle around the location where Lara had last been sighted.

All of which meant, in turn, that so far things could still go either way. No evidence to suggest she'd come to harm, and none to say she hadn't. Ben's open mind would have to stay open a while longer.

'Ask her the name of the detective in charge of the case,' he said to Stefan.

Olivia heard his voice on her phone and sounded perplexed by it. 'Are you on speaker? Who's that with you?'

'My friend, Herr Hope,' Stefan explained. 'He's come to help.'

'Oh. I see.' Olivia didn't ask how Herr Hope could do that. She replied instead, 'Detective Lin is her name. She's very nice. And she speaks English, which makes it easier for me. My Mandarin still isn't so great.'

'What about Dan Chen?' Ben asked. 'Have they found anything out about him, where he might have gone?'

Again, Stefan didn't need to relay the question. 'There's been no more mention of him,' Olivia said. 'What I've told you is all anyone's told me.'

Ben was doubtful that she'd have much, if anything, more to tell them in person than they'd already learned. The next couple of hours might well turn out to have been a wild goose chase. Once they'd finished their business in Qingjiacun their next port of call would have to be to try and speak to this Detective Lin, to find out if Dan Chen's employers had reported him missing from work or whether the guy had been given time off for a short break or a holiday. If it turned out to be the latter, Ben was thinking that this so-called missing persons case could be over very quickly.

But Ben was about to discover that he was wrong. Dead wrong. Because things were going to take a turn he could never have foreseen.

Chapter 10

Without the onboard GPS they'd have become hopelessly lost – and at times even that technology seemed to be leading them nowhere. A succession of roads leading haphazardly away from the smooth modern highway became increasingly rough and rural, shrinking into potholed single tracks where the big luxury Mercedes must have looked strangely incongruous among the primitive and scabby old trucks that occasionally came rumbling by in the opposite direction, forcing an unhappy Sammy to pull tight into the dusty verge to let them pass.

When at last they found it, the little village was just the way Sammy's cousin had described it to him. Qinjiacun was surrounded on three sides by tall forested hills and on the other by a fast-flowing river crossed by a rickety wooden bridge that was the only vehicular access and seemed barely up to the job of supporting their car's weight, let alone that of the local bus serving this tiny community.

Sammy drove slowly through the village. There were few people about, other than a pack of kids enjoying some kind of street game that resembled hopscotch and an old bent man with a staff walking an equally old, bent dog. The houses were mostly wooden-framed and traditionally styled on just two or three narrow winding streets of compacted earth that sloped up from the water's edge. Some homes were encircled by walled yards and gardens filled with lotus flowers and peach blossoms; others were somewhat dilapidated, modern satellite TV dishes a strange sight among the vegetation growing from walls and uneven tiles. The more important buildings, like the small village temple and community hall, occupied the higher ground and featured the classic Asian hip-and-gable roofs that curved up like horns at the corners. There could be no mistaking the fact that you were in China.

Following the directions that Olivia Keller had given them, Ben and his two companions left the car and walked up the dusty street to the small bungalow where the two young women lived. It was one of the more modern houses in the village, with a tiny yard out front dominated by a tree with fragrant yellow flowers whose petals were strewn over the pathway and the roof. Stefan, looking pale and tense, took a deep breath and knocked on the front door.

'She doesn't seem to be at home,' said Sammy after four knocks and no response.

'Damn it, she said she'd be here,' muttered Stefan. They were contemplating what to do next when the bungalow door creaked open and the face of Olivia Keller peered cautiously out of the gap at her three strange visitors.

'Miss Keller? I'm Stefan Hartmann. I—are you all right?'

It was the sight of the young woman's reddened eyes and tear-wetted cheeks that had made Stefan interrupt himself before he could say more. She looked unsteady on her feet and her long dark hair was dishevelled on one side, as if she'd been lying with her head buried in her pillow. Ben and Sammy exchanged glances. None of them had expected to find Olivia Keller in high spirits, under the circumstances, but she seemed much more upset than she'd sounded on the phone less than an hour ago. Something had clearly happened in the meantime.

'Miss Keller, please tell us what's the matter,' Stefan repeated, but she could hardly speak more than a few mumbled words they didn't understand.

Ben had seen this before. 'She's in shock.' Stepping past Stefan he gently took the young woman's arm and spoke softly and reassuringly to her in German, 'Take it easy, now, Miss. Let's get you inside.'

Olivia still said nothing as they led her back through the house to a small, low-ceilinged living room. She was wearing a pair of colourful cotton trousers and a loose-fitting ethnic top. Studenty, like the interior of the cottage. There were a couple of chairs at a small table, some cushions strewn about the floor, pictures and posters on the walls. The two housemates had done all they could to make their home pleasant and comfortable on a low budget. One fixture that the pair hadn't provided for themselves was an old cast-iron wood-burning stove in the corner, with a flue through the wall.

They settled her down carefully in a wicker armchair and Stefan crouched on the floor beside her, coaxing her to speak to them. She kept shaking her head and wiping her eyes as more tears poured down her cheeks. Managing to compose herself a little, she pointed at Ben and Sammy and asked confusedly, '*Wer sind diese Männer?*' Who are these men?

'This is my friend I told you about before, who's come to help us,' Stefan explained patiently. 'His name's Ben. And this is Sammy, who brought us here from Beijing.'

'Is he a policeman?'

'No, he's just another friend. We all want to help you. That's why we're here. Now please, Olivia. You can trust us. Tell us what's happened. Has there been more news?' Stefan was so taut with tension as he spoke that his voice sounded constrained. He was desperate to know more, but at the same time he was terrified of what she might be about to tell him.

It took some time to get the facts out of her, because once she'd begun to open up to them the words all began to gush out in an emotional jumble. 'It was just a few minutes after we talked on the phone earlier,' she sobbed. 'I got another call.'

'From who? The police? Detective Lin?' But Olivia had dissolved back into tears and couldn't speak. Stefan looked as if he wanted to grab her by the shoulders and shake it out of her.

'Go easy, Stefan,' Ben said, switching to English for a moment.

'I have to know!'

'Let her talk.'

But Ben could feel his own tension rising fast too, because whatever they were about to learn, it couldn't be good. He knew that Stefan was thinking the same thing he was. That the call from the police had been to update Olivia with the latest news that their search had now uncovered Lara's remains after all. Ben looked at Sammy and could tell that same terrible thought was in his mind as well. They could only pray that wasn't the case, but there seemed to be no hope of a happy outcome here.

Olivia's next tearful words turned Ben's blood cold and made his heart sink into his boots.

'They told me . . .' she sniffed. 'They told me they found a body. Oh God, it's too awful.' Then the tears started flowing again and she started choking up.

Here we go, Ben thought darkly. This was it, then. Any traces of scepticism he might still have been clinging to were now blown away, along with any remaining chance that this situation would turn out to be a harmless misunderstanding. The poor woman was dead. Stefan had lost his little sister to some psycho maniac or rapist. Whom they were now going to have to catch, and try very hard to refrain from beating to death before they handed him to the police.

Ben laid a hand on Stefan's shoulder and could feel him shaking. Stefan bowed his head, utterly drained and defeated.

'I'm very sorry,' Ben said to Olivia. 'Do the police have any leads as to who killed her?'

Olivia stared up at him from her chair, her eyes filled with tears and confusion. She tried to speak, opened and closed her mouth twice without making a sound, then tried again and this time managed to say, 'Killed her?' She looked even more horrified, as though this was some new idea that hadn't even occurred to her.

Ben stared back at her. Now it was his turn to be totally confused.

'No, no,' she blurted out. 'You don't understand. It wasn't . . . wasn't Lara's body they found. It's Dan.'

Sammy's jaw fell open. Stefan's bowed head snapped abruptly back up. The words had tumbled out of her in such a rapid flow that for a second Ben couldn't be sure he'd heard right.

'Dan Chen? Lara's boyfriend?'

Olivia grimaced and nodded. 'He's dead. But it's worse than that. He was all messed up. I mean, really, *really* bad. The police say someone must have tortured him to death.'

Chapter 11

Suddenly the whole picture had changed. The shock of this unexpected twist made Ben speechless, but already his mind was on fire with all its new implications. If for whatever unknown reason Dan Chen had been violently, gruesomely murdered, then there could be little doubt that something equally bad could have happened to his missing girlfriend. It also meant that this was far more than just some run-of-the-mill rape attack or opportunistic kidnapping, which until now had been the worst-case scenario Ben had been working with.

And if both Lara and Dan were somehow implicated together, the only conclusion Ben could draw was that they'd been involved in something dangerous. Something they'd both known about prior to this happening.

He was the first to break the stunned silence in the room. There was a wooden chair nearby, and he pulled it up to sit close by her armchair so he wouldn't be standing towering over her. Looking straight in the young woman's eyes he said in a firm but gentle tone, 'Olivia, I know how hard this is for you, and I know you've already spent a lot of time talking to the police. But to help us figure out what's going on I need you to go through this again. From the start, as much as you can remember. Are you okay with that?'

Her lip trembled and she seemed about to burst into tears again, but she controlled it. 'I'll do my best.'

'So let's go back to last Friday, when Lara went off on her run. Was there anything unusual about that? Anything you might have noticed about her behaviour, or anything she might have said at the time?'

Olivia nodded. 'She didn't say anything. It's more what she didn't say.'

Ben's eyes narrowed. 'Can you tell me what you mean by that?'

'I don't really know for sure,' Olivia replied uncertainly. 'It was just an impression, really. I thought she seemed kind of preoccupied, withdrawn, not talking much, as if something was troubling her. She's usually so bright and cheerful.' A tear rolled from the corner of Olivia's eye and she wiped it quickly away.

'Did you ask her what that might be?'

'I thought about asking, but I had the feeling she wouldn't want to talk about it. Which I thought was strange, too, because normally we talk about everything that's going on in our personal lives. If one of us is upset, the other is a shoulder to cry on. There've never been any secrets between us. This seemed different.'

Ben asked, 'And how long had she been acting that way?'

She replied, 'All that day. And all of the day before. In fact she'd been a bit odd ever since she got back home on Wednesday afternoon. That's the day she always gets the bus into Xi'an for her weekly lectures. Then afterwards in the late afternoon, when he can get off work an hour or two early, she and Dan sometimes meet up in a park in the city, near the college.' Olivia frowned. 'I mean, that's what they *did*,' she added softly. 'Normally they'd spend the whole evening together. But this time she came back much sooner than usual. And she'd been strange since. I thought maybe they'd had a quarrel, but I didn't ask. I thought if she needed to talk, she would.'

'Did you mention her strange behaviour to Detective Lin?'

'Yes. But she didn't appear that interested. I suppose it didn't seem relevant at the time.'

Stefan had been listening intently to all this, and now a thought had come to him. He said to Olivia, 'When you spoke to my family you told them about an entry in Lara's diary saying her boyfriend had given her something, the last time they met. That would have been the same Wednesday afternoon, correct?'

Olivia nodded sadly. 'Who even keeps a written diary any more? I used to tease her about it. But then as I was getting so frantic with worry I started thinking there might be some secret she was keeping from me. Something that might explain where she'd gone. Maybe it would explain what had been bothering her the last couple of days, too. I knew she kept the diary in the drawer next to her bed. So I went in there and read it, and that's how I learned about this thing he gave her, like a package of some kind.'

'Do we have any idea what was inside the package?' Stefan asked.

'She didn't say,' Olivia replied. 'It all sounded weird to me. If I'd known about it before she disappeared, I'd have asked her about it, and if that's what was bothering her.'

'Where's the diary now?' Ben asked. 'Can we see it?'

She shook her head. 'The police took it away, along with some of her other stuff.'

Something else they would have to try and speak to Detective Lin about. Ben sighed. 'Okay. Is there anything else you remember?'

'There is one thing. Something weird she said to me the day before she disappeared.'

Ben asked, 'Weird how?'

'Maybe it's nothing. Probably just a silly idea.'

'Tell me anyway.'

'Neither of us is a smoker,' Olivia said. 'I mean, I tried it one time at a party back in Switzerland, but I nearly coughed my lungs out and never tried again. But as far as I know, Lara's never even tried it.'

Ben couldn't tell where she was going with this, but he stayed silent and let her talk.

Olivia went on, 'So it seemed odd when she asked me if I had a lighter or a match. I think she was so stressed over whatever she was holding back that she must have bought cigarettes. Hoping that might relax her, you know? But that wouldn't be like her at all. So I don't know. I can't understand what she was thinking.'

It did seem like an off-the-wall kind of detail. Ben didn't know what to make of it. He pointed at the iron wood-burning stove in the corner. 'Maybe she was thinking about lighting a fire? She was feeling cold?'

'We've never lit that thing. There's a man in the village who sells firewood but we don't have any. The weather's been so warm.'

'Okay,' Ben said. 'So it's not that.'

She tried to smile through her tears. 'I told you it was a silly idea.'

'Everything's worth thinking about. Even the smallest detail that stands out as different or unusual can help us understand more.'

She fell quiet, running the tip of her tongue between her lips. 'Different or unusual. Like the thing with the backpack.'

'What backpack?'

'I'd forgotten all about it until you said that just now. There was something different the evening she went off on her run. Normally she carries a little pouch to keep her phone in. You know, like the kind you strap around your middle? A bum bag, or whatever you call it. Well, this time she took a different bag with her. A backpack with shoulder straps, smaller than a ruck-sack but bigger than the one she normally uses. I've got one exactly the same. We bought them together at a market in Xi'an.'

'Could you show it to me?' Ben asked. Olivia got up from her chair and left the room to go and fetch it.

'Why would she have needed to do that?' Stefan wondered while Olivia was gone. 'Was she planning on going somewhere?'

Before Ben could reply, Olivia came back holding a bright pink backpack. It would have been too small to use as an overnight bag. You couldn't carry much at all in there. But at the same time it seemed unnecessarily large to take jogging, unless it was for some other purpose.

Sammy had been silent until now. 'Perhaps she intended to pick up some groceries from the village store?' he offered helpfully.

'I don't think so,' Olivia said. 'We always do our food shopping together. Deciding who's going to cook what.'

Ben knew that was a blind alley. He was thinking about Dan Chen and the mysterious parcel. The enigmatic diary entry. The sudden unexplained change in Lara's mood and her secretive, perhaps furtive, behaviour. He asked, 'Olivia, were Lara and her boyfriend dealing in drugs?'

Olivia's eyes snapped wide in horror. 'No! No way!'

Stefan turned to stare at him too. 'Ben?'

'What if the reason she took the larger backpack was because she was carrying Dan's parcel inside?' Ben said. 'What if the parcel was the reason she was taken, and he was killed?'

'I can't believe my sister would be capable of such a—'

'Then there's the thing with the matches or lighter,' Ben said. 'We know she didn't smoke cigarettes. But there are other things apart from tobacco. You can tell us, Olivia. You won't get into any trouble, I promise. We just need to know what she might have got herself involved in.'

'We're only students,' Olivia protested.

'And students have never been known to do drugs?'

'Lara would never have got mixed up in anything criminal,' she insisted.

'Not knowingly, maybe,' Ben said. 'What about her boyfriend? How well did you know him?'

'Dan was a lovely person. Friendly, warm, so gentle and kind.'

'Yeah, well, whoever tortured him to death and dumped his body like so much dog meat wasn't such a sweetie pie,' Ben said. 'Nice guys don't tend to last long in that world.'

Sammy was shaking his head in disbelief. 'Drugs? You really think?'

'Right now I don't know what to think,' Ben replied. 'But I'm damned if I'm not going to find out.'

Chapter 12

There was no telling where she was, and the more time passed by since she'd been taken, the harder it became to be sure how long she'd been locked in this place. Her captors had taken everything – her shoes, her backpack, her silver necklace, her earrings, even the watch Dan had bought her for her birthday.

Her prison was a bare, windowless stone-block room with a rough concrete floor and ceiling. The only light came from the wind-up lantern her captors had given her, so that she could find her way to the slop bucket when she needed it, to the little washtub and water jug, and to the dishes of cold rice and noodles that they brought her from time to time, which she had to eat with chopsticks. It wasn't as though they'd completely deprived her of any comforts. Her mattress on the floor had been supplied with soft wool blankets that smelled freshly laundered. At least they wouldn't let her freeze to death when the temperature dropped at night. But the lantern was useless, a full minute of frantic winding providing barely that long of dim glow, and so she sat, ate, prayed, sobbed and slept mostly in darkness.

There was nothing else to do. For the first hours of her incarceration she'd pounded on the cell door and screamed until her hands bled and her voice was hoarse. Nobody came, and at last she'd given up in despair and found her way to her bed to curl up and cry herself to sleep. She'd had no idea how long she'd lain there before she woke in the pitch darkness and the reality of the nightmare came back. Winding up the hopeless lantern to give herself a few moments' light, she'd started exploring the confines of her prison in the hope she might at least be able to work out where she was, if not find some way of getting out.

Neither was possible. The iron door was recessed into the stonework and immovably solid, while the walls themselves were so thick that she couldn't make out the tiniest whisper of sound through them. For all she could tell, her prison could have been far out in some remote wilderness, or deep in the heart of a busy city surrounded by people, streets and traffic. Wherever it was, it was a grim and horrible place and her yearning to get out of here was even more intense than her confusion as to who could have done this to her, and why.

She knew that her original captors numbered at least five, because she'd seen them at the cherry blossom grove before they took her. As far as she could tell, though, only three people had the job of looking after their prisoner. Every few hours she'd hear the scrape of the bolt and the creak of the hinges, and there would be one of them framed in the doorway, dimly lit from behind as they entered the cell to bring food and water, or take away her empty dishes and her bucket. It was hard to make them out because they always shone a bright light in her face, but she thought one was a young, tall man with longish black hair, another man older and shorter, and the third a dumpy middle-aged woman. None of them ever spoke to her, not even when she swore and screamed at them, demanding 'Where am I?' and 'Who are you people?' She wanted to attack them, but she was too afraid that they'd hurt her and so mostly she stayed quiet and just cowered in the corner of her cell and waited for them to go away.

Everything seemed hazy and faraway now as she tried to think back to the events leading up to her being taken. But there was no doubt in her mind that the reason she'd been taken prisoner had something to do with whatever was inside the package Dan had entrusted her with and asked her to pass on to his 'friends'. The hastily hand-written note he'd given her along with it had been as clear and specific as the object itself was mysterious. His instructions had read:

LARA,

DO NOT OPEN THIS PACKAGE. TELL NOBODY ABOUT IT AND PLEASE MAKE SURE THAT U DESTROY THIS NOTE AFTER READING IT. 2 DAYS FROM NOW AT UR USUAL TIME, TAKE THE PACKAGE TO THE PLACE U TOLD ME ABOUT, THE CHERRY BLOSSOM GROVE IN THE FOREST NEAR THE VILLAGE WHERE U GO RUNNING. U WILL BE MET THERE BY MY FRIENDS. THEY WON'T HARM U. DON'T SPEAK TO THEM OR ASK QUESTIONS. GIVE THEM THE PACKAGE AND LEAVE. EVERYTHING WILL BE OK. I'M SO SORRY FOR EVERYTHING THAT'S HAPPENING. I KNOW U MUST BE VERY FRIGHTENED AND CONFUSED BUT I PROMISE IT'S FOR THE BEST POSSIBLE CAUSE AND I WILL EXPLAIN EVERYTHING WHEN I SEE U AGAIN SOON.

I LOVE U. DAN XXXXX

After carefully reading it over and over until she'd memorised every word, she'd disposed of the note by scrunching it up and hiding it, with the intention of destroying it more properly and permanently when she had a chance. Then on Friday evening around seven, just as he'd requested, she'd set off on her usual run along the riverside and away from the village into the forest, carrying the unopened package in her backpack. She'd been terribly nervous and somehow felt she was doing something wrong or illicit, but kept reminding herself of what Dan had said, that these people were her friends, that it was for a good and important cause, there was nothing to worry about, and that all these confusing and bewildering questions would soon be answered.

She'd been jogging along the track towards the cherry blossom grove, the scenic spot where she often paused to catch her breath and admire the beauty of nature, when the three men had appeared from the trees. She'd been expecting them, of course, but her heart jumped at the sight of the black balaclava masks they were wearing. With only their eyes and mouths visible they looked intimidating, like terrorists. Weren't they supposed to be Dan's friends? Why did they have to hide their faces – was it for her good, or for theirs? And why the black leather gloves they were wearing?

Still, wanting to do the right thing for Dan, she'd dutifully asked no questions as she stopped, unzipped her backpack and taken out the package to hand over to them as required. They'd seemed pleased to have it, and she'd been glad that she'd completed her task whatever its purpose was.

That was when things had gone badly wrong. Because instead of letting her turn around and leave as Dan's note had implied they would, they obviously had other ideas. After glancing at one another with a nod of agreement, they'd stepped quickly towards her and grabbed her by the arms. Her cry of fear and protest was stifled by a gloved hand clamped over her mouth, and suddenly she was being dragged off the track and into the trees. She'd struggled and resisted for all she was worth, but she wasn't strong enough to tear free of their grip. What the hell was happening?

Her blood turned to ice water as she saw the black van parked on an adjacent track through the forest. She could see two more men sitting in the cab, also wearing the same black masks. As the first three men dragged her towards the van, the two inside opened their doors and stepped out. One of them was holding something in his hand that she saw was a roll of strong, broad tape. The other was carrying a cloth bag.

Lara had been convinced then that she was about to be gang raped, and then probably strangled or stabbed to death and left here for her body to be found in the forest. The terror took her breath away and made her feel weak at the knees. But rather than throw her to the ground and start ripping off her clothes, instead they held her upright while they bound her wrists and ankles with plastic cable ties and clapped another length of sticky tape over her mouth. Seeing her chance, she bit the hand of the man doing it, and felt a surge of triumph at his yell of pain and the taste of blood on her lips. But it was short-lived, because then they pulled the bag over her head and she was swept helplessly off her feet and bundled into the back of the van. The doors slammed, she heard voices, and then moments later the engine started and she felt the lurch of the vehicle pulling away and U-turning back down the forest track.

That was when, lying on the hard metal floor, she'd known she was being kidnapped.

The journey went on for an hour or so before the van stopped moving. The back doors were wrenched open, strong hands reached inside and grabbed her bound ankles and she was dragged out, wriggling like a fish. The sound of nearby traffic told her she was in the city now – it seemed to be coming from overhead, as though they were in some road underpass – but the impression lasted just seconds before her captors bundled her into another vehicle, a car this time, which took off with a squeal of tyres. Almost immediately there was a crunch and the car stopped. From the sounds of angry voices, she realised they must have collided with another vehicle. Seeing her moment she tried to scream for help, but the tape over her mouth and the bag on her head stifled any sound.

Then the car took off again, and this time it kept going. She stopped trying to fight them, and lapsed into state of helpless resignation. A much longer period went by, maybe two hours, before she felt the car pulling off the road and onto what seemed like another bumpy track. A few moments later, it rolled to a halt and she heard the doors opening. They'd arrived. Now what?

What happened next was very strange. She'd expected that the car would stop near to whatever place, presumably some building, where the kidnappers were intending to keep her. Instead they lifted her out and carried her on foot, horizontally as though she were a rolled-up carpet, for the longest time. She'd started struggling again, then stopped, so that she could try to figure out where she was. The sounds of birds, and of rustling trees, told her they were in a forest, though it seemed to her it couldn't be the same one they'd been in before. Her captors were carrying her on and on, their footsteps scuffing along a path. She was only light, but the effort of carrying her such a long way was hard work for them. Twice they had to lay her down on the ground while they caught their breath. The second time, she tried to resist them again but they just picked her up and kept on moving. Sometime after that she heard the rattle of a padlock, the clink of a chain and a metal gate creaking open and clanging shut behind them. Then a while later, she felt herself tilt up at an angle and realised from the different motion that they were carrying her up steps. Lots of them. Up and up, as if the steps went on for ever. It was like some weird, hazy nightmare. Except it was really happening.

Then at last, it seemed as if they'd reached wherever it was they were taking her. Echoing sounds told her they'd entered a building. The jostling movement of negotiating more steps, going down this time, and not so many of them. Next the thud of a heavy door, followed by others; then at last she was here in the dark, echoing space of what was to become her cell.

The ties had been cut away from her ankles, then from her wrists. The last thing to come off was the hood and the tape gag. Bright light shone in her eyes so she couldn't see. Then she was shoved down onto the mattress in the corner, and by the time she sprang to her feet again the door was slamming shut and she was alone.

She'd been here ever since. Time drifted. She thought about Dan constantly. She couldn't believe that these people were his friends. He must have been tricked somehow, or betrayed. Which made her wonder even more about what he could have got himself mixed up in. Had the same people taken him, too? Was he perhaps being kept in another part of this place, wherever it was? He might be just the other side of this wall, in a cell of his own, wondering the same about her.

Lara needed to believe that Dan was all right, but a terrible voice in her head kept telling her that something awful had happened to him.

And that she was going to meet the same fate.

Chapter 13

Ben, Stefan and Sammy left Olivia's place soon afterwards, having learned nothing more. Their trip to the village had only raised more unanswered questions and deepened their confusion. Stefan was visibly upset by the news of Dan Chen's grisly murder. 'How am I going to tell my family about this?' he groaned as they returned to the car. 'Mum and Dad will go crazy.'

'Don't tell them anything,' Ben said. 'Not until we find out more.'

'How are we supposed to do that?'

'By talking to Detective Lin,' Ben replied. 'If she's heading up the investigation, she should be interested to meet the missing girl's next of kin. Sammy, can you make the call and tell them we need to speak to her?'

Sammy was taking out his phone when it rang in his hand: his assistant in Beijing, calling to say that she'd booked them a suite at a good hotel in Xi'an. Now at least they could worry and fret in luxury.

The next part of Sammy's duties proved to be a tougher task. Speeding towards the city it took him twenty minutes to get through to anyone with any authority at the Public Security Bureau, which was the official name of the police headquarters in Xi'an. After wrangling with several layers of admin personnel, to whom he had to painstakingly repeat the whole story each time, he was finally put through to Detective Lin. Over the car speakers she sounded somewhat terse and snappish, as though she had far better things to do than talk to him. Sammy explained the situation one more time, and after her initial reluctance she agreed to see them.

En route, Sammy explained that every city had a number of different administrative PSB centres dealing with different aspects of public security such as fire, traffic, VIP protection, crime control and public order and information: for which read the office of state censorship, propaganda and quelling civil disobedience, Ben thought. The offices were clustered close together in the same area of the city, to which Detective Lin gave them directions. The police HQ was a large austere building with a traditional curved-roof entrance portal heavily guarded by armed cops. Their car was flagged through a series of barriers, and paperwork was carefully scrutinised by guards who looked more inclined to shoot these western strangers on suspicion of terrorism than to let them inside an official building.

'What's it to be?' Ben wondered out loud. 'A quick pat-down to check for weapons, or the full rubber-glove treatment?' Sammy put his finger to his lips and whispered, 'Watch what you say.'

After being made to pass through a scanner they were finally admitted into the building and escorted through corridors and up in a lift to a neat, large third-floor office in which they met Detective Lin for the first time. As a uniformed cop ushered the three of them inside, a slender, petite woman of maybe thirty rose up from a desk to greet them. She was dressed all in black, with long hair scraped tightly back in a ponytail, dark penetrating eyes and finely sculpted features that would have been attractive if her face hadn't been set in a hard expression – somewhere between extreme distrust and outright hostility – barely hidden behind her formal manner.

This interview might not go quite as well as they'd hoped, Ben thought as he was introduced and shook the detective's tiny but surprisingly strong hand. He wondered if she always wore the chunky black pistol in the belt holster on her hip, or had only strapped it on for their benefit.

Detective Lin wasn't alone in the office. Also present was a middle-aged, equally unsmiling superior with greying hair, baggy eyes and a paunch, who if anything looked even less pleased to make their acquaintance and didn't bother to get up from his seat or shake hands, keeping his arms folded. She introduced him as her boss, Chief Zhao. It wasn't obvious to Ben at first whether the chief spoke any English, because he remained silent for a long while as the detective talked. Hers was highly fluent, and she spoke quickly and aggressively. It was hard to tell whether that was just her usual manner or was just adopted for the occasion. She seemed much more interested in Dan Chen's killing than in Lara's apparent abduction, but expressed a polite modicum of sympathy towards Stefan as the next of kin to the missing woman. All Ben got from her were the most suspicious looks and raised eyebrows as Stefan introduced him as a friend and business associate who also happened to be an international kidnap expert come to offer the family his help and support in this crisis. The chief looked even more dubious.

Ben was pretty used to getting the tough treatment from police. A few rare exceptions aside, he'd never quite managed to get on too well with their profession. But the undisguisedly hard-boiled attitude of Detective Lin and her superior towards him made him think he'd have an especially challenging time staying on the right side of these two.

From the start, it was clear that Detective Lin would have no truck with any western outsider sticking his nose in their business. 'I can assure you that's not why I'm here,' Ben reassured her. 'I'm just doing whatever I can to assist the family during this difficult time.'

'That's good to hear,' said Detective Lin. 'Because I must warn you any attempt at unauthorised outside interference in this case will meet with a most severe response from the Chinese authorities and could result in your being immediately deported from the country. I hope that is very clearly understood.'

'In Technicolor, Detective,' Ben replied with the most charming smile he could muster. 'As if we would even dream of such a thing.'

Her expression didn't melt a fraction. 'Now perhaps you can help us to clarify what is going on here. Please tell me again in what capacity you are acquainted with the murder victim.' They'd already been through this, first with Sammy on the phone and at least three times here in person. It was the classic police interrogation tactic, to keep repeatedly asking the same question in the hope of exposing a weakness or contradiction in the witness's statement. Stefan hadn't been expecting such a grilling, either, and he looked nonplussed.

'None at all,' Ben replied, feeling his patience beginning to ebb. 'Neither I nor Mr Hartmann, nor our associate here, have ever met him. As we've explained already several times, we understand that Dan Chen was romantically involved with Mr Hartmann's sister Lara. Whom you don't seem to be having much success finding, I might add.' If charming smiles weren't going to soften her up, Ben was thinking, then maybe it was time to get a little tougher.

That was when Chief Zhao finally broke his silence. 'No chance to find girl,' he said, in English that was almost impenetrably accented and with a cold bluntness that made even Detective Lin blanch. Maybe she did have a human soft centre, after all, Ben thought. 'Not alive,' the chief added.

Stefan had turned a couple of shades paler than the detective at the chief's words. He blinked, swallowed hard, collected himself and managed to reply, 'And what makes you so sure that you can give my sister up for dead already? It's only been a few days.'

'Because people who take her, they do to her same thing did to boyfriend,' Zhao said with a casual wave of his hand. As if to emphasise his eloquent point, he leaned his head to one side, hawked something up from his throat and spat on the carpet.

Ben had known in advance that spitting in public was considered totally normal behaviour in China, indoors or out. He wasn't as shocked as Stefan, who obviously hadn't been prepared for anything like it and got up from his chair, stunned into speechless fury by what he took as the chief's utter disrespect.

'Let's get down to brass tacks, Detective,' Ben said, stepping in before Stefan could explode at Zhao. 'We were told that Dan Chen was tortured. That doesn't sound like any normal kind of murder. Which I'd think would narrow your field of enquiry somewhat. So what's being done to find the perpetrators?'

'Yes, it seems that he was tortured,' replied Detective Lin. 'But I'm afraid that it's worse than that. On examination of the victim's body our forensic team soon found out that the mutilation was more extensive than we realised at first.'

Now Stefan was gaping at the two cops, and so was Sammy, who'd hardly spoken a word throughout the interview, growing more and more visibly concerned at the tension in the room. Ben narrowed his eyes and asked, 'More extensive in what way?'

'We'd show you the pathology images,' she said. 'But they don't make very pleasant viewing. He received an extremely severe beating to the face, and his arms and legs had been systematically broken by hammer blows from the fingers and toes upwards. Indicating that the perpetrators were intent on extracting information before they killed him. Whether they got what they wanted from him or not, that's impossible to say.

They were certainly going to kill him in any case. Death was inflicted by a razor or knife cut that severed the windpipe and arteries to each side. It seems this was done while he was hanging upside down, because his body was drained of blood. There are ligature marks on his ankles where they suspended him.'

'They slaughtered him like a pig,' breathed Stefan. He was still on his feet and clasping his fists tight.

'Then I'm afraid it gets worse again,' Detective Lin told them. 'Much worse. You might want to sit down, Mr Hartmann.'

'I prefer to stand. Let's hear it,' Stefan said tersely.

'There was a longitudinal cut to the torso, stretching from the upper chest to the groin,' she said. 'Made perhaps by the same very sharp blade that was used to cut his throat, or possibly by a scalpel. At first glance it seemed as if it could have been inflicted during the torture, except that it had been sewn up afterwards, which puzzled the pathologists until they removed the stitching to examine the wound more closely. What they discovered indicates that it was made after death, or so we hope for the victim's sake. The ribcage had been sawn open to get at the heart and lungs. They're gone, along with all the other major organs.'

'What do you mean, *gone?*' Stefan asked, shaking his head in confusion.

'I mean that his internal body cavity was almost completely emptied out, everything removed but the stomach, intestines, bowel and bladder. The heart, lungs, kidneys, liver, spleen and pancreas have been surgically removed. By someone quite skilled, according to our examiners. They reported it was a very clean job, as clean as a professional autopsy. We can surmise that the reason the cut was sewn up afterwards was to prevent the rest of his internals from spilling out while the body was being transported to where it was dumped.'

'Oh, my God,' Sammy gasped, doubled up and clutching his stomach as though he wanted to vomit. Stefan was reeling on his feet. Ben gripped his arm and helped him back into his chair.

Detective Lin explained grimly, 'Now perhaps you understand why, if Miss Hartmann has fallen into the hands of the same people, then I'm afraid to say our expectations have to be realistically negative.'

The chief nodded. 'Human organs worth lot of money on black market,' he agreed in his garbled English. 'Girl gutted too.' He looked as if he wanted to spit again, but catching the look on Ben's face he seemed to think better of it and swallowed audibly.

Stefan clapped a hand over his mouth. 'I'm going to be sick.'

Detective Lin called for an officer to help him to the nearest bathroom. Chief Zhao sat there watching the show with a look of mild amusement.

'That's what I love about the police,' Ben said. 'That sympathetic touch when it comes to breaking bad news to loved ones.'

'We're sorry,' she said, looking as though she might actually mean it. She kept darting glances at her superior.

'So what now?' Ben asked her. 'Do you have any active lines of investigation going, or is this all still a guessing game for you guys?'

'The police are doing all we can,' Detective Lin assured him. 'And we have reopened the search for the missing girl. That is all that is possible for now. But I will keep you informed if we learn anything new.'

'If,' Ben said. He'd stopped trying to be charming a couple of minutes ago.

Reading his meaning, she frowned and said, 'I understand your frustration. But I must repeat my warning about getting involved. You must let the police handle this. Otherwise the authorities—'

'I get what the authorities will do,' he cut in. 'We can't have too many experts poking around, can we? Might risk showing up the boys and girls of the illustrious People's Police.'

'I am very good at my job,' she said defensively.

'I hope so, Detective. We'll soon find out.'

The two of them were standing almost toe to toe, glaring at each other. Except Ben was about nine inches taller, and she had to hold her chin high to maintain eye contact. Small, but dangerous. She looked as ferocious as a mongoose about to attack a cobra. The muscles in her face were tight and she was almost quivering with fighting spirit. Ben might have admired it, if he hadn't wanted to throw both her and her chief out of the window.

'Let me give you the name of our hotel,' Sammy said, keen to defuse things before they escalated into something Ben could be thrown in a gulag for. He pulled a business card from his wallet, scribbled where they were staying on the back of it and laid it on the desk. Chief Zhao ignored the card, made a dismissive grumping noise and breezed out of the office. Moments later, Stefan was escorted back from the bathroom, looking pale and ill.

'Do you have a number we can contact you on?' Sammy asked the detective. 'I mean, just in case we happened to stumble across anything you might find useful. Without getting involved in the case, of course,' he added sheepishly.

'If you need police assistance or want to report a crime you can dial 110 like everyone else,' she replied icily. 'Other than that, I don't expect to hear from you. We'll be in touch.'

Ben couldn't wait.

Chapter 14

'Well, that was just wonderful,' Sammy muttered irritably at Ben as they got back in the car to be ushered the way they'd come through the security barriers. 'You really know how to ingratiate yourself with the people in authority.'

'Yeah, I'd get on great living in China,' Ben said.

'I thought you had been in the army. Don't they teach self-control and discipline there?'

'Just drive, will you.' Ben had no time for discussion right now. He was much more concerned about Stefan, who looked gaunt and weak and was moving like a man twenty years older. As Sammy grumpily punched their hotel address into the sat nav, Stefan slumped in the back seat, turned towards the window and stared into space. He was grimly uncommunicative until they were more than halfway to the hotel and passing a large liquor store on a busy boulevard through a modern part of the city. Then he mumbled, 'Pull over, Sammy.'

Minutes later they were on their way again, armed with several bottles of something called Baijiu, which was just about the only kind of spirits available for sale. This presumably wasn't how Sammy had envisioned them spending their expenses cash. Ben wasn't sure that it was a good idea, either, because it was painfully obvious what Stefan's intentions were.

'I don't care,' Stefan muttered in reply to Ben's suggestion that he take it easy with the hard stuff. 'I mean to drink until I'm able to forget everything, for ever, so I never have to think about any of this again. And I'm going to get started the moment we get to the hotel.' Then he fell silent again and lapsed back into whatever tormented thoughts were swirling around his head.

You couldn't blame the guy, Ben thought. A missing sister was bad enough without the threat of ghoulish organ rippers lurking in the background, knives and scalpels at the ready. Ben wasn't sure how he'd have handled it himself. Perhaps in much the same way, seeking solace at the bottom of a bottle. God knew he'd been there before now.

The hotel was much more upmarket than they needed it to be, especially under the present circumstances. Sammy's assistant had picked out the most opulent suite available, with three separate bedrooms, its own small kitchen area, a large living room complete with all the comforts and a balcony offering a view of Tang Paradise Park.

None of them could have cared less. Taking no notice of his surroundings whatsoever Stefan flopped into a big leather armchair with his jinking carrier bag of spirits bottles at his feet, and without bothering to fetch a glass from the kitchen he set about making good on his promise. 'For Christ's sake, Stefan,' Ben said, thrusting a tumbler into his hand, 'if you're going to drink yourself into oblivion at least do it properly.' Meanwhile Sammy, declaring that he was feeling too depressed to talk to anyone, skulked miserably to his room and wasn't seen again for a long time.

Over the next couple of hours, Stefan managed to polish off much of a bottle of Baijiu before it got the better of him and he passed out with his chin on his chest. Ben relieved him of his bottle and glass before he could spill the remaining liquor all over his lap, then delicately covered him with a blanket from his room. Out of curiosity, he took a sniff and then a sip of the Baijiu himself. 'Jesus,' he muttered, pulling a face. It was like drinking rocket fuel. The guy in the liquor store had enthusiastically told them it was by far China's most popular alcoholic beverage. If that was true, Ben thought, then Chinese doctors must be seeing more than their fair share of patients with advanced liver rot.

No wonder clean healthy organs were at such a premium on the black market around here.

Ben was going to slosh the rest of the booze down the sink, but then he thought *fuck it* and poured a glass for himself, which he carried out to the balcony. Evening had fallen, the air was cooler and lights were twinkling over Tang Paradise Park and its lake, the moon climbing over the distant mountains.

Now for the hard part. He didn't want to do it, but it had to be done. Ben took out his phone with a sigh. Whatever time it was in Switzerland, Ruth must have been anticipating his call because she snatched the phone up on the second ring.

'What's happening?' she asked urgently. 'How's Stefan?'

'Sends his regrets that he can't come to the phone right now. He's been sampling the local firewater.'

'Stefan? Drinking?'

'Only to the point of unconsciousness. He's had a tough day. We're not any closer to finding Lara yet. And there's something else you need to know about.'

He updated her on the latest developments, but she sounded so shocked that he couldn't bring himself to tell her about Dan Chen's involuntary organ donation. Just his being dead was enough bad news for the moment.

'My God. What am I going to say to Conrad and Leni?'

'That you're still waiting to hear from me,' Ben said. 'Who knows, maybe tomorrow will be a better day.'

'Call me if it is, won't you?'

'As soon as I know more,' he promised.

'And Ben?'

'Hm?'

'Take care of him. And of yourself.'

'Good night, Ruth.' He ended the call, took another sip of Baijiu, decided *enough* and tipped the rest of his glass over the edge of the balcony. You could almost hear it frazzling a hole in the lawn below. Then he went back to thinking. There was a lot to think about.

Setting aside all the things that Detective Lin had told them, he reflected back on their meeting with Olivia Keller and the more baffling details she'd come out with. The mystery of Lara's backpack was clear enough to him now, because it was almost certain that she'd used it to take Dan's package to whomever she'd given it to. The contents of the parcel, and the ID of its recipient, were still burning questions. And the thing with the matches was perplexing him, too. If not to light the wood stove, and if not to smoke a cigarette or something more illicit, then what the hell could Lara have needed them for?

Ben hated not knowing the answers to these things. And he hated it even more when he was stuck here wasting time in a luxury hotel suite when he could be out there learning what he needed to know. *Fuck it*, he thought again. He'd had enough of trying to work things out by guesswork. Time for some action.

He went back inside and checked on Stefan, who was still pretty much comatose and would be for a while yet. Too out of it to notice Ben removing his phone from his pocket. Next Ben slipped silently into the darkness of Sammy's room, where its sleeping occupant was sprawled face down on his bed, dead to the world and softly snoring. Ben tiptoed across to the chair over whose backrest Sammy had carelessly slung his jacket, felt in the pockets and soon found what he was looking for, the key to the Mercedes.

Sammy wouldn't like it that his guest had taken it upon himself to drive around without him. But that was Sammy's tough shit. Ben slipped out of the hotel suite and headed down to the car.

Chapter 15

The reason Ben had taken Stefan's phone was that it had Olivia Keller's number on it. Carving fast through the night on his way back towards Qinjiacun he tried calling her. There was no reply, so he left a message.

'This is Ben Hope. I know it's late but I have to talk to you again, because we need to thrash this out some more. I'm on my way to you right now. Be there shortly.'

He wondered why she hadn't answered the phone. Unlikely that she'd be out partying, in her present state of mind. Hopefully not zonked out on booze like Stefan, either.

Qinjiacun was mostly all in darkness and even more deserted this time of night. Moonlight rippled on the river and a gentle, warm breeze whispered through the forest leaves. A nocturnal monkey with a long curly tail darted across the village street, startled by his approach. He dimmed the car's lights so as not to disturb the human residents, coasted quietly the last few yards to Olivia and Lara's cottage and parked beside the tree with the pretty yellow flowers.

As he walked up towards the little house he could see a shaded light peeking from a narrow gap in the living room window blinds. That was something, he thought. She was at home and he wouldn't have to wake her. He wondered if she'd got his message and was waiting for him to turn up.

Then as he stepped towards the front door, he noticed that it was lying open a crack. Maybe she'd anticipated his imminent arrival and opened it for him. He might find her in the kitchen, brewing a pot of that jasmine tea of hers to share with her late-night visitor.

Or not. Moving closer to the door, he stopped. Listening. Not just for sounds coming from inside the house, but listening also to his sixth sense, that little voice in his mind that he'd been relying on for years to alert him whenever something was wrong. That inner voice of his was seldom wrong. And it was talking to him now, in a tone that was rapidly rising in pitch and volume as his hand moved towards the door. Telling him he was walking into danger.

Which wasn't an unusual or unfamiliar experience for a man with his background and skills. But it was at times like this that an operator like him was uncomfortably reminded of how naked he felt without a weapon. That hollow space behind his right hip, all but moulded into his body by the years of his trusty old Browning Hi-Power nestling comfortably where he could snatch it from its holster in a split second, felt suddenly very empty.

His fingers touched the cool, smooth surface of the cottage front door. It was made of lightweight wood, like balsa, and needed only a breath of a nudge to push open wider.

Ben stepped into the dark, narrow hallway. His little voice was screaming at him now, but he ignored it and focused on listening for sounds coming from inside the house. The silence was absolute, heavier than air.

He called out, 'Olivia?'

No reply.

'Olivia?' he repeated. 'Are you there? It's Ben Hope. I called to say I was coming.'

Nothing.

Except there *was* something. Not perceptible to his ears, but to another of those acute senses that he'd often relied on in the past to alert him to imminent trouble. That was the sense that could pick up on the slightest telltale waft of cigarette smoke or aftershave while creeping up on an enemy hideout, warning him hostiles were near and all hell was about to break loose.

He paused in the dark hallway and sniffed the air. What he could smell wasn't smoke or toiletries, and it sure as hell wasn't jasmine tea either. This brand of perfume was the kind that brought back the worst memories. Memories of death and carnage. It was a natural partner to that leaden silence that filled the house. And its source was right behind the door just a few steps away from where he was standing. The door to Olivia and Lara's little living room.

Ben took a deep breath, dreading what he might be about to find on the other side of that door. Then he stepped quickly towards it and shoved it open.

The shaded glow he'd been able to see through the gap in the blind was coming from a small table lamp near the window. It was the only light in the room. But it was all the light that was needed to show what was lying on the floor. Ben had returned to Qinjiacun to see Olivia Keller, and here she was. He wouldn't have to go to the trouble of waking her up. He wasn't going to get much more information out of her, either.

Whichever person or persons had neglected to close the front door probably hadn't done so on purpose, although they likely hadn't cared much about how they left things on their way out. They'd paid their social call to the house maybe two or three hours ago, and they'd been here a while. Ben could tell that first fact from the colour, texture and coppery tang of the blood that covered much of the floor. It was still fresh and only just beginning to dry and brown around the edges, and where it was smeared thick over the furniture and over the half-naked corpse of Olivia Keller. The duration of their visit,

115

he could make an educated guess at, too. Because it must have taken them at least an hour to carry out the amount of surgical mutilation that had been done to the young woman's body, if they wanted the organs to come out intact and reusable.

The living room was a slaughterhouse. Olivia lay at its centre, stretched out on her back with her arms outflung to the sides and her legs straight out, like someone who'd been crucified, only horizontally. She was still wearing the colourful cotton trousers as earlier, but the ethnic top was gone. Her upper body, from below the navel to the base of the throat, had been sliced cleanly open by sharp blades and some kind of surgical circular saw to bisect the ribcage, whose halves had been prised apart like the jaws of a Venus flytrap and held in place by the kind of clamps that Ben imagined surgeons using for major heart operations. Not as major as the one that had been performed on Olivia Keller, though, because there was only a gaping bloody hole inside her chest cavity where her heart had been entirely removed. Along with her lungs, her liver, and various other parts that Ben could only guess at and didn't really want to know about.

How much of her ordeal she'd had to endure while she was still conscious, he couldn't say, but he hoped it had been over quickly for her. If the last expression of utter terror and unspeakable agony frozen on her face was anything to go by, he knew he was probably hoping in vain. A length of tape had been stuck over her mouth to stifle her screams.

He closed his eyes. 'Christ.' He'd witnessed some pretty gruesome sights in his life, and while this one maybe wasn't the very worst, he wouldn't be forgetting it any time soon. He could only be thankful that Stefan hadn't been here to see it. As her brother would have done, now Ben was thinking about Lara and trying very hard not to picture her the same way.

He stood there for a few moments, then stepped out of the room and back into the hall where he didn't have to see her or breathe in the smell. As far as how to handle this turn of events, he had two options. The first was to just walk away and act as if it hadn't happened. Which was impossible, for all kinds of reasons. The second was to call his new friend Detective Lin. Which he was reluctant to do for other reasons, but on consideration there seemed no other choice.

If you want to report a crime, dial 110 like everyone else, she'd said. The emergency number took him to an automated service in Chinese and English, and then to an operator. It took a while to get through to the police headquarters in Xi'an. Ben gave his name and said this was an urgent message for Detective Lin. 'Tell her I'm calling from the village of Qinjiacun. She'll know where to find me. Tell her it's happened again and she needs to get over here as fast as she can. Bring a cleanup crew, a mortuary van and all the officers she wants. But there'll be no need for an ambulance.'

He reckoned he had a little over an hour before the might of the Xi'an police descended on the village en masse. That was all the time he needed to poke around the crime scene himself. With a weary sigh he walked back into the living room, stood and looked around him to take in more details. The floor was smooth stone tiles, with a rug in the middle where Olivia had died. There was so much blood that it had completely saturated the rug almost black and then pooled outward, reaching one wall to one side of her and almost as far as the doorway to the other. As the blood became slowly tacky and congealed it showed traces of footprints where the killers had padded around the room carrying out their grisly work. The prints stopped short of the doorway and there were none in the hall, which told Ben they must have been wearing plastic overshoes that they'd removed on their way out, to avoid leaving a trail out into the street. He guessed they'd have been wearing plastic aprons, too, and taken them away with the overshoes for disposal. The stolen organs themselves would have been packed into polythene bags or maybe some kind of freezer box, to keep them fresh. If the killers were really on the ball, they'd be driving a refrigerated van. These sultry subtropical summer nights could be really tough on meat preservation.

All in all, a neat job, professionally carried out. That was, except for the shockingly messy state in which they'd left the body. By strange contrast, Dan Chen's remains had been so carefully sewn up that the forensic pathologists had had to reopen his body before they even noticed the missing body parts. Ben wondered about it as he started hunting around the house for whatever he might find.

The house phone was sitting on its base station on a side table near the doorway. Noticing the flashing voicemail notification LED he picked up the handset and played back the message he'd left her earlier. Then he wiped his prints off the phone and replaced it where he'd found it. Two other doors off the hallway led into Olivia's and Lara's bedrooms. It was easy to tell whose was which, as they'd both left passports, student cards and other ID lying prominently around. Olivia's room was a mess, the bed rumpled, clothes strewn over the floor, junk everywhere, but it didn't have the look of a room that had been ransacked. Lara's bedroom was just the opposite, the bedclothes drum-tight and all her belongings tidied away. The only thing not in its place was the diary, the bedside drawer in which Olivia had said Lara kept it being empty apart from a makeup case and a nail file. Ben wasn't surprised to find the diary missing. Olivia had already told them the police now had it.

Having learned nothing from his search so far, he went back into the living room and returned to reflecting on other questions that had been his reason for wanting to come here tonight. Such as, *why would someone need matches if they don't smoke and aren't thinking about lighting a fire?*

He looked over at the wood-burning stove in the corner of the room. He'd seen it on his previous visit, and there'd been nothing especially remarkable about it then either. Just an old-fashioned rugged firebox cast out of mild steel in the bowels of some Chinese iron foundry, maybe fifty years ago, maybe a hundred. A classic piece of ultra-low technology built to provide good, simple service for a lifetime and more. Certainly not the kind of object to inspire much passion or interest from a couple of millennial students whose world revolved around phone apps and social media.

But it had Ben's interest, and he observed it closely. Working stoves usually had flecks of wood ash and little bits of bark and kindling swept under them, in those nooks and crevices the vacuum cleaner missed. This was totally clean. And as Olivia had said, they didn't have a single piece of firewood to burn anyway. The iron log rack by the stove was empty.

But you could burn other things than logs in a log burner, he thought. Just as there were other reasons for burning something than to keep warm. Out of curiosity he stepped around the edge of the blood pool and went over to the corner where the stove was. He put a hand on its flat, cold iron top and crouched down to examine it. Mounted on solid hinges was a fire door with no glass, just an ornate design cast into the metal, and a latch for opening it. The paint on the wall around the hole where the black iron flue went through was clean and fresh and undiscoloured from contact with hot metal, further confirming that the stove hadn't been lit in some time. Ben lifted the latch, swung the heavy little door open and peered into the sooty brick-lined firebox.

And saw something inside.

Something that someone had thrown into the stove with the intention of returning to burn it later when they got the chance. Except that chance had never come about.

'Hello,' he said.

Chapter 16

What Ben had found inside the wood-burning stove was the reason why Lara had asked her friend if they had any matches or a lighter. It was a single sheet of paper, crumpled into a tight ball and chucked into the firebox to be permanently disposed of in the near future. Just as soon as a lighter or a box of matches came to hand.

And when Ben retrieved the paper and uncrumpled it to read, he soon understood the reason why. Dan Chen's handwritten instructions to his girlfriend had been as clear and detailed as anyone could have made a hastily-scribbled note. He'd specifically told her not to open the package he'd given her, but to pass it on to his 'friends' at an exact time and place: the cherry blossom grove, two days later. Ask no questions, he'd said; make the drop and walk away, and you won't be touched. He'd expressed from the heart how sorry he was to have to ask her to do this. Assured her that although she must be very scared and confused, she needed to understand it was all for the best possible cause. He'd promised to explain everything soon, when he saw her again. Told that her he loved her.

And most importantly of all, he'd specified that she was to destroy the letter immediately after reading it. Which Lara had clearly failed to do, or else Ben wouldn't have been holding it in his hands at this moment.

Hmm, Ben thought. Back in the days of so-called 'HUMINT' or human intelligence, when covert communications often came in the form of coded messages slipped into a folded newspaper left on a train seat or dead-dropped in a litter bin, an experienced operator wouldn't have delayed in getting rid of the incriminating evidence. Lara Hartmann wasn't – or hadn't been, depending on whether or not she was still alive – an experienced operator, by any means. Whatever this was about, she'd clearly been left in the dark and had no idea what her boyfriend was getting her to do for him.

It definitely looked like a drug deal, as far as Ben could see. What other reason could there be to employ your unwitting, naive girlfriend to deliver an unknown sealed package to your 'associates' – read customers – in a secluded setting like a forest in the middle of nowhere?

Unless . . . Dan Chen had worked for the government, albeit in some harmless enough capacity for the Ministry of Culture or some such thing. But knowing what Ben knew about the way governments worked, and especially the more secretive, duplicitous and totalitarian governments of which the modern Chinese state was a prime example, the apparently innocuous grey man working in some low-level department could easily be a sleeper agent involved in something far more shadowy. Was it feasible that Dan could have been a spy of some variety, dealing in sensitive secrets – or a whistleblower exposing corruption, or even a double agent playing one side against the other? That could potentially explain the sticky end he'd come to, even if it didn't account for what his killers had done to his body afterwards. Now maybe those same killers were on a mission to track down and eliminate anyone they believed to be Dan Chen's associates.

Which would mean Lara was certainly dead, as Chief Zhao had predicted. Ben hated to admit the guy might be right.

He was getting into the realms of crazy guesswork here, and he knew it. Nothing was making any sense.

Now people were getting eviscerated in quick succession, and there was no telling who might be lined up next to receive the same treatment. Ben was going to have to come up with some answers, and fast.

He was still puzzling over the questions when the distant wail of police sirens reached their crescendo outside and swirling blue lights appeared through the crack in the living room blinds. He stepped out of the cottage to meet the whole fleet of rapid response vehicles pulling up in a long line, accompanied by a black van he took to be the coroner's. All up and down the street, windows were lighting up, front doors were opening and residents were gathering outside in pyjamas and dressing gowns, gaping at the strange spectacle of a mass police presence descending on their sleepy village in the middle of the night.

At the head of the convoy was a dark grey unmarked saloon car that parked by the tree with the pretty yellow flowers, up behind the Steiner company Mercedes. The driver's door opened and out stepped Detective Lin. *Here comes trouble*, Ben sighed inwardly.

He'd thought she'd looked mean and sour enough back at police headquarters, but judging by the angry scowl she was wearing on her face, she must have been in one of her better moods then. She was wearing no makeup and had thrown on a pair of tight-fitting jeans, immaculate white trainers and a short tan leather jacket. The same chunky black service pistol she'd been wearing at the office was riding on her right hip. A phalanx of uniformed officers formed behind her as she came striding up to meet Ben outside the cottage door. She halted and stared at him, jaw clenched and eyes glinting as if she was giving some serious consideration to unholstering her weapon and emptying the magazine into his chest.

'Sorry for getting you out of bed,' Ben said.

A thousand retorts showed on her face but all she said was, 'You and I will speak later. Get out of the way.'

Ben obligingly stepped to the side as she motioned at the officers to follow her. 'I'd wear something to protect your shoes,' he advised. 'It's a mess in there.'

'You think we haven't been to a crime scene before?' she snapped back, then stalked into the hallway with uniforms jostling in after her.

Some of the locals were still out in the street, peering anxiously at the goings on. Officers urged them back inside, barking orders in quick-fire stentorian Chinese. Ben was totally ignored as he stood leaning against the wall of the house, breathing in the cool night and the sweet bouquet of the flowering tree. The stars were twinkling above the forest and shimmering on the river. It was far too beautiful a night to be sliced to death and butchered in your own living room.

He lit a Gauloise and smoked it slowly as the police went about their work, joined by the mortuary team in their overalls pushing a gurney. It was a nasty task they had to carry out, but no worse than, say, the one his SAS unit had experienced having to reconnoitre an African village after every man, woman and child inside had been hacked apart and dismembered by marauding militia troops. All part of the job.

Ben had taken just a few puffs of his cigarette when one of the cops came bursting out of the house and made it halfway to the street before he bent double, clutched his belly and threw up. Must have been the first time he'd ever seen a young woman torn open and gutted like a fish, obviously. A few minutes later the mortuary team wheeled her out on their gurney, zipped into a black plastic body bag, and trundled her off towards their waiting van. More officers emerged from the house in their wake, looking somewhat pale and shaky. One of the last out was Detective Lin. The scowl had left her face. She was breathing hard.

'I warned you about the shoes,' Ben said, looking down. Those nice new white trainers would never be as white again.

'To hell with my shoes,' she shot at him, the anger quickly returning. 'Let's talk. And you'd better tell me the truth. What are you doing here? Didn't I warn you about meddling with a criminal investigation? And put out that cigarette. It stinks like shit.'

Some people. Ben shrugged, dropped his half-smoked Gauloise and crushed it out with his boot heel. Down the street, the mortuary team slammed their van doors and set off, escorted by two police cars to the front and rear. Faces were watching from nearby windows. 'I wasn't meddling with your case,' he replied. 'I left my sunglasses behind when we were here earlier. Came back to get them.'

Detective Lin pursed her lips doubtfully. 'In the middle of the night?'

'Insomnia,' he said. 'It's a terrible thing. I'm not the only one. Poor Olivia was having trouble sleeping, too.'

Now she looked even more suspicious. 'Really. And do you mind telling me how you know that?'

'Come now. Surely the great detective wouldn't be asking for my amateur insights into her case?'

'I asked you a question. You could be in a lot of trouble, you know. It would be wise to cooperate.'

He shrugged again. 'I don't mind telling you. I'd called Olivia in advance to say I was on my way here tonight. When she didn't answer, I thought maybe she'd gone to bed. But it turns out she hadn't, because she was still dressed when the killers appeared. It's possible she'd got my phone message and was staying up to wait for me. But I think she was already dead by the time I called. Because that would explain why they were in such a hurry to get the job finished.'

'And what tells you that?'

'The fact that they didn't stitch the body up to take it away to be dumped, like they did to Dan Chen's. I suspect they weren't planning on leaving her the way they did. They work more neatly than that, based on what we know of their MO. You understand "MO"?'

'Just keep talking,' she said tersely.

'But they were on the clock, because while they were busy they heard my message come over her answerphone and they knew an unexpected visitor was due to turn up. That might have been inconvenient.'

She thought about it for a moment, then nodded slowly. 'Okay. That makes sense to me. But I'm still not buying this bullshit about coming back for your sunglasses. Prove it. Show them to me.'

'Wish I could. Genuine Ray-Bans. The killers must have taken a fancy to them.' As if no self-respecting torturer could do without the real thing.

'Hm. And what were you doing here earlier anyway?'

Ben was ready for that one, too. 'Stefan's idea. He wanted to pay his respects to his sister's friend. That's all it was, Detective. We wouldn't have dreamed of asking her any questions concerning the case.'

'Oh, of course not. And how did you get here tonight?' Her suspicious eye scanned along the kerb, past her own grey sedan to the Mercedes behind. She pointed at it accusingly. 'Is that your car?'

'Technically, no. It doesn't belong to me.'

'But you drove it here from the city. Yourself, alone, a foreigner. If you don't have the proper authorisation for that, I could arrest you on the spot.'

'But you wouldn't really want to do that,' Ben said with a smile.

'Wouldn't I?'

'I don't think so. Because then you wouldn't get to see what I found here tonight.'

'You found what?' she asked, pretending to be less interested than the glimmer in her eye betrayed.

'Your first real bit of evidence,' he replied.

Chapter 17

He handed Detective Lin Dan Chen's crumpled note, explaining where he'd found it and his theory about why Lara hadn't got around to destroying it the way she'd been instructed. The detective's eyebrows rose as she read.

'Pretty sensational, don't you think?' Ben said.

She said nothing until she'd re-read the note twice more. Then looked up at him, frowning now. 'What does it mean?'

'Well, for a start, it means that whoever snatched Lara Hartmann, kidnap wasn't part of their plan at first. All they wanted was the package Dan had given her. After that they were going to let her walk away, going by what the note says. But then something must have changed.'

Detective Lin eyed him curiously. 'How do you know about the package?'

'Olivia described how Lara had written about it in her diary. Which I also know you've read, because the police took it away.'

She nodded. 'I've read it, but there's nothing of any use to us in it. We still have no idea what he gave her, or why.'

'Then we'll just have to work it out the hard way,' Ben said. 'Good old-fashioned sleuthing work, following the clues step by step. The first step being for you and me to take a walk down to the cherry blossom grove where we now know Lara went to meet Dan's so-called "friends". We can assume that's where she was taken. Sounds like a nice scenic spot. I'm sure someone in the village can tell us where to find it.'

'Hold on a minute. "We"? "Us"? You and me?'

'Why not? Are you still going to arrest me for driving without the appropriate authorisation?'

'No, I'm not going to arrest you.'

'Then I don't see any reason why we shouldn't pool our resources. Tell me you've worked cases like this before, Detective.'

She seemed about to fling back some kind of defensive retort, but then her expression softened and her shoulders sagged a little. It was clear she couldn't shake the horror of what she'd seen tonight from her mind's eye. Ben knew the feeling. She sighed. 'Honestly? I can't say that I've ever seen anything this bad.'

'That's what I thought,' he replied. 'I've seen plenty, and worse. I was seeing things like this when you were still a little schoolgirl in pigtails and sandals.'

'I never had pigtails.'

'And it seems to me that we can help each other here.'

She shook her head adamantly. 'It's out of the question. Even if I agreed in principle, Chief Zhao would go insane if I allowed a civilian to get involved. Especially a foreigner.'

'What about a foreigner who's a former Special Forces officer with years of expertise in tracking missing people and smashing organised crime rings? Let's face it. You need someone like me to guide your moves. And seeing as I'm a stranger here, I need someone with the local contacts and the authority to make things happen. You told me you're a good detective. I believe that. I think you and I could make a pretty good team.'

'I thought you were only here to support the Hartmann family.'

'That was before. Now I'm here to find out who's murdering innocent people and stealing their organs. And to stop them from doing it to anyone else. Meanwhile if there's even a ghost of a chance that Lara Hartmann is still alive, I mean to locate her, rescue her and get her home safely to the people who love her. That's the job I'm trained for. I've been doing it a long time, and I'm not too bad at it. But the clock's ticking and I can't do this alone.'

'And if Lara Hartmann isn't still alive?'

'Then whoever killed her has to pay,' Ben replied. 'That's something else I'm pretty good at making happen.'

Detective Lin was looking at him very intensely. There was a lot going on behind those sharp, intelligent eyes as she chewed over what he'd said.

'Besides,' Ben added. 'What Chief Zhao doesn't know can't hurt him.'

'Are you suggesting I shouldn't even tell my boss I let you work together with me?'

'That's exactly what I'm suggesting,' Ben replied. 'Let's be practical, Detective. The clock's ticking for you, too.'

'What's that supposed to mean?'

'It means that this isn't exactly an open country. Not exactly transparent about matters of domestic policy. You don't have to be a political analyst to know that your authorities are very hot on stopping anyone on the outside from knowing too much about what goes on inside your borders. There's nothing they'd hate more than to have to let western law enforcement agencies poke their noses into their affairs. But that's what's going to happen, because now you've got at least one murdered European on your hands and the other missing presumed very likely dead, their families back home are going to want answers and not even the might of the Chinese state can keep the lid on this situation for long. You have maybe two days, three maximum, before this cosy little crime investigation of yours starts to blow up into one hell of an international incident. And unless you can solve the case very fast indeed you'll have those nice guys and gals from INTERPOL swarming over your turf like ants, whether your government likes it or not. Which is going to put the local cops on the ground in a difficult position with their top brass. You don't want that, neither does Chief Zhao, and neither do I. We have a saying back home, "Too many cooks spoil the broth".'

'We have the same saying.'

'And trust me, the moment this hits the international news, your perpetrators are just going to disappear into the woodwork and you'll never catch them. So before this thing turns into a United Nations circus it's in both our interests for you to work with me. My way.'

'Your way,' she repeated. 'Which is what exactly?'

'Which is to move hard and fast, so the bad guys don't know what hit them. No hesitation, no mercy. When we're done, if there are any still breathing it's your arrest and you get all the credit.'

'And you?'

'Me? I was never here.'

She shook her head again, mulling it all over, but this time the adamant look had gone. He could hear the wheels turning inside her mind. She knew it made sense. She was wavering. A new look of resolve came over her face as she arrived at a decision. But then, just as she was opening her mouth to reply, one of the uniformed cops appeared, looking contrite for breaking in on his superior's conversation. A few steps behind him at the kerbside, lit by the glow from the cottage window and the flashing blue of the police vehicles, stood a short, reedy civilian of maybe sixty, wearing slippers and an oversized silk dressing gown with a red dragon motif on it. The little man was shifting nervously from foot to foot, afraid to make eye contact and nervously wringing his hands.

Detective Lin and the uniformed cop had a few brief words in Chinese. The cop pointed at the little guy in the dressing gown. Detective Lin looked at him and nodded.

Ben asked, 'What's he saying?'

'He's saying that this man lives in the village, that he claims to be a witness to something important and he wants to speak to the officer in charge.'

'Then let's speak to him,' Ben said.

They walked over to where the nervous little villager stood cowering. Either the poor guy was scared rigid of the police generally, or else whatever it was he wanted to talk about was making him deeply uncomfortable. The uniform cop backed away a few steps to let his superior question the witness. It didn't take long to find out what he wanted to tell them. The exchange was conducted in the same rapid-fire Chinese, with Detective Lin pausing between answers to translate for Ben.

'I'm the officer in charge here. You said you wanted to talk to me?'

'Th-that's right. I have information.'

'About what happened here tonight?'

The little guy shook his head. 'N-no. It's about the other girl. The first one. I saw the men who took her.'

'How did you come to see them?'

'Because I was there in the forest watching when it happened.'

Chapter 18

The name of the witness was Mr Chung, and he lived just down the street. He spoke haltingly and it took him a few minutes before he would make eye contact and started to relax in the presence of the police detective and the blond-haired westerner with her, whom he took to be another officer – probably someone even more important who'd been brought in to investigate these shocking incidents. Yes, of course everyone in the village had known Lara and Olivia well by sight, if not to talk to. They were liked by all their neighbours and known to be polite, quiet, well-mannered and respectful. Not like some of the stories people told about visiting foreigners in the city, and their degenerate behaviour.

Asked by Detective Lin what exactly he'd seen, he related the story in detail while she stopped him now and then to put his words into English for Ben. Mr Chung knew the cherry blossom grove well; it was a favourite spot in the woods and he went there fairly often, to walk his dog or to ruminate and enjoy the stillness of nature. And just by chance, he'd happened to be at that very spot on the Friday evening that Lara Hartmann disappeared.

It had been a few minutes after seven, Mr Chung said, when he'd seen the familiar figure of the young student come jogging down the track through the forest. It was well known that she took regular runs along there, and he'd recognised her instantly. He described that she'd been wearing a bright orange sweatshirt, jogging pants and carrying a backpack. He didn't remember having seen her wearing a backpack before, but he hadn't made anything of it.

'Did she see you?' asked Detective Lin.

'No, I was walking among the trees, some way from the track. The branches are quite thick there, so I was hidden from her view. She ran right past without seeing.'

'What were you doing off the track?'

Mr Chung looked a little thrown by that question, and couldn't quite hide the look of discomfort that flashed over his face. 'I was hunting for the *lingzhi*,' he blurted out after a few beats. 'The mushrooms of immortality. My wife makes medicine from them.'

'Okay,' Detective Lin said. 'Please go on. What else did you see?'

'It was just a little further down the track. That's where the men appeared. Three of them.'

'You were able to get a good look at them?'

'Yes, except for their faces. They were wearing masks. The kind that goes over your whole head and just has holes for the eyes. That's when I knew something strange was going on.'

'How did the woman act when she saw these men?'

'I thought that she looked a little scared. But she didn't run away from them. She stopped running and walked up to them. Then she took off her backpack and opened it. There was something inside. She took it out and gave it to one of the men.'

When Detective Lin related all this to Ben, he asked, 'Did he see what the package was?'

'I was going to ask him that,' she said irritably. 'I'm only translating this as a favour to you.'

'Sorry.'

Yes, Mr Chung had got a clear glimpse of the item as it was taken from the backpack. It was all wrapped up with paper and tape and so he couldn't be sure of what it was. 'Only that it looked like a tube of some kind.'

'A tube?'

'About this long,' Mr Chung said, spacing out his palms some eight inches apart.

Ben wondered what could be hidden inside a tube that size.

'So she gave this wrapped-up tube to the three men,' Detective Lin said, 'and then what? Did they give her money?'

Mr Chung seemed quite sure of his reply, shaking his head. 'No, no money changed hands. She just gave it to them, and they took it. They seemed glad to have it. Holding it as if it was something very precious. Like this.' He mimicked it by clasping his bony hands against his chest, like cuddling a newborn kitten.

'Then what happened?'

'It looked like she was just going to turn around and walk away. That's what she seemed to think was going to happen, too. But then the men sort of looked at each other and nodded. Then they grabbed her. She tried to struggle, but they dragged her off into the trees. By this time I had managed to creep a little closer through the bushes. I was terrified that they might see me, but I couldn't stop watching.'

'Did they harm her?'

'I thought they would. I was wondering whether I should jump out and start yelling at them, in the hope it might scare them off. Only I was afraid they'd kill me. But then I realised they weren't going to hurt her, at least not there.'

'How did you know that?'

'Because they had a van waiting nearby, where the track splits into a fork. If you follow the fork it takes you around in a big loop, all the way to the road. I've walked along it before.

So that's where the van must have come from. The men dragged the woman towards it.'

'How well could you see the van?'

'Quite well. It was white. Two more men were in the front. They got out and I saw they were wearing the same kind of masks. They opened the back doors and helped the others to drag her towards them. She was fighting and screaming at them. They put some tape over her mouth to make her quiet.'

Mr Chung's voice was wavering and he looked close to breaking down as he described it. Ben almost didn't need the translation. 'They put a bag over her head and tied her up, and put her into the back of the van. Then they drove off, in a real hurry. But I managed to get the registration number. When they were gone I ran all the way home repeating it to myself over and over so I wouldn't forget. As soon as I got back to my house I wrote it down on this piece of paper. Here.'

Mr Chung reached into his dressing gown pocket and pulled out the torn-off slip to show them. Detective Lin took it from him and examined the scribbled number. 'Thank you, this is very useful. But why didn't you report the incident to the police right away? Don't you know it's illegal to fail to report a crime?'

'I didn't want to get into trouble,' he muttered, hanging his head in shame. 'I was afraid to say anything. Because . . . because . . .'

'You were afraid the men would come back to punish you? But how could they, if they hadn't seen you?'

'Yes. I mean, no. I . . . I . . .'

Detective Lin raised an eyebrow. 'I've a feeling you're not telling me the whole truth, Mr Chung. You weren't out in the forest that evening to hunt for mushrooms, or enjoy the scenery. There's some other reason, isn't there?' She was no fool, that

Detective Lin. 'I think you were there with someone, weren't you? Someone who wasn't your wife? That's what you were doing in the bushes, away from the track.'

Mr Chung was cringing so pitifully that he seemed about to collapse out of sheer unhappiness. Tears leaked from his eyes and ran down his leathery face. He swallowed hard and nodded. Then it all came out, with Detective Lin translating in chunks for Ben's benefit. Yes, he admitted ruefully, it was true. He'd been having an affair with another woman in the village. She was married, too, and they all knew each other. The last several months, the secret lovers had been regularly sneaking off into the forest together for their trysts.

Ben was amazed that anyone would risk their marriage by carrying on with this wizened little guy. But then, he hadn't seen the others.

'That's why I didn't say anything at the time,' Mr Chung confessed abjectly, as if he expected the detective to whip him for his sins. 'I was afraid I would be found out. But then when I saw all the police cars tonight, and then when they brought that poor girl's body out of the house . . . It's so terrible what's happening. I couldn't stay quiet any longer. Please don't tell Mrs Chung. If she knew about me and . . . she'd take a knife and cut my throat.'

Ben and Detective Lin exchanged glances. This was the most important lead that had come their way yet, and all thanks to the amorous intrigues of the village of Qinjiacun. So much for skilled sleuthing work.

'Am I in trouble?' the little man asked, trembling with apprehension.

'No, Mr Chung,' she assured him. 'This is very valuable information. It was a commendable and upstanding act of good citizenship to come forward like this. And your secret is safe.'

Relief flooding out of him, Mr Chung pressed his hands together and bowed his head up and down in humble gratitude. 'Thank you, Detective, thank you! May I go home now? Mrs Chung will be wondering what I'm doing out here.'

'Just one more thing I need to ask of you,' she replied. 'Show us the way to the cherry blossom grove.'

Chapter 19

In a hurry to get back home, Mr Chung led them at a trot along the riverbank to where the beaten-earth track wound into the woods. There was enough moonlight to see by, but as a precaution Detective Lin had fetched a pair of torches from her car. 'This way, this way, please, just a little further,' Chung kept saying, beckoning them on as he scurried ahead through the trees. Ben admired Detective Lin for the way she'd handled the guy. Tough on the one hand, kind-hearted on the other. She was right: she was a pretty good cop.

While they were making their way along the track, she took out her phone and called the police headquarters to get a trace on the vehicle registration number Chung had given her. 'They won't take long to identify the owner,' she said to Ben. 'Chinese police are very efficient.'

'I'm sure they are.'

The path was barely wide enough for two people to walk side by side, and rough in places with old gnarled tree roots like half-buried snakes jutting from the ground. It was on one of those that Detective Lin tripped in her haste to keep up with their guide, and would have fallen if Ben hadn't caught her by the arm to steady her. She felt light and delicate as a bird. He withdrew his hand immediately. 'Sorry,' she murmured.

'So do you have a name,' he asked her as they walked on through the darkness, their torch beams bobbing ahead, 'or will I have to address you as "Detective" the whole time?'

'What's wrong with Detective? That's what I am. I worked hard to achieve that grade and I'm very proud of it.'

'It's just a little formal,' he replied. 'If we're going to be working together.'

'I'm Chinese. Formality is important in our culture. As for working together, I haven't decided if I agree to that yet. And anyway, I don't want to tell you.'

Ben smiled. 'That's okay. Not everyone likes to tell people their name. It was the same in the army. I had a good friend there. He's still a good friend now. Everyone called him Boonzie. It wasn't until years later I found out his real name, Archibald.'

'"Archibald",' she repeated. 'Why did he not like it? Does it mean something bad in your language?'

'Only that his parents didn't show much appreciation for the future psychological trauma they were inflicting on their little baby.'

'What about your name? It must mean something.'

'It's short for Benedict,' he said. 'It comes from Latin. Meaning "blessed".'

'Then your parents must have loved you very much,' she said.

Ben found that a strange and surprising thought. He asked, 'Does your name have a meaning?'

She hesitated. 'Yes, it means "poem cloud".'

'That's nice. So how do you say "poem cloud" in Chinese? Or do you still not want to tell?'

'Shi Yun.'

'Nice meeting you, Shi Yun.'

He caught the brief flash of her smile in the moonlight. She might have been blushing, but in the darkness it was hard to tell.

By now they'd wound their way deep into the woods. In some places the trees encroached closely on the path, but up ahead the foliage opened up into a clearing and Ben could see where the track split into the fork that their eyewitness had described. 'This is the place,' Mr Chung said, turning around and pointing. He showed them where he and his lady friend had been when he first spotted Lara running along the track, then led them to the spot where the three masked men had appeared. 'This is where she gave them the tube,' he said. By now he'd understood that the tall blond European policeman didn't speak Chinese, and he mimicked the movement for his benefit. 'And over here is where the van was waiting.'

'Thank you, Mr Chung,' said Detective Lin. 'We'll take it from here.'

'I can go home now?'

She nodded, and replied with a long stream of Chinese that brought a wide grin to Chung's face. He thanked her again, scurried off back down the track and disappeared into the darkness.

'What did you tell him? Sounded like more than just a "yes".'

'I told him that if Mrs Chung asks him any hard questions about what he was talking to us about, he's to say he was chosen as a representative of the village to help the police with our enquiries. That will be an honour for her.'

'That was good of you, Shi Yun. Am I allowed to call you Shi Yun?'

'I suppose,' she said coyly.

'Now the formalities are out of the way, let's get to work,' he said, shining his torch down at the ground around him. He fell silent as he ran the light slowly along, scouring every inch.

'What are you doing?'

'Tracks are more than just footprints in the dirt,' he said. 'They can draw an accurate picture of what happened, if you know what to look for.'

'You learned this skill in the army?'

'Some of it.'

'I don't see anything.'

'Yes, you do. Look.' He showed her where the long grass was bent and a couple of slender twigs broken in the area where the men had dragged Lara towards the waiting van. 'There's a whole trail here. She was fighting them all the way. And see over here?' Following the fork in the path he dropped down into a crouch and carefully brushed back some dead leaves and trailing bits of shrubbery to examine the ground. 'You can see the indentations from where the van was parked. It hasn't rained in a long time, or else they'd be clearer. And here, scuff marks in the dirt. Notice that pebble, the way it's been dislodged? This is where they stopped to gag and tie her up before they put her in the back of the van. She was kicking out at them like crazy, trying to get free.'

'You can tell all this from a pebble?'

'To you, it's a pebble. To me, it's like CCTV footage. But if you want something more concrete' – bending down and fishing to retrieve something he'd spotted in the bushes – 'check this out.' He laid what he'd found in her small palm. It was an unused plastic cable tie, the kind of standard item available from every hardware store in the world and also widely used for trussing up kidnap victims, military battlefield prisoners and apprehended crooks.

'We use these in the police,' said Detective Lin.

'It's what they tied her wrists and ankles with. Probably had a whole packet of them and this one fell out in the struggle. They also brought along a roll of black duct tape to gag her with.'

She looked at him in astonishment. 'How can you tell that?'

'Because they left that behind too,' he replied, holding the half-used roll up for her to see. 'You might be able to get a print from this, so handle it carefully.'

'I have a bag,' she said, and produced one from her jeans pocket to store the evidence in.

Ben turned back towards the spot where the first three men had met Lara on the track. 'So that's where they appeared, from behind those trees,' he said half to himself, reconstructing the scene in his mind's eye. 'Which means they must have been waiting there for a while, because they couldn't know exactly when she'd turn up. If it was me, I'd have arrived at least an hour sooner. Let's take a look.'

When he examined the spot among the trees where he guessed they'd been waiting hidden for her, he could see from the further signs of flattened grass that his guess was right. And that was where he found something else, too. 'Well, one thing we know for sure,' he said as Detective Lin came over to see what more he'd discovered. 'Whoever these guys might be, they're a long way from being professional kidnappers. They're dropping evidence all over the place. Look.'

'Cigarette butts,' she said, peering down.

'Four of them. Tells us they were here for a little while before she appeared. And it also suggests that one of the three doesn't smoke. The other two got bored, lit up to pass the time and didn't think to clean up after themselves. Amateur night. Add these to the bag. Your lab can run a DNA analysis.'

'This is good evidence,' she said, smiling.

'Happy you brought me along?'

She was about to reply when her phone went. 'I told you they would be quick to trace the vehicle,' she said contentedly.

'I get it. Chinese police are the most efficient in the world.'

But her look of satisfaction turned to a scowl as she listened to the call. 'Shit,' she muttered, putting the phone away.

'What?'

'The van's owner is a Mr Wen Yongjian, in the city of Baoji. He reported it stolen that morning.'

'Then all we have to go on for now is Dan Chen's note,' Ben said. 'Come on, we've seen enough here. Let's head back to the village and talk about it along the way.'

'All right,' she said as they walked. 'So what can we surmise from all this?'

'A lot of contradictions,' Ben said. 'Dan's note describes these people as his friends, but then they turn up to the rendezvous wearing ski masks and they snatch his girlfriend using force. Meanwhile, they've got to be the sloppiest kidnappers of all time, making all kinds of elementary mistakes that no pro would dream of making, but when it comes to cutting people's organs out they're as clean and precise as a top-class surgeon. Then there's something else in that note doesn't ring true to me either, the more I think about it. Dan told Lara in his note that this was "all for the best possible cause". What could he have meant by that?'

'You could be reading too much into it,' she replied. 'To a lot of people, the best possible cause is the one that makes them richest.'

'But no money changed hands,' Ben said. 'Before they grabbed her, Lara was about to turn and walk away after she delivered the package, just like the note told her to. Not your typical kind of criminal deal, then, with no payment involved.'

'Maybe there was money inside the package,' Detective Lin said. 'Rolled up in the tube. Some kind of payoff.'

'And then they decided to take her, too?'

'It's clear she was deceived into thinking they'd let her go. But maybe she was part of the deal, without realising it.'

Ben was unsure. 'You think this humble government employee, who people call sweet and gentle, would really do that to his own girlfriend? Apart from anything else, he must have known her disappearance would cause a stir.'

She shrugged. 'Who knows what people are capable of?'

They explored a few more tentative ideas as they walked back to the village, but still nothing was making sense and by the time they got to the house they had both fallen into silence. Ben wanted to light a cigarette, but what she'd said about them smelling like shit put him off the idea. It was deep in the night and they were both tired and worn out from trying to figure out unanswerable questions.

By now most of the police cars and uniformed cops had left, just a few stragglers hanging around. Crime scene tape had been stretched across the doorway of the cottage, with police warning signs to keep out. Ben blipped the locks of the Steiner Mercedes, and she did the same with her grey saloon.

'Well, I suppose I have to thank you again for your help tonight,' she said. 'Perhaps tomorrow we might learn more from the evidence we found.'

'Will you call me?' he asked.

'I'll think about it.'

He supposed that would have to be good enough. 'Maybe I'll see you around, then. Good night, Shi Yun. Get some rest.'

She smiled. 'Good night, Benedict.'

Detective Shi Yun Lin watched his taillights shrink away into the night. Wondering about him, she couldn't help but find the man intriguing. As she stood there deep in thought, her second-in-command came over to ask if she needed anything more from him. 'No, Sergeant Honglei, you can go home now. I'm about to head back myself.'

With a last glance in the direction Ben Hope had disappeared, she climbed into her car and drove pensively to her apartment in Xi'an. Nobody was waiting there for her, except for her Siamese cat. Shi Yun took a long hot shower, trying to wash away the haunting memory of the dead woman's blood. Then she got into bed with the cat curled up near her feet, and lay awake for a long time thinking about what to do about Ben Hope. He'd found the note from Dan Chen when the police had completely missed it. And he was excellent at interpreting clues. From what he'd said about his background, he had far more experience at solving this kind of case than she did. What if she couldn't solve it on her own?

She was still working those thoughts over in her head when she rose at six after far too little sleep, ate a rushed breakfast on the hoof, fed the cat and headed off for an early start at the police headquarters. After submitting the new pieces of evidence from last night's investigations, she'd been at her desk barely three minutes when an email pinged up on her screen from one of her fellow detectives, telling her a piece of interesting news about the first murder victim, Dan Chen.

Shi Yun was digesting that information and wondering what it could signify, if anything, when her phone rang.

The moment that call was over, she dialled Ben Hope's number.

Chapter 20

As he drove back through the night towards Xi'an and their hotel, Ben debated with himself whether or not to tell his two companions the news of Olivia's death. It was more than just the knowledge of what Stefan's reaction would be that made him wonder if it was such a good idea. Ben's warning to Detective Lin hadn't been all bluff to persuade her. He was all too aware of the opening of the political floodgates that this development would be liable to kick off, once wind of it reached home.

And yet, how could he keep it a secret? The only thing more unthinkable than telling them would be not telling them. Deciding that he had no option, Ben lit another Gauloise and resigned himself to doing the necessary.

It was after four by the time he got back to the hotel. He parked the car and let himself quietly back into the suite, half hoping that his roommates would be still sleeping, so he might be able to delay the inevitable while he grabbed a couple of hours of badly needed sleep for himself. No such luck: Stefan and Sammy had been wide awake for some time, deeply worried about where he'd slipped off to and bursting with questions. Sammy was predictably unhappy about Ben's unauthorised use of the car, while Stefan was upset that Ben had gone off on his own and excluded him. He seemed to have forgotten that he'd been comatose at the time.

Ben cut them short with a stern look. 'Shut up and sit down, the two of you. Stefan, you might need to open another bottle of that Chinese rotgut. I've got some news you're not going to like.'

And then he broke it to them. He'd expected it to be a bad moment. It was worse. He thought that Stefan's outburst of disbelief and denial was going to wake up the whole hotel. Ben was glad he'd taken the guy's phone, because it would have been difficult to prevent him from using it to call home immediately without resorting to force. Sammy slumped on a sofa, beyond depression, and reached for the Baijiu.

'What the hell are we going to do now?' Stefan asked numbly, after the first wave of shock and emotion had subsided. He looked like a grey ghost.

'We're going to stick to our plan,' Ben told him. 'We're going to figure this out. But we need the space to do it without the world breathing down our necks.'

'That's insane. How can I keep this from Ruth, and my parents? And what about Olivia's family? Don't they need to know?'

'Telling them won't bring her back any time soon,' Ben said. 'But one thing it will do is to change their lives for ever. They'll be crushed. Do you want to drop that hammer on them, or do them the kindness of a few days' reprieve?'

'We can't keep this a secret,' Sammy protested, waving the bottle at him. 'It's immoral.'

'It's what the police want to do,' Ben replied. 'And for once in my life I have to agree with them.' He turned back to Stefan. 'We make the wrong move now, we'll never catch the people who took your sister. It's a bullet to the head. Do you understand?'

'She's dead anyway,' Stefan muttered. 'I know it.'

Ben stared at him. 'Do you? Really?'

'Tell me you don't!' Stefan replied, his voice rising suddenly to a shout.

'I'll know she's dead when I see her dead,' Ben said. 'Not before.'

Stefan slammed his fist into the arm of his chair, so hard that the wood cracked and a flash of pain contorted his face. 'That's so easy for you to say!' he yelled. 'It's not your sister that's gone missing!' Even as the words came out, his eyes filled with horror to hear himself saying them.

Ben made no reply for a second or two. Then he grabbed Stefan by the neck, propelled him backwards out of his chair and drove him hard against the wall behind it, pinning him there helpless and gasping. Ben's face was three inches from his. He spoke without emotion, in a voice as hard as blued steel.

'Now you listen to me like you've never listened to anyone in your life before. You think I don't know what you're going through at this moment? You're wrong. I know what it feels like, and believe me, I spent a long time feeling exactly like you are. When Ruth disappeared from our lives the way she did, it was like getting your guts ripped out. But I never gave up on her, Stefan. Never. Not for years, not even when there seemed like no hope we'd ever find her. Not even after the stress and the grief of losing her made both our parents die of a broken heart. I always believed, against all the odds. And now you're going to find it within yourself to believe, too.'

Ben let him go. Stefan slumped down the wall and fell in a heap on the floor. 'I'm not you, Ben,' he groaned, tears in his eyes. 'I don't have your strength.'

'Maybe you're right,' Ben said. 'In which case, then maybe you're not the guy I thought Ruth had chosen to spend the rest of her life with. That would be disappointing.' He took Stefan's phone from his pocket and chucked it down on the floor next to him. 'It's your choice, Stefan. You want to make that call, go for it. But it'll be on you. Now I'm tired and I'm going to bed for a while. If I wake up and find out you just went ahead and killed our best chance of finding Lara, then I'll be on the first plane home to France.'

With nothing more to say and feeling suddenly overwhelmed with fatigue, Ben walked into his bedroom, locked the door behind him, kicked off his shoes and dived into the bed. It was soft and comfortable. Within instants of his head hitting the pillow he was swimming, but even as he let the warm waters of sleep start to envelop him, he was being jerked awake again by the indelible vision of Olivia Keller's slaughtered carcass lying pale and empty on the blood-spattered floor and he couldn't keep out the thoughts that flooded into his head. It was all fine to tell Stefan they were going to stick to their plan, but if Shi Yun Lin decided she wasn't going to let Ben in on her case, those promises were little more than fighting talk. And then maybe he might as well be on the next flight to France anyway.

But he needn't have worried about her. Because by seven that morning, when he'd given up trying to get any proper sleep and was sitting in the suite's little kitchen area revitalising himself with as much hot, strong black coffee as he could get down him, his phone rang.

She was calling from the road, with a lot of vehicle and traffic noise in the background. Her voice was brisk and businesslike, and she didn't waste time getting straight to the point. 'I just got two new pieces of information this morning. The first is that a police patrol came across the stolen van less than an hour ago. It was hidden under a section of flyover bridge in an industrial area to the east of the city. I'm on my way there now.'

'The kidnappers probably used the flyover as a cover from overhead surveillance cameras while they switched their victim into another vehicle.' It was an old trick. 'I'm guessing there was nobody inside.'

149

'It was empty, except for a packet of those same black plastic cable ties one of the officers found under the front passenger seat. It must have fallen under there while they were driving. Someone left some cigarettes behind, too. The same Shuangxi brand that you and I found at the cherry blossom grove.'

Ben nodded. It was always welcome when the bad guys went around scattering breadcrumb trails of evidence for you to pick up on. This wasn't much, but it was a start. 'What's the other thing?'

'I'll tell you in the car,' she replied. 'I'm en route to your hotel now, to pick you up and take you to see the van.'

'Does this mean we're working together now?'

'I've been thinking about it, and I decided maybe you were right when you said it could be to both our advantages. You might be able to spot something I can't.'

'I'm honoured.'

'But don't tell the chief, okay? This is a serious breach of protocol. If my superiors find out, I'll be handing out parking tickets for the rest of my career.'

'Not a word. I promise.'

'Good. Or I might have to shoot you,' she said. It was hard to tell if she was being playful. 'I'm ten minutes from your hotel. Get ready to leave.'

'I'm coming too,' said Stefan when Ben told him where he was going.

'And me,' Sammy chimed in.

There was no stopping them, and so it was a gang of three that was waiting outside the hotel exactly ten minutes later when Detective Lin's dark grey plain saloon pulled into the car park. 'Great,' she said, rolling her eyes. 'The whole contingent. All right, get in.'

The morning traffic in Xi'an wasn't as crazy as that of Beijing, but it wasn't far off it, and she handled the car with skill as hazards flew at them from all directions at once with no regard for the rules of the road. It was probably the only time the Chinese citizenry got to flout the regulations a little, and they all seemed to want to make the most of it.

'So now you're going to tell us the second thing you learned this morning,' Ben reminded her.

'I don't know if it means anything for us,' she said. 'But it got me wondering. It turns out from the records of Shaanxi Lintong Kangfu Hospital that a couple of days before he went missing, Dan Chen was treated there for a minor concussion he'd sustained in that earthquake we had.'

'I didn't know there'd been one,' Ben said.

'We get them from time to time. This was only a smallish tremor, but it was enough to cause some structural damage to buildings. Dan Chen was at work the night it struck, overseeing an important cultural conservation project with his team at the Museum of Qin Terracotta Warriors and Horses.'

'As in, *the* terracotta army?'

She cocked an eyebrow at him. 'You know about it?'

'As much as the next person,' he replied. 'I'm no archaeologist, but who hasn't heard of that one?'

'You amaze me,' she said dryly. 'I thought I would have to explain. This was to be a very important event, the most extensive exhibition of the terracotta warriors outside China since their discovery in 1974. Dan Chen and his team had the task of giving the artefacts a last check to ensure they were in a condition to travel, before they were loaded into their transportation crates and put on a cargo aircraft bound for London.'

'Big responsibility.'

'He was very serious about this work, by all accounts. Anyhow, when the earthquake happened without warning he was alone in a room with a collection of exhibits. Thankfully the damage to the pieces was only slight, but the tremor took out the power and Chen was trapped inside the room for several minutes before his colleagues got him out and they evacuated the building. One of them, a woman called Mei Pinyin, drove him to Shaanxi Lintong Kangfu Hospital to be checked for concussion, but they sent him home with just a few stitches for a cut. Afterwards the transportation of the exhibits was delayed for a few days, and then by the time they called Dan Chen in to resume his work, he'd disappeared and was found dead shortly after.'

'Okay,' Ben said. 'And why does this matter?'

'Here's the interesting part,' she said. 'In the meantime, the team who were given the job of clearing up the debris and moving the statues safely out of the damaged building to a new warehouse location have found that one of them was broken open in the earthquake. It turns out to have been hollow inside. Apparently they're all like that, because of how they were made.'

'One of the statues Dan Chen was left alone with?' Ben asked, hunting for where this was going.

'For five or ten minutes at least. The cavity inside the warrior's body looks as if something could have been concealed there, which it's possible he could have discovered by chance when it broke open.'

'Are you saying he took it? Whatever "it" was?'

'We don't know that,' she replied. 'But I also have a report from Mei Pinyin, his colleague who drove him to the hospital. She's on record as stating to the police that she thought he was acting very oddly. And when she took him back to his apartment, she was certain he was trying to hide something from her. An object of some kind, though she didn't get a proper look at it. But his behaviour seemed suspicious.'

'And if these suspicions proved correct, you think maybe this "something" was the item he gave Lara to pass on?'

'If so, it would be a very serious offence. He'd have been certain to lose his job, and perhaps face an additional prison term. Whatever this thing was, it would have had to be highly valuable to justify taking such a risk.'

'It's still hypothetical,' Ben said.

'I'm not sure. Remember the description that Mr Chung gave us? He said it looked like a tube, about this long.' She took her hands off the wheel to hold them eight inches apart. The car swerved slightly off line in the fast-moving pack of traffic and a horn wailed past, inches away.

'Steady,' Ben said.

Unfazed, Shi Yun replied, 'I got a number for the team member who discovered the damaged warrior, and called him to ask if something that size would fit into the hollow space. He said in his estimation it would, easily.'

Ben thought for a moment. 'How old are these things?'

'In terms of Chinese history, not that old,' she replied nonchalantly. 'They only date back to around 200 BC. In our culture that's almost like yesterday. But the terracotta army warriors are still regarded as one of China's most precious ancient treasures.'

'And as such, they'd be pretty closely guarded.'

'Anyone who tried to steal them wouldn't live very long.'

'Then it's unlikely that our mystery package contains cash or drugs,' Ben said. 'Why go to the trouble of bypassing a ton of armed security to hack into one of these statues and plant the goods in there, when there are a thousand other much more practical ways of passing them on? And even if they did, and Dan Chen was "supposed" to find the tube inside, that was depending too heavily on chance. How could they have guaranteed he'd find it, and not one of his team? And who could have predicted that the earthquake would happen just at that moment and give a pretext to his movements by breaking the statue open? If that was just a lucky coincidence, it was a one in a billion shot.'

She nodded. 'Agreed. I say we need to ditch that hypothesis and look at this from another angle. Perhaps, instead, whatever's inside the tube is something very old and historically important in its own right.'

'That would make more sense,' Ben said. 'Or a little more, at least. By a stroke of pure luck, Dan Chen happens to find this amazing thing inside the broken statue. Being an archaeologist, he's aware of what an incredible discovery he's made. It's worth a fortune, and he's the only one who knows about it. Suddenly he's thinking about quitting his humdrum life for one of wealth and luxury. But he's got to act fast. There are alarms sounding off all over the place, his colleagues are banging on the door and the whole building could collapse at any moment. And so on the spur of the moment he takes a huge gamble. He decides he's going to steal it. Now, this guy's no master thief. Probably shoved it down his trousers in the hope nobody would notice. Then he manages to smuggle it past his colleague who drove him to the hospital, or thinks he does. It's a narrow escape but eventually he's safe and sound back at his apartment with his trophy. He's home free. But next he does a very strange thing.'

'Two very strange things,' Shi Yun said. 'First, why doesn't he keep it for himself? Who are these "friends" he decides to pass it on to?'

'Stolen art fences?' Ben had encountered the world of illegal antiquities trading enough times in the past to have a rough idea of how things worked in their business. When you needed to offload a hot item quickly for as much money as you could grab, you often needed the help of specialist dealers.

'But why doesn't he pass it on to them personally? Why get his girlfriend to do it for him? That's the second strange thing.'

'He was afraid of them,' Ben suggested. 'They're crooks and he isn't.'

'Is that why they snatched Lara?' she asked. 'Just a bunch of really, really mean and vicious bastards jumping at another opportunity? How on earth did a guy like Dan Chen hook up with such people? And come to see them as his "friends"? Was he really that naive?'

'Still doesn't explain what he meant by "the best possible cause",' Ben reminded her. 'What kind of cause? Sounds more like an idealistic thing than a criminal enterprise.'

'And then somehow, in the middle of it all, two people are murdered for their organs.' Shi Yun gave a sigh. 'I can't make that part fit into the rest of it.'

'We're missing something,' Ben said. 'One extra piece of the puzzle that'll make the rest all fall into place.'

'But we're getting closer to the truth,' she insisted. 'I can feel it.'

'I'm confused,' said Sammy. 'None of this makes any sense to me at all.'

'Nor me,' admitted Stefan, who was slouched in the back of the car looking pasty and ill.

'There's our flyover,' she said, pointing ahead. It had taken a while to hack through the chaotic traffic and it was now nearly ten a.m. Pulling off the main boulevard she sped down a sharp incline, scraping the underside of the car chassis as the suspension bottomed out, and pulled up with a squeal of brakes next to where the recovered kidnap van was parked under the shadows of the massive concrete overhang. Beside it were two marked police squad cars and four cops in uniform, waiting for their superior to take over. They'd coned off the area around the van, leaving a narrow lane for other traffic to trickle through the underpass.

Ben was first out of the car. He said, 'Let's see what we have.'

Chapter 21

The kidnappers' stolen conveyance had been a plain white Dongfeng panel van, a few years old, unmarked and unremarkable with nothing to distinguish it from a million others on the roads of every Chinese city. The uniformed cops watched Ben detachedly and he ignored them as he walked around the vehicle, taking in details. Stefan and Sammy had climbed out of Shi Yun's car and were hovering uncertainly in the background. The detective herself stood by with her arms folded and a serious expression.

What Ben was seeing all seemed to fit with what they'd learned so far. The registration tallied with what Mr Chung had told them last night. The van's lower skirts were spattered with dirt, and some trailing bits of vegetation from the forest track were stuck in the plastic trim. Ben yanked open the passenger door, opened the glove box and saw the half-empty cigarette pack that the cops hadn't yet taken away. As Shi Yun had said, they were the same brand as the stubs they'd found in the forest.

'Shuangxi,' Ben said. 'Do a lot of people in China smoke them?'

'A couple of billion, perhaps,' she told him.

'That narrows our search right down. What does the name mean?'

'It means "double happiness".'

Double happiness. Ben thought he could do with some of that. He took one from the pack, pulled out his Zippo and lit it up.

'Hey! That's evidence!'

'Oh, please.'

Ben went on with his tour of the van. The rear doors were open, revealing the cargo space inside which had been lined with heavy-duty plywood, presumably by its legal owner, little knowing that his modification would transform it into the perfect kidnap vehicle. Apart from that, there was nothing to see here.

The cigarette was something of a disappointment, too. Ben couldn't say it was giving him twice as much happiness as his trusty Gauloises. Maybe not even half as much. But he went on smoking it anyway as he stepped away from the van and looked keenly around him. Sure enough, the location under the flyover had been chosen as a surveillance camera blind spot. The van hadn't been alone under here; nearby were some tyre marks where a stationary car parked beside it had taken off in a hurry. That would be the getaway vehicle, Ben thought. Possibly stolen, like the van, or possibly belonging to one of the kidnap crew.

Further across from the van, out in the middle of the narrow lane beyond the cone barrier, he noticed a dark patch where oil or some other automotive fluid had been spilled, and a couple of scratches on the road. That got him curious.

The occasional vehicle was coming through the underpass, with one of the uniformed cops diligently signalling them by. There seemed to be relatively little traffic using this route. Ben thought that the kidnappers would have been easily able to transfer Lara from the van to their getaway car unnoticed. He waited for a small rattly truck to pass, then stepped out between the cones for a closer look at the oil patch. On examination it was still wet, and smelled like two-stroke oil, the kind he mixed into his chainsaw fuel back home. Still fresh, like the scratch on the road next to it.

'It's just some oil,' Shi Yun said.

'To you it's oil,' Ben could have replied. 'To me it's an action replay of what happened here.' But he said nothing. Then as he crouched there thinking, he noticed something else, something colourful lying in the gutter on the other side of the van.

Plastic fragments. Some were no more than little shards, but the largest covered his palm. The colour that had caught his eye was part of a graphic design. The way they were lying in the gutter looked as though someone had carelessly swiped them there with their foot.

Ben was wondering where they might have come from when a little delivery scooter entered the underpass and slowed for the cops. The rider was some skinny kid with an oversized orange crash helmet that made his head look like a giant pumpkin. Scooters and small-engined motorcycles were a ubiquitous sight on the city roads, and normally Ben wouldn't have given it a second glance. Except for two things. The first was the way the rider slowed right down to a crawl, turned to peer at the spot where the oil spill on the road was, then shook his pumpkin head and accelerated onwards, the nasal buzzing of his two-stroke engine echoing under the concrete flyover. The second was that the rear-mounted top box on the scooter had the same colourful graphic on it as the fragment in Ben's hand.

'Are you going to talk to us at any point, or are we supposed to guess what you're thinking?' Shi Yun asked impatiently, arms still folded.

'Yeah, Ben, what have you found?' Sammy called out.

Ben told them, 'The driver of the getaway car was in such a hurry to get out of here that he pulled out without looking and hit something.'

'Hit what?' Shi Yun asked.

Ben pointed at the disappearing delivery scooter. 'One of those,' he said.

They found the fast food outlet nearby. It was a busy, greasy little joint currently cooking up mid-morning brunch and coffee orders to send out to nearby offices and building sites. Shi Yun flashed her police ID for the girl at the serving counter and asked her if their scooter riders used the flyover underpass on their delivery route. The girl blinked nervously back at the stern lady detective and her three male companions and stammered that yes, she thought they used it as a shortcut.

Shi Yun asked, 'Tell me, please, did one of them have an accident there last Friday evening?'

The girl looked suddenly twice as nervous, biting her lip. 'You'd better talk to Mr Wang.'

Wang was the manager, a scraggy little guy who came out of the kitchen wiping his hands on his apron and wearing an ugly leer that became uglier when he laid eyes on Shi Yun's detective badge. He led them into a grungy office where she repeated her question. Wang was cagey at first, but then was forced to admit that yes, there had been a minor incident under the flyover that evening, involving one of their delivery riders and a car. He was even cagier when asked why the accident hadn't been reported to the police. Under her steely-eyed pressure he had to confess that the delivery kid had been underage to be riding a scooter. Wang had had to drive over there in his three-wheeler truck and recover the stricken machine personally.

'Seems like nobody reports anything to the police any more these days,' Shi Yun commented in English to Ben and Stefan. Pressing Wang for more information, she got out of him that the scooter hadn't been irreparably damaged but that its top box had been broken and all the food inside was scrambled.

The kid himself had been shaken but unhurt. Then after a brief argument, the bastard in the car had driven off. But the kid had been smart enough to get the registration number.

'Could I have that?' she asked.

'I don't have it,' Wang said dourly. 'You'd need to talk to the kid.'

'Then give me his contact details.'

'Don't have them either.'

She pointed at the filing cabinet behind the desk. 'You don't keep records on your employees?'

Wang spat. Spat right there on the carpet, in his own office. A real charmer, this guy. 'He's just a kid. Working off the books, you know? That's business.'

Shi Yun gave Wang a card. 'Make sure he calls me very soon. Understand? Or I'll have you arrested for employing minors, and the government will close down your premises and strip all your assets, and you'll spend the next six months in a state re-education facility. And believe me, all the nasty things you've heard about those places are true.'

Wang spat again.

'That was good work,' Shi Yun told them contentedly as they left the fast food place. 'Come on, I'll treat us all to a late breakfast somewhere with a bit more class than this dump.'

'If they can sell us some aspirin,' Stefan groaned, clutching his head, 'that'll be even better.'

'I tried to warn you about drinking that terrible stuff,' Sammy chided him.

Ben was still thinking about what she'd said to Wang. 'Re-education facility?' he asked her on the way back to her car. 'I thought your government's lovely internment camps were mainly just for torturing and indoctrinating the ethnic Muslim community.'

She looked at him. 'I was just saying that stuff to scare Wang. I don't believe those places even exist, and you shouldn't believe it either. It's all just anti-China propaganda cooked up by your western media. Anyway, you think the British and the Americans are so ethical and pure? It was your country who invented the concentration camp, long before there were Nazis.'

Ben could find no reply to that.

They got back in Shi Yun's car and set off again, ploughing through the city traffic with her characteristic driving style. Stefan was still bemoaning his hangover and Sammy was scolding him like a mother hen, while Shi Yun had reverted back to her cheerful, smiling mood and was telling Ben about the pleasant little café-restaurant she was taking them to not too far away across town, where they served her favourite kind of steamed rice breakfast dumplings. The more she dropped the hard-boiled cop act and showed her real self, the more Ben found himself liking her.

'You can get any kind of filling you want,' she was saying animatedly as she slowed for a red light. It was a busy, wide four-way intersection with traffic hurtling by in all directions. The signal lights were up on tall masts. Modern high-rises in the background, with a few traditional Chinese buildings inter-spersed. She added, 'They do a special kind of spicy red bean paste that's really delicious, if you don't like meat.'

'Meat every time for me,' Ben replied.

'Then you should try the pork and chestnuts filling. It's a little fatty for some people, and a little salty, but it's the b—'

Then the side window behind her head as she sat turned towards him suddenly imploded into the car. A stunning, violent impact like being hit by an express train sent them spinning weightlessly into the air.

Chapter 22

The articulated truck had been just one of the countless vehicles roaring by the intersection when it suddenly veered out of lane and, without warning or slowing down, slammed right into them.

The massive collision sent the car spinning and tumbling like a tin can kicked down the street. It came down on its roof, bounced, and righted itself to land back on its wheels, broken glass and bits of bodywork strewn all around. The truck's momentum had been reduced almost to a halt by the impact. Now the unseen driver floored his throttle and the huge cab came on again with a diesely rasp, closing in for a second impact. This time the car was smashed over on its side and spun like a top on the road.

For its occupants, there hadn't been time to register what was happening before they were being helplessly flung about inside. Both front airbags instantly deployed, trapping Ben and Shi Yun securely in their seats during that first crunching impact. In the back, neither Sammy nor Stefan had been wearing a seatbelt.

Disorientated and stunned, it took Ben a few moments to understand what had happened. There was a high-pitched ringing in his ears that drowned out all other sound, and his vision was blurry. As his senses quickly began to return he realised that he was lying on his side against the passenger door, which had now become the floor under him. Shi Yun was sprawled half on top of him, partly suspended between the front seats by her seatbelt. The airbags had deflated after the initial collision and were hanging spent from their panels on the dash and steering column. Broken glass was everywhere. Above them, what had been the driver's side of the car was completely smashed in with all the windows gone.

Struggling to twist around, Ben reached up to grasp Shi Yun by the arm and shake her. Her eyes fluttered open and hazily focused on him. She tried to speak, but was too stunned to make any sound.

That was when Ben realised that he was spattered with blood. So was his seat, the roof of the car and the dashboard. It wasn't hers. And as far as he could tell it wasn't his, either. Where had it come from? His mind was still confused from the shock of the collision and he couldn't understand. A groan from behind made him crane his head around to peer with difficulty into the back, wincing at the pain in his neck and shoulder from where the seatbelt had restrained him in the collision. And that was when Ben came fully alert again and realised with a cold shock of horror whose blood he was covered with.

In the rear passenger's seat directly behind Shi Yun when the truck had slammed broadside into them, Sammy had taken the full brunt of the impact. He must have been sitting with his head close to the window, because now that whole side of his face and skull had been caved in flat like a dropped eggshell. As the car had flipped over on its side he'd been flung across the back seat and now was lying on top of Stefan. His remaining eye seemed to be staring right at Ben between the gap in the front seats, with an expression of pure amazement, as if to say, 'What happened?' Except Sammy wasn't thinking that, because he was no longer thinking anything at all.

Poor Sammy. But there was no time to lament him now.

The groan Ben had heard had come from Stefan, who was trapped between the rear door and Sammy's body on top of him. Ben managed to release his seatbelt catch, reach between the seats and haul the dead man's weight off him. Stefan was all spattered in blood, but that was mostly Sammy's too. At first the only wound Ben could see on Stefan was a gash on his cheek where he'd been hit by flying glass from the imploded window. Then he saw the grimace of pain on Stefan's face and the way he was holding his arm.

Stefan hissed through clenched teeth, 'I think it's broken.'

Before Ben could reply, he heard the snorting rasping growl of the truck engine, and all he could do was brace himself for a third impact. The massive bumper slammed into the capsized car and once again they were flying weightlessly through space for a moment, spinning over and over before they crashed down again and this time rolled onto their roof. The impact had shaken Shi Yun free of her seatbelt and thrown her on top of Ben. He was able to peer out through the shattered windows and saw the truck's radiator grille backing away from them. He thought it was going to come piling towards them again, but it didn't.

He yelled, 'Stefan! Shi Yun!'

'I'm okay,' she groaned. Her voice sounded thick and indistinct.

'Ben, you have to do something!' Stefan yelled back at him.

Outside the stricken car, the scene was one of total mayhem. Cars and vans and scooters and motorcycles speeding unaware down the road only to come across the carnage in front of them were swerving panic-stricken out of the way, many of them skidding and crashing into one another and blocking the road with more wreckage. The articulated truck was halted just fifteen yards away from Shi Yun's wrecked saloon, revving its engine, biding its time before the next attack like a mad bull pawing the ground with its horns lowered. The windscreen reflected a dazzle of sunlight, masking the faces of the men in the front. Was the driver going to come surging towards them for a fourth impact, this time maybe an attempt to get those huge truck wheels to roll right over them and crush them flat?

It was a serious concern – but so was the thick dark smoke that had started pouring from under the car's crumpled bonnet. At any moment Ben expected to see flames appearing and licking up the car's sides, ready to set light to the spilled fuel he could smell leaking from their ruptured tank and consuming them all in an inferno.

Cars were still skidding to a halt at the intersection and more piling up behind them, while the drivers of crashed vehicles were getting out screaming and yelling in panic. Now Ben realised that the truck driver wasn't going to content himself with crushing the capsized saloon flat with them inside. The attackers had other plans.

The truck doors flew open and two men jumped out, followed by three more who emerged from the crew cab behind them. All five were wearing black combat gear, bulletproof tactical vests and three-hole ski masks. And all five were carrying military-grade assault weapons.

As if Ben had needed any convincing that this wasn't just some kind of demented road rage incident directed at a random victim. It was an orchestrated hit job. The rifles in the shooters' hands were the latest model issued to Chinese troops, a home-grown variant of the US Bushmaster. Thirty-round banana-curved magazines, folding stocks, fully-automatic capability. Enough high-velocity firepower to chew through all but the most heavily armoured vehicle and riddle everything inside.

Meanwhile the smoke pouring from under the car bonnet was growing ominously thicker and darker. The seconds were ticking by much too fast.

Stefan was right. Ben had to do something, and he had to do it very soon indeed or they were all dead.

Chapter 23

What Ben needed at this moment was a weapon. And he suddenly remembered that, of course, there was one just inches away, still strapped into the concealed holster at Shi Yun's right hip. Depriving a police officer of their duty sidearm was probably a capital offence in China, but she was still half in shock and her responses were sluggish, so he took the initiative. Thrusting his hand between their bodies where she was jammed against him, he groped around and his fingers closed on the grip of her pistol. At the same moment, the five gunmen were stepping up to the car and lining themselves up in a row with their rifles pointed at the shattered windscreen and side windows, preparing to unleash a storm of firepower on the three living occupants inside.

With a flick of his thumb Ben unsnapped the holster's retaining strap, and then the weapon was drawing free, instantly ready for action. Shi Yun's sidearm was some police version of the standard Chinese military QSZ-92 semi-automatic pistol. Polymer frame, chunky black steel slide, double-stack mag holding fifteen rounds of standard nine-mil Parabellum plus one up the spout. The kind of generic device that worked and felt almost exactly like any of the other plastic fantastics on the modern arms market – especially to someone like Ben who'd devoted thousands of hours of range time with them in his life and had depended on weapons not very unlike this one to save his own life and those of the people around him in many combat encounters. It was just a tool to him, a practical marriage of form and function. But in his hands the functional tool became like a craftsman's precision instrument.

The five gunmen opened fire on the car, all at once in an enormous continuous overwhelming thunder. Bullets smacked into the bodywork and howled off the upturned belly pan and smashed away what little remaining glass was in the windows. At this close range it was like a shooting gallery. But now the odds were at least a little bit rebalanced.

Lying flat on his belly on what had been the roof of the car and firing through the shattered windscreen, Ben squared his pistol sights on the man in the middle and squeezed off two shots at the small but vulnerable target area above the edge of the guy's bulletproof tactical vest. His first shot punched out the man's trachea and the second drilled him neatly in the centre of his forehead, two inches above the bridge of the nose. Before the man was crumpling dead to the ground Ben was already swivelling his weapon ten degrees left to engage the next target and firing again. The guy saw Ben's aim diverting towards him and tried to writhe out of the way, so that Ben's first shot only tore through his shoulder. The man gamely let off another rattling stream of fire that hammered into the car and passed dangerously close to Shi Yun, before Ben's next shot caught him in the side of the neck and blew out his jugular in a messy red burst that spattered over the shooter standing next to him. He went down flailing and collapsed on his back.

The shooters had obviously come unprepared for this kind of determined resistance. Maybe they were more used to going up against unskilled and defenceless victims, like Olivia Keller and Dan Chen, maybe Lara Hartmann and any of the other innocent people they and their cronies went around murdering. As every combat fledgling quickly finds out, it's not the same when your targets are suddenly shooting back at you. The intensity of their fire wavered and then spluttered to a halt as the three remaining men hurried back towards the cover of their truck. Ben chased them with four more shots as they ran and one of them stumbled, but they made it to the truck and hunkered down behind its cab to resume pouring fire at the car. Now they were engaging their target from a different angle, and the way the car was lying upside-down presenting its underside to them was making it harder to place accurate shots into the kill zone.

Shi Yun was fully alert now, as tense as a cat ready to spring. She'd seen what had happened to Sammy and her face was grim. Ben pointed to Stefan and said to her, 'Help me get him out before this thing goes up in flames!' She nodded, and crawled quickly into the back, completely undeterred by the blood and gore. She shoved Sammy's body aside and started helping the groaning, agonised Stefan out of the glassless rear windscreen, easier than trying to clamber out from the crumpled door and less visible to the enemy. Meanwhile Ben pumped four more rounds of covering fire in the direction of the truck, to ensure the shooters stayed pinned down while his companions made their escape.

By his count he'd now chewed through twelve of his sixteen rounds, and the remainder weren't going to last long. Unlike him, the enemy seemed to have no shortage of ammunition from their multiple high-capacity magazines. He clambered over the upside-down roof and out of the back window to join Shi Yun and Stefan, crouching low behind the shelter of the rear passenger-side wheel. Stefan's head was bowed, his eyes were screwed shut in agony and he was gently rocking himself as he cradled his broken arm. He was covered all down one side with Sammy's blood.

Next to him, Shi Yun was getting on her police radio and urgently calling for assistance for an officer under fire. Even if the cavalry only took minutes to get here, that could be minutes too late. 'Do you carry a spare mag?' Ben asked her urgently, and she looked blank and shook her head no.

'What are you doing?' she asked wide-eyed as he jumped up and started moving away from the car. But he was already running towards the bodies of the two men he'd shot. The nearest was lying just a few strides away, spreadeagled on his back with the side of his neck blown out and his fallen weapon on the ground next to him. Ben could hardly see for the thick smoke pouring from the wreck of the car, which momentarily hid him from view of the shooters behind the truck. The first tongue of yellow flame shot through it. Then another. He crouched down low beside the body, his eyes streaming tears and his lungs burning. Snatched up the dead man's assault rifle and tore open the pouch on his tactical utility belt that contained his spare magazine. That was the equaliser that Ben had been looking for. He stuck Shi Yun's near-empty pistol in the back of his jeans, jammed the spare rifle magazine in his pocket, and stood up clutching the weapon.

That was when a gust of wind whipped the smoke curtain away, and suddenly he could see the enemy again. One was kneeling behind the shelter of the truck's crumpled bumper and massive radiator grille; the second had clambered up onto a front wheel arch and was pointing his rifle over the bonnet; and the third had crawled along the ground to lie flat like a sniper beneath the trailer chassis. Whichever of the three Ben had hit as they ran for cover, he reckoned he'd only winged him or just put a dent in his bulletproof vest.

Crashed vehicles sat all around the truck at various angles, several with caved-in body panels and smashed glass, a couple whose horns had jammed on, one that had overturned onto its side and was leaking oil all over the road. Their occupants had mostly fled, but some terrified citizens were still cowering in their cars, some desperately covering their heads, others clutching at one another for protection, others wailing loudly.

This was what made an urban street battle such a different proposition to the kind of action in remote and wilderness areas that Ben much preferred. The crowded intersection was a minefield for collateral damage. One stray shot could mean the death of a helpless bystander, and he could not allow that to happen.

But the enemy weren't going to have such scruples when it came to endangering innocent lives. The instant the smoke started blowing the other way, all three of them resumed firing. The one under the trailer snapped off bursts at the overturned car, while the other two concentrated their attentions on Ben. He dived for cover behind an empty minivan whose driver had managed to beat a safe retreat. Bullets poked through flimsy door skins and shattered the windows, blew out the lights and ruptured the tyres. A wing mirror exploded into fragments, showering him with tiny glass shards. The bodyshell couldn't offer him much protection, but by crouching close to the front he could use the solid mass of its engine block as at least some kind of shield.

Now to give these guys back a taste of their own medicine, he thought.

Chapter 24

Ben's assault rifle was set to fully-automatic, but he flipped the select-fire switch to single shots to conserve his ammunition. Marking his targets, he decided to go for the one under the trailer, who had Shi Yun and Stefan relentlessly pinned down behind the wrecked car. It was a difficult angle; the shooter was half hidden by the iron trellis framework of the trailer chassis and Ben couldn't get a clear shot without risking a ricochet that might find its way to an unintentional target.

That was where his mastery of the art of combat came in. Instead of firing directly at his enemy, calculating the rebound angle as carefully as a snooker player about to make a winning pot, Ben aimed the reticule of his rifle's optical sight at the road surface a few inches from where the man was hunkered down prone and squeezed off a single round. The bullet ricocheted with a howl off the asphalt, kicking up a puff of dust, altered its course forty-five degrees upwards and struck the steel trailer chassis with a resounding clang, uncomfortably close enough to the guy's head to make him flinch and scramble away in jittery panic on his knees and elbows, dragging his weapon along the ground with him. Ben had predicted the angle perfectly; and *now* the guy had moved into a position where he had a clear shot at him without endangering any of the occupied vehicles on the other side of the trailer. He fired again, and this time he nailed his target dead on. The shooter collapsed flat under the trailer and lay still.

Three down, only two left. It was always a highly demoralising moment when you realised the tide of the engagement was unexpectedly turning against you with more than half your force taken out. And now the two remaining shooters behind the truck did what Ben suspected they might. They broke for cover and ran. But instead of trying to get into the truck cab where they knew they'd be an easy target for him, they abandoned their vehicle and made their escape behind the length of the trailer towards the other stationary cars on that side.

There was no way Ben was intending to let them run. He was about to give chase when the thing he'd been anticipating for the last couple of minutes now finally happened. With a flat percussive *whoomph*, the flickering tongues of flames that had been gradually starting to show through the smoke from the car now erupted into a fierce blaze. Fanned by another gust of wind the fire quickly engulfed the whole front end. Through the rippling heat haze Ben saw Shi Yun hauling Stefan urgently away from their hiding place before they were swallowed up in a fireball. Burning trails streaked along the road where fuel had been leaking from the car's damaged tank. In a few instants the wreck had become an inferno, its upside-down shell barely visible behind the flames. Nothing to be done about Sammy inside.

Ben had been momentarily distracted from watching where the two retreating shooters had gone. Now hearing a frightened, high-pitched screaming, he turned and saw the men violently grabbing an elderly woman from the driver's seat of a small hatchback. She must have been hiding ducked inside her car, either too terrified to try to get away or not physically capable of making her escape. She was tiny and frail and looked about eighty. The guy manhandling her had his rifle slung over his shoulder and was holding a knife to her throat while he bundled her into the back seat. He jammed himself in there next to his hostage, his associate diving behind the wheel and restarting the stalled motor. With a screech of spinning wheels they took off, pulled a hairpin U-turn leaving rubber all over the road and accelerated off up the highway.

If they managed to escape, then Ben would never know who'd tried to take them out here today. Worse, the poor old woman they'd taken hostage might end up meeting the same sickening end as their other victims. Even eighty-year-old organs must fetch some kind of price on the black market.

The minivan driver had fled the scene without removing his keys from the ignition. Ben wrenched open the sliding side door, then jumped into the driver's seat, threw his rifle in beside him, got the engine going again and crashed it into gear and went skidding through the smoke and flames to where Shi Yun and Stefan were scrambling away to safety. He screeched to a halt and yelled at them to get in.

'I need to wait for the police to arrive!' she yelled back.

'No, you need to come with me,' Ben told her. He was going to try and keep at least one of the bad guys alive, and he couldn't arrest or detain them without her help. Shi Yun hesitated, but the absolute authority in Ben's voice and in his eyes won her over, and she helped Stefan through the sliding door and piled into the minivan after him. Ben stamped on the gas and they took off again in pursuit of the escaping hatchback. A heartbeat later, the petrol tank of Shi Yun's burning car ignited in the heat and exploded like a bomb, tearing what was left of the vehicle in half and hurling pieces of flaming wreckage far and wide, some of them cannoning off the side of the minivan as Ben accelerated hard away. Had she and Stefan still been standing anywhere within the blast radius, if they hadn't been scorched to death by the flames they might have been sliced to bits by the shrapnel.

But this was far from over yet, because now the chase was about to begin in earnest. Leaving the ailing Stefan in the back, Shi Yun battled her way to the front of the swaying, lurching vehicle to join Ben as he went weaving through the chaos of stationary cars and trucks and the unsuspecting new arrivals still coming down the busy highway. Seeing the pall of smoke up ahead, drivers were trying to turn back the other way, so that every lane of the road was all but clogged. Ben narrowly avoided a dozen collisions in as many seconds, but he couldn't avoid the delivery truck whose driver had slammed on his brakes in panic and broadsided them with an impact that very nearly sent them spinning through the barrier and down ten metres of steep concrete embankment. He somehow managed to control the gyrating van, hammered the accelerator and kept going.

The fleeing shooters had an eighty-yard head start on them. The old lady's hatchback had been slightly damaged in the pile-up at the intersection, but the minivan was in a much worse state with one tyre blown out and flapping on its wheel rim. The steering was wild in Ben's hands but he pressed on as fast as the vehicle would let him go, and as they sped onwards he was slowly beginning to gain on the escaping car. There was no sign of the police among the oncoming traffic that streaked by, horns blaring angrily. Shi Yun was back on her radio, talking fast to update her police colleagues on the developing situation.

Now just sixty yards in front, the hatchback went veering crazily down an exit ramp and headed the wrong way down a narrower road taking them into the more densely built-up part of the city. Its driver was on the brink of losing control, careering madly from kerb to kerb and forcing oncoming traffic to swerve out of his path. A motorcyclist trying to avoid being flattened hit a parked car and he was flung over the handlebars of his crumpled machine, landing on the pavement and scattering terrified pedestrians. Ben wished he could have stopped to check the guy was okay.

Shi Yun had ended her radio call and was staring intently at the road ahead. Ben pointed at the rifle in the passenger footwell. 'Do you know how to use that?' She nodded wordlessly and snatched it up. The weapon looked oversized in her small hands. Almost at the same moment, the man in the back of the fleeing car emerged hanging half out of its rear passenger window, clutching his own rifle. The car was swerving so violently from side to side that it was impossible for him to aim it with any kind of accuracy, but a random blast of fully-automatic fire could easily hit the mark just by chance.

A rattle of shots and the minivan's windscreen dissolved into an opaque white spider's web of fissures. For an instant Ben was driving totally blind, until Shi Yun reacted by punching out the screen with the muzzle of the rifle. Bits of glass and a hurricane of warm wind billowed into the cabin.

They were still gaining on the car ahead. Thirty yards, twenty-five and closing. But the closer they got, the greater the danger from the man still hanging from the window with his assault weapon. Another burst of fire raked the front of the minivan and Ben felt the steering judder and become less controllable as their remaining front tyre was blown out. Shi Yun pointed her rifle out of the smashed windscreen, tracking the wildly gyrating car in her sights but not daring to return fire for fear of hitting the hostage inside.

'Stefan, are you okay back there?' Ben yelled over his shoulder without taking his eyes off the road. Stefan replied with an indistinct groan that Ben took to be a qualified 'yes', and he returned his focus to trying to keep the minivan from going into a terminal skid that would take them out of the chase, and maybe out of the game entirely. Meanwhile, the shooter hanging

177

from the car window seemed to have run out of ammo. He dropped the empty weapon, which bounced off the road and slammed against the front of the minivan as he ducked back inside the car. Ben could see no sign of the elderly woman. He could only hope to God they hadn't hurt her.

Now the road narrowed further as they came speeding into an older area of the city, where the modern offices and high-rises give way to tightly-packed houses and small businesses. An auto rickshaw driver appearing suddenly from a sidestreet stumbled into the path of the hatchback and was swiped brutally out of the way, his flimsy vehicle bursting to pieces while the driver was flung free, luckily unhurt. But the carnage was about to intensify tenfold as, moments later, a street market appeared in their path. The road was crowded with people and stalls selling everything from fresh fruit and vegetables to herbs and spices to teas and traditional medicines. Ben wanted to shout 'Out of the way! Take cover!' but there was nothing he could do as the hatchback went careening into the market without slowing down. The crowds scattered, screaming in panic, women snatching their children, shoppers and stall vendors alike running for safety. The car went smashing into a stall that until a fraction of a second ago had been offering richly colourful displays of apples and citrus fruit and peaches and mandarins and lychees and loquats, all of which erupted into the air amid the flying splinters and torn cloth of the shattered stall. The vehicle went ploughing right through, rolling destructively over everything in its path. Flying fruit cannoned off the pursuing minivan. A half-squashed watermelon landed in Ben's lap and he knocked it aside.

Just ten yards in front and now totally out of control, the car went rampaging through a fresh fish display as the vendor in his apron flung himself desperately out of the way. An oily mess of pulped fish spattered everywhere. Tyres slithering, the car went into a skid, slammed headlong with a loud crunch into the wall of a building behind the stall, and came to a sudden halt.

Ben narrowly avoided slamming right into the back of the crashed car. He was flinging open his door and jumping out before the minivan had even come to a full stop, snatching the rifle from Shi Yun on his way. If the scene in the street market had been one of total chaos before, now the appearance of a man with an assault weapon drove it into pandemonium as people fled screaming for their lives. It had to be some kind of miracle that nobody had been hurt yet.

Nobody, except for the one of the two shooters who'd been at the wheel of the hatchback. The car had hit the wall with enough force to rip him out of the driver's seat and pile him head and shoulders through the windscreen. He was lying draped over the fish-smeared bonnet, bloody and still. Even with the ski mask on, it was plainly visible that his face had been caved in from the impact. Ben didn't give a damn about him.

The second shooter and their hostage in the back of the car had had a softer landing, thrown against the seats and a little banged up but neither appearing seriously harmed. For the moment, anyhow: because the man kicked open the rear passenger door and dragged the elderly woman out, one arm clamped tightly around her chest and the other hand clutching the long, gleaming blade of his knife to her throat. His eyes were wild in the holes in the mask. She was struggling in vain against his powerful grip and gasping in terror as though she was about to go into cardiac arrest. The shooter-turned-knifeman saw Ben standing there with the rifle and started screaming at him in Chinese. You didn't need to speak the language to understand the universal meaning in his voice: 'DROP THE WEAPON NOW OR I'M GONNA SLICE THIS BITCH'S HEAD OFF!!'

Which wasn't the first time Ben had been threatened that way, in similar situations in the past. He hesitated. The guy was holding the hostage with her back closely pressed against his chest, like a human shield. She was probably no more than about five feet tall, but he wasn't a big man himself and he was well hidden behind her, with no clear shot to be had. Ben hesitated just a moment longer, then relented, let the rifle drop with a clatter to the ground and held up his hands to show they were empty.

The masked man seemed unmoved by Ben's gesture of reasonable cooperation and went on screaming, still clutching the knife against the hostage's throat. Shi Yun was out of the van and reasoning with him in Chinese, her tone low and placating, the way a negotiator speaks to a deranged person about to blow themselves up or leap off a tall building. Ben still couldn't understand a word but he had a pretty good idea what she was saying. *'Just let the lady go and talk to us, okay? We can fix this.'*

But Ben could also sense that the guy wasn't going to let her go. His eyes were demented and he was quivering with fear and desperation. People in that state of mind were capable of doing crazy things, and this one looked close to the point of madness. He was clutching the old woman so tightly against his chest that she was lifted bodily off the ground, her legs kicking in empty air. He was going to slice her. Then maybe he'd stab himself or cut his own throat. It would only take him a second to take the two of them out. Two flicks of the blade. A scumbag like him wouldn't be missed, apart from the fact that Ben needed him for information. But for a sweet old lady to have lived all these years just for it to be ended like this . . . not going to happen.

So Ben lowered his hands, reached behind him and took Shi Yun's service pistol from where he'd stuffed it into the back of his jeans earlier. Four rounds left, but he'd only need two. Faster than the knifeman had time to register what was happening let alone react, Ben had the sights lined up on the only critical part of the guy's anatomy that was visible behind his hostage. That was, his lower legs.

Ben fired. BLAM-BLAM, one knee and then the other, in such rapid succession that it sounded and looked as if a single shotgun blast had taken his legs out from under him simultaneously. The guy went down like a wet blanket falling from a washing line. Ben and Shi Yun dashed over to him. She grabbed the old woman and yanked her away to safety while Ben got control of the knife, twisted it out of the guy's hand before he could do anything harmful with it, and tossed it into the gutter. The guy tried to resist, but he was in too much shock to do much. Ben hit him twice in the face, hard, to subdue him, then clamped the sides of his neck in a chokehold that cut off the blood supply to his brain and rendered him quickly unconscious.

'You killed him!' Shi Yun gasped, staring at the limp body. It certainly looked that way. Ben had perfected these kinds of chokeholds years ago, and he was pretty good at staying on the right side of that fine line when he wanted to.

'He'll be all right. You can arrest him when he wakes up.' He handed her back her pistol. 'All yours, Detective. Job well done.'

Now at last they could hear the police sirens in the distance, growing steadily louder. Shi Yun helped the old woman back to her car and sat her down in the passenger seat, speaking softly and reassuringly. Stefan had managed to clamber out of the minivan and was sitting in its sliding doorway, nursing his arm. 'You saved my life,' he said to Ben.

'I was mostly thinking about saving my own,' Ben replied. But he wished he could have saved Sammy's, too. Poor Sammy. That was going to be another hard call to make to Ruth.

The sirens were getting louder. Some of the market crowd were slowly, furtively filtering back from their hiding places. The owners of the wrecked stalls were shaking their heads in dismay at the destruction to their stock. It was going to take days to clean up the mess. Some of the stallholders laid a canvas tarp over the body of the dead man. A kindly woman who lived in one of the neighbouring houses brought a blanket and a glass of water for the old lady while the ambulance was on its way, and Shi Yun thanked her. Meanwhile, her police-issue handcuffs had been left behind in the glove compartment of her car, so she used a piece of twine from the stall wreckage to bind the unconscious prisoner's wrists.

'Who are these people, Ben? Who are they working for?'

'Someone who isn't too keen on our line of investigation,' Ben replied. 'I doubt whether our friend here has much clue who hired him to kill us. But maybe you'll get something out of him under interrogation.'

'What if he won't talk?'

'Then you could always send him to one of those re-education camps that don't exist. Alternatively, leave me alone with him in a locked room for twenty minutes.'

She made no reply to that. 'I can't believe what you did.'

'You mean choking the guy out? That's just a simple little trick. I'll show you sometime.'

'No, I mean the way you defended us back there, when they attacked us. How you handled the whole thing. Just one person against five men with machine guns. I've never seen anyone move like that. It's incredible.'

'Just lucky,' he said. 'I've always been lucky in a fight.'

'I'm so sorry about your friend. He seemed like a good person. What was his name?'

'Samuel Tsang. He worked for my sister's company. I didn't really know him that well. But I liked him.'

She sighed. 'What a mess. Too many people are dying and I don't understand why.'

'We'll understand,' Ben said. 'I promise.'

'And what am I going to tell Chief Zhao? I disobeyed a direct order from my superior officer. I'm going to be in terrible trouble.'

'Screw Chief Zhao. You've just taken down a vicious murderer. They'll give you a medal.'

'I doubt that very much,' she said, anxiously shaking her head.

Either way, they'd soon find out. Because a moment later the first police cars arrived on the scene.

Chapter 25

The next few hours were a dragged-out, difficult and frustrating time. As the police set about sealing off the scene of the incident at the street market, ambulances arrived to ferry the body of the dead shooter, his surviving associate and their rescued hostage to their various destinations. Stefan was attended to by paramedics who ushered him into another ambulance, in which Ben accompanied him to hospital. By the time they got aboard, Ben had lost sight of Shi Yun, who was deep in discussions and explanations with her peers. Chief Zhao was yet to make his dreaded appearance.

Meanwhile, across the city, the logistical nightmare of cleaning up the aftermath of the battle at the highway inter-section was underway. Four bodies, including whatever remains of Sammy Tsang they were able to extract from the burnt-out wreck of Detective Lin's car, had to be carted off to the police morgue, while the bullet-riddled articulated truck used in the attack was towed off by a giant recovery lorry and dozens of other vehicles were cleared out of the way so that the enormous tailback of traffic clogging up that whole area of the city could start to flow again.

Ben saw none of this, and wouldn't have wanted to. As much as he disliked hospitals, he was much happier riding in the ambulance with Stefan and watching as the highly capable medical staff at Shaanxi Lintong Kangfu Hospital whisked his future brother-in-law off to have his arm reset and plastered.

He remembered the name of the hospital as being the same one where Shi Yun had told him Dan Chen had been treated after the earthquake, although he doubted he'd be able to learn anything more about that episode that might help to understand what it was Dan had been trying so carefully to smuggle out of the museum that day. Ben felt strangely lost without Shi Yun's presence as his guide and interpreter. He'd begun to depend on her being around. It occurred to him that he'd begun to find her company not unenjoyable, either. He quickly dismissed that ridiculous idea.

After half an hour sitting in a crowded waiting area he was able to find a Doctor Ho who spoke flawless English and told him that Mr Hartmann was doing well and should make a full recovery. They wanted to keep him in for observation for a few days, however, as it seemed he'd been involved in a very serious road accident. Dr Ho had also been informed that the police wanted to interview the patient in connection with the incident, and would be arriving shortly. It hadn't escaped the doctor's notice that this Mr Hope he was speaking with also looked slightly the worse for wear. Ben had been so busy dealing with Stefan that he hadn't even realised the state he was in, scuffed and bruised from the crash and still flecked with Sammy Tsang's blood.

'Might I suggest—' the doctor began, but Ben held up a hand. 'Thank you, if I require any medical assistance I'll be sure to let you know.'

It was another half-hour before Shi Yun came bursting through the hospital doors, spotted him and hurried over. By then, Ben had already tried calling Ruth to break the news about Sammy and reassure her Stefan was all right. Her line was engaged so he'd left a brief message saying to phone him as soon as she could. Not a conversation he was dying to have.

Shi Yun had swung by her apartment en route to the hospital, cleaned herself up and changed into a light dress that transformed her whole appearance from the formally-dressed authoritarian police detective Ben had come to know. It was the first time he'd seen her wearing her hair loose. It came down past her shoulders, jet black and glossy from the shower. 'You look a mess,' she said, wrinkling her nose at the dishevelled sight of him.

'It's my natural state,' he replied.

'How is your friend?'

'He's going to be fine.' Ben repeated what Dr Ho had told him. Shi Yun looked pleased. 'What about you?' he asked her. 'You've been through a lot today.'

'No more than I can handle,' she insisted. Ben wasn't the only one who stubbornly refused to be fussed over.

They grabbed a coffee from a vending machine and she gave him a quick update on the surviving shooter. Fingerprint database records had already identified him as Zhu Tianyong, a.k.a 'The Shrimp', a notorious underworld assassin and killer-for-hire, whom the police had been seeking in connection with several other murders and armed robberies. Two of the dead attackers had been known criminal associates of his, with the rest pending identification. Tianyong was being treated for his wounds at a different hospital, and the moment he was out of surgery and able to talk they'd be pressing him for all the information they could get.

'So you landed a big fish,' Ben said. 'Even if he was just a shrimp.'

'Let's not pretend I actually did anything,' she replied with a knowing half-smile. But then she glanced past Ben in the direction of the lobby doorway and the smile disappeared. 'Oh, shit.'

Ben turned as the lobby doors swung open and the burly form of Chief Zhao came marching in, flanked by two other plain-clothes detectives who looked as severe and grim as he did. Zhao was obviously looking for someone in particular. His implacable gaze scanned the lobby and landed on Ben and Shi Yun. Ben thought, *Here comes trouble.*

But Ben was wrong. Because as Zhao came striding across the lobby towards them, his hard expression softened and a broad grin spread over his face. It wasn't a look that sat well on him, like a piece of perished old rubber that hadn't been stretched in years. Judging by the way she was staring at her boss in disbelief, Shi Yun must have been seeing it for the first time.

'Ah, there you are, Detective,' Zhao said in his fragmented English, for Ben's benefit. It appeared from his warm smile and the jollity in his manner, then, that the chief hadn't come here to scream at his subordinate that she was being fired from the police for her wilful disobedience of his orders. Turning to Ben he thrust out a hand. 'Major Hope, I am very happy to see you again.'

Ben peered down at the hand, hesitated an instant, then thought, *What the hell* and shook it. The police chief's grip was clammy and soft. 'The pleasure is all mine, Chief Zhao,' Ben replied with a totally disingenuous smile of his own.

'Not at all. It is honour to shake the hand of the man who has done our police force such a service and saved life of most valuable officer,' Zhao said, still grinning like the Cheshire cat and pumping away for all he was worth.

He must have been rehearsing that line all the way here, Ben thought. He couldn't resist replying, 'Thanks, Chief. So I take it you're not going to deport me out of your country for failing to respect the regulations, driving a car without due authorisation, getting involved in an active police investigation and all manner of other heinous crimes against the state?'

Zhao boomed with laughter, so loudly that a few heads in the lobby turned to stare at him. 'No, no! Please forget all that. If you were Chinese citizen you get special commendation and top social credit rating. Very great honour for Chinese people.'

'Damn,' Ben said. 'Is it too late for me to change nationality?'

Zhao didn't seem to get the humour. His expression changing to one of solemn gravity, he went on, 'Rest assured that we catch criminals behind this terrible attack. And of course,' he added gravely, 'you have my sincere condolences for loss of your colleague. You tell me what I can do for you, I do it. Like this.' He snapped his fingers with an air of supreme authority.

To Ben this all came over as utterly fake and he could only wonder what hidden motive lay behind Zhao's apparent about-face. But he had nothing to lose by playing along with the pleasantries. And maybe something to gain. 'That's very kind of you to say, Chief,' he replied. 'Now maybe there is something you can do for me, and for both of us. It seems to me it'd be in all our interests if you could use your powers to keep as much of this story out of the media as possible. Otherwise I'm worried that the people who organised the attack will become much harder to catch. Would you agree?'

Zhao considered for a moment, then grinned even more widely and nodded his agreement. 'This very good idea,' he replied. 'I make possible, yes. China media only report what authorities allow.'

'That's what I thought,' Ben said. 'It's no different in the west. All the world's a village, as they say. So if you can dress up what happened today as some kind of gang warfare incident and keep our names out of it, it would be tactically a good move.' It wasn't every day you got to dictate what went into the state newspapers. How nice to have such influence, he reflected.

Just then, the same Dr Ho Ben had spoken to earlier reappeared in the lobby and came over. With a courteous nod to the police detectives he said to Ben, 'Please pardon me for interrupting. But Mr Hartmann is able to talk now and has been asking to see you, if you have a moment.'

'In that case, if you'll excuse me, Officers.' With a phony smile for Zhao and a real one for Shi Yun, Ben left them and followed Dr Ho out of the lobby.

There was a shrewder look in Chief Zhao's eyes as he watched the foreigner disappear through the swinging doors. 'An interesting man,' he said to Shi Yun, reverting to Chinese. 'Don't you think so, Detective Lin?' Without waiting for her reply he went on, 'A man of considerable skills, as we have seen demonstrated today. In fact I've been giving the matter a great deal of thought. And on reflection I've decided that we should allow this Hope to work alongside us in this investigation. I feel that the case is exceptional enough to justify granting him certain discretionary powers to act as your unofficial partner.'

Shi Yun sensed that Chief Zhao wasn't asking for her consent to his new plan. It was another direct order, one she was more than happy to obey to the letter. 'Of course, Chief,' she replied. 'If he hadn't been there today, I'm sure I would be dead now. But I have to say I'm a little surprised. May I ask why you have changed your mind about him?'

Zhao pursed his lips. 'It's partly a matter of diplomacy. Whatever the hell's going on here, this damn case risks getting out of hand and we can't afford to lose face in front of these Europeans. Besides which,' he added with a sly smile, 'he might actually be useful to us.'

Leaving the hospital a few minutes later, Chief Zhao was driven back to the Public Security Bureau and returned upstairs to the privacy of his office on the third floor. He told his secretary to hold his calls and bring him tea. When it arrived he locked his door and sat for a while pensively sipping his cup and gazing at the phone on his desk.

This was the same place he'd been sitting late that morning when he'd got the unexpected call that had forced his complete change of plan. The call hadn't come from any of his superiors within the police. Nor had it come from any recognisable government department. The voice on the line belonged to a man nonetheless so high up in the administration that very, very few people would have had the temerity not to obey his commands.

These particular commands had been issued to Chief Zhao within minutes of that morning's dramatic incident in Xi'an, long before any news of it could break in the local media. Zhao knew that his all-powerful caller had access to police radio communications, and had learned of the developing situation virtually the moment Detective Lin had made her request for emergency assistance. The caller also knew very well who it was who'd organised the attack as a means of wiping out not only Detective Lin herself, but also the two Europeans and the Beijing corporate executive who were helping her investigation.

'What are you trying to do to us, Zhao?' the voice on the phone had asked. His tone was smooth and calm, but underlain with the chilling menace of someone who could make you and your entire family disappear for ever at the press of a button.

'These people are a threat to us,' Zhao had tried to protest. 'Especially Hope. He's the really dangerous one. What if he were to find out the truth about—?'

'Quiet,' snapped the voice, instantly silencing him. 'Remember who you are, and to whom you owe your position. You have neither the authority to make such decisions, nor the intelligence to devise even the simplest of strategies. If not for the fact that it was so poorly carried out, your idiotic scheme might have deprived us of our best chance of finding the Hartmann girl.'

'I . . . I . . .'

The voice harshly interrupted him again. 'Do you realise how close you have come to ruining our plans? Has it not been made clear to you what would happen if you displease us? Not only to you personally, but your wife and those three charming children of yours? Do you really want their screams echoing in your ears as you suffer your own agonising death? What was done to Dan Chen and the others can be done to anyone we so choose.'

Zhao said nothing. He had a very clear understanding of what Dan Chen had been put through. His torture had been especially inhuman because of the information they'd wanted from him. He'd held out for a long time. But nobody could hold out against these experts in cruelty. They were masters of their trade and knew exactly how to cause the most unbearable agony and prolong it beyond endurance. The pain had been so horrific in the end that he'd had to crack and tell them everything, in return for a merciful death. Now they knew it all.

'Now listen to me very carefully, Zhao,' the voice said. 'There will be no other warning. The only way you and your family survive this is if you do exactly what I tell you.'

'I'm listening,' Zhao mumbled, feeling shrivelled down to the size of a small and helpless child.

'Hope is dangerous, as you say. And his skills and background make him highly capable. A man like that is worth having on your side, at least for as long as he may prove useful. That's why instead of eliminating him at this stage, we are going to embrace him. You will give him all the freedom and power he needs. And then he'll lead us straight to what we're looking for.'

Chapter 26

To a stranger China might seem oddly different from Europe in many ways, but one thing they shared was that universal smell that seemed to permeate all hospitals, the same sharp tang of disinfectant and soapy chemicals that never quite managed to sterilise away the underlying odour of sickness and death and all the unpleasant associations and memories it triggered for Ben.

Dr Ho led him through the shiny-floored corridors to the private room where Stefan was sitting alone. Ben's future brother-in-law was propped against his pillows, wearing a hospital gown and an impressive fibreglass cast that encased his right arm up to the shoulder and hung elevated by a cable and pulley. There was a drip stand by his bedside and all the usual bleepy electronic equipment monitoring the patient's vital functions. Some colour seemed to have returned to his cheeks, no doubt mainly thanks to pain medications, but he looked anxious and perplexed. Dr Ho told them gently but firmly that they had five minutes, then left them alone.

'Our friend Zhao is here,' Ben told him. 'Along with a couple of his plain-clothes goons who are probably going to want to talk to you.'

'I've been expecting they would turn up before long,' Stefan said glumly. 'That's why I wanted to speak to you first. How do you suggest we handle this situation?'

'Discreetly,' Ben replied. 'The less anyone on the outside knows, the more breathing space it'll allow us.' He repeated the reasons he'd explained to Chief Zhao. 'He seems to be on the same page, thankfully. Wants us in on the case. Full police co-operation.'

Stefan didn't appear all that reassured. 'Do you trust him to keep this quiet?'

'I wouldn't trust the bastard as far as I could throw him,' Ben said. 'But whatever political game he's playing, if it suits him to keep our names out of the papers then yes, I think he'll do that. So his goons won't need to ask you more than a few questions, just as a formality to confirm your version of what happened.'

'And your officer lady friend, she's on board with this new plan?'

Ben wondered about the 'lady friend' part. Was there something he was missing here? 'Totally on board. Her, I trust.'

Stefan frowned. 'What worries me most is what we should do about poor Sammy. He had no wife or children, thank God, but the company people back in Beijing will soon learn that he's dead. They'll be devastated, I'm sure. We can't keep the facts from them, can we?'

'For the moment, they don't need to know more than the bare bones. Which is that Sammy died in a car accident. That part is true enough, after all. As for the rest of it, we need to buy as much time as possible without alarm bells ringing all over the place. That's the last thing we need, so we can focus on our main priority of finding Lara.' He didn't want to reveal too much of his own concerns about what exactly they might find, if anything.

Stefan nodded. 'Agreed. I only wish I could be out there with you and not stuck here in this stupid room with this stupid broken arm. Damn it, why did this have to happen?'

'You just take it easy,' Ben said. 'Let me handle it.'

'Then there's Ruth,' Stefan said, about as far from taking it easy as it was possible for a man to be. 'Apart from the fact that I hate lying to my own fiancée, she's got to find out the truth sooner or later and she won't be happy that we hid it from her, to say the least. You know what she's like. Quick to anger, slow to forgive and strong on principle. Honesty is the first rule of our relationship.'

Ben did know what she was like, from experience. 'It's an expedient lie,' he reassured Stefan. 'Don't worry about Ruth. When the time comes, I'll smooth things out with her. Trust me, she'll understand.'

'I hope you're right. Or she'll never forgive me.'

And so it was settled, albeit with some misgivings on Stefan's part and a few privately-held ones on Ben's, too. He was glad they'd had their talk when they did, because the dreaded return call from Ruth came just two minutes afterwards, as he was heading back towards the lobby.

'Where are you?' she asked urgently, desperate for news. 'What's happened?'

The parts he was able to tell her, he needed to tell straight. 'I'm at the hospital in Xi'an. There was an accident. Stefan was hurt, but nothing serious.' He gave a brief, heavily diluted account of the smash.

'What about you?' she interrupted before he could get to the inevitable worst part.

'Hardly a scratch. But Ruth, there's something you need to know. It's about Sammy.'

It wasn't as tough a call as it would have been if he'd had to come clean about everything, but nonetheless he was glad when it was over. The news of Sammy's death didn't leave Ruth in tears, but there was a telltale tightness to her voice that told him she would have a hard time of it over the next few hours, the worst of which would be having to notify the Beijing office. Putting his phone away with a sigh as he walked back into the hospital lobby, Ben found Shi Yun alone with the two plain-clothes goons. She looked uncomfortable in their presence. 'The chief went back to HQ,' she explained.

'Do Tweedle-Dum and Tweedle-Dee here speak any English?' Ben asked her, waving a finger in the direction of the goons.

'We do,' one of them said, giving Ben a sullen eye. 'And those are not our names.'

'Well, whatever your names are, if you want to go and talk to Mr Hartmann, now's the time. But you'd better clear it with Dr Ho first. And whatever questions you have for the patient, keep it snappy and to the point. He needs to rest. Got it?'

'Got it,' said the other.

'Outstanding. Now Detective Lin and I have got more important business to take care of. Let's go, Detective.'

'You're pretty used to being in command, aren't you?' she said as they pushed out of the lobby doors into the sunshine.

'Those two are the kind that need their marching orders spelled out,' he said. 'I've dealt with them a thousand times before.'

'I get the impression you don't like the police very much.'

'Oh, I'm willing to make the occasional exception.' Spying a taxi rank, he headed towards it, Shi Yun striding quickly along to keep up.

'I'm pleased to hear it,' she said. 'So where are we going?'

'Back to the hotel, for now,' he told her, opening the taxi door. The driver was a little whiskery guy in a woolly cap, who peered up at them curiously. 'It's as good a base as any for me. Once I've cleaned up a little I can give you a lift home, now you don't have a car any more.'

Shi Yun spoke in Mandarin to the taxi driver, and they set off. 'I have a better idea,' she said. 'That hotel's really out of the way. Instead of being stuck out there on your own, why don't you just pick up your car and your things and come and stay with me at my place?'

He looked at her.

'Don't misunderstand me,' she said. 'I suggest it because it's the most practical arrangement. If we're going to be working together, it suits us to have a shared base of operations. My apartment has a spare bedroom. And it's not far from the office, in case we need anything.'

Ben agreed that it was a good plan. At the hotel, he took a quick, cool shower, binned his clothes and changed into fresh ones. Then he checked out of the suite, they collected the Mercedes and Shi Yun directed him across the city to the drab modern apartment building where she lived.

To Ben, her home seemed about as spacious as a rabbit hutch, but she explained that for a single person to have a two-bedroomed apartment was really quite a privilege, one of the special perks of her profession. She kept the tiny space meticulously organised and uncluttered. Her compact but diverse library surprised him with all its books on western history and philosophy, as did the prints of Impressionist paintings on the walls. 'Did you think it would all be Chinese dragons and propaganda posters of our Dear Leader?' she laughed. She played a kind of Oriental harp that he was curious about and which she explained was called a guzheng, and kept a collection of beautiful little jade sculptures. The apartment smelled of flowers and scented tea.

'This is Chan,' she said, introducing him to a small but proud-looking blue-eyed Siamese cat that prowled over to disdainfully check out the unexpected guest. 'Don't try to pet her. She doesn't tolerate anyone touching her except me.' Putting that notion to the test, Ben reached out a hand to the cat and she let out a strangled spitting yowl, ears laid flat and her eyes turning a startling red. 'Yikes,' he said, withdrawing his hand before it got lacerated to ribbons. 'Looks like you don't need to worry about burglars.'

'Oh, no, I'm not concerned about security,' Shi Yun replied nonchalantly. 'This is China. People are generally very safe here.'

'Until they get a surprise home visit from the organ rippers,' he said.

'Besides,' she said, ignoring that comment, 'I have lots of protection.' Taking her holstered pistol out of the small handbag she'd been carrying, she opened a tall, narrow cupboard unit to reveal a hidden gunsafe inside, with a fingerprint-activated smart lock that she tapped to access the steel-lined cabinet. She slotted a ready-loaded magazine from the safe into her pistol and stowed it away. Ben couldn't help but notice the pump-action riot shotgun that also lived in there, which he recognised as the police and military version of China's Hawk model 97. She had several boxes of solid slug and buckshot ammo to feed it with. 'I can see that,' he replied.

'Only police and army personnel are permitted to keep fire-arms,' she explained. 'Ordinary citizens found in possession of unauthorised weapons are sentenced to hard labour or death.'

'Sounds like the UK,' Ben commented.

'I'm hungry,' she said, stepping into the minute kitchenette. 'Do you like Chinese food? I'll make us a snack.'

Ben's energy levels needed replenishing too, after their busy day and a missed lunch. 'I'll help.'

'No, but you can stay in here and keep me company if you like. It's not often Chan and I have a visitor.' She tossed him a bottle of Tsingtao lager from her fridge, and he leaned in the kitchenette doorway, sipping the cold beer and watching as she deftly cooked up a dish of fried chicken, mushrooms, beansprouts and noodles in a heavy cast-iron wok. Her 'snack' turned out to be a mountain of unctuous, delicious-smelling cuisine. He wondered if she always ate like this, and where she must put it all to remain so slender. She served two generous helpings into a pair of flat bowls and they sat on stools at a fold-down table in the kitchen. 'You prefer a knife and fork?' she asked. 'I'm so used to the sticks.'

'The sticks are fine by me,' he replied, and she watched with an expression of approval as he used them. 'Not bad,' she said. 'You're quite an expert.'

'And you're a great cook. This is fabulous.'

Chan watched him too, her head cocked to one side, then hopped up on his lap.

'Shoo her away if she bothers you.'

'She's fine,' he said, stroking the cat's silky fur. Chan started purring loudly.

'I can't believe she likes you. She seems to want to scratch most people's eyes out.'

'I'm just naturally charming, I suppose.'

Shi Yun laughed. 'So tell me, Mr Charming. What's next after this?'

He laid his chopsticks down on his empty bowl. 'When you've finished up your meal I think you should call our friend Wang. Find out if the kid who was knocked off his scooter is working today, and if he is, then we'll pay him a visit.'

The kid was indeed working that day. His name was Dylan Li and his shift wouldn't be over for another several hours. 'Sounds like a plan, then,' Ben said. 'Let's go.'

'First I want to stop off at headquarters.'

'What for?'

'To get another car from the police pool,' she replied. 'One with the proper equipment and a radio. Besides, I don't like that Mercedes. It's too flashy.' She disappeared into her bedroom for a few moments, and reappeared changed out of her dress and back into jeans and her tan leather jacket, once again the tough, no-nonsense lady detective. She returned to her gunsafe, took out the holstered pistol and strapped it on. 'I'm sorry I don't have one for you,' she said.

He pointed inside the safe at the Hawk 97 riot shotgun. 'No?'

Chapter 27

Late that afternoon, Shi Yun at the wheel of her new unmarked police car, they cut back across the city to the flyover where the stolen van had been found, and from there to Wang's fast food joint. En route she phoned in to learn whether anything had yet been gleaned from the interrogation of Zhu 'the Shrimp' Tianyong. It seemed that the tough little guy was holding out and still refusing to talk. 'Let's hope we have more luck with the kid,' she said to Ben.

Wang's young employee Dylan Li was in the kitchen storeroom hauling sacks of rice around and seemed happy to take a break from his shift to talk to them, once he understood he wasn't in any trouble for working off the books. 'Sure,' he said brightly. 'I still have that piece of shit's registration number. Is he in serious trouble?'

'He's a suspect in a kidnapping and several murders,' Shi Yun told him.

'Cool. I hope the fucker gets the needle.'

Dylan happily handed over the grubby delivery receipt on which he'd scribbled the registration, and provided a description of the car and driver. It was a shitbox of an old model Volkswagen Bora, something between puke green and piss yellow according to the kid, with a broken headlight and a taped-up wing mirror probably from the last time he'd knocked into someone. The culprit was a few years older than Dylan, hard to say but maybe about twenty-five, with long floppy hair and a stupid-looking face. Back in the police car, Shi Yun wasted no time talking to HQ, and very soon afterwards the database matched the number to a 2004 VW Bora.

'Registered owner is one Jia Wenguang,' she said with a smile. 'Twenty-seven years of age, resident of Xi'an. We can access his whole file right here from my phone. Social credit status, financial history, details of relatives. He works part-time in a print shop that makes T-shirts, and also has a job working in a restaurant. Parents are deceased but he has an older sister, now married and still living in the city.'

She showed him their suspect's government ID mugshot. Dylan Li's description of his stupid-looking face might have been a little prejudiced, but he'd been right about the floppy hair. 'Looks like our man,' Shi Yun said with satisfaction.

Ben studied the image and tried to picture Jia Wenguang as a masked kidnapper snatching a young woman in the woods and dragging her into the back of a van. The face in the photo looked more like that of a college student than a hardened criminal. Yet appearances could be deceptive, and the evidence spoke for itself. Sometimes it was the innocuous-looking types you had to watch out for.

'Any previous criminal history?' he asked.

'None that he's ever been caught for,' Shi Yun replied, scanning the file. 'But our records show he has zero social media profile, no WeChat account, nothing. That's suspicious in itself.'

'I don't have any social media profile either. Am I suspicious?'

'I don't know. Perhaps you have something to hide. That's how our government regards it, anyhow. Citizens who don't engage online are seen almost as vagrants. It's very hard for them to live any kind of normal life, so we tend to assume they're up to something secret and illegal.'

'Welcome to the police state,' Ben said.

'Not so bad when you're on the right side of it,' she replied. 'The address is just half an hour away. Let's go.'

Jia Wenguang's squat, unattractive apartment building was in a poorer neighbourhood of Xi'an City, a long way from the traditional scenic districts or the affluent skyscraper centre. Shi Yun parked in a narrow, dirty street where small shops and squalid residential buildings clustered in the smog. Most of the vehicles along the littered kerbside were older and in bad condition, but none of them was a greenish-yellow 2004 Bora.

Ben and Shi Yin got out of the car and walked towards the building. A drunken guy peeing against a wall yanked up his flies and staggered away when she flashed her police ID at him. Some kids on the far side of the street were pointing at Ben and yelling something in Chinese that they obviously found hilariously funny. 'What are they saying?' he asked. 'Foreigner,' she replied.

'I suppose I've been called worse things.'

Jia Wenguang lived on the top floor. The building didn't look much better on the inside than it did on the outside, and even if there had been a lift Ben would have chosen to hike the stairs. Arriving at a landing with a long bare-walled passage lined with apartment doors on both sides, Shi Yun led the way, counting off numbers until she said, 'This is the one.'

There was no kind of doorbell or buzzer. Three knocks; four; five; no response or sounds of life from inside. Shi Yun drew her pistol and used the butt to rap more loudly, then pressed her ear to the door, listened carefully and shook her head with the corners of her mouth downturned. 'I don't think he's at home.'

'Or he doesn't want to talk to us,' Ben said. 'Let me try.'

'You can't kick it down,' she warned him, alarmed.

'Honestly. What do you take me for?' He took out his wallet, in which he kept a small set of lock picks for just these kinds of occasions.

'Those are what criminals use!'

'There are criminals on both sides of the law,' he reminded her. It took less than a minute to defeat the simple lock, and then the door swung open and they were inside.

You never quite knew what to expect in these situations. A loaded gun in your face. A silent attack dog just waiting for the chance to sink its fangs into you. A primitive booby trap wired to the pin of a grenade or the trigger of a shotgun tied to a chair and pointing at waist height as you stepped through the door. Or the decomposing remains of the person you'd come looking for making a very nasty smell, with or without their internal organs removed.

This time was different. Not only was Jia Wenguang not at home, either alive or dead, it seemed that his apartment had been vacant for some time. There were no clothes in the wardrobe or drawers, no toiletries in the bathroom, no personal effects of any kind, and nothing in the kitchen cupboards or fridge. Even the litter basket and garbage bin, those repositories of information often useful to the meticulous detective, had been emptied.

'He moved out,' she said. 'Damn. Another blank. What now?'

'Dan Chen's apartment,' Ben said. 'I'd like to have a look around inside, in case there's anything the police missed.'

She looked mildly offended. 'What makes you think we would have missed anything?'

'Humour me.'

Shi Yun shook her head. 'I think it's a waste of time. But you go if you want. We can pick up your car from my place.'

'Where will you go?' he asked, surprised.

'To check out Jia Wenguang's sister. She might know where he went. He could even be living with her.'

'I don't like the idea of splitting up,' Ben said. 'It's risky.'

'But we'll be twice as efficient that way,' she replied. 'And in China—'

'I know. Efficiency is everything.'

Chapter 28

He shouldn't have agreed to the plan, Ben was thinking as he set off alone from Shi Yun's place in the Mercedes. The more time he spent with her, the more important it became to him to be there to protect her if anything else happened. The unknown threat against their lives was still out there and could be planning another strike at any moment.

Then again, he reasoned, she would theoretically be quite safe as she drove off to pursue her own thread of their investigation. The new police car she was driving, picked out at random from the police pool and signed for only that afternoon, couldn't possibly be traced to her by anyone on the outside, and certainly not so soon. On top of which it could only have been his being with her, along with his two companions, that had made her a collateral target in the truck attack. Whoever had tried to take them all off the table, they had no reason to be interested in a middle-ranking female detective who was only incidentally connected to the Lara Hartmann affair. In short, Shi Yun was better off without him.

With those reassuring thoughts in mind, and the equally reassuring presence of the loaded Hawk riot shotgun hidden under his jacket on the rear seat, he followed the sat nav directions eastwards across the city towards Dan Chen's former address.

He found it in a quieter and more pleasant suburban area than the district where Jia Wenguang had lived, where the streets

205

were wide and clean and the apartment buildings were taller and more modern. Dan Chen's apartment was located on the thirteenth floor of a well-maintained tower block with its own gardens separating it from the street, the perfect abode for a young, upwardly mobile and ambitious government employee. Nobody in the street was staggering about drunk or urinating in public, and there were no gangs of nasty little urchins to point and call out unimaginative insults at him. Ben rode up in the lift with a nice little old lady who smiled constantly at the tall blond foreigner, and whom he'd have liked to be able to ask if she'd known the late Mr Chen, in case she knew something interesting. No such luck. She got off on the eleventh floor and he reached Chen's alone.

The thirteenth-floor landing was airy and bright, a broad L-shaped corridor with a large plate-glass window overlooking the streets and muting the rumble of traffic from below. The apartment doors were spaced far apart, with neat little brass nameplates on them. Dan Chen's nameplate had been removed, and the police had stuck their yellow crime investigation tape around the door. It must have been there since their last search of his apartment, now lying sad and empty in the wake of his unsolved murder.

But more recently, Ben noticed as he approached the door, someone had taken a sharp blade to the tape, cutting all the way around so that the door could be discreetly opened. Less discreet was the way someone – the same someone? – had forced the lock. It had been levered open very recently, judging by the freshly cracked, splintered wood of the jamb and the little flakes of paint on the carpet at its foot. The door was hanging slightly ajar. He very carefully, very quietly peered through the gap and was able to see part of the entrance hallway, a short white-painted corridor with three internal doors leading

206

off it and a little chest of drawers to one side, on which lay a stubby steel wrecking bar. A splinter from the forced door jamb was still stuck between its jaws.

The door at the end of the hall was open. And someone was moving about in the room beyond. Ben saw a figure flit past the doorway, too quickly for a clear look, except to make out that it was a tall, thin man with long black hair tied in a pony-tail. He disappeared from sight but Ben could hear him rummaging around the room, opening drawers and cupboards.

Ben had two basic options here. The more direct and instinctively appealing was to enter the apartment and confront the intruder. Behind closed doors he could use all the force necessary to find out who the guy was, and what he was doing inside the dead man's home. Or, more strategically, he could pull back, wait for the guy to leave, follow him and see where the trail led.

The younger, brasher and more impulsive Ben would certainly have opted for the first plan of action, every time. But the more experienced and perhaps slightly wiser man he'd grown into had learned the hard way that the heroic strong-arm approach wasn't always necessarily the most productive. If he played this right, he might be able to learn a lot more useful information than simply whatever lies or confessions of ignorance he might be able to beat out of some paid lackey. The tall thin ponytailed intruder was unlikely to be a high-up player in whatever organised crime gang had hired him to break into Dan Chen's apartment. But he might lead Ben to someone who was.

It was a dangerous decision, because of the risk of letting the guy slip through the net. But Ben made it anyway. He stepped back from the door and retreated down the corridor, past the mouth of the lift where he could hide around the corner of the L and observe the intruder leaving the apartment.

He was prepared to wait there as long as he had to. But as it happened, he wasn't waiting for long.

Less than three minutes later, the intruder emerged from the taped-up doorway. If he'd taken anything from the apartment he must have it in his pockets, because all he was carrying as he walked towards the lift was the steel bar. If Ben had confronted him inside, he might have been able to force the guy to give up his name – but in hindsight that wouldn't have been necessary. Because Ben already knew who he was. A couple of years had gone by since the government database mugshot had been snapped and the floppy hair had grown out a few inches, but there was no doubt that the man who'd been lurking inside Dan Chen's apartment was Jia Wenguang. The same Jia Wenguang who'd been seen at the wheel of the getaway car used in the abduction of Lara Hartmann. The same Jia Wenguang who'd mysteriously moved out of his own shithole apartment and was now about to lead Ben to wherever he'd been hiding out since.

Jia paused at the lift doors. He pressed the button with his knuckle, waited for it to come whooshing up from a lower floor, then stepped inside as the doors glided open.

Ben waited for the doors to close, then raced for the stairs. The fire escape was at the other end of the L-shaped passage. Thirteen floors to descend in the time it took for the lift to shoot down the shaft. It was a long way to run, but gravity was on Ben's side – and so was the banister rail that allowed him to go sliding down one landing at a time. Reaching the ground floor he burst out of the fire escape exit at the side of the apartment block just in time to see Jia Wenguang strolling casually down the street away from the building.

Ben followed at a distance, careful not to be seen. As his quarry rounded the corner of a building and disappeared down a sidestreet he quickened his step to catch up, then peered around the corner and saw him walking up to an empty car parked at the kerbside. An early model Volkswagen Bora painted a sickly tinge of greenish yellow. It had a broken headlight and one of the wing mirrors had a makeshift repair with black tape. The getaway car. Jia unlocked the driver's door, jumped in and started the engine with a cough of smoke from the exhaust.

Ben had tailed a lot of suspects in his past hunts for kidnappers' lairs and safehouses, and this was the first time he'd ever known one to drive around the streets in their own ropey third-hand car that had been recently used to abduct one of their victims. It wasn't what anyone could have called a hallmark of professionalism. Just who the hell were these people? But he didn't have much time to dwell on the question, because he had to run fast back up the street towards where he'd parked the Mercedes. He blipped the locks at a distance, leaped behind the wheel and fired it up, slammed into drive and squealed away from the kerb just as the yellow Bora appeared from the sidestreet junction up ahead. Jia Wenguang turned right and continued up the road, merging with the traffic.

Ben eased off the gas and allowed a few other vehicles to slip into the gap between himself and the yellow Bora. The only sure way to maintain a tail without getting spotted was to use multiple cars, vans and motorcycles relaying one another and staying in radio contact. Failing that, you just had to hang right back in the traffic, not do anything to draw attention to yourself, keep your eyes open and hope you didn't lose the chase at a traffic light.

Jia headed south and west, maintaining a sedate pace as he drove through different districts of the city, and Ben stayed with him. Street names and road signs were all in Chinese and he would have had no idea where he was, if the sat nav hadn't provided translations of the city district names: Xinzhuang Village, Dazhao Neighbourhood, Dongsima Village. It was after six p.m. and the chaotic early evening traffic was only gradually starting to thin out. A large truck emerged from a junction ahead and got between them, belching smoke, its wide trailer blocking his view of the yellow Bora for long enough for Ben to start to worry that he'd lost him; but then he caught sight of him again, moving into another lane, and punched the accelerator to close the gap up a little.

It went on like that for another half-hour as the sun sank into the western sky; now speeding along stretches of fast highway, now threading through densely built-up areas separated by increasing areas of greenery and agricultural land as they drew closer to the outer edges of the city. Twice Ben tried to call Shi Yun, but she wasn't picking up. The second time he left a message, saying, 'It's me. I'm on our guy. Looks like we're heading south-west. out of Xi'an. Call me when you can.'

By the time they'd been driving for almost an hour, with still no word from Shi Yun, the yellow Bora had led him out of the remote suburbs and into open countryside. Forested hills loomed high above the winding road. Smaller villages flashed by, some with ancient traditional houses and temples whose beauty would have merited stopping for a closer look if he hadn't needed to keep doggedly ploughing on in pursuit of his target. By now the traffic had diminished considerably, with far fewer headlights in the mirror and virtually nothing coming the other way, and it was hard to keep a safety buffer of other vehicles between them; while with the fading light came the growing risk of mistaking another pair of taillights for the Bora's. Ben was beginning to flag from sustaining his concentration so intensely for so long, and he was relieved when at last the Bora turned off down a narrow rural road and its flaring brake lights signalled that it was stopping.

Turning off the main road three hundred yards behind, Ben killed his lights and engine and let the Mercedes coast quietly to a halt. The Bora had come to a halt but its headlamps were still on, and in their beams Ben could see no sign of a house or building of any kind on that whole stretch of road. Nothing but dense forest rising up to the hills on each side, whose outlines were just faintly visible in the soft glow of moonlight filtering through the trees overhead.

Then the Bora's lights went out. Jia Wenguang was definitely stopping here, and Ben wondered what was coming next. Was he due to meet someone in this remote place? Was Ben about to be introduced to another of the gang? Only time would tell. For the moment they were alone, and nothing was happening. Other than the moon and the occasional wash of passing vehicle lights behind them on the main road, the lane was all in darkness. As Ben sat watching and waiting, he could just about make out the tiny glow of a mobile phone screen through the Bora's rear window. Maybe Jia was checking messages, or perhaps he was calling someone. The associate he'd come here to meet?

The call, if that was what it was, only lasted a few moments. Then the Bora's lights came back on, and Ben thought Jia was about to drive on. In that case, Ben would wait until he was a good distance ahead and then follow, with his own lights off. Driving blind in the darkness would be tricky.

But instead of continuing up the road, the Bora turned into a narrow opening in the trees that Ben hadn't been able to see from this angle, and disappeared. It would be all but impossible for Ben to follow him in there by car without being seen or heard. He turned off the switch on the driver's mirror to prevent the cabin light from coming on, grabbed the shotgun from the rear seat and got out of the car.

At a slow, silent trot it took less than half a minute to reach the opening in the trees where the Bora had disappeared. Ben peered into the darkness of the forest and could see no glimmer of a light in there, only a winding track through the trees not unlike the one near Qinjiacun where he and Shi Yun had found the abandoned van. This one was only barely wide enough for any vehicle to pass through. Judging by the faint tracks in the dirt, though, the Bora wasn't the only one to have travelled along it recently.

But where had the car gone? For the first time since leaving Xi'an, Ben was beginning to worry seriously about losing Jia's trail. Then his gamble would have failed and the long pursuit would have been all for nothing. There was nothing for it but to explore the track on foot, finding his way by moonlight and hoping it might lead him to something.

He stepped towards the opening in the trees and was about to start off down the track, when he suddenly stopped.

He'd heard something. He turned and looked in the direction of the strange sound.

And that was when Ben realised that he, too, was being followed.

Chapter 29

It wasn't another car that was following him. Nor was it another person on foot. It wasn't even a human being.

The whirring electric motor buzz overhead might have been barely noticeable against the constant ambient sound backdrop of the city, but out here in the silence of the countryside it would have been hard to miss even by someone with less acute hearing than Ben's. The small drone was hovering about two hundred feet above the lane. All that could be seen of it was an X-shaped silhouette against the dark sky, and little blinking lights like those of a miniature aircraft. It seemed to have come out of nowhere, but its appearance couldn't be without a reason. Ben had no doubt that it was following him. And most likely filming him, too, using a tiny night-vision camera and transmitting real-time video footage back to some unseen controller who therefore knew exactly who and where he was, and what he was up to.

Not good.

There was no way such a small drone could have had the range to follow him all the way from Xi'an. Someone must have been tailing his car in another vehicle, unwilling to get too close, and then launched the device from not too far away so they could track his movements. But who?

He had to assume it was another of the same gang Jia belonged to. Which meant they must have known all along that he was on their tail. He felt like kicking himself for his foolishness. But he knew it was too late to cry about it now.

He also knew that letting the drone continue to follow him wasn't an option. Would the dense tree cover allow him to give it the slip, once he entered the forest? Maybe, but it couldn't be guaranteed. These pesky little bastards could fly almost anywhere, zip through the smallest gaps and record everything below in ultra-fine detail, even in low light conditions. That was what made them so useful for military purposes, and especially for Special Forces units, that their role in combat and military intel operations was expanding every day. Ben had come up in the old-school way of doing things, but he'd always known that one day people in his profession were going to have to deal with these tough new adversaries as a matter of course.

In short, the damn drone had to die. And Ben just happened to have the perfect means of achieving that.

So he unslung the riot shotgun from his shoulder, pumped a round into the chamber, raised the weapon upwards, let the combat sights fall on the dim, murky X shape hovering over-head, and squeezed the trigger. A short-barrelled shotgun that was essentially intended for close-range combat was pretty ill suited to taking down flying game, whether of the living or robotic variety. But Ben's aim was good, and as the gun let out its ear-splitting BOOM and kicked savagely against his shoulder he saw the dim target vaporise satisfyingly into a million tiny pieces.

Obviously not one of those armoured versions made for military use, then. 'That was fun,' he muttered to himself as the fragments of drone rained down and scattered across the road. It was so comprehensively destroyed that there would have been nothing to learn from checking out the remains.

Not so much fun was the knowledge that the last moments before the drone's destruction would have been neatly captured on its camera, along with the face of the perpetrator. On top of which, a shotgun blast in the dead stillness of night would have been sure to reach the ears of Jia Wenguang and whoever else he might have come here to meet. It might not have been tactically wise for Ben to signal his presence to the person or people he was trying to pursue – but he'd had no choice, and in any case they probably already knew anyway. At least there was no longer anyone watching him, he thought.

He slung the weapon back over his shoulder and set off down the track. Deeper among the dense tree cover the light of the moon was less able to penetrate the overhead canopy, and he groped his way through the inky shadows with twigs whipping at his face and outstretched hands. The ground felt mossy and spongy underfoot, deeply rutted and trenched here and there from vehicle tyres sinking into the soft dirt. The foliage was so thick on both sides of the track that there seemed little chance of Jia's having deviated off it. Wherever the car had disappeared to, Ben was as sure as he could be that he was following the right trail.

And sure enough, within a couple of minutes' trek from the road, his vision now adjusted to the dark, he made out the shape of a stationary car twenty yards ahead. Two more vehicles sat nearby, where the track widened out slightly into a small clearing. All three were unoccupied, but as a precaution Ben had the shotgun ready. As he reached them, he recognised the yellow Bora, its engine still warm and ticking as it cooled in the night air. Of the other two vehicles, one was a smaller hatchback of Chinese manufacture, and the third a motor scooter whose rider must have had some difficulty negotiating the soft rutted track.

If Jia and the kidnap gang had gathered here in the forest tonight for a secret rendezvous, there was no sign or sound of them. The track seemed to continue a certain distance into the trees and so Ben followed it, clutching the shotgun tightly and scanning constantly left and right in the knowledge that they might well be lurking in the dark ready to ambush him.

No bright lights suddenly dazzled him, nobody jumped screaming from the trees brandishing knives and machetes or started shooting out of the shadows. He walked on, until a little way further up the track he came to a wooden gate, ten feet high and barring his path. He soon realised that it was part of a security fence sectioning off an area of the forest. Possibly a very large area, it seemed to him. Attached to the gate and the wire mesh of the fence were signs that he could make out in the faint moonlight. They were big and red and intimidating, and while he couldn't understand the Chinese characters printed on them, skull-and-crossbones symbols communicated their stark DANGER – KEEP OUT warning clearly enough.

Ben had no idea who'd built this perimeter or why, except that they must have had their own good reasons for wanting to seal off, hide and protect whatever was inside. The gate was held shut with a thick chain and a large steel padlock, both of which would have been strong enough to withstand a shotgun blast even if he'd been willing to risk more noise.

One way or another he needed to get past the fence. If he couldn't go through it or around it, he'd have to go over it. The thick, strong mesh provided plenty of footholds and handholds for him to scale up the gate. Easy enough to negotiate, until ten feet off the ground he came to the coils of barbed and razor wire running along its top. Clinging to the mesh he tossed the gun to the other side, shrugged one arm out of its sleeve of his leather jacket, then the other, and laid the jacket over the sharp coils so he could scramble over. He dropped to the ground, put the slightly lacerated jacket back on, snatched up the gun and kept moving.

The track continued deeper into the exclusion zone, rising as the ground sloped gradually into a hillside. The dense forest seemed to stretch for ever on both sides. From deep among the trees came the screech of some night bird. Then after several hundred more yards, the track stopped. A shard of moonlight shone on the craggy stone stairway that rose steeply in front of him.

The fence and gate had been erected comparatively recently, but the stairway looked as if it had been there for ever. Like the stonework of medieval castles Ben had seen, but far, far older. Maybe two thousand years, maybe three. A feat of engineering that must have taken hundreds of stonemasons a very long while to build. And they'd built it to withstand the ravages of time, climate and nature throughout the whole span of human history that had elapsed since their long-gone era. The steps were crumbled and split in places, choked with weeds to each side and worn smooth in the middle by the passage of countless feet.

Ben had little doubt that the last person who'd been here before him was Jia Wenguang. And that Jia must have had a key to the security gate to get in here. Whatever the perimeter had been created to hide from the outside world, he and his associates were privy to the secret.

Ben paused at the bottom and looked up. The stone stairway seemed to go on an awfully long way.

Wherever it might lead him, he began climbing.

Chapter 30

Up and up he went, step after step after step until he'd lost count and his calf muscles were burning. The ancient stairway carried him higher and higher up the steep hillside until, at last, the trees crowding thickly on both sides began to thin out and the summit of the hill was drawing nearer. He'd been moving fast all this way, in the hope that he might soon catch sight of Jia – and maybe the person or persons Jia had come all this way to meet up with – but there was still no trace of another living soul anywhere to be seen. Turning around to catch his breath and gaze at the view behind him he could see the faintly moonlit sweep of forest below stretching out for miles.

There was just a short way to go now before he reached the top. He clambered up the last few steps, and now the slope was flattening into the bald, treeless crown of the hill where another, even more bewildering, sight was waiting for him. As he left the stairway behind him he could see a faint light up ahead, the soft amber glow of a lantern. Above it, silhouetted black against the night sky, stood a solitary archway that rose out of the remnants of what Ben realised was some kind of temple, as ancient as the stone steps that had led to it. Judging from what he could make out of its crumbled walls and toppled columns, far back in history this had been a large and imposing building that would have dominated the landscape from its high perch. Now all that remained was this sad, empty ruin.

Except it wasn't quite as empty as it appeared at first sight. Because sitting under the glow of the lantern suspended from the archway was the first other human being Ben had seen since he'd set out through the forest.

As Ben approached, he could see in the soft light that the man sitting under the arch wasn't Jia Wenguang – in fact few people could have looked more different from the lanky, dark-haired twenty-something Ben had followed from Xi'an. This man appeared at least fifty years older. The hair he had left was long and wispy and as snowy white as the goatee beard that hung down his chest. Clad in what looked like a rough sackcloth robe he was seated cross-legged on a stone plinth, as still as a statue. For a few moments Ben couldn't be sure that he *wasn't* a statue.

Ben stepped closer to the old man. He looked as though he might be deep in some kind of meditative trance, or maybe asleep. His eyes were closed and he didn't seem to be breathing. Was he even alive?

'Hello?' Ben called out to him. The old man didn't give a flicker of a response. Maybe he was dead, Ben thought. He called out again, 'Hello?'

The old man still didn't so much as twitch a muscle until Ben was standing just a few feet away. Then, suddenly, his eyes snapped open and he looked at the newcomer with absolute clarity and focus. Moving with astonishing agility for someone his age, he unfolded his legs and hopped quickly down from the stone plinth and stood in the middle of the archway, blocking the way through. His intense gaze stayed locked on Ben the whole time, though because he was at least eight inches shorter he had to raise his head to maintain eye contact. The rough cloth robe hung from his narrow, bony shoulders almost down to his feet.

Who was the old man? For all Ben knew, he lived up here like some kind of strange old hermit. Or was he connected to the same group of people Ben was tracking? That seemed unlikely, somehow, and for the moment Ben decided he should give the wizened old geezer the benefit of the doubt. He spoke to him patiently. 'I don't know if you can understand a word I'm saying, but I came up here looking for someone. Have you seen him? Young, dark hair in a ponytail. His name is Jia Wenguang.'

'I understand what you are saying,' the old man said, looking at him curiously. His English was accented but fluent enough.

'Then perhaps you can help me,' Ben told him. 'Or if you can't, then I'll have to ask you to get out of my way so I can find him myself, okay?'

The old man's face showed no expression. He didn't move aside and said nothing.

Ben took a step closer. He had no wish to act hard or intimidatingly towards a defenceless septuagenarian, but he was in a hurry and fast losing patience. 'Look, sir, if you can understand me, then please don't waste my time. I have important business to attend to, and I need you to step aside.'

'I know who you are looking for,' the old man said to Ben. His face was still and his voice was soft and calm.

'You do? Then where is he?'

'He is here,' said the old man. 'He arrive here a few minutes before you.' He slowly pointed back at the moonlit ruins behind him.

Ben peered past him through the archway but couldn't see any sign of anyone else around. There were still a few parts of the temple left standing, but they appeared empty. 'Then you'd better let me talk to him. He's involved in something bad and he's got some explaining to do.'

The old man slowly shook his head. 'There are many things you wish to understand, yes? But you cannot go any further, until you can prove your good intentions.'

Ben stared at him. 'My good intentions?'

'For start, put down weapon,' the old man said, nodding in the direction of the shotgun slung over Ben's shoulder. 'No weapons allowed in sacred temple.'

If that was all it was, Ben was willing to compromise just to placate him. He shrugged, unslung the gun and propped it butt-down against a crumbled pillar. 'There. Happy? Now get out of my way. I won't ask you again.'

But still the old man refused to step aside. Calmly but adamantly he shook his head and repeated, 'Must prove good intentions.'

'I put the gun down. What more do you want?' This was getting ridiculous. Ben was going to have to push past him, but he'd have to do it gently so as not to hurt the guy. Someone so frail and bony as this could all too easily get broken in two from the least bit of force. Ben reached out to lay a hand on his shoulder, intending to brush him aside.

What happened next came as a shock. Because the old man was so slightly built that Ben had expected him to weigh nothing and be as easy to push past as a flimsy weed. Instead, it felt as if Ben had tried to shove a mature oak tree out of the way. It was as though the old man were made of concrete and planted immovably deep in the ground. He might have been one of the stone columns that had once held up the temple roof.

Then as Ben tried to apply more force, the old man reached up a bony hand and touched his wrist. It was only the lightest of taps, barely more than a brush of a fingertip, but it felt like getting jolted by a high-voltage cattle prod. A startling shock of pain shot through Ben's arm and he snatched it away.

'Not touch me,' the old man warned him. His voice and expression were completely placid. 'That no way to prove good intentions. Sifu T'ao ask you nicely. Not so nice next time.'

Ben's extensive unarmed combat training had taught him all about the various nerve centres that could be activated in various parts of an opponent's anatomy to inflict pain, numbness and even temporary paralysis. He'd used those techniques himself many times, to good effect. The tingling agony that was burning through his arm was like nothing he'd known before, but he was convinced that the old man had just triggered the nerve point by a fluke. Now he needed to get this interfering hermit, or whatever the hell he was, out of his way so he could move on with his purpose for being here. He went to shove him again, harder this time. And was proved wrong.

Dead wrong.

In his long and extensive experience of hand-to-hand fighting Ben had nearly always proved to be faster, more reflexive and more skilled than his opponent. On those few occasions when he'd had his hands full it had always been in going up against other Special Forces-trained men, sometimes multiple combatants at once, with superlative expertise in various combat systems like Krav Maga or Jiu-jitsu. This time around, dealing with a small, apparently frail and weak opponent several decades his senior, Ben was in for a shock. As he stepped quickly towards him to plant the flat of his hand against his chest and knock him back, the old man reacted more quickly than any human being Ben had ever seen. A striking cobra could scarcely have moved that fast. Before Ben could lay a hand on him, before he'd even had time to register what was happening, the old man's own hand flashed out and struck a counter-blow high up on Ben's chest. It landed just below where the outer edge of the collar bone met the muscle of the right shoulder.

Like before, the old man had used just the tips of his fingers, more of a darting jab than a strike – but its effect made Ben stagger backwards. It felt as if the life energy had suddenly been sapped out of him, completely drained away. In the same instant a volcano of unbelievably intense pain erupted inside his chest, filling his whole upper body and almost making him pass out. He drew a sharp breath and struggled to remain on his feet. What the hell had the crazy old geezer just done to him?

A lesson you soon learned in fighting was that you will always get hurt to some degree, and that pain was something to deal with and ignore as best you could until the fight was over and your opponent was put out of action. Ben steeled himself, marshalled his energy and stepped quickly back in for another attack. This time he came in with a double push-grab, intending to wrench the guy off his feet and dash him to the ground. It should have worked, but it didn't. As though it were nothing, the old man deflected his attack with a sweeping two-arm opposite movement that was almost too fast for the human eye to follow, knocking his hands out to the sides. Then again out came the darting cobra strike, two-handed this time, aimed at both sides of Ben's chest. Now the old man used his bony knuckles instead of his fingertips. He aimed for a point just a couple of inches higher than before and hit it with what seemed, and felt, like surgical precision.

The explosion of pain first time around had been severe. This time it was doubled, like a fireball blossoming inside him and ripping his internal organs to pieces. Ben's vision flashed spangling white and then went murky, and for a fleeting instant he was convinced he was going to lose consciousness. His whole body felt cold and he could barely gather a breath but he blinked away the agony, gritted his teeth and summoned every shred of power he could to launch himself back in for a third attack.

Changing his strategy from an upper-body strike to one aimed lower down, he lashed out with a straight stamping kick at the old man's legs. It was a move that could break an opponent's knee, although all Ben wanted to do was sweep his feet out from under him – and if it had landed, the old man would have had no chance of staying upright. Then Ben would have wasted no time in moving in to stun him with a few more solid but non-lethal blows, and finally taken him out of the fight by applying the same strangle technique he'd used on the Shrimp.

At any rate, that was Ben's plan. The old man had other ideas, however, and exactly as if he'd read Ben's intentions a microsecond before he launched the kick, he skipped daintily out of reach and the sole of Ben's shoe connected with empty air.

'You are too slow,' the old man said with a sly smile, the first expression that had shown on his face until now.

Very funny. Then try this on for size, Ben thought. If there was any strength left in his body at all, he was determined that he'd use it to land a good hard blow on his opponent. This time he didn't intend to pull his punches. No more messing around. No more misguided allowances for his opponent's inferior size and advanced years. This was the endgame, right here and right now.

Ben feinted right with a curving fist towards the side of the old man's head, then diverted the strike for a left jab to the jaw instead. Even the best fighters could have been fooled by it, and the old man almost fell for the trick. Ben actually felt the silky brush of the old man's hair on his knuckles as his fist came close to making contact – the closest he'd come yet, and the closest he ever would.

Now it was the his opponent's turn to stop dancing around and bring matters to a conclusion. Before Ben could react, he was darting back like a snake and his wiry arms were lashing out from the folds of his robe to deliver a double blow to both sides of Ben's neck, right below the ears at the rearward corners of his jawbone.

And that was it. After that, Ben felt no more. A dark mist rolled up from the ground, from above, from all around, swallowed him up and carried him away to a different world where nothing could reach him. He never even felt himself falling.

Chapter 31

When consciousness slowly filtered back into Ben's mind, at first he had no idea how long he'd been asleep. It could have been days, weeks. He felt dizzy and disorientated, and it took several seconds to realise that he was no longer outside, among the moonlit ruins of the temple. Now he found that he was inside a stone-walled room or chamber, lying on a hard wooden bench with only a cushion under his head. The light came from flickering lanterns and filled the space around him with a soft glow and the smell of paraffin fumes.

After a few more seconds, Ben's slowly returning senses told him that he wasn't alone inside the chamber. The figures of four people stood peering down at him. One of them was a woman, and in his jumble of confusion he imagined at first that she was Shi Yun – but then he blinked and focused and realised that her older, unsmiling face was one he'd never seen before. By contrast, of the three men standing over him, two were familiar. The youngest was the same Jia Wenguang he'd followed all the way here from Xi'an, and the most aged was the crazy old man he'd encountered beneath the archway, now standing here as calm and still as when Ben had first seen him.

Both memories felt like a million years ago in some strangely altered reality. But no, they'd really happened, and Ben really was lying here having come off badly from that encounter. A dull ache pounded through his skull and his body felt as if he'd gone fifteen rounds with a heavyweight champion. He groaned and tried to sit up on the bench, but he could hardly move or even raise his head from the pillow.

'Who the hell are you people?' he managed to mutter.

It was the third, unfamiliar, man who replied. He was a few inches shorter than the tall, gangly Jia Wenguang next to him, and maybe twenty years older, putting his age at around forty-eight or fifty. He was neatly dressed in a dark suit, wore little round wire-rimmed spectacles and his thinning hair was slicked back in an old-fashioned style that made him appear quite dapper. He spoke carefully and deliberately in well-schooled English, with only the slightest accent.

'My name is Jun Ming. These are my colleagues Jia Wenguang and Sifu T'ao, whom you already know, and this is Shoi Hie' – motioning at the woman on his right. 'You are here at our refuge, part of the temple that is below ground where our enemies cannot find us, or so we hope. Doubtless you have many questions to ask us, which will be answered in due course. First, allow me to apologise for the rough handling you received earlier. I'm afraid it was really your own doing, as you gave Sifu T'ao no choice.'

The old man offered Ben a knowing smile and a courteous bow of his head. He asked, 'You are feeling all right?'

'Oh, never better,' Ben muttered back.

'As it happens,' said the man called Jun Ming, 'we were expecting your visit. We have people watching the forest, and they observed your approach all the way from the road. One of these guards saw you shoot down the enemy surveillance drone, which was what helped to dispel our initial concern that you were one of their operatives. We now know for a fact that is not the case, having taken the liberty of ascertaining your identity by going through your pockets while you were, ah, *resting*. Your reason for being here in China is clear to us.

Though all the same, you could have helped yourself considerably by offering Master T'ao your assurances that you had indeed visited our temple with peaceful intentions and were only seeking to gain knowledge, rather than to inflict violence. Violence is abhorrent to our values, and those of our creed.'

That's bloody rich, Ben might have commented, lying there suffering from the humiliating treatment he'd been dished out by a dwarfish psychopath nearly old enough to be his grandfather. But he couldn't get past something else Jun Ming had said a moment earlier. He frowned and replied, 'Wait a minute. Enemy drone?'

Jun Ming nodded, looking perfectly earnest. 'Yes, of course. Why, did you think it was ours? Then I'm afraid you really have no idea what is going on.'

'I think that's fairly clear,' Ben said.

'In which case, allow me to shed as much light on the matter as the limitations of time will permit. This is a war, my friend. We may be on the losing side for the moment, but we are fully committed to defending ourselves as best we can. And believe me, if we had been persuaded that you were one of the enemy, we would never have allowed you to enter our temple. Sifu T'ao would have killed you with his Dim Mak.'

Ben's head was still a little fuzzy and he didn't understand what Jun Ming was referring to. Seeing the blank look on his face Jun Ming went on, 'Dim Mak, I should explain, is the ancient Chinese martial art of the death touch, an esoteric discipline harking back thousands of years to the earliest eras of our civilisation. Few practitioners have ever gained full mastery of this long-forgotten technique, and no man alive is as skilled in it as our wise friend here. He has not earned his title of "Sifu" lightly. It is only bestowed on the most eminent exponents of their craft. You are lucky to have survived the encounter.'

'That's just wonderful,' Ben said, fixing them with a fierce look as the anger rose up inside him. 'Now, enough of this bullshit. If you were watching me through the woods then you know I was tracking this scumbag here.' He pointed at Jia. 'Which means you also know why I dragged my arse all this way to your quaint little refuge. So where's Lara Hartmann?' By an effort of sheer willpower his voice had regained some of its strength, but the effort of speaking made him feel dizzy again, and once the words were out he lowered his head to the pillow.

The younger man showed no response to being called a scumbag, which either meant he was supremely well-adjusted or didn't understand English. Jun Ming tutted disapprovingly. 'It's regrettable that you should resort to insulting language, when you remain so ignorant of the situation. I hope all will soon become clear. As for the young lady, I can assure you that she has been well looked after. The additions made to the temple, courtesy of our patron, allow us to provide a certain amount of simple, but adequate, accommodation.'

Whoever this mysterious patron might be, Ben neither knew nor cared at this point. Jun Ming's revelation made him want to sit bolt upright on the wooden bench, but again the dizziness and nausea overwhelmed him and he slumped back down. 'She's here?'

Jun Ming looked at him benevolently. 'I sense you are in some difficulty. It will take a little time for the Qi to return to your system. Perhaps you would like some water? Tea?'

'I don't suppose you have whisky,' Ben muttered in reply.

'Sadly, no alcohol is permitted in the temple. Let us bring you some water, and perhaps something to restore your strength. Then we will talk more.'

They all left the chamber, except for the old man, who stayed quietly watching over Ben. Ben had the feeling he was being guarded in case he tried to escape. But even if he'd been in a fit state to attempt it, he was too intrigued and excited to want to.

So Lara was alive, after all his doubts and fears. The relief flooded through him as the news sank in, along with the renewed feelings of mingled sadness, disgust and anger that others hadn't been so fortunate.

Sifu T'ao was looking at Ben with an enigmatic half-smile and a twinkle in his eyes. 'I am sorry for your discomfort,' he said. 'Effects of Qi drainage will not last very long.'

'Qi?' Ben tried to pronounce it the way they did, like 'chee'.

'Qi is life force,' the master replied. 'Govern all living creatures and everything in the universe. Just as knowledgeable healer able to balance and restore Qi to sick patient, true art of combat allow us to deplete life force of opponent at will.'

'Just with a touch?'

Ben was genuinely interested, partly out of professional curiosity, in understanding what had been done to him. The old man looked pleased to be able to have a conversation with a fellow warrior, albeit one whom he'd made to look like a raw apprentice. He pointed at the spot on Ben's upper chest where the first serious strike had, quite literally, knocked the energy out of him. 'That is first lung point,' he explained. 'In Chinese we call it *Zhongfu*. You would call it Central Palace. In acupuncture, very powerful healing point. But in art of Dim Mak, practitioner use it to drain the Qi from opponent's lung meridian. Felt great pain, yes?'

'Like nothing on earth,' Ben replied quite truthfully, and the old man looked satisfied. 'But then you hit me again on both sides, two inches higher. What was that?'

'Ah. That is *Yunmen*, or, as you would say, Cloud Door. More pain. Strike here will also cause Qi drainage, but for whole body. Loss of so much energy so suddenly can bring unconsciousness. Skilled practitioner able to use it to cause delayed death.'

'*Delayed* death? You mean you can determine when your enemy would die?'

The Sifu nodded sagely. 'After one day, two day, five day, opponent drop dead from exploded heart. Just so.' He snapped his fingers. 'Everyone scratching head wondering what happen, but only Dim Mak master know real reason.'

'So if my heart suddenly explodes two days from now, I'll know who to blame.'

'This not happen. I not want to kill you. I only want to cause more pain. That why I change finger strike into fist, to hit muscle and sinew channels.'

'It worked,' Ben said.

The old man smiled again. 'Normally no man can fight on after this, but you are strong. I very surprised. So then I strike point called San Jiao seventeen, *Yifeng*, for final knockout. We name this one the Windscreen.'

Ben asked, 'The neck points?' The area below both ears was still very tender and sore.

Sifu T'ao nodded. 'This point very deadly. If struck with true intent, light blow able to cause knockout if direction of strike come from correct angle. Just so.' He showed with his slender, bony hands, tracing an imaginary line of about forty-five degrees from each side of the neck through to the opposite side, about halfway up the jaw bone. 'If struck from behind ear and into jaw bone on same side,' he warned, 'it cause instant death. All depend on skill and intention of practitioner. Easy for novice to make mistake. I decide to angle strike to knock you out, but not kill.'

'Thanks for holding back,' Ben said.

'You are welcome,' the old man replied, bowing.

Seconds later the door opened and Jun Ming, Jia Wenguang and the woman called Shoi Hie returned to the chamber. Shoi Hie was carrying an ornate enamelled tray with a glass of water and a porcelain cup containing some kind of strong-smelling and steaming hot concoction. Taking the cup from the tray, Jun Ming explained, 'Shoi Hie is a master herbalist, and has prepared you this powerful tonic that will aid in your recovery and encourage the depleted Qi to quickly return to the system. Here, drink it while it is hot. Then we will talk.'

Ben managed to prop himself up a little on the bench, accepted the cup from Jun Ming's hands and took a sip of the scalding liquid. It tasted horribly bitter, but he persevered, and to his amazement within a minute or two he was already starting to feel recovered enough to sit up.

'All right, so let's talk,' he said. 'But first I need some proof that you're telling me the truth.'

Chapter 32

Jun Ming spread his hands in a gesture of acquiescence. 'I understand. You wish to see the young lady? A perfectly reasonable request. I will have her brought from her quarters right away, so that you can see for yourself that we're true to our word.' He turned to Jia and spoke a soft command in Chinese. Jia nodded, headed for the door and disappeared.

Turning back to Ben, Jun Ming said with a smile, 'I really cannot blame you for having formed the wrong impression of us, Mr Hope. It was natural to assume, under the circumstances, that our associates had abducted the poor girl for some nefarious purpose. And no doubt that was also her conviction, when we first brought her here. To begin with, we were concerned that she might try to escape, and so we had no choice but to house her in a rather unpleasant cellar that, sadly, must have confirmed her impression that she had indeed been taken prisoner by vicious kidnappers. Having managed to persuade her of the reality of her situation, more recently we were able to move her to somewhat better quarters.'

His expression became grave as he went on, 'Needless to say she was, and remains, extremely distraught as a result of the terrible news we had to break to her. Not only has she learned of the sudden and violent death of the young man with whom she was romantically involved, but also that of the friend who was like a sister to her.'

'It was me who found the body,' Ben said.

'We know that, from our contacts within the Xi'an police. I should add that these contacts, who must remain anonymous for reasons that will become clear, have no knowledge of Miss Hartmann's whereabouts. As you'll also understand, we are compelled to operate with the utmost secrecy, protecting certain sensitive information even from our own people. But returning to Miss Hartmann, she has taken the news as well as could be expected. She understands it was necessary to bring her here for her own protection.'

Ben's mind was much clearer now that Shoi Hie's herbal brew was working its magic, but still none of this was making any sense to him. He asked, 'Protection from whom?'

'From the evil people who continue to persecute us and our faith,' Jun Ming replied with the utmost sincerity and a look of deep regret. 'The same monsters who are responsible for the murder of our dear friend Dan Chen, another of our brethren. And who also killed Olivia Keller, mistaking her for her housemate.'

Ben's memory flashed back to the phone image Stefan had shown him of the two young women together, and how similar they'd looked: *they could be twins*, Ben had commented at the time. Now the realisation hit him. Like so many obvious truths, it was both simple and horrible. 'They thought she was Lara?'

Jun Ming nodded sadly. 'And butchered the poor girl without a second thought, stealing her organs in order to further profit from their crime. You understand, Mr Hope, these are the most brutal men imaginable, utterly devoid of humanity. They will do anything, anything at all, to acquire the secret information that poor Dan Chen was luckily able to pass into safe hands shortly before his own death.'

This explained why Olivia's killers had also ransacked the house in Qinjiacun, in search of this supposed secret. But that was about all it did explain. 'Who the hell are you people?' Ben asked again.

'We are devotees of Falun Gong,' Jun Ming replied simply.

Ben had no idea what he meant by that, and his mouth was open to ask when he was interrupted by the return of Jia Wenguang, accompanied by the young woman whom Ben had almost given up hope of ever seeing alive.

Stefan's sister was barely recognisable from that one picture Ben had seen of her. It must have been the shock and stress of the last few days that had stripped so much weight from her that she looked thin and gaunt. Her hair was bedraggled and her eyes were red from crying. She was wearing a traditional Chinese silk gown that hung too loosely from her skinny body.

'How are you feeling, my dear?' Jun Ming asked her fondly.

She stepped into the chamber after Jia, then halted in her tracks at the sight of Ben and stood staring at him. The pallid leanness of her face made her eyes look huge. 'My God, then it's true,' she gasped in English, the language she'd been mostly speaking with her hosts. 'You're '

'A friend of your brother's,' he finished for her. 'My name's Ben. We came to China together to look for you.'

Lara let out a sob of relief and joy. 'Stefan! Where is he? I've thought about him so much!'

'He's not far away,' Ben told her. 'Come back with me and you can tell him yourself. He'll be pretty darn happy to know you're all right. It's not exactly been easy, finding you.'

'But I can't leave here,' she protested, shooting anxious looks at Jun Ming and the others. 'It's not safe. After what happened to ... to ...' Her eyes suddenly filled up and the tears overcame her, so that she couldn't say any more. Jun Ming patted her shoulder affectionately, and Shoi Hie hurried over to hug and console her. Definitely the most sympathetic kidnappers Ben had come across in his career.

'I'm afraid you're right, my dear,' said Jun Ming. 'In the present situation this temple is the only safe refuge for any of us.' He explained for Ben's benefit, 'It, and the area of forest enclosed around us, was gifted to our organisation by another of our loyal followers, the Chinese billionaire Chang Han Yu. He purchased the land to create a secret haven and meeting place for our fraternity. So far he has been able to conceal his allegiance from those in power, and he has many useful connections at high levels. It's thanks to him, for example, that we knew that Stefan Hartmann and an associate from Europe had landed in China and were searching for his missing sister.'

Lara was still weeping bitterly in Shoi Hie's arms. 'Stefan's family to me too,' Ben said. 'He's my future brother-in-law.'

'I admire such strong loyalty to blood kin. But as I understand it, you also have some special skills. We heard about the incident in Xi'an.'

'I was with the British SAS,' Ben admitted, uncomfortable as ever when it came to talking about his past. 'After which I went freelance rescuing kidnap victims. That's why I was asked to help. I only wish I could have done more.'

Jun Ming nodded. 'A man of your experience is a useful ally in such times of danger. And make no mistake, we are in grave danger. All of us, even here in this remote hiding place. Our enemies have thus far been unable to find our secret base, but I fear they are getting closer. Thankfully you were able to destroy the drone before it could pinpoint our exact location, but it's only a matter of time before they do. The ears and eyes of the state are everywhere. We can only assume that must be how Dan Chen became their target, even before he ever realised he was being monitored.'

'I think you'd better tell me more about this brotherhood of yours,' Ben said. 'I've never heard of Falun Gong, but it sounds like it's pissed off some of the wrong people.'

'It is a twentieth-century variant of the ancient health-giving and martial practice of Qi Gong, whose history can be traced back thousands of years to the foundations of Chinese culture,' Jun Ming explained. '*Falun Gong* means "Discipline of the Dharma Wheel", and it also incorporates elements of Buddhist teachings. It aims at bringing the devotee to a higher level of spirituality and morality through meditation exercise and the cultivation of the key principles of Truthfulness, Benevolence and Forbearance. We preach a message of peace, healthful living, and harmony with the divinity of Nature. You could describe our movement as a religion, of sorts. One that has become the target for destruction by ruthless elements within the Chinese Communist Party who are hell bent on eliminating it. They have mobilised the full might of their propaganda machine to brand us as an evil cult, a sect of heretics. Their campaign aims to eradicate us completely, a goal that has been openly stated by the official media and backed with an onslaught of lies and disinformation via television, radio and the internet, intended to brainwash the rest of the Chinese people against us. They have the weight of the police, the military, the judiciary system, the education system and a vast network of informers behind them. As a result many of our people have been murdered or imprisoned, incarcerated in labour camps, forced to work until they dropped dead of exhaustion or were brutally executed, so that their body parts could be sold on the black market.

'This practice is rife in our country,' he added, his voice becoming tight with anger. 'How do you suppose our authorities are able to supply so many harvested organs to the medical industry? The persecution has been going on for years and continues unabated to this day, despite the fact that we represent no threat to anyone and only wish to be allowed to pursue our spiritual faith in peace and tranquillity.'

'And to hold on to this secret that you keep talking about,' Ben said. 'I'm guessing it's somehow connected to the object, or artefact, or whatever it was that Dan Chen found inside the terracotta warrior statue, the night of the earthquake.'

Jun Ming looked impressed. 'You have learned a good deal. That is correct.'

'Had Dan become afraid they were onto him?' Ben asked. 'Is that the reason he got Lara to pass it on to you instead?'

'He believed he was being followed,' Jun Ming replied. 'Lara was the only one he could trust to pass the package on safely, without any risk to herself. Or so he genuinely thought.'

'I only wanted to help him,' Lara blurted through her tears, pulling away from Shoi Hie's embrace. 'It seemed so important to him. I had no idea what it was he was asking me to give them.'

'You and me both,' Ben told her. 'There's a lot I don't know yet. I'm hoping that's about to change.' That last part was directed at Jun Ming, with a meaningful look.

Jun Ming nodded. 'Indeed. Seeing as you have come this far, my colleagues and I have come to the agreement that you should be told the whole truth. You see, Mr Hope, the discovery Dan Chen made that night, the thing that our enemies so badly wish to acquire from us, holds the key to the ancient and long-lost secret of the Golden Library.'

Chapter 33

'The Golden Library,' Ben repeated, and waited for someone to offer an explanation. The chamber had suddenly gone quiet, as though the mention of this baffling new element in the mystery had plunged the four Falun Gong devotees into a state of solemn reverence. Even Jia Wenguang, who apparently didn't understand a word of English, was standing there hanging his head like a devout member of a religious congregation receiving a sermon. Sifu T'ao had gone back to doing a creditable imitation of a statue.

'Lara,' Ben said, turning to her. 'Do you know anything about this?'

She looked uncertain, stammered a couple of syllables and then closed her mouth and shook her head. Ben turned back to the others and asked impatiently, 'So is there more to this Golden Library thing, or am I supposed to guess?'

Jun Ming pursed his lips and said to Shoi Hie, 'This discussion may take some time. Perhaps Miss Hartmann would like to return to her quarters?' Then he spoke a few words in Chinese to Jia and motioned towards the door, obviously telling him to go with them.

'Am I going to see you again?' Lara asked Ben on her way out of the chamber.

'You can count on it,' he assured her. 'And soon. We're getting out of here and you're going home.'

'That may not be such a straightforward matter,' Jun Ming said to Ben when they were alone with Sifu T'ao.

'We'll see,' Ben replied. 'First, I think you were about to explain to me what this is all about.'

Jun Ming shrugged. 'Very well. What is the Golden Library? Its legend dates back to the earliest era of Chinese civilisation. Created thousands of years ago, it was supposedly our greatest repository of philosophic wisdom from a golden age of enlightenment and high culture, rivalling in wealth and size the great lost libraries of Alexandria, of Aristotle, of Pergamon and Constantinople. Some would call the Golden Library not so much a legend as a myth, pointing to the lack of evidence that such a place ever existed. And until Dan Chen's discovery, one would have had to admit that they might have been right. All this has now changed. The importance of what he found . . .' He shook his head in wonder. 'It cannot be overstated.'

Jun Ming hesitated, looking grave. 'Before I go any further, Mr Hope, I must ask: how much do you know about our nation's past?'

'No more than a few scraps,' Ben said. 'I know that the country went through a lot of different dynasties and had an advanced civilisation dating way back to when we Europeans were living in mud huts and only starting to learn about farming. And that it all got turned upside down during the twentieth century when the cultural revolution happened and the new Communist state took over.'

'That's a fairly simplistic, though more or less accurate, condensation of over four thousand years of recorded history,' said Jun Ming with a thin smile. 'For the purposes of explanation, the part I would like to take us back to is the very beginning of the Qin Dynasty. This was the reign of China's first emperor, dating between 221 to 206 BC. He is remembered as Qinshi Huangdi the First. The fact that he styled himself as the divinely luminous god-king of Qin may give you an insight into the egocentric nature of his character. He was in fact a ruthless and bloodthirsty tyrant, so notorious that another of our history's most murderous despots, Mao Zedong in the twentieth century, welcomed comparisons between his own reign of terror and that of the first emperor. Both were responsible for the murder, starvation, torture and incarceration of countless innocent Chinese men, women and children.'

'Not one of the good guys, then,' Ben said.

'That would be putting it mildly,' replied Jun Ming. 'On the other hand, Qinshi Huangdi is credited with having done much to consolidate early Chinese culture. He was the first to introduce a standard written form of the language, and he also ordered the building of the original version of the Great Wall of China. Another of his major accomplishments was the creation of the famous terracotta army.'

'The same one that Dan Chen and his team were working on,' Ben said, remembering.

'A most important detail, which I will come back to later. Now, prior to the reign of the first emperor, the prevailing philosophy of this time had been that founded by the revered scholar and sage Confucius, who had lived between 551 to 479 BC, and whose ideas on human nature are still central to Chinese thought. Confucius had a very positive concept of human nature. In his opinion, human beings were basically good, and social harmony could be cultivated and maintained if people in authority set a good moral example for everyone to follow.'

There's the rub, Ben thought.

Jun Ming went on, 'A key concept of Confucian philosophy was "ren", meaning "civility", "goodness" or "humanness". The

241

idea being that if everyone cultivated this virtuous quality of "ren" within themselves, such personal self-improvement would collectively result in a well-ordered, happy society. It also meant that the state itself need have relatively little involvement in everyday civic affairs, since the citizens did not need constant oversight or heavy-handed policing in order to maintain order. It was to these ideas that most past Chinese rulers had always looked as a guide for how to govern the land. Nobody can claim they created a Utopia, of course – no society is ever perfect – but to a greater or lesser degree, they were successful.

'And then Qi Huangdi came along. When he seized power in 221 BC he ushered in a whole new paradigm for how China should be ruled. The new emperor believed in another, very different philosophy that set itself in stark opposition to the optimistic and pro-human ideas of Confucius. This new philosophy was known as "Legalism". The Legalists believed that human nature was fundamentally flawed, corrupt and wicked, and that the only proper and effective way to govern society was by means of fear, coercion and the ever-present threat of punishment – in other words, the establishment of a police state.'

'Sounds familiar,' Ben said.

'To Qi Huangdi these ideas seemed self-evident, and he followed the doctrine of Legalism to the letter. He passed many restrictive new laws that were to be enforced by a very extensive police force with sweeping powers. As well as this, he established a secret service and wide-ranging spy network, in which citizens were strongly encouraged to participate by spying on their neighbours and family members, and reporting any transgressions to the authorities. Informants were rewarded, while those found guilty of even the slightest misdemeanour were generally sentenced to execution. Death was the punishment for virtually anything, even for such crimes as turning up late for work.

Those lucky enough to be spared that fate might find their sentences commuted to torture, punitive mutilation or forced labour on one of the many large-scale public projects instituted by the emperor. There was no right to trial, no court system. The word of Qi Huangdi was absolute and final. His reign of terror swept the whole of China.

'Now,' Jun Ming continued, 'you can imagine that this oppressive new regime was not universally loved by the people. Most were too afraid to speak out for fear of the consequences, but not all. Many intellectuals and scholars, especially Confucian thinkers who were appalled by the ideas and practices of the Legalists, dared to voice their opposition to state policies, and to the emperor personally, either publicly or in writing. Needless to say, Qi Huangdi would not tolerate the least criticism of his divine greatness. Enraged, he ordered brutal reprisals against the Confucian scholars' protests. They were arrested, imprisoned, cruelly tortured and executed by the hundred, while the books they had dared to write voicing their insurrectionist ideas were piled into great heaps and burned. Not only those, but in his rage against the rebel scholars the emperor ordered that any book or piece of writing that espoused the philosophies of Confucianism was to be destroyed along with them. This, in effect, would have erased a great part of the centuries-old literary legacy of pre-imperial China.

'But that is where our story takes an interesting twist,' Jun Ming said. 'Because the legend tells that, while the emperor doubtless destroyed many, many precious writings, he did not destroy all of them. Even as the bonfires blazed, it is said that thousands upon thousands of books were secretly taken away to be hidden in a vast underground library that Qi Huangdi had dug out of solid rock for just this special purpose. Ironically, many of the slave labourers set to work on this enormous task were the Confucian scholars he had previously imprisoned for their thought crimes. According to the story, he lavished unlimited resources on its construction, ordering that its walls, ceiling and columns be magnificently decorated with precious metals and stones. It was said that, when finished, the whole of this huge subterranean space gleamed like gold.'

'The Golden Library,' Ben said. 'I get it. But if the legend's true, why would he have gone to such trouble building it, only to store a bunch of books he hated for their ideas? Makes no sense to me.'

'It makes no sense at all,' Jun Ming agreed, 'without understanding that the emperor had another secret, one that haunted and tormented him.'

Chapter 34

'You see,' Jun Ming went on, 'as he grew older, Qi Huangdi had become increasingly terrified of the prospect of his own death. He couldn't accept that, as a mere man and not the god he had styled himself as and so desperately craved to be, he would eventually reach the end of his days; and that despite all his vast wealth and unlimited power, he could do nothing to escape the same fate as the lowest peasant. But he was wise enough to understand that among the literary treasures of past centuries, in addition to the many thousands of philosophic works on Confucianism, Daoism and much else, was a vast body of writings on medicine and the healing arts. Much of it was devoted to ancient mysticism, occult science, magic and the murky world of Chinese alchemy, which had been of interest to esoteric scholars since the fourth century BC and perhaps even earlier, long before it reached Egypt and India.'

'Alchemy,' Ben said, nodding. He'd come across that bewildering, arcane subject before, and remembered something about it. One of the strangest aspects of alchemy, it seemed to him, was the fascination it had held for so many believers through the ages – everyone from medieval monks to high-ranking Nazis – and still did today. What gave this purported science of transformation such alluring power over even some of the most intelligent minds was its contention not only to be able to turn base matter into gold but to bestow the greatest gift of all: human immortality. After all, it wasn't just emperors who were afraid of dying.

'Let me guess,' he said. 'He wanted to live for ever?'

'A perceptive insight,' said Jun Ming. 'You are absolutely correct. For much of his adult life the emperor was obsessively devoted to the search for a magical elixir that would enable him to transcend his own mortality. Many of the Confucian scholars who had been spared execution and survived the hard labour of building the great library were then forced to spend the rest of their lives there as his researchers, poring over mountains of ancient texts in pursuit of his goal.'

'I'm also guessing they never found it,' Ben said.

'Given that Qi Huangdi never saw his fiftieth birthday, I would say you are correct there, too,' Jun Ming said with a smile. 'Sometimes it is not only the good who die young.'

'Couldn't have happened to a better guy. But what does this have to do with Dan Chen's discovery the night of the earthquake?'

'It has everything to do with it,' Jun Ming replied. 'Every brutal, repressive dictatorship that ever existed in history has always spawned resistance movements among its people. This was no different, and the feeling against the first emperor was very strong, not just among philosophers and scholars but among the ordinary working population too. Not all those opposed to the emperor's tyranny were caught and punished. Some managed to remain undetected, and one such rebel must have learned of the existence of the secret underground library. How he himself made that discovery, we may never know for sure, just as we will probably never have any clear idea who he was. Did he belong to some popular movement who believed the library's contents should be available to the public? Nobody can say. What did he do for a living? Again, we are in the dark, except to surmise that he was likely employed as one of the many sculptors and stonemasons who were set to work creating that other of the emperor's great projects, the terracotta army. Perhaps that was how he learned of the library's existence, from the rumours that must have been circulating among the workers.'

Jun Ming held up a finger. 'But one thing we *do* know, thanks to Dan Chen, is that this anonymous Chinese citizen of the second century BC found out much more than he should have. So much so, that he was able to draw a detailed map of the library's location, which he then sealed in an ebony cylinder and concealed in a place where nobody could have thought of looking for it.'

Suddenly all the loose fragments of information came together in Ben's mind, and he understood. '*That's* what this is all about? A map showing where some old library was?'

'Please. It is hardly appropriate to dismiss one of the great lost cultural treasures from our history as merely "some old library".'

'My apologies,' Ben said. 'So this guy, this stonemason or whoever he was, he hid the map inside one of the terracotta soldiers. Why?'

Jun Ming gave a shrug. 'Who can say? Did he hide it there for posterity, hoping that one day it might be found? That seems unlikely. Or perhaps, did he instead choose that hiding place as a temporary measure to avoid being caught with it by the emperor's spies, which would have certainly meant his death? If so, what could have happened to him that meant he never returned to retrieve it? That is something else we may never know. So many questions without answers.'

'I have a few more for you,' Ben said. 'Cut to the present day and, for whatever reason, this map has resurfaced, and it just so happens to have fallen into the hands of Dan Chen, a government employee and a follower of this outlawed religion of yours. The first question is, how did the bad guys know what he'd found? Especially when he'd gone to such lengths to keep it a secret from anyone except Lara?'

'The simple answer is that he was betrayed,' Jun Ming replied. 'By his colleague, a woman named Mci Pinyin.'

'I know about her,' Ben said, remembering what Shi Yun had told him. 'She thought he was acting strangely that morning after the earthquake. That's what she told the police, but I assumed she'd been interviewed after he died, as someone who'd known him.'

'I'm afraid you assumed wrongly. In actual fact we suspect she is a paid state informer who reported him to the authorities *before* he was apprehended. China is full of them. Acting on that information, certain elements that were already suspicious of his possible connections with the Falun Gong movement now began to question what he might have found that night, and its possible significance.'

'And they pulled him in just on that suspicion?'

'This is China,' Jun Ming said. 'As in all tyrannical regimes, the slightest whiff of doubt is often enough to tip the balance between freedom and incarceration. Then once they had him . . .'

Now Ben could see why Jun Ming had been so keen for Lara to leave them, cleverly anticipating that the conversation was bound to shift into areas that would be too distressing for her to hear. 'They pressured him to find out more.'

'That is a rather polite way of putting it,' Jun Ming replied. 'To be blunt, prior to his death they subjected him to the most unspeakable and hideous torture, the likes of which nobody could resist without breaking. I'm afraid he must have suffered horribly at their hands, and I can't judge him for having told them everything. But that is what he certainly did. That led them to realise the momentous discovery we stood to make, thanks to him.'

'And that's why they targeted Lara,' Ben said. 'Because now they knew that he'd told her the secret, too.'

Jun Ming nodded sadly. 'And given her the scroll to pass on. Yes. Then they came for her, but they got Olivia Keller by mistake, simply because of their physical resemblance. That, in a nutshell, is the whole story of what happened.'

A moment of heavy silence filled the room. Ben broke it by asking, 'I still don't get what could be so important about this Golden Library to you people that you'd risk so much over it? And by the same token, why would the Chinese government be so hot on wanting to suppress it?'

Jun Ming shook his head. 'It is not the government per se that we fear. Regardless of how you in the west may perceive our nation, not all of the leaders of modern-day China are tyrants and despots. Many of them are moderate and progressive in their beliefs, and honour our Chinese traditions and heritage as highly as we do. But sadly, their influence is overshadowed by that of the hard-line idealists who continue to exert such a grip over the state. At their core is a rogue cabal of immensely powerful radical communists who will stop at nothing to enforce their principles. *They* are our enemy, and a very dangerous enemy that will not rest until we are destroyed.'

'Why you? Why Falun Gong?'

'Not for anything we have done. How could a creed of peace, harmony and compassion be a threat to anyone? No. They hate us simply because of what we represent, in their eyes. You see, Mr Hope, wherever communists have gained a foothold in the world they have always sought to erase and rewrite the history of that country. Their fervent desire is to eradicate all trace of ancient cultures, philosophies and religions, anything that predates their own ideology. It's in the nature of their revolutions to wipe the slate clean and start again from zero. At the dawn of the cultural revolution in 1966 they called on the people to "sweep away all cow demons and snake spirits", that is to say, to completely eradicate all the old ideas, old culture, old customs and old habits that they regarded as having infected China for thousands of years. They called these things "the four olds" and unleashed a storm of systematic destruction against them. The Red Guards almost completely destroyed the sacred tomb of Confucius, and even disinterred the remains of our later and more beloved emperors so that they could be publicly dishonoured and burned as a symbol of a new beginning. They carried out a frenzied campaign of violence involving mass lynching, beheading, stoning, drowning, boiling, raping to death, ritual disembowelment and even cannibalism against anyone they considered to be dissidents or counter-revolutionaries. Sifu T'ao here witnessed the cruel and brutal murders of many of his family members at the hands of the Red Guard. Their ideology spread to all corners of our culture. Chairman Mao banned the spiritual aspect of traditional Chinese medicine, and masters of ancient practices such as Tai Chi had to flee the country to avoid persecution and execution.'

'But it's not like that any more, is it?' Ben said. 'I've seen people doing Tai Chi in the park in Beijing. Nobody was giving them any trouble.'

'No, it's true that much has changed since those terrible times,' Jun Ming agreed. 'At least, on the face of it. But a dark and sinister undercurrent still very much remains, waiting for the day when it can reassert power. If they did it once, be assured that they are quite capable of doing it again. And meanwhile, as we know, the atrocities continue behind the curtain. These people are truly evil. It is a disease of the soul,

Mr Hope. Like a cancer that has affected every nation where it has been allowed to gain a hold. Look at the history of the Soviet Union, or Cuba. Even France, in its revolutionary period in the late eighteenth century, became prey to a kind of proto-Marxist fervour that sought to literally reset the nation's calendar from the year one, reorganise every aspect of its citizens' lives under a reign of terror, create a new secular monoculture in place of centuries of Christianity, do away with everything that was recognisable from its rich historical traditions and forcibly re-educate the people to worship the state, the state, and only the state. The result, as always, was bloodshed and disaster. How many hundreds of millions of corpses has the madness of communism left in its wake? How many more must die in the future?'

Jun Ming sighed and shook his head in sorrow. 'As for those of us in the Falun Gong fraternity, why, *of course* we would risk everything, even our own lives, to protect the secret of the Golden Library from the hands of these dangerous radicals who would not hesitate to destroy it. Our spiritual beliefs are in keeping with the traditional Chinese wisdom of the ages, bringing together the philosophies of Buddhism, Daoism and Confucianism. For us, the rediscovery of the Golden Library is a momentous event.'

'You talk as if you've actually found the place itself.'

Jun Ming smiled. 'We have.'

All this time Ben and Jun Ming had been talking, Sifu T'ao had been hovering silently on the edge of the conversation as if he'd slipped into another meditative trance, showing no flicker of expression even when Jun Ming had mentioned the murder of his family members by Mao's hated Red Guards. But then suddenly his eyes snapped open and came into sharp focus, and he cocked his head like a cat. He'd heard something.

So had Ben. It was only the faintest of sounds, dim and distant, coming from outside and above.

'What is that?' Jun Ming said anxiously, peering up towards the chamber ceiling.

'Are we underground here?' Ben asked.

'Yes, in part of the old temple's cellars, where the monks used to store their produce.'

'Show me the way out of here,' Ben said. 'And let me have the shotgun.'

Chapter 35

They hurried out of the chamber. Ben, who'd been unconscious when he was brought down below, was seeing the narrow stone corridor and upward-leading steps beyond the doorway for the first time. The murky passage was half-lit by a pair of flickering paraffin lanterns that hung from iron hooks each side and gave off heavy, eye-watering fumes. 'This way,' Jun Ming said, snatching one of them from its hook and leading up the staircase. The ancient stone steps were as worn smooth in the middle as the much larger ones that had brought Ben up the hillside. He followed Jun Ming, with Sifu T'ao moving nimbly along right behind.

The steps led up towards a roughly round opening like a well mouth, showing a dark circle of night sky above. Only a faint glow of moonlight penetrated down the stairway shaft. The strange sound could be heard more clearly as they approached the top. 'Douse your lantern,' Ben said. Jun Ming understood, nodded, and before he turned down the flame and blew it out he motioned to where Shi Yun's police riot gun had been left propped against the staircase wall. Ben grabbed it as the stairway went dark. He checked by feel that the chamber had a round in it, and nudged past Jun Ming saying, 'Better let me go first.' Clutching the weapon in a combat hold he emerged into the coolness of the night air.

The sound that had drawn their attention from below was fully audible now. And disconcertingly recognisable. It was the same airborne buzzing, whirring sound Ben had last heard earlier that evening, before he'd ventured into the forest. Craning his neck upwards, he saw the blinking lights and the same hovering X-shaped silhouette of a second surveillance drone that had somehow managed to pick up the trail of the first and continued over the treetops and up the hillside to the temple.

Whether the drone was being remotely controlled or whether it was working autonomously, it had found them. And whether or not Ben did something about the flying eye in the sky, it was too late to avert the damage that had already been done. Even if it hadn't just caught him on camera as he emerged from the underground shaft, these ruins mysteriously hidden behind a tall wire security fence would have been far too interesting for the enemy to ignore.

This was a scouting mission. It would soon be followed up by a party of armed men. And there was no telling how close by they might already be. They might be sitting in a vehicle just the other side of the forest at this moment, preparing for the attack. How many? Six? Eight? More?

Ben turned and shouted to Jun Ming behind him, 'Stay back! Stay out of sight!' But Jun Ming had already emerged from the mouth of the stairway shaft into the moonlight, blinking up in confusion and consternation at the hovering drone. Sifu T'ao appeared next to him. Now both their faces would have been captured by its high-resolution digital eye too. If the enemy hadn't already had them down on record as targets for destruction, they sure as hell did now.

Ben felt a renewed pang of guilt at the knowledge that if he hadn't followed Jia Wenguang here tonight, they might never have found them. But that was something else it was too late to worry about.

Maybe Sifu T'ao was able to destroy the drone by the power of intention, or beaming mental death rays at it. Mere mortals like Ben had to resort to other, cruder means. But still fairly effective. For the second time that night he raised the shotgun to his shoulder and angled it upwards and squeezed the trigger. Same result as before. The hovering lights went dark and the X-shape overhead shattered into a million tiny fragments that rained pattering down over the temple ruins. The echo of the crashing gunshot rolled over the hillside and the forest below.

'Looks like your friends are back,' Ben said.

Sifu T'ao was impassive and silent. Jun Ming bent down, picked up a larger piece of shattered drone that had landed at his feet and examined it in the moonlight. 'This is very bad,' he said, frowning. 'Now our refuge has been compromised they will be coming for us all very soon. Unless we evacuate the temple immediately there will be no chance of escape. We can only hope they are not already advancing through the forest, where we could run straight into their path.'

'What about that way?' Ben asked, pointing beyond the ruins towards the rear side of the hill. That might offer an alternative escape route, although how they'd be able to circle back around to their vehicles was another problem they'd have to deal with.

Jun Ming shook his head. 'An earthquake many centuries ago took away that whole face of the hillside, leaving nothing but a sheer cliff edge and a vertical drop. Only a mountaineer could scale down it, with ropes and equipment that we do not have. No. The only way out of here is the way we came up, by the long steps. Come, we must get moving immediately, while there is still time. I will go and alert the others.'

But that wasn't necessary, because the booming report of the shotgun had already been heard from below ground and within seconds they were joined by Jia and Shoi, both looking alarmed. Jun Ming quickly explained the situation to them. With a gasp, Shoi hurried back down below and reappeared moments later with Lara in tow. Lara was dopey and tousled and had clearly been fast asleep in her quarters. 'What's happening?' she asked anxiously.

'Time to get out of here,' Ben told her.

'But where to?'

'We can worry about that later. Jun Ming, you said you had more people watching the forest.'

'They will either remain hidden from the enemy or make their own separate escapes. I can contact them by radio to tell them what happened.'

'Do it. Then let's get moving.'

There was no time to pack up whatever possessions they'd be leaving behind. Jun Ming glanced wistfully back at the temple ruins as the six of them hurried away towards the giant steps. Because he had the only weapon Ben went first, keeping Lara close to him. The forest below was dark and quiet and seemed totally empty, but there was no telling. The steps were just as steep going down as they had been coming up. One stumble, and a person risked tumbling all the way down to their death unless they managed to grab a handful of weeds and gnarly old tree roots to arrest their fall. Ben wasn't about to let anything happen to Lara, having come so far to find her, and he kept a tight grip on her hand. 'Are we going to see Stefan?' she asked breathlessly. 'Soon,' he promised. 'Then this will all be over and you'll be going home.'

Down and down, hopping from one step to another. Ben was cursing his sore limbs for the agony the exertion was causing him; cursing himself even more for having let himself get so easily beaten up earlier. He wasn't a proud man and was always happy to defer to another's superior skills, on those very rare occasions when he encountered them. But all the same, he was feeling a certain grudging resentment at being shown up the way he had – while he couldn't resist a certain curiosity to know more about the Dim Mak moves the wild old man had pulled on him.

The forest gradually rose up around them as they worked their way towards the bottom. Shoi let out a yelp as she caught her foot in a tangle of weeds and nearly fell. Jun Ming snapped at her to be careful, then moments later pitched forwards as he missed his own footing, and only Sifu T'ao's quick, strong hand rescued him from taking the fast way down. But the rest of the descent happened without incident, and within a few minutes they'd made it safely back to the foot of the steps. The moon had shifted across the sky and was now veiled behind the trees, plunging the forest into dark shadows. Ben wouldn't have risked using a torch if he'd had one. They picked their way with urgency along the forest track. Ben was ready with the shotgun and constantly anticipating an attack, but none came. The security fence seemed much further going back than it had coming out. Still no sign of anyone approaching through the woods. Jia reached inside his shirt and took out a large key on a string around his neck, which he used to undo the gate padlock.

Ben could feel his tension rising with every step as they left the perimeter fence behind them and headed for the road. He expected to see lights ahead at any instant, followed by yelling voices and the sound of gunfire. Lara kept tripping over the rough ground and he yanked her along by the hand. 'Ouch! You're hurting me!' she complained, but he ignored her. Behind him he could hear Shoi's little sounds of anxiety and Jun Ming's ragged breathing. Jia was in better shape than the older man, but the eldest by a wide margin, Sifu T'ao, was as fresh as if he'd been out for a gentle stroll in the park.

At last, Ben made out the dully gleaming shapes of the parked vehicles ahead. Jun Ming pointed. 'We should go in Jia's car. It's the most reliable.'

Ben guessed that Jun Ming's was the little hatchback, and that the motor scooter belonged to Shoi. As for Sifu T'ao, he probably had no truck with such modern technology and had teleported here by magic. What a motley bunch they were, he thought. And their vehicles were something of a rag-tag assortment as well. He looked doubtfully at the rusty old Bora. True, it had managed to lead him here without falling to pieces. And before that, it had played its amateur role as a kidnap vehicle well enough. But Ben didn't trust the damn thing not to break down on them just when they needed it most, and anyhow there was far more space for six people in the Mercedes.

'Wait here,' he told them. 'I'll be right back. Stay in the shadows and don't move. Then when you see me flash my lights three times, start heading quickly for the road. Got it?'

He set off at a fast sprint along the track and reached the opening in the trees in under a minute. Slowing the last few steps, he stalked out into the moonlight and gazed up and down the road. The debris from the first dead drone still littered the verge, and there was the Mercedes parked a distance away, exactly as he'd left it. It didn't look as though anyone else had been here in the meantime. The main road beyond the junction was dark and quiet. Relieved but still cautious he ran to the Mercedes, then piled in behind the wheel, dumped the shotgun in the passenger footwell, fired up the engine and went tearing the short distance to the opening of the track. He flashed the lights three times and sat impatiently waiting for nearly ninety seconds before he saw Jun Ming emerge from the trees followed by Lara and the others.

'Hurry,' Ben called to them, but while his companions were edgy and nervous nothing on earth seemed able to impress any sense of urgency on Sifu T'ao, who ambled casually over to the car, gazing at it as though he rode in one of these every day. Ben got out, opened the doors and helped Lara into the front passenger seat, while Jia and the old Dim Mak master got into the back and Jun Ming and Shoi took their places in the middle row. Filled up with bodies, the Mercedes looked like a minibus. Ben dived back into the driver's seat. So far, their escape from the temple seemed to be going so smoothly that he almost wondered if they might have overreacted to the second drone's appearance. He said to Lara in German, 'Hold on to that gun but don't fiddle with anything, and pass it over to me quickly if I need it.'

'I do speak English, you know,' she replied sourly. 'And I also hate guns.'

Sometimes, you didn't necessarily get along with the people you were on a mission to save. 'So do I,' he said. 'When they're pointing at me.' He slipped the transmission into drive, U-turned the car briskly around to point towards the main road, and accelerated away.

And that was when the four pairs of headlights appeared from the junction ahead and came racing towards them, widening out to fill the whole road and blocking their exit.

Chapter 36

Ben hit the brakes hard and the Mercedes slithered to a halt. The four approaching vehicles kept coming right at them until they were just fifteen yards away, then stopped in neat formation, spaced out from verge to verge with no way past. The four identical black Chinese SUVs could have been unmarked police cars, but Ben's instinct told him otherwise.

'It's them!' gasped Jun Ming.

'You don't say,' Ben muttered in reply.

'What are we going to do?' Lara said, turning to Ben with panic in her eyes.

'Exactly what we planned on doing,' he told her. 'Pass me that, would you please?'

Lara suddenly didn't seem to hate guns any more. She handed it eagerly over, and he snatched it from her hands and kicked open his door and stepped half out onto the road, pressing off the weapon's safety and pointing it at the middle two SUVs. In his experience, the team leader always liked to take the centre position. Also in his experience, the best defence against an enemy ambush like this was to turn the attack straight back at them and start shooting first, with all the speed, surprise and firepower you could bring into play. In this case he was lacking on the firepower side, but Ben intended to make full use of what he had.

He fired off three loud rapid shots, working the pump action like lightning in between, hitting them hard and aggressively.

The bright muzzle flash erupted from the shotgun's short barrel and the empty shells kicked out of the receiver. His first two shots blew out a windscreen apiece. His third ripped a huge hole in a radiator and flipped up the vehicle's bonnet, a plume of white steam hissing violently and coolant spurting from ruptured hoses and pipes underneath.

There was nothing like giving a clear signal of your intent to the enemy. But now they replied, bursting out of their vehicles and opening a determined return fire. In the chaos Ben counted eight men scurrying for cover and training their weapons on him before he was forced to duck for his own cover behind his open door. Like the hit crew who'd staged the assault at the intersection in Xi'an they'd come heavily armed, this time equipped with stubby black submachine guns. The ferocious crackle of shots reverberated over the road as bullets slammed into the bodywork of the Mercedes. He pumped another round into the Hawk's chamber and fired again. Then another. Saw one of the figures stumble and go down, clutching at his chest; saw the glitter of flying glass like diamonds in the dazzle of the headlights.

Choices. He could either make a heroic stand here and wait for his ammunition to run dry and the enemy close in for the kill – in borrowing Shi Yun's shotgun he hadn't reckoned on needing to fill his pockets with extra cartridges – or he could take the necessary action to get himself and his charges out of the field of fire and away to safety. As more shots peppered the Mercedes and dissolved its windscreen into a web of cracks he leaped back behind the wheel, slammed the vehicle into drive and stamped the pedal violently to the floor. The engine roared as he sped straight towards the blockade of vehicles ahead.

He barely had time to shout 'Hold on tight' before they slammed into the narrow gap between two of the damaged

SUVs with a metallic crunch as loud as a grenade exploding. The jarring impact threw everyone forwards in their seats except Sifu T'ao, to whom the normal laws of momentum and inertia didn't seem to apply. Ben kept his foot down hard on the gas and the Mercedes' tyres spun against the road as it ploughed on through the gap between the vehicles, shunting one of them sideways so that one of the attackers was crushed between it and the one to its other side. He caught a glimpse of an angry face and a submachine gun muzzle pointing towards his shattered driver's window from not two feet away. Before the man could fire, Ben poked the shotgun through the window and loosed off a blast at point-blank range that knocked him reeling backwards with a screech, blood spattering off the vehicle behind him. And then the Mercedes' spinning, smoking tyres regained traction on the road surface, the free-revving howl of the engine dropped in pitch and they were through, overturning the SUV to their right as they surged towards the open road ahead. More shots rattled off the tail of the Mercedes and the rear window shattered, making Jia duck in terror.

In moments the wreckage of the breached barricade was behind them and rapidly shrinking in Ben's rear-view mirror. Keeping his head low to peer through the section of windscreen that wasn't opaque with cracks and bullet craters he sped away towards the junction ahead, and went skidding out onto the deserted main road. By his reckoning they'd taken at least three of the enemy vehicles out of action, along with several of the attackers. He'd have been surprised if they still had the fight left in them to give chase, although he wasn't taking any chances.

It had been only a brief little skirmish, but a pretty hot and intense one. If they'd used Jia's car they'd most likely not have made it. By contrast, for all the punishment the Mercedes had taken it was solid enough to have suffered no loss of power, brakes or steering. Their one remaining headlight was enough to see by as Ben hammered down the main road, putting as much distance between them and their now distant attackers as possible.

'Is everyone okay?' he asked urgently. 'Anyone hurt?' Lara was cringing low in the passenger seat beside him, pale and badly shaken up but uninjured. The panic-stricken gibbering from the rear told him that Jia was all right too. Sifu T'ao cuffed the young guy over the back of the head, shutting him up without triggering any fatal nerve points. Shoi nodded dumbly, wide-eyed. Jun Ming still had his screwed tightly shut, with his hands clasped over his head. 'Is it over?' he managed to gasp. 'Have we survived?'

'No, we're all dead and this is heaven,' Ben replied. 'What do you think?'

Jun Ming took his hands off his head, sat up straight and looked around him, blinking. Sifu T'ao reached forward to check his pulse and murmured something reassuring in Chinese.

'W-who were those men?' Lara asked.

Ben noticed that at least she wasn't complaining about him shooting people. He explained, 'They're the folks our Falun Gong friends here have managed to provoke into wanting to kill us all.'

'We have provoked nobody,' Jun Ming protested indignantly. 'They declared war on us.'

'Then you'd better start getting your act in order,' Ben said. 'Because if not, this war of yours will be over before it even began.'

'We are committed to whatever comes. If it has been written that we must die for our cause, then so be it.'

Ben shook his head. 'Sorry, Jun Ming. That kind of fatalistic thinking isn't something you'll find in my book. I'm interested in affirmative action. Such as, where we go from here. If you'd stayed out of sight of that bloody drone like I told you, it wouldn't have got a picture of your face. Now that it certainly has done just that, it means that if you or any of your known associates – that means all of you happy little gang of four – try to go back home you'll find the bad guys have laid out a welcome committee for you and been sharpening their knives while they were waiting. Which means we need somewhere to hide, and fast, because I have no intention of driving around half of China in a shot-up car that's like a big billboard screaming for the authorities to come and pick us up. So you'd better start coming up with ideas.'

Jun Ming fell into a long, thoughtful silence that showed he knew Ben was right. As the shock of the sudden violence subsided and he was able to gather his thoughts he said at last, 'It is not our personal safety that concerns us. But we must survive in order to protect what is most important for posterity, and the values for which we stand. If we cannot go home, then I can think of only one remaining safe refuge. Somewhere our enemies cannot possibly find us, as long as we are careful. And as long,' he added in a significant tone, 'as nobody else leads them to discover our whereabouts.'

Ben ignored that jab. 'I'm all ears.'

Jun Ming peered at his watch. 'We still have several hours of darkness before it would become necessary to ditch this vehicle and find another less noticeable. That should give us all the time we need to make the journey I am thinking of, sticking as much as possible to the back roads to avoid drawing attention to ourselves.'

'A journey to where?'

'To the place that Dan Chen rediscovered for us,' Jun Ming told him. 'Let me take you to the Golden Library.'

Chapter 37

They were hurtling through the darkness along the mostly empty road. Ben badly wanted to try calling Shi Yun again, and was anxious that he hadn't been able to get through to her earlier. But first he needed to hear more about their destination that night.

Jun Ming said, 'It is not a long journey to get there. Qi Huangdi's principal residence was situated in Xianyang, the location of the modern city of Xi'an. He built his mausoleum there, and of course it was the home of the terracotta army that was to accompany him into the afterlife. For this reason many historians and sinologists searching for the whereabouts of the lost Golden Library have believed that it must be somewhere in the same vicinity, accessible by means of one of the hidden tunnels linked to his great palace.'

'Tunnels?'

'A morbid fear of his own mortality wasn't the only peculiar foible of Emperor Qi Huangdi,' Jun Ming explained. 'Our first imperial ruler was also terrified of malevolent spirits that he believed haunted his footsteps and threatened to harm him wherever he travelled in the open. And so, he had built an entire network of subterranean roadways connecting all of his two hundred and more palaces. The spirits could not get to him below ground, you understand.'

'It seems so obvious,' Ben said. 'Makes you wonder why you hadn't thought of it yourself.'

'For someone of quite literally unlimited wealth, it would have seemed simply a practical solution to an everyday problem. Sadly, many of those tunnels have collapsed over the centuries and proved impossible to excavate, gone for ever. And with their loss, the route to the secret library was also erased.'

'But Dan's map showed where it was,' Lara said, with a mixture of sadness and pride. A tear glistened in the light from the dashboard. She wiped it away.

'Yes, my dear,' Jun Ming replied tenderly. 'His sacrifice and courage will always be greatly honoured for their inestimable contribution.'

'So where is it?' Ben asked, keen to get past all the elegiac stuff and back down to brass tacks.

'In the Qinling Mountains,' Jun Ming replied. 'The same area of Shaanxi Province is also home to Qi Huangdi's mausoleum and the museum of the terracotta soldiers and horses where Dan worked, close to the foot of Mount Li. Some distance away, about seventy-five miles east of Xi'an, is another mountain belonging to the same range called Mount Hua. That is where we found another way into the tunnels, by means of what might once have been an escape exit.'

'Mount Hua,' Ben said, reaching for the sat nav.

'In some ways it was the perfect location,' Jun Ming said. 'It is a very important mountain in Chinese religious culture, with a variety of ancient temples and monuments built on its slopes. For many centuries it was all but cut off, as the giant plateau with its five major summits could only be reached by the treacherous ridge known as Canglong Ling, translated as the Dark Dragon Ridge, until a new path was created some forty years ago. Once the refuge of monks and hermits, the region is now a tourist attraction with numerous hotels and restaurants.'

'So we can always pop out for a bite, or maybe order in some stir-fried chicken and noodles while we catch up on our reading of sacred Daoist scriptures,' Ben said, driving one-handed as he keyed in the search destination MOUNT HUA.

'Is is not as cosy as I made it sound,' Jun Ming replied. 'Parts of the mountain remain highly remote and inaccessible, their ascent considered by professional climbers to be one of the most dangerous in the world. Some of the most precipitous paths have been closed off, for safety reasons. It is along one of these that, not without some difficulty, one comes to the entrance of a cave whose shaft, narrow at its mouth, opens wider and leads deep into the mountain. There it connects with the remains of the ancient secret tunnel that allowed Qi Huangdi to travel there unseen by the evil spirits. As you go deeper through the shaft you descend lower and lower, until you arrive at the vast chamber cut out of the solid rock by the emperor's slave army more than two thousand years ago, and almost completely unseen since that time.'

It might have sounded like something out of a fantasy tale, if Ben hadn't already seen some pretty strange and weird sights in his time. 'And you're telling me that you've actually been there and seen it?' he asked.

Jun Ming nodded, smiling at Ben in the darkness of the speeding car. 'Oh, yes, my friend. And to say it is a spectacular sight would be something of an understatement.'

The sat nav had calculated a long and convoluted route skirting around the city and meandering eastwards. 'It's going to take us a few hours to get there,' Ben said.

'We should be able to make the journey before dawn. But allow me to suggest a different route, as the one offered by the satellite navigation will take us dangerously close to 22 Base.'

Ben glanced back at him in the rear-view mirror. 'Now *that* sounds like something I need to know about.'

'As long as we give it a wide berth, it should not pose too much of a risk. 22 Base is the military zone occupied by the Chinese People's Liberation Army Rocket Force. That is—'

'I know what the Rocket Force is,' Ben said. 'It's the new name for what used to be called their Second Artillery Division. They're the unit in charge of guarding China's nuclear warhead stockpile. And you're telling me these same mountains we're headed for are loaded with enough nukes to blow the top off the planet.'

'It is a big mountain range,' Jun Ming said with a dismissive gesture. 'More of a concern for us is the amount of security that surrounds the camp. The facility is heavily protected, as you might imagine, and civilian vehicles entering the area are often randomly stopped and searched by the military police. We luckily escaped interrogation. But of course there is no telling whether we would be so fortunate next time.'

'Sounds like just the kind of fun outing I came to China for,' Ben said. 'How bad can it be? Let's do it.'

With about ninety miles to cover, the sat nav could guide them for the first leg of the journey with Jun Ming's alternative directions to follow. Conversation dropped to a minimum, and for a time the only sound was the thrum of the engine and the whistle of the wind through the cracked and broken windows. Lara was slumped in the front passenger seat with her head on her shoulder, breathing softly. With the danger behind them for a while, Ben allowed himself a few moments of deep relief and satisfaction at having found her safe and alive. All he wanted now was to get her home – but something told him there was still a long way to go.

His thoughts returning to the immediate present, he took out his phone to try again to make his call to Shi Yun.

'Where *are* you?' she burst out at the sound of his voice. 'Where have you been all this time? I was trying to call all evening and wondering what could have happened to you!'

Ben smiled. It was good to hear her voice. 'I got a little waylaid, that's all,' he replied, speaking low to not be too overheard by the others. 'You okay?'

'I'm fine. At home, pacing up and down wondering when you're coming back. I spoke to Jia Wenguang's sister but it turns out she hasn't heard from him in weeks and doesn't know where he is. But I was thinking—'

'I found him,' Ben told her. 'And not just him. I have Lara.' Then interrupting the flood of astonishment and the many questions that instantly started pouring out of her, he said, 'I'll tell you everything when I see you again. In the meantime I need you to call the hospital and speak to Stefan.'

'It's the middle of the night.'

'That's why I can't do it. Use your police authority, say it's a matter of national security or something. Tell Stefan she's safe and well, and that he's to phone Ruth and start arranging for us to get out of China as fast as possible.'

'I'll do that. I was worried about you, you know?' she added in a lower voice after a pause. 'You shouldn't have gone off like that.'

'I'm sorry, Shi Yun. I was worried about you, too.'

'When are you coming back?'

'Soon, I hope.'

She sounded as if she wanted to say more, but changed her mind and repeated, 'I'll call the hospital right away,' and hung up.

Ben put his phone away, feeling strange about their conversation and the effect that hearing her voice again was having on him. He sighed. *Stupid.* This was not the time or the place to start getting romantic about someone. Someone he'd only just met and would soon leave behind, thousands of miles across the other side of the world, never to be seen again.

He settled in his seat and rechecked the sat nav. Still a good few miles to go before their backroad route would have bypassed the city and taken them towards the mountains to the east. So far, so good, with only the occasional solitary vehicle on the road and no sign of any police, not to mention any hordes of gun-toting, organ-ripping, state-sanctioned communist assassins chasing after them.

'Please forgive me for eavesdropping on your conversation just now.' Jun Ming's voice broke in on his thoughts, speaking softly in the darkness close to his ear. 'But I should remind you of what I mentioned earlier. I am afraid that it will not be such a simple matter for you to get out of China.' He pointed at the sleeping Lara. 'The poor innocent child has seen and heard too much for the sinister elements within our government to permit her to leave. And as for you, you already knew you posed a serious threat to them. After tonight's events, far more so. They will hunt you like the rest of us, my friend.'

'I'll find a way,' Ben said.

'I may be able to help,' Jun Ming replied enigmatically. 'We will talk more about it when we reach our destination.'

Chapter 38

Ben drove on in silence, his thoughts drifting between thinking about Stefan, about Ruth, about Shi Yun, about what he was going to find at the end of this road trip and, most of all, about how this was all going to end.

Lara stirred now and then in the passenger seat, and once in her sleep became agitated and muttered, 'Dan? Dan?'

Ben reached across the console, put a gentle hand on her shoulder and she settled back into more peaceful dreams. Behind them, Shoi Hie and Jia had managed to give in to sleep too. With Sifu T'ao it was hard to say, but he was his usual still quiet self as the Mercedes ploughed on through the night and Jun Ming prompted Ben with occasional softly spoken directions.

'We are nearly there now,' he said after another silence, leaning forward to stare intently ahead. How he knew that was anyone's guess, since all they'd been able to see in the last few miles was empty hills and winding mountain road with no landmarks to speak of except for a couple of lonely rural settlements they'd passed by some time ago. On top of which, a heavy mist had been gradually descending on the landscape and was making it even harder to see through the damaged windscreen. Faint looming shapes, no more than darker patches against the darkness glimpsed here and there through the drifting fog, were all that could be seen of the Qinling Mountains. But there was no doubt they were quickly gaining altitude as the road climbed steadily, narrower and rougher to the point where some stretches of mountain pass were little more than tracks littered here and there with the rubble of minor rock slides from the steepening cliffs either side. By now Jun Ming's alternative route had rendered the sat nav completely obsolete and Ben had turned it off a long time ago. If he'd been out here on his own, he'd have had to admit to being totally lost.

Lost, but not alone. They were snaking through another misty pass when a long and slow-moving tail of vehicle lights in the distance ahead, cutting through the fog like laser beams, told Ben that they were about to encounter a military convoy. 'No doubt from 22 Base,' whispered Jun Ming's voice behind him. 'This is the closest our route takes us to it.'

'That's the best news I've heard all day,' Ben muttered in reply as he quickly killed his own lights and pulled off the road onto an adjacent track half shielded by straggly bushes and dead trees. He could only hope that the fog would hide them from view, or else this journey might soon come to an untimely end.

They waited for several minutes in tense silence, Jun Ming breathing hard and Ben sitting with his hand on the shotgun, until the convoy had rumbled by and its seemingly endless procession of great lumbering transport and armoured troop vehicles, like giant monsters in the darkness, had finally vanished into the mist. Ben waited another full minute, in case of stragglers, before he restarted the car and they continued on their way. After that breathless moment the monotony gradually returned, and they seemed to have been travelling on for ever when at last Jun Ming tapped Ben on the shoulder and said, 'Stop here. This is as far as we can travel by road.'

The sleeping passengers reluctantly shaken awake and blinking and yawning, they gathered what few items they'd brought with them and left the car to continue on foot. The night was chilly and the fog drifted around them like smoke. Through breaks in the wispy curtain all that was visible were large rocks and crags and poor scrubby vegetation. 'There's nothing here,' Ben commented to Jun Ming.

'We thought the same, when the map first led us to this spot. But we were wrong. Come, let's go.'

The road had brought them a long way up already, but the steep track ahead was going to take them much higher. Jun Ming explained that this was one of the paths that had once been open to hikers and climbers, before safety concerns had prompted the authorities to close it off. A few hundred feet up, they had to clamber over a ramshackle wooden gate covered in danger signs. The cold night air was made more biting by the breeze, and Lara in her flimsy silk gown was hugging herself and shivering. Ben took off his jacket to drape over her shoulders. Shoi Hie was much more stockily built and well fleshed out, and seemed fairly resistant to the elements. By contrast Jia looked dogged and miserable, plodding along in their wake and not speaking to anyone. Whenever he started lagging behind, Sifu T'ao would turn on him like a sergeant major and encourage him to step up his pace with a swift boot up the backside.

'If I am going to make a regular habit of visiting this place,' Jun Ming panted, pausing to catch his breath, 'I had better get myself into shape. And these shoes were definitely not made for hiking.' As they kept on up the boulder-strewn path he was soon limping, though he was too stoical to complain openly. Ben found the slim but sturdy post of an old, weathered danger sign, broke it off and gave it to him to use as a walking staff.

He found himself reflecting on his last trek in the mountains, back in Switzerland when his life had seemed so much simpler, albeit fleetingly, and the most dangerous things to be met on his path were eagles. The slopes and crags of the Qinling range seemed infinitely more stark and menacing. The higher the path took them, the more crumbly and treacherous it became. Things became decidedly more interesting when the track ended and was replaced by a rickety plank walk fixed to the side of the mountain by means of crude iron supports, with an apparently infinite drop into the misty abyss to one side.

'I'm terrified of heights,' Lara moaned, shrinking away from the edge. Ben replied, 'Then it's just as well we can't see anything.' But he kept a very secure grip on her arm. '*Sorry, Stefan, your little sister took a tumble down the mountain*' was not an option he was willing to allow. To his relief the walkway continued for only a few hundred metres before they found themselves back to trudging over solid rock once again.

After another half-hour or so, the track split as the mountainside divided into twin peaks, with one fork cutting to the left and the other continuing close to the cliff edge to their right. Jun Ming paused, seeming undecided, then waved them towards the left fork and said, 'This way.' They scrambled on after him. But it wasn't long before he paused again, and congregated with Shoi Hie and Jia for a discussion that quickly became a furious whispered argument with lots of gesticulating and sour looks. It was clear to Ben that they'd taken the wrong turning or lost the thread of their route.

Jun Ming won the debate and they pressed on regardless, with Jia muttering to himself and shaking his head. Then some time later, as the first smudges of the red dawn were beginning to bleed through the drifting fog, they came to the cave mouth.

'This is surely it,' Jun Ming said, turning to beam happily at them. 'Everything looks so different in this fog that I became confused for a moment. But I was right! Or at any rate, I think I was.'

'Let's find out, shall we?' Ben said. He ducked his head under the low cave entrance and stepped inside, peering into the shadows where the red rays of the dawn couldn't penetrate. He took out his Zippo, flipped the lid and thumbed the striker to light their way by the glow of its flame. The floor of the cave was deep in rubble and the going was difficult as they threaded their way through in single file.

'Yes, yes, this is the place,' Jun Ming kept saying, his confidence now fully restored. When the Zippo got too hot to hold, Ben set it down on a ledge while he ripped a strip of material from his shirt.

'Jun Ming, I need to borrow your staff.' He wound the material around one end, soaked it in what was left of his supply of lighter fluid and lit it from the flame to make a rudimentary but effective torch.

Now they were able to make better progress as the flickering firelight illuminated the way ahead. Deeper and deeper, the cave floor sloping downwards just as Jun Ming had described it. There was no longer any doubt that they were in the right place. They passed a junction where the natural cave connected with the wide, perfectly rounded and smoothed shaft of the emperor's tunnel. Jun Ming explained they'd tried to follow it back along itself as far as they could, confirming their prediction that the sheer pressure of millions of tons of rock, perhaps together with some historic seismic or climatic event, had sealed it off in a massive collapse of rubble.

From here on, Qi Huangdi's slave workers had widened the natural cave shaft into a man-made tunnel in its own right, which led them still deeper until it opened out into a much larger excavation, an antechamber which in turn led to a huge stone archway inset with an ancient wooden door, thick with cobwebs and dust. They stopped and gazed up at its height, and

275

at the Chinese character markings chiselled into the rock arch. This really was it. Ben was hardly able to believe what he was seeing. Judging by the expression on her face, neither was Lara.

'Are you ready to witness something truly amazing?' Jun Ming asked Ben with a smile.

Chapter 39

Jun Ming turned the great iron handle and heaved his weight against the door, and it swung open slowly with a groaning creak. Ben could see nothing except darkness beyond it. He was about to step through and shine his torch for a clearer look when Jun Ming gently blocked him with a hand on his chest and shook his head.

'Please. We can allow no naked flames inside the library. Please wait a moment.' He ducked through the dark doorway and came out a moment later clutching a pair of rechargeable camping lanterns that certainly hadn't been here since the second century BC. 'We left these behind on our previous visit,' he explained, turning one on and handing the other to Shoi Hie as Ben dropped the burning torch to the floor and stamped out the flame. 'Now, if you'd like to step inside, I think you will find the journey was worthwhile.'

Ben followed him through the high archway. The electric light was bright and made him blink after the dullness of the fire torch; but then, as his vision adjusted, he was able to make out his surroundings. He'd travelled to a lot of unusual places before now, and seen things that most people would have hardly believed possible. But this was one sight that made even him draw a breath.

The space he found himself in wasn't some rough dug-out stone chamber, like others he'd known. It was like an underground cathedral, and none that he'd ever seen before or would ever see again. As far as the lantern glow could reach in all directions, everything gleamed with the reflection of burnished gold. Gold everywhere, more gold than he'd ever seen in one place before. The dully glittering walls rose up and up to the vaulted ceiling, which shone down from on high with the same lustre of precious metal and was supported by tall thick columns made not of stone but of shiny smooth marble, lapis lazuli and more gold, all of it worked to the highest degree of perfection by master craftsmen. And on and on it went, stretching ahead as far as the light could reach as they stepped deeper into the chamber.

Ben had to tell himself he wasn't dreaming. Standing at his shoulder, Lara was staring around her open-mouthed with amazement. The material value alone of the building would have run into multi-millions. As a piece of China's lost heritage, inestimable. That was without even reckoning on the library's breathtaking hoard of contents. Not books, of course, as books hadn't existed then – but scrolls, thousands and thousands of them, piled on ornate gold shelves that ran all the way to the ceiling and along the entire length of the walls that Ben could see. The collected intellectual, scientific and philosophical wealth of an ancient society that was already far advanced when his and Lara's European ancestors were still barely emerging from the Neolithic age, sharing their living quarters with pigs and goats and learning how to smelt iron in charcoal pits.

'I told you it was an impressive sight,' chuckled Jun Ming. All four of the Falun Gong associates were grinning in amusement at the expressions on the newcomers' faces. 'And now let me show you the artefact that made such a discovery possible. Lara, my dear, you have seen it before but never up close.' His steps echoed to the ceiling as he walked over to one of the lower shelves and picked up an object that he brought over to them. It was a glossy black cylinder, richly inlaid, from which he removed the lid to reveal the rolled-up silk parchment inside. Very delicately, he drew it out of its protective tube and unfurled it to show them.

What Dan Chen had found inside the body of the terracotta soldier was more than just some hastily scrawled treasure map where X marks the spot, but a work of beauty in its own right, rich in detail and painstaking delicacy of line and colour. It showed the route by which Jun Ming had led them through the mountains, and the slope they'd come up, marking the entrance to the cave with a set of Chinese characters inked in gold. In the corners were finely-drawn depictions of the interior of the library itself, exact in proportion, showing that whoever the anonymous artist had been, he or she must have seen this place with their own eyes. As for their identity, that would likely remain a secret for ever.

Ben finished examining the map and looked around him again, finding it hard to tear his eyes away from so much beauty. He shook his head in wonder and asked Jun Ming, 'But what can you do with this place, now you've found it? Surely you can't be thinking of keeping it hidden, all to yourselves? What good would that do?'

'And yet what option do we have?' Jun Ming replied sadly. 'I would sooner live here like a hermit for the rest of my days, sworn to protect its secret with my life, than to turn it over to the authorities. Even if the more civilised and progressive members of our government saw fit to recognise the value of this rediscovered treasure, what of the destructive elements who still hold so much power and influence over the destiny of the nation? What if another cultural revolution were to occur one day, another swathe of devastation at the hands of maniacs only too happy to smash China's ancient heritage? There is so much to risk. Count yourself lucky that this is someone else's responsibility, my friend. But then, you have plenty of responsibilities of your own to take care of, no less challenging by any means.'

Ben understood what he was talking about. 'I've been thinking about what you said,' he admitted frankly. 'And I think you're right. Getting Lara out of China and back home safe to her family won't be easy, now that we've stirred things up so much. You said you might be able to help. If that's still the case, then I'm open to suggestions.'

'I'm glad you have come to that conclusion,' Jun Ming said. Behind him, Sifu T'ao nodded gravely. 'I would say it is not just difficult but impossible, even despite the western corporate ties that enabled you to enter the country. Getting in was the easy part. I doubt very much whether your connections are strong enough to get you out.'

'But yours are?'

'I believe they are your best chance of success. You recall I mentioned our secret supporter and patron, Chang Han Yu?'

'The Chinese billionaire.'

'One of the richest men in all of East Asia. He would do anything within his considerable means to help and protect our order, and its friends. But even with the benefit of his great power and influence, it would not be as simple a matter as stepping on a private jet. Believe me when I say it would never leave the ground. The authorities are onto you now, as well as your travelling companion and anyone else with whom you have been in contact.'

Ben thought of Shi Yun. He hated the thought of her getting into trouble because of him. 'Are you saying they wouldn't even let Lara's brother leave the country? He's done nothing to threaten anyone.'

Lara burst out, 'Stefan? They mustn't hurt Stefan!'

'It is possible they would hold back in his case,' Jun Ming said. 'But certainly not in yours. One rash move on your part, and you will be made to disappear. Both of you,' he added, looking earnestly at Lara. 'It would be put down as a tragic accident, mere bad luck, just one of those things or, as you say, "shit happens". And I doubt whether the British or Swiss embassies would risk becoming embroiled in a diplomatic incident over the event.'

'Then what do you suggest?' Ben asked.

'That we use our friend's influence to enable an alternative route out of China. Already I can see various possibilities to be considered, though none of them are easy, or safe. It would be too great a challenge for a man of lesser skills than yours. That is, if you are interested in pursuing this option.'

'I'm interested,' Ben said. 'That's if you're sure that this Chang Han Yu would really be willing to stick his neck out like that for a couple of total strangers.'

'If you are asking me whether he can be trusted,' Jun Ming said, 'then I can assure you the answer is yes, unequivocally. Even so, he would be taking a very serious risk. And you must understand that such risks cannot be taken entirely for free.'

Ben looked at him. 'You mean he'd want money?'

Jun Ming shook his head. 'Far from it. Money means nothing to a man like Chang Han Yu, since he already has enough to last him and all his descendants a thousand lifetimes.'

'Then what does he want?'

'Given that we now know who you are and what you are capable of,' Jun Ming replied with a cautious glimmer in his eyes, 'what Chang Han Yu would ask in return for his help is the one thing that you are uniquely able to bring to the deal. Your specialist expertise.'

It sounded to Ben as though the Falun Gong people were gunning for something in particular here. Something important they'd already been discussing and planning among themselves, waiting for the right time to make their move. That time was now, evidently. 'Quid pro quo,' he said. 'You scratch my back, I scratch yours. But just how am I supposed to do that, exactly?'

In the pause before the reply, looks passed between Jun Ming and the others that told Ben his guess had been right. *Here it comes*, he thought.

'Let me tell you about our leader,' said Jun Ming.

Chapter 40

'Her name is Song Yuxuan,' Jun Ming said in a tone of reverence, as though he were talking about a saint or a goddess. 'The most wonderful and heroic person you could ever wish to meet. She has been at the forefront of our movement here in China for over ten years and with her great courage and strength has unified us in ways we could never have imagined. She liaises with many of our exiled brethren overseas and has been tirelessly working to create an international media network to support and promote our cause, also producing literature and DVDs to counter the wickedly dishonest portrayal of Falun Gong in the Chinese official state media. This has also placed her directly in the sights of those who would want to see her eliminated.'

'She sounds like a brave lady,' Ben said, wondering with suspicion where this could be leading. Of course, there would have to be a catch.

'Two years ago, she and five others managed to simultaneously hack several cable television networks in Changchun. For over an hour they televised a counter-propaganda documentary of their own, produced and directed by Song herself, revealing to thousands of households the truth about the persecution, murder, torture and incarceration of Falun Gong practitioners across China. Shortly afterwards, police raided all six of their homes. Three of Song's co-conspirators were shot dead while trying to escape, while of the two who were arrested, one was found mysteriously hanged in custody and the other simply disappeared never to be seen again. Song managed to evade capture for over eighteen months, continuing her work all this time at grave personal risk, until she was finally caught by police in Shanghai, where she was hiding. She was transported to Beijing under military escort, where she was beaten and thrown in prison awaiting trial. Among the falsified charges against her is that she was caught leaking state secrets, which is ridiculous and typical of the corruption of the legal system. How could she, or any of us, possibly have access to state secrets?'

Jun Ming shook his head in disgust and went on, 'Anyhow, it has been nearly four months since her arrest and she has been languishing in solitary confinement all this time. Now our intelligence contacts within the judiciary system tell us she is due to be tried and sentenced two days from now. Needless to say, the verdict is a foregone conclusion. There is no possibility of clemency, no appeals will be heard and no other legal recourse is available. Without a doubt, she will be sent directly from the courthouse to one of the many forced labour camps, such as Xichanping Farm in Beibei District, which is known to contain many Falun Gong followers. If that happens, she is sure to be tortured to death or suffer organ harvesting within weeks, perhaps even days.'

Ben said nothing. He had a pretty good idea what was coming next.

'We cannot let this happen,' said Jun Ming, his voice cracking with emotion. Shoi Hie had tears in her eyes and Jia Wenguang was standing with his head bowed. 'But what can we do against the might of the state authorities? We are pacifists, not warriors.'

Ben looked at him. 'Jun Ming,' he said patiently, 'if I didn't know better I might think you were asking me to spring your leader from prison. Because if you were, I'd have to explain why that's a very, very bad idea.'

'We are realistic,' Jun Ming replied. 'Of course we understand fully that such a plan would have zero chance of success and would effectively be a death sentence for anyone bold or foolish enough to attempt it. But . . .'

'But?'

'It goes without saying that Song's trial, like all such trials, will be a travesty of justice, a piece of pure theatre designed to make an example of her and reinforce the propaganda message to the public that she and all other members of her evil cult are a domestic terror threat to be feared and despised. However it presents us with a small window of opportunity. She is currently being held on remand at the Beijing Women's Prison in Daxing District, an area in the south of the city. The trial and sentencing are scheduled to take place at ten a.m. on the day after tomorrow, at the Daxing District People's Court. According to our sources, at eight-thirty a.m. she is due to be taken from her cell, loaded onto a prison truck and driven to the courthouse, a journey of approximately thirty-five minutes. She will be the only prisoner aboard the truck, accompanied by four armed guards. We have managed to secure details of the exact route the driver will follow. On arrival she will be placed in a secure room to await the start of the proceedings.'

Ben said, 'I see. But going by this plan of yours, she'd never reach the courthouse. And all it takes to rescue her from their custody is for someone to intercept an armoured prison vehicle in the middle of the morning traffic, neutralise four determined and very pissed-off guards with shotguns and rifles, plus the driver and anyone else on board, snatch the prisoner, who of course will be securely chained up to the inside of the truck, and whisk her away through the busy city in broad daylight with about ten thousand police armed response units on red alert descending on them from all directions. Is that the general kind of thing you had in mind?'

Jun Ming shrugged. 'To be perfectly honest, we thought we would leave the exact details up to you, being the expert in such matters.'

'It can't be done,' Ben said. 'It's the most insane thing I've ever heard of. I'm sorry for her. I truly am. But I'm afraid it's too late to do anything to help her at this point.'

'That is very disappointing to hear,' Jun Ming replied with a sigh. 'Enabling her escape from China would have been the greatest coup, not just on a personal level but for the benefit of all of those who have suffered persecution. You see, she more than anyone would have had the power to make a difference. Nobody has amassed more evidence of the past and ongoing atrocities committed against our people. Nobody could present a stronger, more compelling case to the international authorities, the United Nations and the US Commission on International Religious Freedom, among others. Only that kind of personal testimony would be powerful enough to convince the outside world to exert pressure on our government to end this cruelty once and for all. So much more than Song's own life is at stake here. But if you say it cannot be done,' he added sadly, 'then we will have to accept that it is so. I thank you for your candour. There is no more to be said.'

A gloomy silence fell over the library. Only the quiet sobbing of Shoi Hie could be heard in the vastness of the chamber. Jun Ming looked suddenly older, shrunken and inconsolable. His younger colleague wore a grim expression and Sifu T'ao was bowed in sorrow. Even the incredible wealth of gold all around them seemed to gleam with less lustre than before. Lara was glaring at Ben with eyes full of hurt and accusation, as if he'd been caught drowning kittens.

Ben said nothing for a long moment. Then he puffed his cheeks and his shoulders sagged. *Fuck it*, he thought. *What the hell.*

He said, 'A helicopter. It might just about be possible to do it with a helicopter.'

Chapter 41

'But . . . we do not have a helicopter,' Jun Ming replied after a crestfallen silence.

'I didn't expect so,' Ben replied. 'Those are the kind of fancy toys only very rich people can afford. Billionaires, like your man Chang Han Yu. If he's serious about wanting to help his movement, then it doesn't seem too much to ask him to make the small investment required to bring this plan of yours about.'

Jun Ming and the others all exchanged glances. Jia looked clueless until Shoi Hie explained it to him in rapid-fire Chinese, and his eyes opened wide.

The strategic details were forming in Ben's well-practised mind the way they'd done a thousand times before, back in the day when he'd been forced to think on his feet like any strong military commander. It came as naturally to him as breathing and his tone was brisk and decisive. 'So here's what we need to do,' he told them. 'We have less than two days to organise it, so we'll need to move fast. I don't suppose there's any phone reception anywhere nearby, so you, I and Sifu T'ao will scoot back down the mountainside as quick as our little legs can carry us and get to where you can make a call to Mr Moneybags. Then I think a face-to-face rendezvous will be in order, because there's a hell of a lot to talk about and arrange. In the meantime, I suggest we leave Lara here in the library for her safety, along with Shoi and Jia to look after her. Got it?'

'But I want to come with you,' Lara protested. 'Why do I have to stay here?'

'Because you're what we call the principal asset in this situation,' Ben said. 'And principal assets need protecting. So you'll kindly shut up and do what I say, or else I'll tie you to one of these columns.'

Lara glowered unhappily, but Ben's idea seemed to be making sense to the others. Jun Ming's face was beginning to glow with renewed optimism. Sifu T'ao was nodding in approval. Ben asked, 'Do you have all the necessary essentials to last a couple of days? How secure can the place be made in our absence?'

'We brought some things with us when we first came, in case we got lost or became stranded on the mountain. There is food, water, blankets to keep warm at night. The lanterns are all fully charged. And there is a deadbolt enabling the doors to be locked from inside, in the unlikely event of their being discovered.'

'Good. Now, as for what we'll need to pull this off, it's going to be quite a shopping list. It'll involve putting together a team of people and it'll be very expensive and tricky. But pretty much anything's possible when you have unlimited cash resources.'

'Perhaps I should write this down, in readiness for calling Chang Han Yu.' Jun Ming patted his pockets, produced a small notepad and pen, and the Sifu held the lantern close by to give him some light.

'I'll provide a more detailed list when we meet with him, but here are the basic requirements for equipment and personnel. One, the helicopter needs to be small, light and fast. It also needs to be totally untraceable to him or his organisation, if he knows what's good for him. Because we'll certainly have to ditch it after the job is done, to avoid getting shot out of the sky by the flying aces in their J-20 stealth fighter jets, and the cops will be all over it like ants within a matter of hours.'

'I understand,' muttered Jun Ming, scribbling this down on his pad as fast as he could.

'Two, I'll need a hell of a good pilot who can be trusted to keep his mouth shut. Three, a minimum of two large trucks to be used to intercept and immobilise the prison vehicle at a prearranged point along its route, synchronised so as to block it off to the front and rear. Again, those drivers have to be totally reliable and trustworthy.'

'There are many such people we can call upon,' Jun Ming said confidently.

'There'd better be,' Ben replied. 'Four, I want top of the line radio communication equipment for the entire team. Timing's going to be critical and we need to stay sharp. And,' he added with a pointed glance Jia's way, 'they'll all need to be able to speak good English. Unless I'm supposed to take a crash course in Chinese over the next two days.'

'That will not be necessary.'

'Now, point number five, I'll need the correct HRST rappelling equipment to enable a rapid extraction of the prisoner. Six, armament: there'll be very specific requirements for that. Seven, road transportation: a car, fast but not too distinctive, and untraceable like the helicopter; plus another reliable driver who can rendezvous with us on the ground at a moment's notice. It'll take at least one switch of vehicle, preferably two, to reach the safehouse, the last of which should be something with off-road capability in case anything goes wrong and we need to take unorthodox evasion measures. Land Rover, Range Rover or one of your Chinese equivalents.'

Jun Ming stopped scribbling and peered up from the pad with a frown. 'Safehouse?'

'That's number eight,' Ben said. 'Somewhere totally secure, preferably not too far out of the city but not overlooked by any immediate neighbours and offering good vantage points all around, plus a decent escape route if that should become necessary. Rural smallholdings are pretty good for these purposes. Abandoned, derelict ones are even better, because it's less likely anyone would hide there. Assuming all goes well, that's where your leader and I will hole up until the next phase of the plan. For the sake of precaution I'd prefer if we didn't remain there any longer than a few hours before moving on.'

'Very well. Anything else?'

'Yes. A stock of provisions will have to be supplied in advance; doesn't have to be a lot, if we're only staying a short time. Food and water, bedding, changes of clothes and basic medical equipment. She's likely to be physically weakened after months in solitary confinement and might require treatment for dehydration, mental trauma and God knows what else.'

All this was duly scribbled down. 'You mentioned the next phase of the plan?' Jun Ming asked.

'That's where we all regroup at the safehouse, as soon as possible afterwards: Lara here, Stefan, and whoever else is going to be involved in getting us all the hell out of this delightful country of yours. That part, I'm just going to have to trust Chang Han Yu to set up. It's out of my jurisdiction.'

'I repeat that Chang Han Yu can be trusted absolutely. He is a man of great wisdom and ability.'

'Let's hope so.' Ben pointed at the pages of the notepad that Jun Ming had covered in a flurry of notes. 'And if you reckon your brilliant billionaire pal can manage to stump up all that lot in time, then we might *possibly* have a chance of making this work. What do you think?'

Jun Ming gave a dry smile. 'I think we should get down the mountain and speak to him, as you suggest.'

'Then there's not a moment to lose,' Ben said.

Chapter 42

And not a moment was lost, as Ben and his two companions made it back down the mountain in half the time it had taken to come up it, now that the warm rays of early morning sunshine had burned away the last of the fog. Ben was ready with the shotgun as they stalked cautiously back to the hidden spot where they'd left the car, in case some passing patrol from 22 Base might have spotted it, rightly flagged the bullet-riddled Mercedes as suspicious and left a unit to stake it out. Not that he would have been able to do much against Chinese troops, with only a pump-action and a handful of rounds; and he was relieved to find the vehicle undisturbed.

By the light of day it looked even more of a mess. To venture anywhere near civilisation would spell guaranteed police trouble, and somehow Ben didn't think that his friendship with a Xi'an detective, or even the relatively free rein that Chief Zhao had afforded him, would be enough to placate the authorities. But the car would serve to travel a short distance, in the hope of reaching a mobile signal before too long. As Ben sped back in the direction of the main roads, Jun Ming sat glued to his phone avidly waiting for a bar of reception to appear on the screen. After twenty minutes, during which time the only traffic they'd passed was a peasant plodding along in a ramshackle cart pulled by a mule, he suddenly announced, 'I have it. We can stop.'

The call to Chang Han Yu didn't take long, and any misgivings Ben might have had about the billionaire's willingness to help them were quickly settled. By pure luck he'd just landed back in his base city of Beijing after a week's business trip to California; otherwise they might easily have missed him. The number that Jun Ming had was a secure line on which they could talk quite openly without fear of government phone taps. Chang Han Yu listened carefully to the outlined plan and provisional list of requirements that Jun Ming read out to him, and agreed to them without hesitation. He'd been about to fly off again to his business offices in Shanghai, but now was happy to postpone the visit and arrange instead for them to be picked up at their remote location for a face-to-face meeting in the city later that morning.

While they waited Ben tried calling Shi Yun again, but her line was always engaged. He left her a brief message, light on details and saying only that he was going to be too busy to return to Xi'an for a couple of days and not to worry about him.

If only she knew.

This was one of those times when the power of money to make anything happen made extreme wealth look very alluring to those who didn't have it. Less than two hours after Jun Ming's call, the sound of an approaching chopper made Ben look up and shield his eyes from the sun. No, thank Christ, it definitely wasn't a military aircraft from 22 Base come to check them out. In minutes the sleek silver Airbus helicopter with Chang Han Yu's company logo on the side was whipping up a dust storm as it came down to land on the lonely mountain road and they were hurrying over to meet it, heads ducked low under the rotors. Sifu T'ao's long robe crackled and fluttered in the wind blast. Jun Ming had confided to Ben that the old master had never flown before – but he was predictably unfazed by the experience as they climbed aboard and the pilot whisked them into the air.

The Airbus carried them to a private airfield where a small white jet was waiting to speed them the rest of the way back to Beijing. Visiting a major city was to be another first-time experience for Sifu T'ao, who after staunchly refusing all offers of refreshments from the pretty, smiling stewardess sat looking rather unimpressed as he frowned down from his porthole window at the sprawling urban landscape below.

Ben felt a pang of sadness to be back here in the capital, thinking of poor Sammy Tsang; but there wasn't much time for dwelling on the past. On landing at the same runway of Daxing International as his and Stefan's first arrival in China, instead of taxiing to the private terminal building the jet took them around the rear and stopped outside a hangar bearing the same company logo as both it and the helicopter. The three passengers disembarked and were greeted in the sunshine by a silver-haired, immaculately-dressed and extremely elegant Chinese man in his early sixties, or perhaps in his seventies and super-fit. He met them with a strong handshake and a self-assured smile, taking off his mirrored sunglasses to reveal eyes that were as sharp and intelligent as they were strikingly and unusually blue. Ben was always ready to form good impressions of people and he liked Chang Han Yu immediately, the same way he'd felt about Sammy Tsang on first introduction.

In perfect English the billionaire offered Ben his sincere thanks for offering to help the plight of the Falun Gong followers. 'Please allow me to invite you all for lunch. Come, we talk in the car,' he said affably, motioning to a black stretch limousine waiting by the hangar. 'It is like a rolling office for me, and one of the most private places for conversation in all of China.'

The whisper-quiet limousine ushered them along the familiar route from the airport and into the city as they began going through the finer points of Ben's plan. It might have seemed decidedly odd to be sitting in a luxury limo openly discussing such serious criminal activity, but Chang's composure and charm somehow made it feel natural. He listened attentively, interrupting only to ask perceptive questions and offer suggestions, such as his thoughts on the best spot for the trucks to intercept the prison van on its journey to the courthouse. Ben was surprised by his positive attitude to every detail of what he'd suggested.

'It is an excellent plan,' Chang said smiling as they continued their conversation over lunch. The setting was his own private restaurant on the top floor of a glittering company skyscraper in downtown Beijing, whose total privacy, like that of the limousine, allowed them to speak freely. The food was prepared by Chang's Parisian chef and Sifu T'ao seemed content to munch in silence while the others did all the talking. Though Chang and his fellow Falun Gong followers preferred to abstain from alcohol, a bottle of very fine wine had been provided for Ben's enjoyment, which he drank sparingly out of politeness.

'An excellent plan,' Chang repeated. 'As simple and practical as it could be, yet thoroughly calculated in every aspect. It is not without risk, but then I would risk a great deal more to save this very special woman from such a fate as they have in store for her.'

'I am glad you approve,' Jun Ming said. 'And might I add, immensely grateful for your generosity.'

'Please, think nothing of it,' Chang replied with a warm smile. 'My contribution is negligible compared to Mr Hope's. Such courage and skill far surpass anything I could ever dream of doing. The very best of luck, my friend,' he added, raising his glass to Ben.

After lunch, in a boardroom of the same company tower, Ben was introduced to the team of six – consisting of the helicopter pilot and five drivers, two assigned to the trucks and the others to the chain of getaway vehicles that would enable their escape by road – on whom the success or failure of the plan heavily depended. Even before he met them they'd all been thoroughly briefed, and he was pleased with their grasp of their roles.

That evening, Chang took Ben, Jun Ming and the Sifu on a limousine ride to the apartment building in another area of Beijing where a penthouse covering the entire top floor was being provided for their accommodation. Early the following morning, Ben was reunited with his team and the deep-drilling into detail began in earnest. Assembled aboard a discreet minivan they drove south-eastwards through the city to the Daxing District where the women's prison was located: a multi-storey facility on four acres of land, obscured behind high walls and wire fencing and barely visible from the road. 'It was created in August 1999,' Chang had explained to Ben the previous evening, 'and is the only prison in Beijing dedicated to the detention of female Falun Gong practitioners. Four of its eleven sections are reserved for what the authorities like to call their "re-education" – more correctly described as the most brutal, barbaric forms of brainwashing imaginable – while the remaining floors are for the isolated detention of those who refuse to renounce their beliefs. Here they are routinely tortured, beaten, deprived of sleep, disabled or not infrequently killed. The unluckiest ones of all are not kept there but sent to the forced labour camps, facing a life of hellish torment from which they are generally never released alive. Organ harvesting is rife.'

From as close as they could get to the prison facility, the minibus passengers were taken on the same route that Song Yuxuan would follow on her journey to be tried and sentenced. Ben agreed that Chang's choice of location for the truck ambush, a staggered junction from which the intercepting vehicles could emerge left and right at just the right moment, was as good as any. As best they could time it, the spot was fourteen minutes' drive from the prison gates, a little less than halfway to its court-house destination – which allowing for traffic conditions meant the van would reach it at around 8.44 a.m.

'Then this is where we do it,' he told his team, and the two men who would be driving the trucks snapped dozens of images on disposable digital cameras that would later be destroyed.

From there, they drove to each chosen vehicle switch point in turn, examining its strengths and potential weaknesses from various angles until late in the afternoon, by which time Ben was as satisfied as he could reasonably expect to be – perfection in these matters being, as he well knew, an unachievable goal. In an ideal world, the location of the safehouse would have been established before they decided on where the pick-up points would be, to make for the most direct and logical route. But the timing had been so tight that Chang was still busily hunting for a safehouse that met with Ben's requirements. He'd promised to have found one by the end of the day.

Back in the skyscraper boardroom, now redesignated as a war room, Ben spent the evening making every man repeat the details of his part until they were so undividedly focused on the task ahead that they had all but forgotten everything else about themselves and their lives. Around midnight, just as Ben was about to take pity on them and bring the torturous briefing to an end, an almost equally tired-looking Chang Han Yu appeared and led him along the corridor to another room where a collection of equipment had been laid out for his inspection.

'I trust they are exactly as you requested,' Chang said. 'Some items were rather difficult to obtain, but luckily most people become quite amenable when it comes to bribery.'

Ben checked through each piece of kit in turn, examining it closely in silence. Then he nodded and said, 'This is good, Chang. I know you must have put a lot of effort into getting these.'

'As you know, next to the near impossibility of procuring an unregistered aircraft of the correct type, the hardest of all the items on my list to obtain has been a suitable safehouse, fitting with your instructions. However I'm happy to report success, the last of the arrangements made just minutes ago. Would you like to take a drive out with me and see it, to ensure it meets your approval?'

Ben thought about it, and shook his head. It was late, he was very tired and tomorrow was going to be a hell of a long day. 'Don't worry about it. I trust you.'

'I'm deeply honoured by your faith in me. I took the liberty of entering the satellite coordinates into the third escape vehicle's navigation system. Those will take you straight to the property, only a few miles beyond the city outskirts and as close to the final pick-up point as we could make it. I don't think you will be disappointed by my selection. And of course, the necessary supplies will be in place by the time you get there.'

Chang paused, racking his brain. It had been a long, hectic day for him, too, and those bright blue eyes of his were faded and bloodshot. 'Is that all of it? I can't think of anything I might have missed.'

'No, that takes care of everything,' Ben said. 'All that's left is getting the job done.'

'I have absolute confidence in your success,' Chang said with a weary smile. 'Now perhaps you wish to return to the penthouse, in order to get your rest?'

Ben said nothing as they drove through a sudden downpour of rain to the apartment building in Chang's personal Bugatti Veyron. Chang shook his hand, wished him good luck once again and expressed his hope that the weather would have improved by morning. He gave Ben a card with a handwritten number that, like his helicopter, was untraceable to him. 'Please call me at any time, should you need to.'

'I will.'

'I hope we will meet again soon,' Chang said with a last smile, and turned back towards his car. Ben headed up in the lift, went straight to his room and was fast asleep within five minutes.

Then it was the next day, and he was ready.

Chapter 43

By exactly 8.45 a.m., pretty well on schedule and just one minute later than predicted, the slow-moving prison van had made its way through the heavy morning traffic as far as the intercept point. The stormy wet weather had cleared overnight and the sun was already strong and warm as it climbed through the cloudless sky. Anyone hearing the distant dull thud of a helicopter overhead might have squinted up to see the small aircraft hovering high above the city, but such sights were so commonplace over Beijing that nobody was likely to take any notice.

Not yet. In just a few moments, that was all about to change.

From where Ben was crouching near the mouth of the open side hatch with the powerful wind blast swirling around him, the target below was just a small grey rectangle threading its way closer and closer to the critical spot. Seconds counted. His mouth was dry and his body was jangling with anticipation, every muscle as tight as a coiled spring about to be released. *Wait for it . . . wait for it . . . Now!*

And right on cue, the two other small rectangles he'd been expecting to appear at any moment came into play. First the red shape of the heavy articulated truck veering suddenly from its carefully-chosen sidestreet and cutting across the van's path, forcing it to a stop; then an instant later, the second white shape of another appearing from the opposite side to block it off from the rear, preventing escape. A couple of other vehicles were unavoidably caught in the net with the truck. Horns started blaring angrily.

'Go, go!' Ben yelled into his mic. His helicopter pilot was skilled and quick-witted and he obeyed instantly, dropping altitude towards the street. Ben had already been buckled into his rappelling harness ten minutes ago. He was wearing all black: black assault mask, black tactical vest, black gloves. Grenades dangled from the belt around his waist, along with the Browning Hi-Power pistol in its holster, strapped to his back was a kit bag containing more essential items and hanging from its sling around his shoulder was the special military weapon provided courtesy of Chang Han Yu's apparently inexhaustible list of bribable contacts.

Party time. As the helicopter plummeted out of the sky Ben grabbed the rappel cable hanging beside him, clipped its quick-release carabiner hook to the ring on his harness, said his lucky prayer and launched himself out of the hatch into empty space. It was a manoeuvre he'd repeated so many times in his life that it was instinctively drilled into him. The chaotic gridlock of traffic below rushed up to meet him and he hit the ground on bent knees, simultaneously releasing the cable from his belt. Heads turned in disbelief as this black-clad figure dropped surreally from the sky like a Special Forces soldier and instantly rushed towards the immobilised prison van.

Ben knew he had only instants before the guards inside the van recovered from their shock and confusion and began to mount a resistance. The last thing he wanted or needed was to get into any kind of firefight with them or anyone else. He'd insisted from the very start that nobody was to be badly harmed in the attack, unless it was utterly unavoidable. The Browning semi-auto on his belt was only there as a threat and a last-ditch option; while his primary weapon was the grenade launcher that he unslung from his shoulder as he closed in on the van. It was loaded with the same kind of non-lethal stun munitions as his SAS unit had used for storming terrorist strongholds containing hostages who were still living and intended to be kept that way. The grenades worked by filling closed spaces with a shockwave of sound that disorientated and temporarily incapacitated everyone inside, foe and friend alike.

He took aim at the driver's side window, squeezed off the trigger and the grenade exploded from the short fat barrel, smacked through the glass and detonated within the cab with a flat BOOM that made the whole vehicle shudder and rock on its suspension. The prisoner in the back would be briefly taken out of action with the rest, but that was a positive for him as she'd be easier to handle that way. Ben's other stipulation in the planning stage had been that the ambush should be as much of a surprise for her as for the prison personnel, in case she might accidentally give anything away by her behaviour.

Letting the launcher dangle from its sling Ben tore open the driver's door, shoved the guy roughly aside and boarded the van. The head guard was riding up front with the driver, a portly middle-aged man who stared at Ben in horrified confusion as he tried to make a clumsy grab for the shotgun clipped between the seats. Ben clubbed him with the butt of the launcher and tore the ring of keys from his belt.

Two of the remaining four guards were staggering towards him, clutching their weapons but in no fit state to use them, while the other two were on the floor. Ben trampled over the fallen pair, grabbed the other two and knocked their heads together, let them drop senseless to the floor with the others and surged on towards the rear of the van where the prisoner sat slumped against the bars of the cage she was locked into.

She was a small, skinny woman with cropped hair and a blue prison jumpsuit uniform, wrists and ankles securely cuffed together and chained to a rail. The stun grenade had knocked the energy out of her, which was fine by him in case she tried to resist in her panic.

Ben opened the cage, then reached quickly into his kit bag for the pair of gas masks he was carrying. With little time for delicacy he yanked one of them over the woman's head and put the other one on himself. By now one of the guards had recovered enough to get back up on his feet, and was clawing at his holstered sidearm. A pretty tough customer and strongly devoted to his duty – but nobody was tough enough to withstand what was coming next. Ben pulled one of the tear gas canisters from his belt, activated it and rolled it down the length of the prison van where it instantly began spewing white vapour at the guard's feet. By the time the guy had realised what was happening he was engulfed in a cloud of gas and collapsed to his knees, choking and spluttering and desperately rubbing his eyes. Ben tossed another canister into the front of the van, to prevent any further opposition from the rest. In seconds they were gasping like landed fish, totally incapacitated and unable to see out of their streaming eyes. By the time they recovered, Ben and the prisoner would be long gone. Unless an army of police arrived here first.

Working fast but staying calm, Ben tried three keys from the guard's ring before he found the one for the woman's cuffs. He freed her wrists first, then the ankle shackles, then scooped her up and bundled her over his shoulder. She weighed almost nothing after four months in solitary confinement. In two strides he'd reached the side loading door of the van and crashed it open, jumping back out into the warm morning sunshine.

The occupants of the other vehicles trapped between the trucks had long since fled. The chopper was hovering directly overhead, sending down a hurricane blast and a deafening roar from its blades, the rappel cable hanging from its hatch. Ben tossed a third gas canister into the van for good measure, then reached for the dangling cable, clipped it to his harness and yelled GO, GO to the pilot to winch him up. He kept a tight grip on the prisoner, feeling the cable go taut and the upward force snatching him off the ground.

Before they were even fully aboard, the pilot was already regaining altitude. Ben thrust the woman inside, clambered in after her, slammed the hatch shut and pulled off his gas mask and hers. Song Yuxuan was coming round from the effects of the stun grenade and trying to focus on him, terrified out of her wits but obviously beginning to realise that her situation had just taken a strange and radical turn for the better. Tearing off his assault mask so she could see his face, he smiled at her and yelled over the deafening noise, 'You're going to be okay! You're free!' Whether she understood him or not, she made some reply that was lost under the rattling roar of the chopper as the pilot banked the aircraft around and started accelerating the hell out of here.

The street shrank rapidly below them and then they were off, nose down, tail up, full throttle, the floor of the helicopter sloping under them like a pitched roof. The rescue might be over, but the escape was only just beginning.

Chapter 44

Chang Han Yu's unregistered chopper was now the hottest target in China and they'd have just minutes before this whole city was flooded with armed police. After a very short, rushed flight northwards the pilot brought them down to land in a wide grassy area of one of Beijing's many parks, where retired citizens out for their morning stroll stopped to gawk at the unusual sight of a helicopter coming down to land, and the even more unusual passengers who disembarked from it in a hurry – followed by the pilot, who quickly shut down his engines and beat a hasty retreat on foot in the opposite direction leaving the craft abandoned in the middle of the lawn.

Chang Han Yu had chosen this particular park not just for its ease of landing, but for its proximity to a fast two-lane boulevard that cut further northwards across the city in the direction of the second vehicle pick-up point. Ben half carried the weak, stumbling Song Yuxuan across the neat lawns, through a flower bed and a stand of pink and yellow blossoming trees and out of a gated side exit to where the driver was waiting for them, right on cue, to hand over their first getaway car. The young Falun Gong devotee had been one of the sharper and more receptive of the team during their briefings, and Ben had no qualms about his reliability.

So far, everything had been note perfect. But now, as he hurried Song towards the car, he gave an inward groan. Because despite Ben's repeated insistence that the vehicle should be as inconspicuous as possible to blend in with the regular traffic, in his enthusiasm for ensuring a rapid escape Chang had provided them with a bright yellow McLaren GT. Just where the hell he'd managed to get hold of an untraceable example of one of the world's quickest sports cars at such short notice, Ben neither knew nor cared. No use complaining, though – it would have to do.

The car's dihedral doors opened upwards like bat wings and the young driver jumped out, gave Ben a brilliant smile and set off at a wild sprint. Ben bundled Song into the passenger seat, dived behind the wheel and hit the gas and the McLaren took off like a spurred horse, squashing them against their backrests with its acceleration. Once he'd filtered into the free-flowing traffic he settled down to a slightly more sedate pace, turned on the sat nav and saw to his satisfaction that the coordinates for the next pick-up were there as requested.

It was only now that Ben was able to get a proper look at his charge. Song Yuxuan was in her early forties or thereabouts, with strong determined features and the first streaks of grey appearing in her jet black hair, or what was left of it after the prison guards had cropped it short with shears. Solitary confinement and a starvation diet had left her looking malnourished and sallow-skinned, but before that she would have been strikingly handsome. And soon would be again, if she could reach safety and remain free of the authorities' clutches.

Until now she'd been too overwhelmed with shock and astonishment to speak, and in any case the roaring blast of the helicopter had made conversation impossible without a headset and mic. 'And so who the hell are you?' she asked in English, having made the fairly simple observation that Ben wasn't Chinese. She might be in a physically weakened, depleted state after her months of

306

imprisonment, but there was a fire in her eyes. This was a tough, feisty lady. She'd needed to be.

'A friend of a friend of yours,' Ben said. 'They're getting you out of China.'

'Jun Ming arranged this, didn't he?'

'No names. Better that way.'

'In case I get caught again? Don't worry, I'd die before I told those bastards anything.'

'Don't count on it,' he replied.

'This car is ridiculous,' she said acidly. 'Some escape this is.'

'Maybe you'd rather be back in your cell?' he asked, and she fell into a moody silence.

Five very rapidly-covered miles across the city, they made it to the second switch point two minutes ahead of schedule and Ben impatiently counted down the hundred and twenty seconds with his eyes watching in all directions for police, before a bright red Audi R8 appeared and the driver screeched to a halt next to them, instantly getting out and making himself scarce with the engine still running. At least this car was a little less flamboyant than the first. They transferred out of the hot, ticking McLaren and blasted away again.

'Maybe you should slow down a little,' Song suggested. 'Where are we going anyway?'

'Somewhere we can get you out of harm's way, a decent meal inside you, plenty of rest and rid of that stylish prison uniform.'

'The Hotel Eclat?'

'I doubt that very much.'

'Food. Oh, God, I'm so hungry. I can hardly remember the taste of anything except soggy rice and rotten potatoes.' She closed her eyes for a moment, savouring her newfound freedom. 'Well, whoever you are, thank you for getting me out of there.

You have no idea what that place was like. But it was better than where they were about to send me.'

'You're probably right about that.'

No sirens screaming after them, no flashing blue lights in the mirrors. It felt as if they were getting away with it. Ben slackened his speed a little more and began to relax as his own adrenalin levels gradually settled. He lowered his window and lit a Gauloise, fully expecting his passenger to complain. Everyone else seemed to, after all. Instead she said, 'Could I have one of those?' He lit it for her and she greedily sucked in the smoke, gasping 'Oh, that's so good.'

'Not exactly a fit with your Falun Gong lifestyle, is it? Clean and pure in body and spirit, perfectly in harmony with nature and all that stuff?'

She turned to look at him. 'Give me a break. After what I've been through?'

Seven miles later they were nearing the eastern edge of Beijing, where the nav system was taking them to the third and final vehicle switch point. When they got there, he was gratified to see that the car was just what he'd asked for, a boxy big Range Rover, roomy and comfortable, but as quick on-road as it was useful off it. Again, as Chang Han Yu had promised, the coordinates for this last, longest leg of the drive had been provided for him, so that all he had to do was follow the directions to the safehouse.

Less than twenty miles into the countryside east of Beijing, the sat nav finally led them to their destination. It definitely wasn't the Hotel Eclat, but it was just what Ben had been hoping to find. The old farmstead had been lying empty and uninhabited for enough years for the long, bumpy track leading to it to become overgrown with weeds in some places and swamped by a muddy river further down its length, which Ben had to ford with water up to the axles. The house itself stood alone and semi-derelict in the middle of a dusty yard, surrounded by a broken-down porch, its woodwork ancient and windows rotted. The porch was collapsed at one end, part of the old tin roof had fallen in and nobody in their right mind would ever choose to live here. There were no neighbouring properties, and the track and the open ground made for all-round visibility of a good kilometre.

It was perfect.

Ben pulled up outside the house and killed the engine. The silence was absolute as they stepped out, just the soft whistle of the wind. 'I think we made it,' Song breathed.

Ben didn't want to jinx it by agreeing too readily. 'We shouldn't have to hole up here for long,' he told her. 'Just until your friends have finished making the arrangements for getting you out of the country. Then we'll be moving on as fast as we can.'

'You as well?' she asked him.

'I certainly hope so,' he replied with a smile. 'After today, I'm in even more trouble than you are.'

Chapter 45

Once he'd got her inside, Ben returned to the car to hide it under a dilapidated lean-to out back, then started exploring their hideout. Chang Han Yu had delivered once again, by providing all the supplies they needed to last several days if necessary. There were plentiful tins of chicken and fish, packets of dried noodles, gallons of water in large plastic bottles, all the essential pots and plates and cutlery, and a gas-powered camp stove to cook on. No coffee, damn it, but you couldn't have everything. Along with those items Ben found sleeping bags, blankets, soap and towels and more medical gear than he'd asked for, along with fresh clothing for both of them. When darkness came they'd be able to discreetly light their hiding place with a couple of paraffin lamps. Last but not least, that blessed Chang had made up for the lack of coffee by leaving them a bottle of twelve-year-old single malt scotch.

The broken-down house had no running water, and they'd have to clean themselves up the old-fashioned way by heating pots of water over the stove. For Song, even that was a luxury after the squalid conditions in which she'd spent the last four months. She happily ditched the hated blue prison-issue jumpsuit and changed into her new things. Her experiences had erased any sort of inhibitions she might have had about stripping off in front of him, and even though Ben discreetly turned the other way he couldn't avoid noticing the many bruises and burn marks, some of them recent and raw, that the guards had inflicted on her body. Those must be hurting like hell, though she was both too proud and too happy to complain, and so in addition to the glucose drink he prepared to replenish her energy levels he gave her some painkillers from their supply. She gulped down a modest plateful of chicken and noodles, unable to eat too much because the starvation diet had shrunk her stomach.

After her meal Ben gently cleaned the fresher of her burn wounds, treated them with antiseptic and covered them with clean dressings. Then she curled up in a sleeping bag on the bare wooden floor and he covered her with a blanket. She was soon fast asleep with a contented half-smile on her lips, probably her first in a long time. Ben sat watching her for a while, trying to imagine the things she'd been through. Leaving her alone, he wandered outside onto what was left of the front porch and stood gazing up the empty track.

It was over – or, at any rate, this first part was. He allowed himself a celebratory Gauloise and a generous nip of the scotch, and started turning his mind to the next phase of the plan. Everything now hinged on how quickly they could move on, and whatever alternative exit route out of the country their wealthy ally had been able to come up with. Last they'd spoken about it, Chang had assured him he was working on it.

And that was when a deeply unpleasant realisation suddenly came to him, one that hadn't occurred while he'd been so tied up with organising the rescue mission. It was this: if their powerful, influential enemies could conspire to prevent him and Lara from leaving China in the normal way, then there was nothing to stop them arresting Stefan on some trumped-up pretext the moment he tried to step onto his flight home. He was no threat to them, but these people were more than devious enough to detain him as bait – in fact they had every reason to. A tethered goat, providing a means to get to their two main targets, Ben and Lara. And these people had also demonstrated very clearly that they had no compunction about harming innocent lives to achieve their objectives.

With that chilling thought in mind, he flicked away his half-finished cigarette, poured away the last of his drink and took out his phone to call Shi Yun. To his relief there was just enough mobile reception to get through, and this time she answered.

She let out a cry at the sound of his voice. 'Where have you been? What's happening?'

He said, 'Listen, there's a change of plan. Where's Stefan now?'

'At the hotel, getting ready to leave,' she replied, sounding as though she was frowning and unsure. 'Everything's been arranged. Though he was really upset that he couldn't see his sister yet.'

'He will, sooner than we thought. Tell him to stay away from the airport. It's imperative that he doesn't get on the plane, or anywhere near it.'

'Why? What's he supposed to do instead?'

'Bring him over to your place and sit tight. You'll be contacted.'

'And then?'

'And then Stefan and I will rejoin his sister and we're getting out.'

'You mean . . . you're not coming back to Xi'an? I'd thought—'

'Me too. But I can't do it, Shi. The situation's gone a different way now.'

'But then . . . if you're leaving . . . it means I won't ever see you again.'

Her words, and the heartbroken tone she said them in, cut him deep. For the first time he understood fully what she'd come to mean to him, too. He shook his head. 'I'm so sorry. There was no other alternative.'

'I have to see you,' she insisted. 'If only just to say goodbye.'

'I don't know if that's a good idea. For your sake. Things have been happening and it might not be safe here. I can't say more than that.'

'You don't have to cover up with me. I heard what happened in Beijing. I knew, somehow, something so wild and crazy had to be connected with you.'

'I have no idea what you're talking about.'

'I've seen what you can do, Ben. Whatever your reasons were for what happened, I know they must have been good ones, but I don't care anyway. I just want to see you. I'm coming to meet you, too. One last time before you're gone.'

Ben knew there was no point in trying to persuade her not to. His hands were tied and once again he had no choice – on top of which, the prospect of seeing her again was hard to ignore. He felt as though he had a ten-pound ball of lead inside his chest as he got off the phone with her and made his next call, this time to the secret number Chang Han Yu had given him.

Chang was understandably anxious to hear more about the rescue, knowing only what he'd been able to glean from the news broadcasts breaking all over the state media. Ben cut through all that and quickly, urgently explained the rethink of their plan and the need for Stefan to be brought to the safehouse as fast as possible, along with Lara. He gave Chang Shi Yun's number to call.

'I think your strategy is a wise one,' the billionaire replied after a moment's consideration. 'I will speak to our mutual friend immediately and make the necessary arrangements, to be carried out with all possible haste.'

'I appreciate everything you've done for us, Chang.'

'On the contrary, my dear friend, you're the one who deserves all the gratitude. We will talk again very soon. There is still much to discuss.'

After that, all Ben could do was wait, fretting over the complex and ever-changing sequences of moves in his head like chess pieces on an imaginary board, in the hope that it wasn't too late to make this work. He could well imagine the distant frenzy of activity that this change of plan had sparked into action: Shi Yun rushing to the hotel to catch Stefan in time; Stefan calling Ruth to say he wasn't getting on the Steiner plane; Ruth going crazy wondering what the hell was happening over there; meanwhile, Jun Ming having to move heaven and earth to fetch Lara from her refuge inside the Golden Library, down the mountain and back to Xi'an with all the speed and efficiency that their super-rich patron could bring to bear. Having all those fancy planes, trains and automobiles at one's disposal, not to mention limitless cash, certainly did help to grease the wheels a little.

Ben had to smile to himself as he pictured the touching, emotional scene of Lara and Stefan's reunion in the safety of Shi Yun's apartment. But there would be little time for tears and celebrations before they were shooting off again, whisked the six-hundred-odd miles from Xi'an to Beijing for their rendezvous at the unlikely location of this derelict old farm.

It was a lot to make happen in such a short space of time. And stuck here helpless to do a damn thing about it, Ben didn't even want to contemplate all the things that could possibly go wrong.

'What the hell,' he sighed to himself, resignedly returning to the bottle of scotch. 'Let's have another drink.'

Chapter 46

Whether it was just her mind and body relaxing after so much intense stress or the need to catch up on months of sleep deprivation, Song was out of it for the rest of the day. She awoke long enough to hungrily gobble down another meal of tinned meat and noodles and swallow a litre of water, then went back to her sleeping bag and dozed straight off again.

With little else to do, Ben spent his time watching out for any sign of movement on the track or the open land surrounding the farm. Waiting around for something to happen was how SAS soldiers mainly occupied themselves, in between explosive bouts of violent activity, and he was well used to it. But his usual ability to slip into a state of almost trancelike stillness, not moving for hours on end, alert and ready yet totally relaxed, failed him on this occasion. What should have been a brief stay at this safehouse was going on much too long. It made him edgy that the Beijing police, not much over twenty miles away, would be combing the entire city right now for the escaped prisoner and the masked accomplice – a terrorist like her, no doubt – who'd sprung her from custody. Once they'd finished kicking down the doors of every suspected hiding place within the urban zone, they'd expand their furious search to the outlying areas. They wouldn't rest until they found her and made good the humiliation of having let her slip through their fingers. Heads would be rolling otherwise, if indeed they weren't already.

In the meantime he couldn't stop dwelling on the many troubling weaknesses in the rescue plan. It had been impossible to get Song out without leaving a trail of witnesses, like the walkers in the park where they'd abandoned the chopper. For all their precautions, it could just be a question of time before the police found someone, or someone came forward, who'd seen the fugitives heading out this way. Or else, in this land of informers one of the accomplices Chang had had to trust to help them could blab to the authorities, a nice reward and a boost to their social credit score being a more compelling motivator than loyalty to their faith. The more people you involved, the more moving parts you built into your plan, the more there was to go horribly wrong. Ben had never been much of a worrier, but he was worried now.

Come evening, with no sign of any hordes of police units surrounding the safehouse, he told himself to get a grip, and retreated to the small, bare side room that still had a mostly intact roof and where he made his bed for the night, letting Song have the privacy of the main living space. By the dim light of a paraffin lamp he stripped and reassembled his remaining weapon, the pistol he hadn't left behind in the chopper. It was the same old familiar model of Browning he'd known for many years, and which had saved his life and those of others many times. Its fourteen rounds of 9mm were all he'd have to defend himself and Song if something bad did happen. He tucked the weapon under the rolled-up blanket he was using as a pillow. After a few cigarettes and a little more whisky, he was able to relax enough to grab a few hours' sleep.

Up before dawn, he stretched his muscles and took the pistol from under his pillow. He went into the main room to check on Song, softly breathing in her sleeping bag, then stepped quietly outside to resume his watch for a while. Still nothing. To keep his mind distracted from his worries he aggressively pumped out fifty press-ups, fifty pull-ups from a beam of the porch roof, and fifty abdominal crunches, then ran eight circuits of the farm at a pace that was enough to get his heart rate going a little. By now the shimmering disc of the sun was beginning to edge up through a band of streaky purple-crimson clouds in the east.

And that was when the vehicles appeared.

Ben whipped out the Browning and ducked behind the broken-down end of the farmhouse porch, watching as the two large SUVs came splashing through the flooded section of the track. They didn't look to him like police vehicles, but you could never be certain. He couldn't make out how many people were inside. Five or six in each, he reckoned; up to a dozen opponents if this was about to turn into a shooting match. If that happened, he was going to have to make every one of his fourteen rounds count.

The SUVs rolled the rest of the way down the track, drew level with one another where it widened out and pulled up side by side twenty yards from the house. Ben flipped off the Browning's safety. First guy to step out with a weapon was a dead man. Next, Ben would roll under the porch as the firestorm began, and hope he could take as many out as possible before they managed to take cover behind their vehicles.

But the firestorm never came, because as their doors opened and the first person stepped out, Ben saw with a surge of relief that it was Stefan. His arm was still in a sling and he looked dishevelled after the long night drive from Xi'an, but his face was split from ear to ear with a huge, happy grin. From the other side appeared Lara, looking radiant and joyful for the first time since Ben had known her. An instant later, Jun Ming appeared from the driver's door.

Good old Chang Han Yu had delivered on yet another promise. Ben flipped his safety back on, quickly hid the weapon in his waistband and stepped out from behind the porch to meet them. Jun Ming waved. Stefan pointed and said something to Lara, who looked even happier at the sight of Ben.

He was about to call to them when, to his surprise, Chang stepped out of the second SUV. He hadn't expected the billionaire to escort the others here in person. In the passenger seat was the diminutive, familiar white-haired figure of Sifu T'ao, no longer wearing his long monastic robe but clad instead in a neat black outfit that looked like a martial arts uniform. Chang was smiling and grinning, and Ben smiled back; then his smile wavered as the last passenger got out.

Shi Yun was wearing the same light dress as she had that day in Xi'an when he'd visited her apartment. Her hair caught the colours of the dawn light as she came hurrying towards him. Ben could see the knowing looks on the others's faces. He stepped from the house to meet her and she flew into his arms with a tight embrace. It was a strange moment, like two long-lost lovers meeting again.

'You don't look so happy to see me,' she said, pulling self-consciously away from him.

'Of course I am. But I told you, I don't know how safe it is here.'

'Well, if you thought I was going to be left behind, you don't know me. I wanted to see you and nothing was going to stop me. I'd have arrested everyone first.'

'I'm glad you came,' he told her, surprised by how earnestly he meant it. 'I wanted to see you, too.'

Behind them, a sleepy-looking Song had emerged onto the porch. Her face lit up when she saw who the arrivals were. The next few minutes were taken up with animated chatter and

318

laughter as they were all united for the first time. Stefan gripped Ben's hand warmly, lost for words and palpably emotional, while Shi Yun hung on to his other arm as though she'd never let go. Sifu T'ao had allowed his famous deadpan composure to slip, and couldn't stop grinning. Even Lara suddenly wanted to hug.

As they all stepped inside the house, suddenly it was quite a little crowd in there. Ben wondered for a moment whether the half-rotted floorboards would take their weight. 'Where are Jia and Shoi Hie?' he asked Jun Ming.

'They remained at the library,' Jun Ming replied. 'Soon to be joined there by others of our circle. We intend to set up a permanent presence there, to protect it.'

'Well, my friend, you fulfilled all our expectations and more,' laughed Chang, clapping Ben heartily on the shoulder. 'Our dear Song appears in excellent shape, considering her terrible ordeal. Oh, but what a rescue! Masterfully done! You have to tell me everything, down to the last detail.'

'What you and I need to talk about is where we go from here,' Ben said. 'We're still a long way from the finish line.'

'Indeed we must,' Chang said more soberly.

That discussion finally took place a few hours later, as the happy little crowd gathered seated around the floor to share a hearty lunch, not one restricted to tinned chicken and noodles this time as Chang had brought a luxury hamper full of delicacies with him, along with bottles of champagne in an icebox for those who could have it, and traditional Chinese tea for those whose religion proscribed alcohol. Chang certainly liked his food (if not his drink) and so, it seemed, did Sifu T'ao who once again tucked into the feast with silent relish. It was a highly unusual event to be taking place in such surroundings, but nobody cared. Shi Yun sat pressed close to Ben's side as they ate. Song and Jun Ming were deep in conversation, and seemed to have known one another a long time.

'Now let me tell you what I propose,' said Chang through a mouthful of one of the delicious little savoury cakes and waving a tea cup in one hand, while Ben, Stefan, Lara and Song listened intently. 'The journey will consist of three parts, the first being potentially the most hazardous although I foresee no real problems. This will involve cutting directly across much of China to Macau on the south coast. You might ask why, and the answer is that being an autonomous region independent of Chinese control it is by far the nearest, and in fact the only, safe port from which to leave the country.'

'Makes sense to me,' Ben said. 'How do we get there?'

'I would think it prudent to stagger the overland trip into stages as we did before, using a combination of aircraft and road vehicles. I would strenuously avoid train travel, being far too risky for our purposes. Everything is being arranged as we speak.'

'No Ferraris or Rolls-Royces though, Chang,' Ben said.

'Of course. I apologise if I perhaps got carried away. Now,' Chang went on, 'the other reason I chose Macau as your departure point from China is that I happen to have some good contacts there. On arrival you will be met by a trusted friend of mine, who manages one of the region's major casinos of which I am a principal stakeholder. After a short stay in Macau you will embark on a tanker headed for Taiwan. I should perhaps mention that the vessel in question belongs to my own commercial shipping line, Han Yu Global.'

Ben smiled. 'You capitalist, you.'

Chang shrugged off the accusation. 'At least it means that your voyage will be undisturbed, and more comfortable than if you had been mere stowaways. Yet it seems I'm not the only one with useful connections. Your friend Stefan here has already arranged with his fiancée – who I gather is a close relation of yours—'

'Ruth, my little sister.'

'—for the family jet that would otherwise have flown from Xi'an to meet you instead at Taiwan Taoyuan International Airport. From there to Europe, and then on to the United States with our dear Song. That part I leave up to you.'

'Song is welcome to travel anywhere she likes in the world aboard our Steiner aircraft,' Stefan said.

'I hope I have left nothing out,' said Chang. 'I regret that there will be a slight delay of perhaps twenty-four hours before you can leave here, to enable us to finalise the last of the details. A couple of our helicopter fleet are currently in for repair and it's not always easy to find replacements at short notice.'

The trials and tribulations of the super-rich. 'I understand,' Ben said. Though privately he wasn't very pleased at the thought of having to stay put for another whole day. His sixth sense was still jangling alarm bells at him from somewhere in the back of his head.

By the time all the food was gone, the group had fragmented into separate conversations. Stefan and Lara had a lot to talk about, although her mood had darkened with the still very raw grief over what had happened to Dan and Olivia. Stefan did all he could to console her. Meanwhile among the Chinese the subject of conversation had moved on to the less immediate future, and the support that the Falun Gongers hoped Song would be able to attract to their cause once she reached the US. Ben was listening in and trying to catch the odd word, but the language was still totally impenetrable to him and Shi Yun quietly translated, whispering in his ear. North America was their best bet, they all agreed, with its very large Asian population and an already established following. Jun Ming was especially excited about what she could achieve there, though Song herself was cautious in her optimism. 'It's all very well to think their government authorities would get seriously involved. But do you really believe they'd risk starting a diplomatic cold war with China over the likes of us? To say nothing of a hot one.'

'Even just by helping to shine a spotlight on what goes on—' Jun Ming repeated, before Song interrupted him by saying, 'Then why don't you come too, if there's so much we can achieve? They'd listen to you.' But Jun Ming was adamant that he needed to stay here and do his bit to protect their precious Golden Library, along with Sifu T'ao who would be living there full-time as its guardian, as he'd been doing at the temple.

'Then I should stay too,' Song said, 'instead of running off to America like a coward when there's so much to be done in my own country.'

'It's far too dangerous for you here, you know that. And then who would spread the message to the outside world?'

Presently Ben had had enough of listening to them argue, and slipped away from the group to wander back outside. The afternoon had gone quickly and the sun was already starting its long dip into the west. He stood looking up the track and all around, wondering why he still felt so edgy, telling himself he was just seeing ghosts and that there was nothing to worry about. He was so preoccupied with his thoughts that he didn't sense her presence until she was close beside him.

'So it's tomorrow,' she said in a low voice, reaching for his hand. Her fingers felt small and delicate laced between his. 'Then you'll be gone. That doesn't give us a lot of time to say goodbye.'

'You could always come with me,' he joked.

'And leave my cat all alone to look after herself?'

'You have your priorities straight. That's good.'

'What's happening between us, Ben?' she asked, suddenly much more serious, looking into his face as if searching for answers that couldn't be put into words. 'After you suddenly went off like that, I realised I . . .' her voice trailed off. She shook her head, looking down at her feet. 'I never felt that way before.'

'Something that could have happened,' he replied. 'If things had been different. But they aren't. And so it can't. That's just how it is. We don't really get a say in the matter. However we might feel about it.' The words felt as awkward as they sounded. He wished there could have been a more poetic, eloquent way to express the mixed, bittersweet emotions he was feeling.

'Fate,' she murmured sadly. Falling silent for a few moments she gazed off into the distance, then heaved a sigh. 'Damn it, why couldn't you have been Chinese?'

'Just unlucky, I suppose,' he replied with a smile.

'Still,' she said, squeezing his hand. 'We have the rest of the day. It might not be much but it's ours. Let's walk a while.'

That evening's meal was a more subdued affair than before, and the group spoke much less as they sat around to eat. Knowing that tomorrow many of them would be parting ways, perhaps never to meet again. As night fell, they scattered into the nooks and corners of the old house, sleeping bags and blankets strewn about the floors like a dosshouse. Ben retired to the little room where he'd made his camp, and lay there thinking about tomorrow.

He'd been lying there alone in the darkness for about thirty minutes and was beginning to fall asleep when the soft creak of the door woke him. He instinctively reached for his pistol, sitting up and blinking. The door creaked shut. The small shadowy figure that had crept furtively into the room came padding over to his bed.

'Shh,' said the figure. 'It's me. Don't want to wake the others.'

'What are you doing?' he asked, half awake and stupid as she slipped naked into the sleeping bag beside him.

'Saying goodbye,' she whispered.

Chapter 47

It was sometime after three in the morning when Ben was jolted awake again. This time it wasn't the soft creak of the back room door opening that roused him from sleep. It was another kind of unexpected visitor. The kind that arrived in the dead of night in silent electric vehicles, so that all that could be heard was the muted crunch of tyres over the dirt yard outside. The kind that turned off their lights before they came into view of the house, so that no glare of headlamps would wash across the windows and their arrival would come as a complete surprise to those inside.

The kind that Ben's sixth sense had been warning him about.

How they'd been found didn't matter at this moment. But found they had been.

He lifted the sleeping Shi Yun's arm away from where it had been lying across his chest and rolled out of the sleeping bag, grabbing his clothes from the rumpled pile on the floor. She stirred and murmured, 'What is it?'

Ben said nothing. Moving fast, listening hard. Outside, the rolling crunch of tyres had become more diffused, telling him that at least two vehicles and more likely three had spread out to surround the farmhouse. He pulled on his trousers and buckled the belt. Snatched the Browning from under the pillow. She was wide awake now, and frightened. He could see the gleam of her eyes in the darkness. '*Ben?*' she hissed.

'Get dressed. Quickly, quietly.'

Barefoot and shirtless, he strode for the door and peered through. The windows of the main living space were dark, only a glimmer of moonlight penetrating the dusty, grimy glass. The huddled shapes under their blankets around the floor were still. Someone was snoring softly. Shi Yun had pulled on her dress and joined him by the doorway. He took her hand and whispered, 'Police.'

The options were coursing through his mind. None of them were good. First because of the impossible situation Shi Yun now found herself in, torn between two sides. Second because, connected to the first, it wasn't feasible to get into a shootout with the cops. Springing a prisoner from custody had been bad enough. Gunning down a bunch of police officers would serve to ramp up the seriousness of his crimes to off-the-charts levels and make anyone else inside the house an accomplice to be sentenced to death. If they were caught. Which was the third bad thought running through his mind, because the chances of them all escaping from this were essentially nil.

'My pistol,' she whispered. 'It's in my handbag.' It sounded as if Shi Yun had already taken sides, without hesitation. She slipped past him, moved silently through the dark room to where she'd left her handbag, and pulled out the weapon.

'Now arrest me,' he whispered back to her. 'Arrest all of us.'

She drew in a sharp breath and stared at him.

'I told you you shouldn't come here. Now this is the only way you get out of it.'

'But what about you—?'

'Never mind me. Do it.' If she walked him out into the porch with her gun to his back and showed them her detective badge, she might have a chance of persuading them she'd found the fugitives first. As for the others, they'd got themselves into this voluntarily and nothing could help that now.

'No,' she said. 'I won't.'

Ben whispered urgently, 'For Christ's sake, Shi. This is no time for arguing.'

'I *won't!*' she repeated much more loudly, loud enough to wake the others. Jun Ming sat up in his sleeping bag, dazed and dopey from his deep sleep, gasping, 'What is happening?' Across the room, both Chang Han Yu and Song were rapidly waking up, too, and seized by sudden panic. Lara let out a small cry of fear. Stefan's voice in the darkness said, 'Ben?'

Only Sifu T'ao's little nest of blankets in the far corner was lying there undisturbed. Ben realised that was because the old man wasn't in it.

'A police tactical raid team are outside and we're all about to be arrested,' Ben announced to the shocked gathering.

Breaking the stunned silence, Stefan said, 'Can't we fight them?'

'You want to die?'

'Better than going back to prison,' said Song.

'There's no debate here, people,' Ben said.

And he was right. But not in the way he thought he was. Because in the next instant, whatever argument there might have been one way or another was settled by the crackle of automatic gunfire from outside. The police, if that was who was out there, hadn't rolled up to arrest them.

They'd come here to kill everyone inside.

And even as Ben was grabbing Shi Yun and pulling her down to the floor to duck the bullets that were suddenly flying through the windows, that struck him as being a little strange.

Ben and Shi Yun hit the floor, belly down, both with their pistols outstretched and pointing towards the door as thundering steps came racing up the porch outside. The door burst open and a black figure appeared in the doorway, another one right behind. Blinding, dazzling white light flooded the room to disorient its occupants. The armed attackers were storming the farmhouse – and they were intending to get this clean-up done fast.

But Ben was faster, and his split-second reflex shot took the first man down before he knew what had hit him. As he pitched forward, dead on his feet, the guy behind him let off a blast from his automatic weapon. In his haste he fired high and the deafening rattle only stitched a ragged line of holes in the far wall before Shi Yun's shot went off and slammed into his chest, making him stagger. She'd fired centre of mass, the way she'd been trained to, and she'd hit where she was aiming. But that didn't work so well when your opponents were kitted up with bulletproof vests. Ben followed up her shot with another of his own, blowing off the top of his head with a gory spray that caught the light from behind.

Now the first wave had been beaten back, the running figures outside in the yard retreated to take cover behind their vehicles. One of them was the portly, overweight shape of a middle-aged man who moved more awkwardly than his younger teammates and looked as strangely familiar as he appeared out of place clad in tactical assault gear.

But Ben had no time to dwell on that, suddenly hearing a sound coming from the back room where he and Shi Yun had been sleeping. He made a dash for the door and got to it just in time to see another figure clambering in through the small window. He blasted two more shots and the figure tumbled into the room and sprawled to the floor with a short, sharp scream that was drowned by the boom of the Browning as Ben took down the other man who'd been trying to follow him through the window.

Now there was the sound of more gunfire coming from the main room, very close by. Ben turned and raced again for the door, but was driven back by bullets ripping through the wood, splinters flying. He dived to the floor. All hell was breaking loose the other side of the door. More shots. A scream: Lara's voice. A man's shout of anger, which could have come from Chang or Jun Ming. Then two more shots, the first punching another hole in the back room wall and missing Ben by an inch; the second hitting some other target and immediately followed by another female cry. Not Lara's voice this time. Not Song Yuxuan's.

Shi Yun's.

Ben scrambled to his feet with ice water for blood and crashed through the door, gun raised.

And Chief Zhao said, 'Drop weapon or I kill her!'

Chapter 48

As Ben stood there pointing the pistol, he instantly took in the whole scene and the events of the last few seconds flashed through his mind. During the brief moment he'd been in the back room dealing with the window invasion there, the enemy had staged a renewed attack on the front. Of the three men who'd come crashing through the door, Shi Yun had wasted no time in taking out the first with a dead-centre headshot. His teammate coming up behind him had fired wildly, hitting Chang, before Shi Yun shot him too. But that was when her weapon had failed to cycle properly, causing the partly ejected spent cartridge case to jam up the action and prevent the slide from closing and chambering the next round.

Professional shooters called it a stovepipe jam, because of the way the fired case stuck out of the chamber mouth like a chimney. These things happened. If you want totally reliable ignition every time, go for a revolver. But they only happened once in a million rounds, and she'd been unlucky. Very unlucky, because the jam happened just as the third man had come surging in through the door and she hadn't had time to clear it before his weapon was pointing in her face. He was the portly, middle-aged one who couldn't run as fast as his hit team subordinates. Slow, but big and powerful. Grabbing her and knocking the pistol from her hand, he'd whirled her around to face the door of the back room and was holding her in front of him like a human shield with his gun to her temple. The guy was backlit by the glare of the lights shining through the open front doorway, but Ben had recognised him instantly.

'Well, well, look who's here. You're a bit off your normal stamping ground, Chief.'

'Drop weapon!' Zhao repeated. He jammed the muzzle of his gun tighter against the side of Shi Yun's head. She struggled to break free of his grip and tried to lash at his shins with her heels, but he was too strong.

'Shoot him, Ben!' she yelled.

The last time Ben had faced a standoff with an armed hostage taker had been that day in Xi'an, when the Shrimp threatened to cut the old woman. On that occasion the victim had been so tiny that Ben could get a clear shot at his legs behind her. This time, it was impossible without risking hitting the hostage instead of the bad guy. Ben hesitated.

'I kill her!' Zhao screamed.

Zhao must have known that if he pulled the trigger, Ben would finish him instantly. Would he do it? How much of it was a bluff?

Ben kept his gun level and steady. He hid the tremor of terror in his voice as he said, 'Shoot your own officer? That's a little unconventional, but then I'm guessing this isn't an official police operation, is it, Zhao? You're strictly off the radar here. Which means you're on your own with no backup.'

Playing for time. Hoping his opponent would crack under the stress, and make a mistake that gave Ben an opening to shoot him. But Zhao held firm. 'I kill her!' he screamed again, louder, and there was a look in his eye that made Ben believe he meant it.

No choice. No way Ben was going to risk her life like that. No matter what. He lowered his aim and let the pistol drop from his hand.

The air seemed to have been sucked from the room. The others were all standing or crouched there, frozen like statues in the harsh light shining from outside. Stefan was hugging his sister tight. Jun Ming's mouth was opening and closing soundlessly in horror. Song was staring at the police chief with cold hatred in her eyes. Chang was leaning against the wall clutching his wounded arm, his face contorted in pain and blood dripping over the floorboards. The bodies on the floor weren't moving. Zhao had been the last of them. But now Zhao was on top.

The chief was a cautious man, though. He didn't dare let go of Shi Yun in case she attacked him, and Ben's loaded and cocked pistol was still lying nearby on the floor. He still had too much to lose. He jerked his chin in the direction of the fallen weapon and barked, 'Kick away!'

Ben didn't move. 'I get it now,' he said. 'You had a tap on Shi Yun's phone, didn't you, Zhao? When Chang called her to arrange for Stefan and Lara to come here, you were listening in. Then when she wanted to go with them, you tracked her here from her mobile. You were using police resources, but you had your own private business to take care of.'

'Kick away!' Zhao yelled. The look was back in his eyes. This guy was still quite prepared to kill her if Ben didn't do as he said.

So Ben obeyed, and kicked the fallen pistol away from him. It slid clunking across the floorboards and bumped against the wall. He said to Zhao, 'Now I can't get to it. Let her go.'

But Stefan looked as if he wanted to make a dive for the pistol, with his one good arm. Ben saw his friend hovering on the brink and warned him, 'Stefan, no. He'll shoot you.'

Zhao's ugly face split open in a leer of triumph. 'Yes. I shoot him. I shoot you all.'

'Because you're one of them,' Ben said. 'You were one of them all along. Taking your orders from the same corrupt gang of butchers who murdered Dan Chen and Olivia Keller. Getting your cut of every stolen organ they sell on the black market. Hiring crooks to do your dirty work, like this lot here and the ones who tried to take us out in Xi'an. You killed Sammy Tsang.'

'And now I kill you,' Zhao said with a sneer.

'Go for it, Chief,' Ben said.

A witness to the scene might have thought Ben's composure a little out of place, under the circumstances. That his whole demeanour and tone of voice were strangely calm and collected. And that he was talking too much for someone in his position, who was about to take a bullet and unable to do the damnedest thing to prevent it. They might even have thought that Ben had lost his mind, that he no longer cared what happened to him or his companions.

Stefan and the others were probably all thinking the same. But that was only because they didn't understand that Ben was playing for time again. Except it wasn't a wing and a prayer like it had been moments earlier. Now Ben had a much more solid reason to be stalling for as long as he could. One that nobody else in the room knew about.

That was because all eyes in the room were fixated on him and the police chief, and nobody was paying attention to the front doorway.

The front doorway, through which the diminutive figure of the Sifu was creeping. He was silhouetted in the glare of the lights, all black apart from his wispy snow-white hair. He'd come gliding up the porch steps as silent as a ghost, barely seeming to even touch the floor. Now he was poised just a few steps behind Zhao. A coiled cobra about to strike. Totally calm, yet totally focused. Just the way he had been when Ben had first met him under the archway to the old temple.

And then, before anything else happened, before Zhao could pull the trigger or realise the danger that was coming up behind him, the Sifu struck.

The movement was so extraordinarily, uncannily rapid that it appeared like a film replay with several frames cut out of it, so that one moment the old man was here and the next he was there, with no visible transition between the two points. As for the physical contact that he made with his target, it happened so fleetingly and was over so instantly that Ben barely even had time to register it. Zhao's weapon seemed to fly out of his hand of its own accord and he staggered and convulsed on his feet as though he'd been hooked up to a high voltage cable. His grip on Shi Yun slackened and she wriggled away from him. Zhao's eyes were screwed shut in agony as he clapped a hand to the spot on his neck where the Sifu had struck him. He tried to scream, but the only sound from his mouth was a hoarse gasp. He whirled blindly around as if trying to lash out at some invisible enemy. Then his legs folded under him, he went totally limp and the boards juddered as he collapsed heavily to the floor and lay still.

By then, Ben had already scooped up his fallen pistol. Shi Yun had retrieved her own and cleared the stovepipe jam with a fast rack of the slide. They trained their weapons on Zhao's prone body, ready to pump him full of bullets if he tried to get up.

But the chief wasn't getting up.

Sifu T'ao had backed away a couple of steps and was standing there quite unruffled, impassively surveying his handiwork as if nothing at all out of the ordinary had happened. He nodded his head in a courteous little bow to Ben, maybe just the trace of a knowing smile on his lips. 'Just so,' he said.

'Is he dead?' Ben asked. He certainly looked dead.

The Sifu shook his white head. 'Not dead, but not alive. Dim Mak has drained all the Qi from his body. He is empty shell now.'

'Then we don't need to waste a shot on the pig,' said Shi Yun, looking down at him with disgust. She lowered her pistol. 'I can't believe he could have done this. How could I have been so blind?'

'The cop lady realises the error of her ways,' Song said with an acid laugh. She'd been shooting nasty looks at her ever since that afternoon, when it had slipped out what she did for a living.

Ben held Shi Yun tightly for a few moments, then went over to Chang and inspected his wounded arm. It was bleeding profusely, but the bullet had passed straight through the flesh without hitting bone. A basic field dressing would do until they got him to a doctor. Turning to the Sifu Ben said, 'I'll never understand these things you can do, Master. But I thank you.'

The old man smiled and gave another polite bow. 'If you stay in China, you become student, learn from me the ways of Dim Mak.'

'It'll have to wait for another time,' Ben replied.

Stefan was looking confusedly down at the inert, corpse-like Zhao. 'I never liked him. He was crude and horrible. But I never would have thought he was one of them.'

Ben nodded. 'Their inside man on the force, and not the only one in China, I'll bet. These bastards have their hooks in deep everywhere. Song, would you pass me that first aid kit?'

'Then it was not the police who found us tonight,' said Jun Ming, just now beginning to realise.

'No,' Ben replied. 'But all the same I suggest that the sooner we get the hell out of here, the better.'

Chapter 49

It was Stefan who suggested piling all the bodies in a single heap on the floor of the farmhouse and burning the place down around them to erase the evidence. Apart from the uncharacteristic gruesomeness of such an idea coming from his normally placid, peaceable future brother-in-law, Ben was against it on the grounds that a large fire could be seen from miles away through the night and might attract attention. By the time anyone discovered what had happened here tonight, they wanted to be long gone.

They quickly gathered up the remainder of their stores and piled them into the Range Rover, to be used on the journey out of China. By four a.m. they were speeding away, Ben at the wheel of the Rover and Shi Yun and Jun Ming driving the two other vehicles in which they'd come. The electric SUVs belonging to Chief Zhao's attack team had been dumped in a nearby field where nobody would find them for a long time.

The first priority now was to seek some proper medical attention for the wounded Chang. As dawn broke in all its glorious colours they arrived at a small village near Shuyan in Xianghe County, where some discreet enquiries led to the home of the local doctor. Dr Wu was semi-retired from medical practice and not especially thrilled to be dragged out of bed to see to an unexpected patient – even less so when he examined Chang's arm in the private consulting room adjoining his home.

'This is a gunshot wound,' he commented, looking suspiciously at the motley gang of the patient's friends.

'A hunting injury,' Shi Yun told him, as authoritatively as she could manage. Dr Wu was no fool, but whether he believed the story or not he agreed to do what he could. 'Though he should be in a hospital,' he kept repeating as he got to work. For payment, he turned down the thick wad of cash Chang offered him but was happy to accept his gold watch as a trade before ushering them out of his consulting room as quickly as he could.

With Chang properly patched up and dosed to the eyeballs on antibiotics and codeine, the time was fast approaching for the group to part ways. Saying goodbye was going to be hard, especially for Ben and Shi Yun. But that wasn't the worst difficulty they faced. Now there was the additional concern that the illegal tap Shi Yun's boss had placed on her phone might well have compromised their plans.

Pale and weak from blood loss but still perfectly lucid despite the drugs, Chang soberly advised them, 'I fear it may no longer be safe for you to make use of my company aircraft to cross southwards to Macau. As an alternative I suggest making the trip entirely by road instead. The G4 Beijing–Macau Expressway stretches for more than fourteen hundred miles due south as far as the border city of Shenzen. That takes you nearly all the way to your destination.'

'A long distance to drive in a hot car,' Song said dubiously.

'The Range Rover is untraceable to me,' Chang reassured her. 'Likewise I was intending to provide you with a credit card to safely, anonymously, pay the necessary motorway tolls en route, as well as buy fuel. The only real caveat is that you must get off the road before reaching the Port of Entry at Huanggang, which,' he explained for the benefit of the three foreigners, 'is an extensive customs control along China's southern border. Military guards rigorously check all vehicles and inspect the passports of every traveller in and out of Macau.'

'Then it's simply impossible to get out without being stopped,' Stefan said.

'Macau is connected to mainland China via a long bridge over the Pearl River,' Chang told them. 'That, too, is controlled. But there is another way. The newly extended campus of Macau University on Hengqin Island is accessible via a one-kilometre-long underwater road tunnel. It is unguarded and provides around-the-clock access to Macau bypassing immigration checks and customs. I happen to know this, as the crossing has been a magnet for illegal immigrants wanting to sneak into Macau from China in search of work, some of whom were employed in my casino. But I must warn you that the border guards are very well aware of the trick, and have installed security surveillance on the wall around the campus.'

'That still doesn't help us much,' Stefan complained. Both Lara and Song were tight-lipped and shaking their heads.

'We'll worry about it when we get there,' Ben said. 'In my experience there's always a way.'

'A way that leads straight to prison,' Song muttered. It was hard to blame her for having that on the brain.

'This may come in useful,' Chang said, handing them a small leather pouch. 'I had meant to give it to you earlier, before we were interrupted.'

Ben unzipped the pouch and looked inside. 'Jewellery?'

'Four luxury watches, all genuine Rolexes and much prized as status symbols here in China. There are some other assorted trinkets, gold rings and bracelets, and a small quantity of cut diamonds.'

Ben whistled. 'These must be worth a fortune.'

'A worthwhile expenditure. As you observed from our negotiations with the good Dr Wu earlier, cash bribes are all but useless in our country for the simple reason that nobody uses paper money any more – unlike in Japan where cash is still very much king. These items, however, may prove more persuasive.'

'We'll pay you back for all this,' said Stefan. 'Every penny, just as soon as we get home.'

'If my fears prove correct I might be in prison by then, my friend,' Chang replied with a rueful smile. 'In which case you would be well advised to act as though you were never associated with me.'

Now at last, the time had come to say goodbye. Shaking of hands, wishes of good luck. Ben thanked Sifu T'ao again for saving their lives, and reiterated his gratitude for everything Chang Han Yu had done. Song and her Falun Gong comrades embraced warmly and tearfully, in the hope they might meet again one day, and in better times. Lara hugged them too, the first time Ben had ever seen anyone so grateful to their kidnappers.

Now for the part he'd been most dreading. He held Shi Yun tight for a long moment. There was little more to be said between them, and to say anything much would have been too painful. 'I won't forget you,' was all she murmured. Then wiping a tear and giving him a last stoical smile that would be his memory of her for evermore, she got into the car. Moments later they were gone. Ben stood and watched until they disappeared. He sighed and lit a Gauloise. Stefan put a hand on his shoulder.

'Let's go,' Ben said. And then the journey southwards began.

It seemed counter-intuitive to head back eastwards towards the outskirts of Beijing where the authorities would still be tearing the place apart hunting for them, but it had to be done in order to pick up the G4 Expressway. It wasn't quite the same as zapping south on a nice private jet, but flying safely below the radar in an untraceable vehicle and armed with Chang's magic credit card for toll fees, the fugitives at least had little immediate concern of being stopped by the police.

They joined the vast, broad and bustling expressway to the south of the city and soon settled into the rhythm. Fourteen hundred or so miles equated to something like a twenty-hour drive ahead of them. Ben would be taking the wheel for most of the way, sharing now and then with Song as neither Lara nor Stefan, with his arm in plaster, could drive.

The first fifty miles, then a hundred, then two hundred, went by peacefully. The big, comfortable Rover was the kind of car you could just lounge back in and drive with one toe on the gas and two fingers on the wheel, munching up the miles without the least effort. After spending so much time planning and discussing every detail of the journey it was a welcome relief in some ways to speed along in silence, but left to his own devices Ben found his thoughts kept returning to Shi Yun. He fretted about what could happen to her now, largely thanks to the fact that she'd ever been unlucky enough to meet this total stranger called Ben Hope. Another part of him worried about the welcome that Chang Han Yu might receive when he returned home. They would never have made it without his help and the thought of him losing everything and ending up in jail was tough to bear.

Meanwhile Song, slumped in the front passenger seat, was preoccupied with her own concerns and spent her time turned towards the window, gazing idly at the traffic. Stefan dozed on and off in the back seat, while Lara sat quietly beside her brother, looking dreamy as she thought ahead to being reunited with the rest of her family in two or three days' time. If the journey went smoothly, once she was home and able to get back on with her life her short sojourn in China would eventually fade to no more than a heartbreaking memory.

If it didn't go smoothly, then maybe they'd all end up being shot to pieces or arrested and facing spending the remainder of their days in a labour camp. That was, if they weren't trucked directly to some secret medical facility where they'd be slaughtered, eviscerated and their organs packed into refrigerated boxes for immediate delivery to transplant recipients in hospitals all over East Asia.

Whether or not Lara was fully aware of that possibility, Ben couldn't tell, and it wasn't a subject he'd have wanted to mention to her. He could imagine what Jeff Dekker would have to say about it, though: 'Christ, I feel sorry for the poor bugger who ends up being given *your* liver, mate.'

Ben had to smile at that.

On and on, and the hours rolled by, along with signs for Shijiazhuang, Handan, Zhengzhou, Xinjang and the various other cities they passed by as they cut south through Hebei, Henan and Hubei Provinces. The expressway wasn't the longest in the world by any means, nor even the longest in China – but it had to be one of the busiest, all eight lanes constantly crammed with traffic. Ben stayed right on the edge of the 75mph speed limit wherever possible, except for when the road widened out to an incredible fifty lanes for the inevitable walking-pace snarl-up of toll controls, an endless ocean of motor vehicles like nothing he'd ever seen before. The magic credit card worked fine, and they cruised through the tolls without trouble.

Gradually, almost imperceptibly, the landscape changed around them. By mid-afternoon the sunshine and blue sky had turned to a leaden grey with a fine, steady drizzle. They'd planned on travelling more or less nonstop, eating and drinking on the hoof from their stock of provisions and pausing only for fuel or the occasional switch of drivers. Ben had always travelled light when it came to food, finding that an empty stomach kept his wits sharper. Out of habit he preferred instead to run his motor on cigarettes and coffee and hold out for a proper meal at the end of the day. Coffee was the one commodity he was sadly lacking in this instance, but he still had a few Gauloises left and fired one up now and then, cracking the window an inch out of courtesy for his passengers.

The smell of tobacco smoke lulled Song out of another of her long spells of thoughtful silence and she said, 'I'll have another of those if you can spare it.'

'Looks like you're getting to like them,' he said, lighting one for her.

'It's just to keep my nerves from falling apart. I'll kick the habit when I get to America.'

'Remember what they say,' he reminded her, 'about the road to hell being paved with good intentions.'

'Ha. I know all about the road to hell,' she said with a dark chuckle. 'I was on it a long time.'

'Let's hope we're on a better one now.'

She looked at him more seriously with the cigarette halfway to her lips. 'You think we'll make it?'

'So far, so good. Don't you?'

She shrugged her shoulders, sucked on the Gauloise and blew out a puff of smoke. 'I can't help but think this is all too easy somehow. And there are things about Chang's plan I don't like.'

'If you have other ideas, I'm open to suggestions,' he said.

'I'm working on it.'

She finished her cigarette and fell silent again. Ben drove on. He'd been watching the fuel gauge for a while; now as the Rover's gargantuan tank started threatening to run empty, a sign flashed past for a fuel station and he decided it was time to stop and refill, stretch their legs and maybe grab that much-needed coffee. As the exit came up they pulled off the expressway and rolled into the crowded services.

And it was at the fuel stop that their peaceful journey came to an end and everything suddenly unravelled.

Chapter 50

Stefan and Lara were fast asleep in the back of the car, touchingly resting against one another like a couple of kids. While Ben filled up the Rover, Song climbed out and offered to see if she could find a coffee machine. 'You must have read my mind,' he said, smiling. She smiled back and pushed inside the filling station shop, a miniature mall crowded with shoppers.

Ben finished topping up the tank, moved the car on a few yards to let the next vehicle in line pull up at the pump, then went into the shop after her. The in-store sound system was playing some kind of synthetic Far Eastern pop music that he automatically closed his ears to. He spotted Song among the shoppers and went over to join her. 'There's what we need,' she said brightly, pointing back towards a row of dispensing machines in the far corner.

Ben was happy to see her much more relaxed now than before the start of the journey. Even despite the prison-issue cropped hair and the ravages of her long, lonely incarceration visibly stamped on her face she was a different person. The promise of freedom was beckoning to her and a glow of optimism was gradually spreading through her with every hour she got closer to her new life. He used Chang's credit card to pay for the fuel, and then the pair of them made their way through the throng to the coffee dispensing machine. No coin slots, card only. Welcome to Planet Dystopia. 'How do you like

344

it?' he asked her, picking from the different varieties on offer. 'Strong and black and in the biggest cup possible,' she replied eagerly.

'A woman after my own heart.' Another swipe of the magic card, and the machine glugged thin dark liquid into two foam cups.

'After all these months I'd almost forgotten what coffee tasted like,' she joked at her first sip of the stuff. 'I still don't remember.'

'Pretty grim,' he agreed. 'But better than what they give you in the British army.'

'Shall we get some for the others?'

'I think Lara's more the decaf type,' he said, but Song didn't seem to get his meaning, replying innocently, 'Oh, is she?'

'I'd say she has the look. You can always tell them.'

'That's a pity. She seems like a nice girl.'

It felt good to spend a couple of minutes joking around and exchanging casual banter, like normal folks. But while the two of them were talking and sipping their coffee there in the corner by the machines, they didn't notice the kid watching them from over next to the magazine stand. Especially watching Song.

He was maybe twelve or thirteen years old, morbidly overweight and clutching a tablet device near his chest as though someone had glued it to his hands. He kept glancing at it, and then back at her, and then back at the screen. Whatever he was seeing there, it was making him frown and scowl more deeply every time he looked. A short, corpulent woman who presumably was his mother was grazing the magazine shelves nearby. After a couple more peeks at his tablet the kid turned to her and started insistently tugging at her sleeve in that annoying way of attention-seeking children everywhere. Having managed to distract her, he whispered something in her ear and began pointing a chubby finger, as if to say, 'Over there, see? It's her.'

The woman's gaze followed the kid's pointing finger. She seemed about to dismiss him with some line like 'Don't be so silly, she doesn't look anything like her.' But then she did a double-take at the tablet he was shoving towards her face. Glanced again at Song.

Now she was wearing the same perplexed frown as her kid. She waddled a few steps over to the even more overweight man who presumably was her husband, and prodded his fat arm. He looked up from the copy of *China Auto News* he'd been browsing through, confused at first as his wife jabbered and pointed, then stared across the room at the woman she was going on about. He grabbed the tablet from the kid, studied it for a moment, looked up again at the real-life version of the prison mugshot the state media had plastered all over the internet, and his expression hardened. He replaced the magazine on its shelf and, with a determined spring to his stride, hurried over to have a whispered conversation with the shop manager at the counter. More covert looks, more frowning and pointing. Then the manager got out his phone. As they got wind something was up, others began to turn and gawk.

By now Ben's sixth sense had already started tingling again. The cluster of people gathered over by the counter and paying him and Song an unnatural amount of attention had grown into a small crowd. The shop manager was jabbering urgently to someone on his phone, though from this distance it was impossible to hear what he was saying even if Ben had understood

Chinese. He drained his cup, tossed it into a nearby litter bin and told Song, 'Come on, we're out of here.'

'What's up?'

'I get the feeling you're a little too famous to be walking around in public,' he replied.

'Must be the hairstyle.' Song dumped her half-finished coffee and they started walking quickly towards the exit. The manager watched them coming with a look of alarm, put away his phone and stepped out from behind the counter, hand raised and talking to them loudly. Song's reply to him didn't sound too polite. Ben waved the guy aside, but he'd clearly decided it was his duty to play the hero and he tried to block them at the exit.

Ben didn't know the Chinese expression for 'Kindly get out of the way, sir,' but he was willing to go about this as nicely as possible to avoid a scene. That was, until he spotted the two burly security men in quasi-police uniforms and carrying side-handle batons come banging through an inner door and surging towards them. And so he grabbed the manager by the scruff of the neck, spun him around and sent him spinning into the two guards. All three went down like bowling pins. The fat kid's mother let out a shrill shriek as they sprawled at her feet. The kid's father was yelling and shaking his fist. Half a dozen other people in the crowd were taking out their phones, and it wasn't hard to guess who they were calling.

'That's the thing about being a wanted fugitive,' Song commented dryly as they burst out of the shop doors and ran back towards the Range Rover. 'You can't go anywhere without getting hassled.'

'What's happening?' Stefan cried out, jolted awake as they bundled into the car.

'Place has bad coffee,' Ben replied. He fired up the engine, slammed into drive and the Rover's tyres squealed as they took off towards the services exit. But already the wail of police sirens could be heard rapidly approaching, and they weren't too far away.

'Buckle up your seatbelts, everyone. We're about to have company.'

Chapter 51

Ben went storming out of the services and sped back towards the expressway, in the hope that they could filter back into the heavy traffic and be out of there by the time the cops appeared. Everything that had just happened would have been caught on camera, of course, and now they were a marked target once again – but there might still be a chance.

Then that chance slipped away out of reach before it even existed, because as Ben hit the roundabout from the services slipway the flashing blue lights of two patrol cars were already fast approaching from the direction of the expressway. They must have been close by when they received the radio alert. Lucky for them, but inconvenient timing for Ben and his fellow fugitives. Lara and Stefan were craning their necks to stare in alarm out of the rear window. 'They're coming!'

Ben didn't need to be told that. What he needed to think about was how to evade them, and there didn't seem to be too many options. The expressway was out; he hurtled around the roundabout looking for a different exit, and saw one racing up towards them. It was blocked off with traffic cones and big red signs that you didn't have to understand Chinese to know said CONSTRUCTION AREA – ROAD CLOSED. Beyond the cone barrier was a scene of intensive activity, mechanical diggers rolling back and forth on their caterpillar treads, a giant tipper truck dumping a black mountain of gravel, a lorry spreading hot tar and a small army of busy workers in yellow jackets and hard hats.

Maybe not the ideal escape route. But Ben took it anyway, blasting through the cones and scattering them in all directions. Beside him Song was yelling, '*Are you crazy? This road doesn't go anywhere!*'

Behind them, the two police cars had spotted their target and were skidding off the roundabout in pursuit with their sirens wailing. Ben accelerated through the construction zone, flattening a sign and forcing a group of workers to dive out of the way. There were about a hundred yards of road ahead before another row of cones and a barrier closed it off at the far end. What lay beyond that, he had no idea but reckoned he'd soon find out. If they made it that far. One of the mechanical digger operators, unaware of what was happening, was lumbering across their path towards the mountain of gravel at the rear of the tipper truck. With no other way through and no time for hesitation, Ben stamped harder on the gas and headed straight for the closing gap.

Too narrow. It was a choice of whether to crash into the massive front end of the digger, or the gravel. Ben chose the gravel. The Range Rover hit it with its two offside wheels and the car tilted violently up sideways at a crazy angle as loose stones hammered their underside like cannon fire. He gritted his teeth and ploughed on – not that he could stop now – hoping that if it didn't tear off their steering gear, suspension and exhaust system they might be able to get through. And they did, with the Rover still tilted up on two wheels. In their wake the leading police car had tried for the gap but smashed into the heap in an explosion of gravel. The second, almost too close behind to avoid piling straight into its rear, had somehow managed to swerve around the digger and was still in the chase. One down, one to go.

The Rover slammed back down onto four wheels, throwing its terrified passengers around inside. They'd made it, but now they were fast running out of road as the cones and barriers at the far end of the unfinished section came racing up towards them. All Ben could see after that point was grass and dirt, but worrying about it wouldn't do any good. They smashed through the flimsy barriers; and now Ben found out what lay beyond them as the Rover's front end dropped into empty space. Not over the edge of a cliff, but down the near-vertical slope of the earth embankment on which the new elevated road section was being built.

When Ben had asked Chang for a car with off-road capabilities, this wasn't quite what he'd had in mind. It was all he could do to stop them from skidding out of control as they went careering down the loose dirt incline, tyres scrabbling for grip. The worst thing to do would have been to touch the brakes.

Meanwhile the surviving police car had reached the brink of the drop. In his desperation to catch their quarry its driver flew off the edge with all four wheels airborne, twisted in flight and hit the dirt at a bad angle that sent it cartwheeling and rolling and flipping down the side of the embankment. If it had landed on its wheels without wrecking its chassis it might have had a hope of keeping going. Instead it came down with a crunch on its roof, wheels spinning and the note of the siren dying in an off-key wail.

The Rover had a better landing, though only just, and their luck didn't hold out for long. The terrain at the foot of the slope was so rough and craggy that not even the best off-road car and driver could have negotiated it. They crashed blindly over a series of deep ruts, flew over an earth hump that acted like a ramp and then came down again into a nest of rocks hidden in the long rushes, which flung the vehicle over sideways.

They rolled once and came to a final halt still upright but astride a mound that lifted their wheels off the ground, stuck like a ship on a reef.

'That's one way of doing it,' Song muttered. A glance around the inside of the car told Ben that nobody had suffered worse than a shaking up. 'End of the line. Everyone out.'

The four of them grabbed what they could and jumped free of the stranded Rover. 'Which way from here?' Stefan asked.

Ben had no idea where to head, except to keep putting distance between themselves and the expressway before more police arrived on the scene. They set off at a run, stumbling over ruts and boulders and tearing through the tall grass. Another digger sat empty on the rough ground nearby, surrounded by various bits and pieces of construction material. For a wild moment Ben toyed with the idea of getting the thing started and driving off in it. Then he saw the mouth of the pipe.

It was a huge corrugated metal drainage culvert, six feet in diameter, that the road construction crew had been laying in preparation for the thousands of tons of rock and earth needed to finish the embankment. Much of it had already been buried into the ground, with the remaining section protruding like some monstrous worm coming up for air. Another wild thought came into Ben's mind as he remembered what Jun Ming had told him about the tunnels the first emperor of China had built to allow him to travel about underground, where the evil spirits couldn't get to him.

No evil spirits around here. Just an awful lot of police, who might be about to turn up at any moment.

'That's where we're going,' he said to Stefan, pointing at the mouth of the culvert pipe.

'Where do you suppose it leads?'

'Away from here,' Ben replied. 'That's good enough for me.'

'Me too,' said Song. But Lara stood with folded arms and shook her head in refusal. 'I'm not going in there.'

'Oh yes, you are, baby sister,' Stefan said, grabbing her wrist and yanking her along.

'There might be rats!'

'It's a drain, not a sewer. Now come on.'

Ben went first. It was like stepping into a cave, or a giant pothole. There was more than enough headroom for him, and he was the tallest. The daylight penetrated into the pipe for a dozen or so yards before it receded into total darkness. This time he had no flaming torch to light the way, but the curving sides made it easy enough to follow the direction of the tunnel by feel alone while its dry bottom, new enough to be still free of drainage water or mud, allowed for reasonably rapid progress.

Lara had stopped protesting and focused instead on keeping moving. Their footsteps and voices echoed in the claustrophobic space. No telling how deep underground they might be now, what might be sitting right above them or what they might find at the end.

If there *was* an end. After thirty minutes' uncertain progress through the hot, airless and highly claustrophobic darkness Ben was beginning to worry about having led them, quite literally, down a blind alley from which there might be no escape without having to turn back – or worse, much worse, in which they'd find themselves trapped by police blocking their only exit. But soon afterwards, having grown almost used to the total blackness, he suddenly realised he could dimly make out the line of the pipe wall where it curved around some fifty metres ahead.

Light at the end of the tunnel. Maybe some crazy notions weren't so crazy, after all.

Chapter 52

Emerging from the mouth of the culvert pipe, blinking in the light, they found themselves surrounded by a wide expanse of scrubby, hilly wasteland. This end of the pipe emerged from deep under a tall earth mound piled up months ago by the road construction engineers and now green with sprouted grass and weeds. Ben ran up to the top of the mound and could see the G4 expressway and the part-finished new raised section in the far distance. As he'd been hoping and betting, the half-built drain had brought them a long way. But there was still much further to go before they reached safety. The lights and sirens of a massed police response were dimly visible and audible even from this distance.

He ran back down to join the others. 'Let's keep moving.'

Now began the long trek across country, in the hopes of picking up an alternative and more minor route on which to continue their journey southwards, as well as some kind of vehicle to carry them along it. Ben might be a stranger in a strange land but he'd nonetheless been here many times before, on all those occasions when he and his SAS units had been deployed deep in the hostile territory of whatever war zone they happened to have been dropped into, living on their wits and completely reliant on their own initiative to find the essentials of shelter, food and transportation. He'd become pretty adept at stealing cars, trucks, anything with four wheels that could possibly be made to go, even for short distances.

That said, those had been mostly undeveloped countries, disorganised at the best of times and further plunged by conflict and invasion into a state of chaos, where enemy forces were often scattered and leaderless and the local populations frequently quite amenable to giving assistance to the foreign troops they saw as liberators. With skill and guile you could cover hundreds of miles without so much as a bump with the enemy, always one step ahead of being detected. The situation he was in now, leading a rag-tag bunch of fugitives one of whom was a hotly-sought escaped 'terrorist' through what was probably the most tightly-controlled and organised police state in the world, was maybe a little more challenging.

Hours went by, and as they cut roughly southwards mile after mile through the open countryside Ben was glad of the daylight fading. Dusk found them scrambling down a steep, tree-dotted riverbank and following the course of the river until they came to a natural rock cleft with an overhang where they could make camp for the night and even risk a small fire for when the temperature dropped through the hours of darkness. They ate the last of the tinned provisions they'd brought with them from the safehouse and slept huddled under their blankets beneath the shelter of their rocky ledge. Roughing it to this extreme was coming as a shock to someone like Lara, and to a lesser extent her brother; for Song, it was paradise in comparison to the living death she'd left behind and the even worse fate she'd faced before her escape.

Come first light they were on the move again, still following the course of the river as it meandered more or less due south. They trudged in single file over the flinty, pebbly shale along the edge of the eastern shore, sometimes having to wade through areas of marsh or clamber over fallen trees, carrying their remaining water and bedding rolls, pausing now and then for

Ben to check their direction, speaking little. For hundreds of thousands of years humans had been building their settlements near water – and so sooner or later, Ben expected them to come to a village where they could stock up on provisions. Better still, find transport to enable them to resume their journey.

And so he wasn't too surprised when, around mid-morning, the side of a wooden building became visible among the trees a little way up the slope of the opposite bank. Crossing the shallow river by means of some handy stepping stones, they climbed the slope to investigate, and found the dilapidated wooden shack was one of several scattered around a little rustic house.

'Doesn't look lived in,' Stefan whispered at Ben's shoulder as they peered cautiously through the foliage. Ben was inclined to agree at first, but then a movement caught his eye: a reddish-brown chicken stalking across the yard in front of the little house. It was joined a moment later by another that came strutting from one of the wooden sheds, this one a big fine cockerel with a proud multicoloured tail, which chose the moment to let out a loud crowing. The next of the holding's inhabitants to appear was a stooped old man. He was carrying a bucket of feed and dressed in dirty dungarees, boots and a straw hat. He might have been around the same age as Sifu T'ao, but aged and broken down by comparison.

Ben stepped out of the trees and advanced to meet him, followed by the others. Suddenly spotting them, the old man froze staring, then came to life and started yelling at the strangers in a reedy, frail voice.

'He says we're trespassing on his land,' Song said. 'Telling us to go away.'

In a country like China it was unlikely that the old guy could run inside the house and fetch a shotgun to start peppering them with. But the situation was delicate, because even if he lived like a medieval peasant he was bound to have a phone and it was all they needed for him to call the police. Ben was thinking what they could tell him to calm him down, when he noticed the ancient truck parked by one of the other sheds. It was at least forty years old, streaked with dirt and rust, with a battered aluminium hard top bolted to its flatbed and filled with straw.

'Ask him if we can buy that,' Ben said to Song.

'Who the hell would want it?'

'Just ask him.'

Song relayed the question in Chinese. The old guy put down his bucket and approached a few steps, deeply wary of them especially when he scrutinised them more closely and saw that three were foreigners. His face was as wrinkled as a dried prune. No, was his reply to Song. That was his only truck and he needed it for taking his chickens to market. But he seemed intrigued at the thought of getting some money, and hovered there as though expecting them to say more.

Ben took out the pouch that Chang had given them, unzipped it and fished out a glittering two-tone steel and gold Rolex that he held up to show the old man. 'Tell him that for the value of this watch he could afford to buy himself a much better truck. And a new pair of boots without holes in.'

The old man didn't seem to require a translation. His eyes glittered as brightly as the watch as he stared hungrily at it for a moment, before he came out with another stream of Chinese.

'He says he has a wife,' Song said.

Ben had expected there'd be some haggling involved. 'Fine,' he replied, and took out a smaller lady's watch from the pouch. 'Then the good lady will love this.'

Another long, hungry look, another quick-fire burst of words. 'And he's also got five daughters,' Song translated, rolling her eyes. 'The eldest is sixteen and the youngest is seven. They all need something too.'

'The greedy old—' Stefan began indignantly, but Ben shushed him. He said, 'No problem. There are rings and gold chains and all kinds of baubles here. Something for everyone.'

Instead of being pleased, the old guy appeared warier than ever as though this offer must be too good to be true. Song spent a few moments reassuring him, and he seemed placated. 'But for that price,' Ben said, 'it's only fair that we should get more than just the truck. We need a driver, too.'

After a quick exchange Song reported, 'He says okay, maybe. But he wants to know where we're going.'

'South,' Ben said, pointing upriver through the trees. 'But not on the expressway. We stick to the back roads.'

The old guy took a little more persuading, but after a few more rounds of dialogue with Song interpreting, the deal was done. Ben shook his skinny, frail hand and said with a smile, 'My name's Ben. What's yours?'

'He's Li Feng,' said Song.

'Nice to meet you, Li Feng. Now how soon can we get going?'

'He says what about the stuff?'

'He can have it after, once the job is done.'

Old Li Feng accepted that condition readily enough. Nor did it appear to bother him one jot that this whole arrangement had to be highly suspect. He disappeared into the house for a while, and from outside they could hear raised voices. Then Li Feng re-emerged wearing an old tattered coat over his dungarees and dangling a set of keys, and ushered them all over to the truck.

'Surely you don't expect us to get inside that thing,' Lara complained as she peered with distaste into the covered flatbed.

'It stinks. And everything's covered in filth. Oh my God, it's not just filth, it's *chicken shit!*'

'Shut up, girl,' snapped Song, whose tolerance had been gradually wearing thin. 'What price do you put on your freedom? If your pretty little dress gets dirty you can buy yourself a nice new one in a fashion boutique in Taipei.'

In any case, after their long march along the river Lara was already fairly well muddied and bedraggled. But she was quite right about the chicken shit, which was liberally smeared over most surfaces of the truck inside and out, and gave Ben a new idea. He said, 'Song, tell Li Feng that if he's got a few crates of live poultry he can load in with us, that'll earn him an extra diamond ring for his lovely wife.'

Needless to say it was soon taken care of, with the four clandestine passengers ensconced at the front of the flatbed and well hidden from view by several stacked cratefuls of squawking birds. Li Feng grabbed another loose hen from the yard for good measure, stuffed the poor flapping, struggling creature into the last crate very much against her will, and closed up the rusty tailgate. Lara was no more pleased than the hen, but she sat glowering in silence. Then Li Feng clambered cheerfully into the front cab, the engine fired into life with a choking gasp, and they were on their way again.

Chapter 53

As agreed, Li Feng's route kept strictly to the most minor rural roads. His rattly, smoky truck didn't seem capable of anything over forty miles an hour anyhow, and it would have been positively dangerous to venture into the speeding traffic of the expressway. By the opposite token, anything more than 40mph would have threatened to shake them to pieces as they crashed and lurched over road ruts and potholes that felt as if they were the size of asteroid craters.

Ben had travelled in a lot worse, though, and he was content enough. Whether riding in a private jet or a shitty old poultry wagon, as long as he sensed he was making progress it was all much the same to him. But not all the passengers were happy with the new mode of transport. Even Stefan, who until now had been quite willing to go with the flow, began to grumble. 'This is terrible. We're supposed to travel all the way to Macau in this thing?'

'I doubt that Li Feng's willing or able to take us that far,' Ben said. 'We'll stay with him as long as we can, then we'll improvise something else for the rest of the way. We still have a couple of watches and a few trinkets left.'

That settled the argument for now, and for the next couple of hours nobody spoke again – not that it was easy to speak anyway, over the rattle of the exhaust, the rasp of the engine and the constant clucking and squawking of their avian co-passengers. Ben slipped into a troubled reverie, casting his mind ahead to the most critical point of their journey, when

360

they'd have to make that all-important crossing of the southern Chinese border.

He'd been sitting there for a long time working through every imaginable detail of the plan when he suddenly realised he could no longer feel the bumps and lurches of the truck. Peering ahead through the dusty back window of the cab he saw that, sometime during his protracted period of concentration, Li Feng had turned onto a slightly more major road enabling them to press on more smoothly at a breakneck forty-five. At this fantastic rate of travel they might even reach their destination this month. Stefan caught Ben's eye and gave him a thumbs-up.

But minutes later, nobody was smiling as Li Feng came over the brow of a hill and was confronted by a police road block that was stopping and checking all traffic on the road. The truck slowed to a crawl, then to a halt. Ben and his three companions shrank right down low in the back, up close to the mouldy dirty straw that covered the flatbed floor. Stefan looked at Ben. Ben put a finger to his lips and shot a warning look at Lara. *Not a sound.*

Vehicle doors. The crackle and fizz of police radios. Voices: a stream of terse, harsh commands in Chinese, followed by Li Feng's reedy, warbly reply from the truck cab. Would the old chicken farmer have figured out the obvious by now, that his mysterious passengers were wanted criminals on the run? Would the promise of the goodies they'd offered him outweigh his fear of the police? Would he crack under the pressure? The next few moments would tell.

Ben tensed as he heard footsteps walking around the side of the truck and pause at its rear. The rusty scrape of the tailgate catches; then the gate opened with a creak. From where Ben was lying inert against the stinking straw he had a partial view through the bars of the poultry crates and the chickens inside of the cop's face peering into the back of the truck. He was a pimply youth of only nineteen or twenty, with his cap pulled down low over his brow and a uniform coat a size too large for him. A submachine pistol hung from its sling over his shoulder. Alarmed by his appearance, the caged birds started up their noisy squawking and clucking. The young cop pulled a face at the pungent mixed aroma of chicken shit and mouldy straw wafting out at him. Then apparently deciding he'd seen and smelled enough, he closed up the tailgate and returned to report the all-clear to his superiors.

It seemed as though their camouflage had worked. Moments later, the cops waved Li Feng on and the truck pulled away from the checkpoint. The note of the diesel returned to its monotonous nasal drone as they gradually picked up speed again. Good old Li Feng had come through for them.

'That was too damn close for comfort,' Stefan muttered when anyone dared to speak again. Song slowly let out the breath she'd been holding the whole time. Lara was shaking.

'You know, I've been thinking about what I'd do if they caught us,' Song declared over the noise of the truck. 'And I've decided that I'd let them shoot me before I'd ever go back to jail. I mean it.'

'It didn't come to that,' Ben replied.

'Not this time, but it could again. And I've been thinking about something else, too. You asked me what was wrong with Chang's plan about getting into Macau? Well, here's what I think. Chang's a hero. He's risked everything for me, and I'll always love him for that. But as much as I hate to say it, if he's been compromised like he's worried he has, then the chances are that so has his casino buddy in Macau. Which means if we make contact with him there, or if we try to board that ship, we could be walking straight into a trap.'

Ben nodded. In truth, she was only echoing the same misgivings he'd been having himself. He said, 'I'm listening.'

'It gets worse,' Song went on. 'To begin with, the Pearl River bridge crossing to get into Macau in the first place will be massively guarded. And I don't like the Macau University Campus idea much either. True, it *used* to be a weak point for people slipping in and out of China illegally, but the border control authorities have been wise to it for years and I've heard too many stories of people getting arrested trying that route. The embankment all around the university wall is four metres high and you have to swim across a moat to even get to it, and that's before you even have to deal with all the surveillance cameras.' She shrugged. 'Well, I can deal with a lot. Seeing people shot dead in front of me, I can handle. I'm okay with crashing cars and running through underground drainpipes. I don't even mind sitting in a heap of rotting chicken manure. But there's one thing I can't do, guys, aside from ever spending another day in a cell, and that's swim. Not even just a short distance. I'll drown. Or I'll get caught. Either way I'll be a corpse.'

'You only thought of all this now?' Ben asked her.

'I wanted to get away,' she replied simply. 'More than anything. And any sort of plan would have sounded okay to me at that moment. But now the closer we get to the end point, the more it scares me that I won't make it.'

'I agree, I don't like it either,' Stefan said.

'Nor me,' Lara chimed in.

Ben said, 'All right. Assuming we agree to scrap the Macau plan, what does that leave us with?'

'There's another possible way,' Song said, leaning closer.

'Then you'd better tell us about it,' Ben replied. 'This is your country, after all.'

Chapter 54

Song said, 'The narrowest point between mainland China and Taiwan is from the coast of Fujian Province. If we could keep heading further south to, say, around Wuhan and then cut eastwards towards the coastline, we could get to Fujian in just a day's drive or so. It's probably about nine hundred kilometres, give or take.'

'I don't think I can stand being in this truck for another nine hundred kilometres,' Lara said.

'Assuming it would get that far,' Stefan said.

Ben asked Song, 'Okay, then what?'

'In the circles I move in, I've known quite a few political dissidents who got into trouble with the Chinese government. One of them was a young man called Zhou Haibo.'

'Another of your Falun Gong people?'

Song shook her head. 'Just your ordinary run-of-the-mill human rights activist, who was persecuted after being involved in anti-government protests in Hong Kong and became scared of what might happen to him if he didn't get out of China. That's how I know about the crossing from Fujian Province, because a few years ago he was able to make it from a small fishing port over the Taiwan Strait in a rubber dinghy. It's only about a hundred and thirty kilometres.'

Stefan brightened up a little. 'So he escaped?'

'Only for a while. In the end he was arrested and deported back to China.'

'But I thought Taiwan was safe,' Lara said.

'Even so, the Taiwanese authorities don't like to stir things up too much with the mainland. But the fact is that he got caught. And we're too smart to let that happen to us. Aren't we?'

Ben looked at her. 'You can't swim, and you want to cross the Taiwan Strait in a dinghy.'

'It doesn't have to be a dinghy,' she argued. 'And the whole point of a boat is that you don't *have* to swim. Or am I missing something?'

Ben said nothing.

'It's the best option we have,' Song insisted, seeing the sceptical look on his face.

'There is one slight problem with it,' Ben said. 'Which is that relations between the two countries haven't been too hot lately. A lot of military experts reckon China might be set to invade before too long. And thanks to the heightened tensions, those waters are full of Chinese warships patrolling up and down the coastline. It's tricky.'

'But still worth trying,' she replied.

'Anything's worth trying, as long as you're prepared to take the risks.'

'I am. Are you?'

'I'm the reckless lunatic who jumps out of helicopters and breaks people out of prison in the middle of Beijing, gets into shootouts with rogue cops and smashes up every car he gets behind the wheel of. My opinion doesn't count for much.'

She smiled. 'Then the other three of us take a vote on it. Agreed?'

'Fine by me. Stefan?'

'It's only a hundred and thirty kilometres,' Stefan said. 'Open water, no border checks. As long as we can avoid those warships we're home free. I say we go for it.'

Song nodded and looked at Lara. 'That makes two in favour. The deciding vote is yours.'

Lara hesitated, pursed her lips, looked down at her hands. 'I just want to get out of here and go home. I want to see my family again. If that's the best way, then I'll vote for it.'

The joys of democracy. 'Then it's decided,' Song said. 'We go to Fujian Province.'

But it soon turned out that Lara wasn't the only one who didn't relish the thought of such a long trip in the old truck. A few miles later, Li Feng pulled off the road, got out of his cab and poked his head through the tailgate to tell them he'd come far enough and was anxious to get back. Ben couldn't blame the old guy, and was thankful for the way he'd got them through the checkpoint. They disembarked, paid him his dues and he turned the truck around and set off back the way they'd come, leaving a haze of diesel fumes and some drifting feathers in his wake.

'Well, that's that,' Stefan said as the four of them stood there on the empty road. 'Anyone have any ideas as to how we go from here?'

'Look,' said Lara. She pointed through some straggly trees that lined the roadside. Above them in the distance, something that appeared like a sooty black cloud was hovering across the otherwise clear sky, leaving a slowly dispersing trail in its wake. Except it wasn't a cloud.

'It's a train,' Ben said.

By the time they'd crossed the small patch of woods that separated the road from the railway line, the smoky diesel locomotive had rattled on by and all that could be seen was the last of its cars disappearing up the track. It was moving slowly, but not so slowly that they'd be able to catch up at a run. 'We missed it,' Song said, pulling a face.

'It was a goods train,' Ben said, looking around him. 'And this looks to be a well-maintained line that gets a lot of use. With any luck another might come by before too long.'

Which turned out to be an optimistic statement, because it wasn't until six hours later that the tired, hungry and thirsty group of hikers following the railway track roughly southwards heard the faraway rumble growing slowly but steadily louder behind them. They ducked into the trees to the side of the tracks and waited for the train to come into view. It was moving so slowly that it took a long time to appear; and when it did, they saw it was another goods train like the first, pulled along by the old-fashioned kind of locomotive that was almost obsolete now anywhere else but developing countries in Asia. Its carriages were the antiquated wooden box wagons with sliding doors, the type that had been used for over a hundred years to carry everything from coal and iron ore to sheep and cattle.

The four of them stayed hidden in the trees until most of the carriages had come rolling lazily past, wheels clickety-clacking on the rails. Then Ben said, 'Now!' and they burst out from hiding and ran along the track. Ben hopped on first, yanking open a boxcar door to find it was carrying a load of steel cable, with enough room for them to squeeze in. He held out a hand for Song as she hurried after the train, grabbed her and swung her aboard. Then Lara, and finally Stefan, who with his arm in a sling had to grab a hold one-handed and nearly stumbled and went under the wheels.

'Welcome to our home for the next few hours,' Ben told them. 'Sorry it's not too comfortable.'

'Could have been a lot worse,' Song commented. 'As in radioactive waste or explosive chemicals.'

'Or chickens,' Lara added.

'The question is where it'll take us,' Stefan said, peering out of the boxcar's single-barred window at the countryside rolling by.

'The big industrial belt of Central China is mostly to the south of here,' Song said quite confidently. 'Places like Wuhan, where they're very big on aerospace, building satellites, biotechnology, 5G telecommunications and who knows what else. My guess is this train is heading for that area.'

'Then all we have to do is ride along,' Ben said.

Wherever it was going, the train was no kind of express and it was going to take a long time to get there. After the first few hours they settled into the easy, swaying, clackety-clack rhythm and found places among the huge cable rolls to spread out their blankets on the worn bare planking and get some rest. The last of the water was shared out between them. Food was a luxury commodity that would have to wait until their next stop. When that would be was anyone's guess.

All night long the train kept ploughing onwards; then at dawn Ben looked out of the barred window and saw the landscape had completely changed from pleasant green countryside to a barren industrial wasteland with not a tree or a blade of grass in sight. As the morning wore on they passed vast dumps of derelict cars the height of mountains, giant factory chimneys belching smoke and toxic fumes, construction zones as big as small towns where armies of workers looked like swarming insects.

In his anxiety to know just where the hell they were, Ben was tempted to turn on his phone and get a GPS location. But the night before, he and Stefan had talked about the wisdom, or otherwise, of calling Ruth with the latest update of their progress. After the incident with Shi Yun's phone, they'd decided that mobile use was too risky in case they, too, were being

368

monitored. Soon enough, however, as they rumbled by a factory siding with its name emblazoned in giant characters Song was able to inform them that her guess had been right: they'd reached the heavy industrial zone of the central Chinese city of Wuhan. Before too long it would be time to get off the train and find whatever transport they could to carry them on the eastward leg of their journey to the coast.

What might await them once they got there was anyone's guess. But for the first time since the G4 expressway Ben was feeling as if they might actually make it.

Then again, he'd been wrong before.

Chapter 55

When the goods train stopped to refuel and offload some of its cargo at a rail yard sometime before midday, none of the workers milling around happened to notice the four rather dirty and dishevelled-looking stowaways who slipped out of one of the wagons and made their retreat across the wasteland.

The nearest residential area was a former village, one of many no doubt, that had been swallowed up over time by the expanding industrial sprawl around the city of Wuhan. The streets were rimed with pollution from the massive factory chimneys that loomed over the skyline in any given direction and from which spewed a chemical stink so oppressive that it was a wonder the locals could breathe the air and survive, let alone drink the water. Ben and his companions took turns cleaning themselves up as best they could in a public toilet that was only marginally better than the kinds of squat-holes Ben had seen in the worst Third World backwaters. Once that was reasonably well taken care of, lunch of sorts was provided by a takeout joint reminiscent of Wang's place back in Beijing, but without the gastronomic flair. It was also apparently the last business premises in China that was happy to take cash payment.

'Now let's see if we can't find ourselves some wheels,' Ben said.

Quarter of a mile away they came to a motor garage that looked like a cross between a scrapyard and a panel-beating shop. Its sheds were made of corrugated iron, and the wreck of a 1957 Chevrolet Impala sat incongruously outside, along with a selection of less aged bangers in various states of repair, one or two of them for sale. The owner and sole operator of the place was a surly guy with muscled forearms bulging from the rolled-up sleeves of his oily mechanic's overalls and a tatty baseball cap covering his shaven head. After a lot of cagey negotiations he finally let them agree to drive away in one of the bangers, the cheapest and nastiest of those that were actually running, in return for a valuable gold watch. No paperwork, no questions asked, and a full tank of fuel into the bargain. Ironically, the car he was offering them was very similar to the VW Bora that Jia Wenguang had used in Lara's 'kidnapping' – same year, same dubious colour, same amount of rust.

In any case Ben was too busy watching the mechanic to pay much attention to the cosmetic state of the car. While they talked to him, Song interpreting as usual, the guy kept staring at her in a way that made Ben suspect he'd recognised her face like the fat kid at the expressway services. After he'd repeated the same phrase in Chinese several times over, with a peculiar gleam in his eyes, Ben understood that Song was holding back from translating it. 'What's he saying to you?' he asked her.

She sighed. 'He's asking me if he knows me.'

'It's not some kind of inept chat-up line, is it?'

'No. I think he's genuinely thinking he's seen me before. And I think we know where. He's fishing. He knows who I am.'

That was enough for Ben to decide that this guy could be a liability. And they hadn't come all this way to let some idiot bring them down.

'Tell him that everything he's heard about us is true,' he told Song. 'We're a gang of dangerous terrorists on the run, the most wanted criminals in China. We've killed a load of people and if he causes us any trouble we'll come back here and kill him, too. In fact if he's not careful I'm going to lose what little patience I still have with his stupid questions and do it right here, right now. Tell him it'll be extremely violent and unimaginably painful, and when he's dead I'll stuff his dismembered body parts in the boot of that old Chevy and burn this whole place down. But if he behaves, I'll not only let him live but he'll still get to keep the watch.'

Song looked at Ben with a raised eyebrow. 'Are you sure you want me to tell him all that?'

'Exactly word for word.'

Song translated. The guy turned pale and Ben didn't think he'd give them any trouble.

The car might have been in a rough state, but the tyres still had some miles left in them, the electrics all still worked as they should and there was nothing especially noticeable that could draw the eye of a fastidious traffic cop. The mechanic had retreated to the safety of his corrugated shed out of fear of being murdered by the terrorists, so it was left up to Ben to fill the tank from the single petrol pump on the garage forecourt, check oil and fluids and give the car as much of a clean bill of health as his limited expertise would allow. If the old VW only had another nine hundred kilometres to run before it was due for the scrap heap, that was good enough for him.

Nine hundred kilometres equated to about ten hours' driving at a decent pace, maybe a couple of hours longer if they tried to stick to more minor roads for the sake of prudence. The end of the journey was coming tantalisingly close now, and Song was visibly nervous. They circled Wuhan's ring road in heavily congested traffic, crossed over the imposing Yangtze River Bridge, and headed south-eastwards away from the city.

To Ben's relief the traffic thinned out as they steered a course north of Jiujang on the shores of the winding great river, and plunged down through the more remote province of Anhui. The much quieter road took them across bridges and narrow passes through the high ground of the Huangshan Mountains where low clouds drifted just overhead and masked the tall peaks, whose vista now and then opened up to show breathtaking valleys and lakes below.

'Isn't this such a beautiful country, though?' Song reflected with a tear in her eye. 'To think I'm probably never going to see it again.'

'Things might get better again one day,' Ben replied, though they both knew that was unlikely to be the case.

South of Anhui Province, in the late afternoon they bypassed the city of Shangrao nestling at the foot of the mountains, with Poyang Lake to its west. Come evening, after so many hours of constant driving, they stopped at a tiny ethnic village in Yanshan County, which had dirt roads and ancient little houses so barely touched by time that it felt like stepping into some distant bygone century. They did a trade for some fruit and fresh fish from an outdoor stall that was the village's equivalent of an all-day supermarket and whose owner was delighted with the little gold chain they gave her in return for the goods. It seemed that everywhere you went in China, people were secretly happier dealing on the black market than being enslaved to the forces of the new digital economy.

Finding a secluded spot on the bank of the nearby river, they made a camp fire of twigs and dead wood over which Ben skewer-grilled the fish, a kind of freshwater trout that had been caught earlier that day. As they sat cross-legged around the glow of the fire as night fell, the conversation was much more relaxed than before and it was the first time since Ben had known her that he heard Song laugh openly. After their meal Stefan and Lara paddled in the cool moonlit water. It was good to see Lara gradually becoming a little happier, too, after all she'd been through. She talked less and less about Dan and Olivia, although the pain was still very raw. As for Stefan, now that those terrifying days when he'd thought he'd lost his little sister for ever were behind him, he was like a different person.

'Let's rest here for the night,' Song suggested, and it was agreed they'd continue the journey at first light. As the temperature dropped and a cold wind blew down from the mountains they covered themselves with blankets and sipped the last of Chang's whisky to keep warm. Lara went off to sleep in the car.

Come the spectacular dawn that broke behind the faraway peaks and lit the forest treetops the colour of bronze, they were off again. Now it was back to the high roads as they climbed and dropped, climbed and dropped through magnificent scenery, passing strange rock formations, great lakes, temples and monasteries. From there their route took them almost due south again, through yet more mountainous terrain whose craggy summits, the highest ones capped with snow, alternated with heavily wooded rolling hills as they finally crossed into the north-western regions of Fujian Province. In their caution to keep away from main roads they sometimes found themselves travelling along almost impassably rough tracks, and a punctured tyre forced another mid-morning stop in a misty, remote, lake-filled district of Yongtai County where Ben discovered that their spare wheel was almost completely bald. That was also where the car started making ominous grinding noises whenever he changed gear, which was becoming gradually harder to do. By now they were only an hour's drive or so from the coast, and he quietly prayed the old Volkswagen would last just a little longer.

The carefully-avoided city of Putian, of around three million inhabitants, was the last major population centre they skirted around before they finally reached the coast and had their first heart-lifting glimpse of the sparkling ocean, then started threading their way down the province's eastern shoreline. 'We made it,' Stefan said, grinning.

'We're still in China,' Ben reminded him.

'You worry too much, brother,' Stefan replied, and maybe it was true. But all the same, Ben would hold back his celebratory mood until they were safely across the water in Taiwan.

This side of the water, their final destination was the fishing port of Dongpu, which they reached late that morning. Clustered all up and down the coastline either side of it were various smaller villages each with their own jetties and harbours filled with boats of all shapes and sizes and a great deal of maritime traffic going on. Though something larger and more robust than a rubber dinghy was definitely preferable for their purposes, Ben's opinion was that they should try to seek out the smallest and most modest vessel that could accommodate four people in reasonable comfort. For that reason, and to steer clear of too many prying eyes, he settled for the tiniest of the fishing villages they passed by, and drove down the dirt road to the harbour to investigate their options.

'What do you think?' Stefan asked from the back seat as they sat in the car surveying the little harbour. Even from back here they could smell the tang of fish, oil and diesel fuel.

Ben might have answered, 'I think I've never seen anything so dismal in my life,' but he kept his mouth shut. The main harbour jetty was a dilapidated mess of ancient half-rotted wooden planking, old pallets and assorted bits and pieces of lumber all nailed together pell mell and so infirm that the whole haphazard construction swayed gently from side to side with the force of the tide. The scummy bluish-green waters of the China Sea lapped and gurgled around the ancient posts supporting it above the surface. Of all the scores of fishing boats moored along its sides, most looked as if they'd sink before they even got out of the harbour, let alone had to weather the open sea. The typical design seemed to be a long, narrow flat-bottomed vessel, usually with a steel hull half eaten away with rust and a ramshackle wooden wheelhouse extended the length of the deck by an arched canopy of salt-encrusted canvas or corroded tin sheets. Any remaining space on deck was generally crammed with heaps of uncoiled rope, netting, dirty old fuel drums and assorted rubbish.

'Well, they seem to be able to float okay,' Song said, trying to sound optimistic. 'That's the main thing.'

'Let's take a closer look,' Stefan suggested. 'Something might be for sale.'

Nothing was, though, and as they walked out onto the swaying, creaking jetty, careful where they stepped in case they fell through the many gaps into the water, up close the boats looked so shambolic and unseaworthy that Ben was on the verge of saying, 'Let's go back to the main port and try there.' But Song was on a roll, and not to be outdone she made a line for the first fisherman they spotted. He was a work-hardened and leathery-looking fellow who looked as if he must have spent most of his life at sea, pottering about his deck with a scraggy dog following at his heels. He stopped what he was doing and stared at the four strangers as they approached.

'I'm going to ask him if he'd like to sell us his boat,' Song said. 'What do we have left to trade?'

'About twenty thousand dollars' worth of gold watch and a handful of loose diamonds that probably cost ten times as much,' Ben said. 'But he doesn't look to me as if he'll go for it.'

'Still, I have to try,' she replied. She approached the stern of the moored boat, shielded her eyes from the glare of the sun, and they watched and listened as she made her polite enquiry. As Ben had intuitively sensed, it was met by a flat, hostile refusal followed by a tirade of abuse. Giving up, she made a dismissive gesture and walked back to rejoin them. 'Says who the hell do we think we are and how's he supposed to make an honest living without this boat? Then he said some other things I won't repeat.'

Maybe a rubber dinghy was going to be their best option, after all. 'There's nobody else around,' Stefan said, scanning the harbour. 'Let's try our luck further along the coast.'

They were walking back towards the car when Ben saw the cripple.

Chapter 56

That wasn't a term Ben would generally have stooped to using to describe a person with a disability, unlike his friend Jeff who didn't have such scruples. But this poor man wasn't merely disabled, or infirm, or suffering from mobility issues. He was *crippled*, and as rough as it sounded that was the only word for it. Where he'd come from was unclear, but it must have taken him a long time to drag himself as far as the harbour. He was making his jerky, hesitant way along the smaller of the jetties on two makeshift crutches that just weren't enough to support his meagre weight on his badly twisted legs, while his spine was so distorted out of shape that he couldn't have stood more than four feet tall.

Halting by one of the moored boats, the pathetic figure propped one crutch against its bobbing stern, then the other; then, supporting himself on the deck railing with his useless legs giving way under him, he tried to clamber aboard, failed, fell back down and came dangerously close to slipping off the edge of the jetty and being crushed between its side and the hull of his own boat.

'Wait there,' Ben said to the others, and ran along the clattering walkway to help the poor guy out. He bent down to grab him under the arms and hauled him upright. He didn't weigh much more than the tatty, threadbare clothes he was wearing. Ben helped him over the side, got him sitting safely on an upturned crate on deck and brought his crutches aboard. The man had the face of a seventy-year-old but his body seemed three times older. Ben wondered what his ailment could be: the result of some serious accident, maybe, or a terrible wasting disease. Either way it wasn't doing him any good, or his livelihood either. He clearly hadn't had a good meal in a while.

'Are you okay?' Ben asked. The man seemed to understand his meaning, and made a despondent shrug as if to reply, 'What does it look like to you?'

Song and the others had caught up. She spoke to the disabled sailor in Chinese, and he replied in a long stream that sounded pretty bitter. 'He says he wishes you'd let him drown,' she told Ben.

'Oh, he can't mean that,' Lara said, frowning in sympathy.

'Says he used to love this boat but now he hates it. Can't even look after it any more, let alone sail it.'

Ben and Stefan exchanged glances.

'Are you thinking what I'm thinking?' Ben said.

Their idea appealed instantly to the poor fisherman, whose face lit up in joy at the prospect of exchanging his old boat for the riches on offer. 'Wait until I tell Deng.' Deng, as it turned out, was his elder brother with whom he lived in one of the streets back there behind the harbour. From the way he talked it seemed that Deng ruled the roost. Deng also had a friend who ran a nearby pawn shop. 'Then you'll be rich,' Song said, smiling.

'Yes! Rich!' the fisherman replied, and rocked with laughter at the very thought of his imminent retirement and a life of relative luxury, for as long as the money lasted. He didn't seem in any way curious about Song, certainly didn't recognise her as one of the infamous fugitives from Beijing whose escape was splashed all over the state media. He'd probably been too busy trying to scratch a subsistence living all these years to ever watch TV or follow the news, Ben thought.

When the exchange had been made and the fisherman limped off as hurriedly as he could to tell his brother about the sudden wealth that had come their way, Ben turned his attention to the boat. Underneath all the old car tyres lashed to its sides as bumpers, the thirty-foot steel hull was so eaten away with rust that it was probably only a millimetre thick in places. The deck was badly warped, the awning from the wheel-house was more patches than original canvas and the compartment housing the apparently pre-war inboard diesel engine was black with oil. There was no cabin space below, no heads, no galley. The vessel was basic in the extreme – but, as Song had said, the main thing was that it appeared to float well enough; and all it needed to do was carry them the hundred and thirty or so kilometres across the strait to Taiwan's western shores. After that, it could sink to the bottom.

'Are we ready, shipmates?' said Stefan, in a jocular mood now that the end of their journey was in sight.

'I hope I'm not going to be seasick,' Lara muttered. As though that was the worst thing that could happen on the sea crossing. Then something even more worrying occurred to her and she asked, 'Are there sharks in this ocean?'

'Oh yes,' Stefan assured her with a broad grin. 'All kinds. Hammerheads and tiger sharks and great whites, waiting to snap us up.'

'You're teasing me. Song, tell me he's just teasing me.'

'How do I know what kind of sharks there are?' Song replied irritably. 'I'm not planning on going in the water anyhow.'

While they were bickering Ben was sloshing the contents of a fuel drum into the tank through a hatch on deck. He reckoned they were carrying about a hundred gallons with a few spare drums in reserve, which should easily be enough for their short voyage. *Here goes*, he thought. In the wheelhouse he thumbed the well-worn starter, and after a few asthmatic coughs the diesel rasped enthusiastically into life in a cloud of black smoke.

Stefan cast off their mooring ropes fore and aft and shouted, 'All clear!' The propellers burbled and churned as Ben eased the vessel out of its narrow space, bumping tyres with its closely-moored neighbours. Then they were chugging away through the harbour waters towards the mouth of the bay. It wasn't long past midday and the sun was shining, the sky was clear and blue and the broad horizon of the South China Sea in front of them was as smooth and flat as a mill pond.

Taiwan was just a few hours away. And freedom.

The bay and the inshore waters along the coast were teeming with fishing traffic, consisting mostly of local small boats that stayed within a short range while only the larger commercial trawlers ventured far out to sea. Stefan had piloted his uncle's boat on Lake Thun as a kid and insisted on taking the controls, steering the vessel one-handed while Ben and Song climbed up the rusty ladder to the top of the wheelhouse, which was surrounded by a railing and offered a better all-around view than the deck below.

Song closed her eyes and drank in the sea breeze. 'I'm so happy to be free,' she sighed. Turning around to look back, she gazed for what might be the last time at her native country. 'I'm going to miss the place, though,' she said. 'I've lived there all my life.'

'I'm going to miss one thing about it,' Ben said, partly to himself. He already was.

'I would never have taken a man like you for a big romantic,' she said with a warm smile. 'But you are, really.'

'Never been called that before,' he replied. 'A big fool, maybe. I'd agree.'

They hadn't been sailing more than a few short miles when Lara, who'd wandered to the far end of the bow to lean on the railing there and gaze out to sea with her long hair streaming in the wind, let out a shout and pointed out to sea. 'I see land! Are we there already?'

'No, that's just the Kinmen Islands,' Song called down to her from the top of the wheelhouse. Those had been the topic of earlier discussion, due to their being officially governed by Taiwan and therefore offering a much closer potential landing for the Steiner jet to come and pick them up. But Song had warned them off the idea, because the Chinese government staunchly insisted on regarding the islands as part of Fujian Province. 'Things could get nasty' had been her wise advice.

It wasn't until a long while later, with the coast of China receding far behind them, that the hazy shape of another land mass gradually began to appear over the distant horizon ahead. This time, it was Song's turn to let out an excited whoop. 'There it is!'

Ben was about to speak when something else caught his eye. He turned to look back at the boat's wake, and then beyond to the broadening expanse of calm waters they'd just crossed. That was when his heart sank and his jaw tightened.

Because the beautiful stretch of open green-blue sea between them and China that last time he'd looked had been so empty, such a tribute to the success of their escape, was now filled with the purposeful white shapes of two Chinese navy warships. They were still half a mile back but coming up fast.

And they were headed straight for them.

Chapter 57

Ben knew that if he'd been able to see the sides of their hulls, each of the two warships would be marked CHINA COAST GUARD in big black letters. And that if he'd had a bird's eye view of their decks and superstructure, he'd see they were bristling with heavy weaponry.

He wasn't quite as much of a naval expert as his ex-Special Boat Service friend Jeff, but from this distance he was pretty sure that the ships were of the 056 Corvette class used as patrol cutters by the CCG, displacing 1500 tons, ninety metres long and carrying some eighty-odd crew with a top speed of about twenty-five knots. Designed more for short-range green-water escort or protection missions than for major combat operations, they nonetheless packed a formidable punch with their 76mm naval guns as main armament, backed up by 30mm autocannons mounted in pairs and capable of discharging armour-piercing or incendiary rounds at a fearsome rate of fire. As if that weren't enough, each corvette was additionally equipped with four powerful anti-ship missiles designed to take out anything up to a medium-sized military vessel, eight surface-to-air rockets to deal with enemy jets and helicopters, and a pair of triple-tube torpedo launchers equally capable of sinking hostile ships or submarines.

In short, the occupants of the tiny, fragile, slow and extremely vulnerable fishing boat were in some serious trouble. All Ben had by way of weaponry was the Browning pistol he'd brought from the safehouse, with about half a magazine's worth of ammunition left.

He tapped Song on the shoulder and pointed out the fast-approaching corvettes. 'It's not over yet.'

She gaped. 'Didn't I tell you it was too easy?'

They ran down the ladder to join Stefan in the wheelhouse. He'd been too busy piloting the boat to notice they were about to have company, and he turned pale at the sight of the Chinese ships. 'How the hell did they find us?'

'I can't believe that poor fisherman would have reported us, would he?' asked Lara, who'd come running back in alarm from the bow.

Ben shook his head. 'No, but maybe Deng did, once he'd figured out who his brother had traded the boat to. Looking to claim a nice reward, I reckon.'

'Whatever the reason, they're onto us.'

'How do we know that?' Lara said, fighting her panic. 'They might not be.'

'That's no routine patrol,' Ben replied as he watched the corvettes. 'They're headed right for us.'

'Which means we're sunk,' Stefan groaned. 'Dead in the water. Or headed for jail.'

'I'll jump in with the sharks first,' Song said resolutely.

'They haven't caught us yet,' Ben said. 'And we're not going to let them, if we can help it. Let me take the wheel, Stefan.'

There was little hope of the underpowered fishing tub, with its ancient thumper diesel, outrunning a pair of fast modern cutters, but Ben was damned if he wasn't at least going to give it a go. He jammed the throttle on maximum power and the little boat responded with surprising enthusiasm. The engine note rose a semitone in pitch, white water churning at the stern, and the boat's blunt nose split the surface and sent up a modest bow wave that sprayed up to lash the deck. The canvas awning fluttered crackling in the wind. How long the ancient diesel would stand being gunned full throttle, Ben had no idea. But they were suddenly moving much faster and that could only be a good thing.

'We're losing them!' Lara shouted excitedly.

But a rearward glance at their pursuers told Ben that was just wishful thinking on her part. The powerful corvettes could overhaul them without the least effort. And they were still coming on fast, closing in with every passing minute. He gritted his teeth and leaned harder on the throttle, trying to milk every last drop of power from the little boat. The engine note had risen another quarter tone and sounded harsh and straining. The smoke from their exhausts had thickened to a dark billow that was whipped away by the wind.

'You're going to blow it up!' Stefan yelled over the noise.

'I know,' Ben said. But he kept up the pressure on the throttle. The dark, hazy land mass that was the island of Taiwan was closer now, but still very far away. Meanwhile the advancing corvettes were less than quarter of a mile behind and the distance was constantly shortening. 'Dump everything over the side,' he ordered the others. 'Fuel drums, water barrels, anything that isn't bolted to the deck. Hurry!'

Stefan, Lara and Song ran from the wheelhouse and started pitching whatever they could into the sea, to help lighten the load and encourage the boat to go faster. One after the other the heavy spare fuel drums hit the water with a splash, followed by a whole collection of miscellaneous deck clutter. If it had any effect on their rate of knots, it was so slight as to be barely noticeable.

Ben looked up at the canvas awning, fifteen feet of patched sailcloth flapping madly above them and stealing precious momentum by catching the wind. Anything that could be done, had to be done. And done without an instant's hesitation, if they were to have the slightest chance of getting out of this.

There was an old hatchet lying in the wheelhouse, for cutting lines or tangled netting. He snatched it up and tossed it to Song, pointing up and yelling, 'Cut it loose!' She nodded and instantly set about hacking at the ropes holding the canvas in place at its corners, helped by Lara who'd found a rusty knife. The two of them were staggering on the pitching deck, soaked by spray from the bow wave. The canvas came partly loose, its free end streaming in the wind; then as Song sliced away the last rope it flapped away into their wake and was lost in the white foam.

Now the boat was as streamlined as they could make it without demolishing the wheelhouse. But the increase in speed was still negligible – in fact, they seemed to have lost momentum. Ben looked down at the instruments and saw with a skip in his heartbeat that their engine revs had come down by a fraction. Then a fraction more, the counter needle slowly sinking along with the dwindling engine note. The smoke billowing out behind them was turning blacker and thicker. The engine wasn't going to hold out much longer under this kind of load.

'They're still gaining on us!' yelled Stefan. As if Ben hadn't known that very well already. He looked around him, racking his brain for anything he could do. Nothing was coming to him. The situation was desperate.

Then it got worse. There was a flash from one of the corvettes, and with a puff of smoke and a streak of flaming tail exhaust an anti-ship missile launched upwards from its deck. The rocket arced through the sky, then dived down in a long parabola, altered course and came skimming over the water. Now it was clear: the corvette commander wasn't interested in overhauling the fishing boat and arresting its occupants. He was under orders to sink and destroy them.

One direct hit from a high-explosive missile would blow them out of the water and kill everyone aboard. Ben could only pray that the weapon system wasn't fitted with active radar homing, because if it was there would be no possibility of evading it. As the missile streaked towards them with a terrifying whoosh he held back until the last moment and then jammed the wheel hard over all the way. Again the little boat responded enthusiastically and the deck leaned at an acute angle as they heeled to port.

But still it was close. Very close. The missile shaved by their starboard side, impacted against the sea and exploded in a ripping blast whose shockwave violently rocked the small boat from stem to stern and hurled a crashing torrent of water across the deck. For an instant Ben thought it was going to roll them right over and capsize them. Lara screamed and would have gone tumbling across the deck if her brother hadn't saved her from falling. Song was hanging for dear life on to the side of the wheelhouse. But then the deck somehow managed to right itself under their feet and they were through.

Ben pressed grimly on. One missile gone; only another seven to go. That was without counting the torpedoes, main guns and machine cannon that would pulverise them the moment they were within range. Which could be any moment now, unless he could think of something.

Too late. Another flash from the second corvette, another streak of tail fire and the second missile was hurtling towards them. Again Ben waited until the last moment, then spun the wheel as hard and fast as he could, this time to starboard, and the boat heeled over so tightly that he had to plant his feet wide and wedge his back against the wheelhouse bulkhead to stay upright. Again, the missile flashed by them with just feet to spare and tore up the sea with a shattering explosion that threatened to tear them apart.

. . . Still alive, but for how much longer? Nobody could have that kind of luck more than twice. The bows of the corvettes were looming closer and closer. Just a hundred and fifty metres and closing. Now the machine cannon would open fire on them for sure. Ben braced himself for the final, devastating salvo that would reduce the boat to floating bits of burning wreckage and its four passengers to mincemeat.

Fine, he thought. He'd lived most of his life in the knowledge that, one day, sooner or later, this was what it would come to. He accepted it now, just as he always had. But he wasn't about to die without offering the bastards a fight, for whatever that was worth.

Ducking out of the wheelhouse he pulled the Browning from his belt, steadied his aim on the swaying, pitching deck and squeezed off four shots at the warships. The reports were like popping corks after the ear-splitting missile blasts. A 9mm pistol round would bounce as harmlessly off those massive iron hulls as a child's toy spring gun against the hide of a charging elephant. It was useless. Pointless. Little more than a gesture of defiance. But he squeezed off the rest of the magazine anyway, firing as fast as he could work the trigger. Maybe one of his bullets would find its way, leave some kind of impression.

Most likely not. And it wouldn't change the outcome, either way.

They were dead.

'Oh my God!' Stefan suddenly shouted. 'There's another one!'

Chapter 58

Ben spun around, looked where Stefan was pointing in horror and saw the enormous slate-grey hull of the battleship that was bearing down on their western side, no more than two hundred metres away. In the chaos of the moment, it seemed to have appeared from thin air.

And now they were truly finished, because a third Chinese warship in the game instantly reduced their already minimal chance of survival to less than zero.

Or not.

Because as he looked up at the huge vessel, half blinded by the salt spray from that second explosion, Ben realised with a jolt that from the jackstaff at her bow she was flying a dark blue flag marked by fifty white stars.

Not the colours of the China Coast Guard. Still less those of the People's Republic. It was the Union Jack ensign of the US Navy.

And coming up fast behind the American warship was a fourth, vastly larger vessel. A full-blown Nimitz-class United States aircraft carrier, all hundred-thousand nuclear-powered tons of her, as she was escorted on routine patrol through the Taiwan Strait by the destroyer whose officers had first noticed the highly unusual sight of two CCG corvettes attacking a tiny unarmed cockleshell of a fishing boat – this in a stretch of sea that was considered international waters by all governments except that of China.

With death in his heart, Ben grabbed the wheel and steered right for the destroyer. He had no form of distress signal to draw their attention. All his hopes now were on their commander having realised what was happening. Even then it could already be too late.

Almost touching their wake, the two Chinese corvettes came on like a pair of greyhounds chasing a hare. A very slow, wounded hare. With a last cough, a splutter and then a terminal-sounding bang and a dense cloud of black smoke the fishing boat's over-heated engine finally reached the limit of its endurance and seized solid. Ben and the others were thrown forwards as the vessel suddenly lost all thrust and went dead in the water. The smoke poured dense and choking from its engine bay, drifting over the deck and blotting the American ships from view.

They were sitting ducks. If they abandoned ship and swam for it, they'd have almost no chance of escape. None at all if they remained aboard the drifting, powerless vessel. Now the corvettes finally let rip with their machine cannon, tearing the surface of the sea into a flurry of white water and slamming rounds into their deck and hull, chewing everything in their sights to tiny pieces. But at the same moment a change in the direction of the wind masked the stricken fishing boat in its own thick black smoke, and the Chinese gunners no longer had a precise target to aim for.

The American destroyer was closing rapidly on the scene, leaving the slower-moving giant aircraft carrier far back in its wake. The destroyer's siren was sounding and lights flashing as a warning to the Chinese ships, but they kept on pouring intense fire into the smoking wreck of the fishing boat that was now beginning to break up and settle lower and lower in the water.

Then came a screeching shriek as the two F35 Lightning stealth fighter jets hurriedly scrambled from the carrier's flight deck came streaking low over the sea, closed the distance in a matter of seconds and made a pass over the corvettes, then banked around in perfectly-synchronised twin arcs and came back for another. At the same moment the US warship would be radioing the corvette commanders and their coastal base to tell them in no uncertain terms to stand the hell down, or face the consequences.

The corvettes' guns fell silent but they kept bearing down on the sinking fishing boat and for a few moments it seemed as though they were going to reopen fire. Then, as the Chinese obviously decided that heeding the warship's stark warning might be preferable to getting blown out of the sea and held responsible for sparking a major incident in disputed waters, they slowly turned about and started back towards the distant coast. The Lightnings did two more low overpasses to ram home their message, then screeched off and returned to the carrier. In the meantime, the destroyer was already lowering a pair of rigid inflatable rescue craft piloted by United States Marines, which came surging and bouncing at high speed over the water.

And it was only as they drew up alongside the burning, smoking wreck of the fishing boat, with weapons at the ready and no idea what they were about to find, that they heard the sound of whooping and laughter.

Less than twenty minutes after the Marines picked them out of the water, Ben, Stefan, Lara and Song found themselves aboard the main deck of Navy warship USS *George McClellan*. They were met there by its silver-haired commander, Captain Nathan B. Forrest, and a group of his senior officers who were no less astonished at how lucky all four dripping survivors had been to escape without a scratch. It was to their even greater amazement that Ben told them his name, military rank and unit, before giving his account of why they'd been on the boat and the Chinese authorities were attempting to kill them.

The naval officer called Greeves who'd been noting all this down hurried off to verify Ben's credentials. He was soon back again, and he and the captain spent a few moments conferring.

Captain Forrest had a deeply tanned, heavily lined face that bore the natural authority of a man long in command, but now he looked somewhat bewildered as he finally turned back to speak to Ben.

'Well,' he began sternly in his southern twang, Kentucky or Tennessee, 'I have to say that in all my forty years' service with the United States Navy I've seen some pretty strange things. Done a few, too. But I've never come across anything quite as frankly bizarre as this story you're telling me.'

'Thank you, Captain,' Ben said.

Forrest paused, his steel-grey eyes locked onto Ben's. 'Let me be clear,' he continued, 'the China Coast Guard authorities are perfectly within their rights to fire on any potentially hostile or suspicious vessel that ignores their warning to steer clear of what they consider to be their sovereign waters. However, it would seem to me to be self-evident that they do *not* have the authority to sink a civilian vessel, much less one containing foreign nationals, sailing in what *we* consider to be international waters.'

'It would seem that way to me, too.'

Forrest made a dry smile. 'Unfortunately our countries don't entirely agree on what's what, in that regard. But whatever the case may be, it appears that your credentials check out, Major Hope. And having no wish to get myself or my ship embroiled in some kind of half-assed British Special Forces operation, official or otherwise, it appears to me I have no option but to take you at your word and land the four of you in Taiwan as requested. Hell, you were already nearly halfway there. But be warned, I'm sticking my neck out for you people.'

'It's highly appreciated, Captain.'

Chapter 59

Two days later

Some homecomings were joyful affairs, full of laughter and celebration. Others in Ben's experience had been marked by tragedy and heartbreak. This one was both of those things.

He hadn't expected Ruth to be on the plane that landed at Taiwan Taoyuan International Airport to bring them back to Europe, but she was the first person who greeted them on the tarmac and it was an emotional reunion between her, Stefan and Lara. Ben was the last to be hugged by his tearful sister, but he was hugged the longest. 'I don't know how I can ever thank you.'

There was much more of the same over the next two days, as Lara finally arrived back in Switzerland and was surrounded by everyone she'd ever known, as well as a few she hadn't. Her parents Leni and Conrad had aged ten years in a matter of days, and the safe return of their beloved daughter was like getting their life back. Silvia and Maximilian rolled out the red carpet and laid on a lavish fanfare for the hero who'd saved the day. But as always in these highly-charged situations, there was a limit to how much praise and gratitude the hero himself could handle and he tended to stay on the periphery, saying little beyond what was polite, just happy that they were happy. He had a lot of other things on his mind.

For others, life had changed for ever. The Keller family had suffered a loss that would never go away, having to come to terms with the fact that they might never know who had killed their daughter and now faced the bureaucratic ordeal of trying to bring her body home from China so they could at least have closure. Lara had promised she would do anything to help, and she'd be devoting a lot of time to supporting the grieving family over the next few months. She had her own personal grief to deal with, too. The memory of Dan Chen, the short-lived happiness they'd shared, would stay with her until her dying day.

Meanwhile it was a sombre period for the Steiner office's employees in Beijing, where the irreplaceable and much loved Sammy Tsang was deeply mourned by all who'd worked with him – even if the circumstances of his death weren't fully explained by the official account. Ruth was unable to attend the funeral in person but delivered a moving eulogy via satellite video hookup.

As for Song Yuxuan, the last time Ben would ever see her was at Zurich Airport the same day they'd all arrived. The Steiner plane was taking her directly from there to New York, where she'd be met by a group of the Falun Gong contacts she'd made back in China. 'So here I am, about to start my new life,' she said with a nervous smile as they parted ways. 'Wish me luck.'

'No need to,' Ben replied. 'You're going to be fine.'

'I hate goodbyes.'

'Then don't say it,' he said. 'Take care, Song.' They shook hands, and a short while later she was in the air. Heading towards her future while Ben went off in search of his own.

The question still remained what that future would be. He hadn't been long back in Switzerland when the inevitable moment came, as he and Ruth were walking alone in the grounds of the Steiner estate and she asked him, 'Well, big brother, have you decided yet whether to hang on to that job I offered you?'

To leave Le Val and his friends there, and strike out on a whole new path. It felt like closing the book on everything he'd ever done, everything he'd known. Part of him was ready for change; yet another part was as daunted by it as a child afraid of the darkness.

'I don't know yet,' he told her. 'I need more time to think about it.'

'Take all the time you need, Ben. You've earned it.'

That afternoon he took the cable car back up the mountain and climbed to the same high ridge from which he'd seen the eagle. 'There you are,' he murmured, gazing up with a smile as the great bird appeared and circled far above him in the clear blue sky. It was as if nothing had changed, as if the two lonely predators had been here together in this remote place all along. Lords of the air, masters of their own destiny, answerable to no one.

And maybe nothing had really changed, Ben thought. Maybe for him, nothing really ever could.

It was as he was pondering that imponderable question that, to his surprise, his phone went. Cupping it against his ear to screen out the whistle of the mountain wind, he heard the familiar voice on the line.

'Hey, mate, where are you?'

Jeff sounded as if nothing much had changed for him, either.

'I'm back in Europe,' Ben replied, knowing that his friend would never ask him how things had gone on his travels. If Ben wanted to talk about it, they'd talk. If not, it didn't matter. That was Jeff.

'Well, when you manage to get your arse back to base, there's something I want to run by you. Remember a while back, we talked about expanding the business, building a new premises and all that? A bit of land's come up for sale that I reckon would fit the bill just perfect.'

'Where?'

'I'll tell you when you get here,' Jeff answered. That was Jeff, too.

'I'm on my way,' Ben said.

EPILOGUE

When he came to in the hospital bed, at first he could remember nothing. Where he'd been, how he'd got here, were a mystery like some forgotten dream. Even his name; it took a while for the memory to percolate back into his mind that he was Zhao Hu Ping, chief of police.

'You're awake,' the doctor said soon after.

'What happened to me?' Chief Zhao asked him. 'Where am I?'

The doctor told him that he'd been found wandering in the countryside twenty miles from Beijing. Which was where they'd brought him and where he'd been in something like a coma for the last three days. Though quite what had caused it, or his strange memory lapse, was baffling medically. They were curious about that odd little mark on his neck, too. It wasn't a bruise as such, nor a burn. Nor a birthmark either, as they'd originally thought. Very unusual. They'd never come across anything quite like it before.

'Who cares? I need to get out of here.' Zhao started climbing out of the bed. When the doctor tried to stop him, he said, 'Don't be ridiculous. I'm recovered now. And I've never felt better in my life.'

It was true that he felt full of energy, as though he were suddenly twenty years younger and firing on all cylinders. As the rest of his memory quickly returned, he remembered the treachery of Chang Han Yu, as well as that little bitch of a detective Shi Yun

Lin. Only he knew about their crimes. Only he could see to it that they'd get what they had coming to them.

'Where's my phone?' he asked a nurse as he threw on his clothes.

'You didn't have one on you when you were found,' she replied. 'No identification either. We didn't know who you were.'

'Never mind,' he snapped. 'Have a car sent to take me to the nearest police prefecture. I have important business to take care of.'

As the car drove him through Beijing, he was thinking with pleasure about the fate he was about to arrange for the traitors. He'd personally ensure that Shi Yun Lin was sent to the harshest and most squalid forced labour camp in China, there to spend the rest of her short and very uncomfortable life. As for that mangy bastard Chang Han Yu . . . Zhao smiled to himself, then scratched at the little red spot on his neck. It was maddeningly itchy and there was a burning pain in it as well, which seemed to be getting suddenly more intense.

But never mind it for now. It was just an insect bite or something. What did doctors know?

The local police chief stepped out to greet him on his arrival at the police prefecture. 'Chief Zhao, welcome to Beijing. What brings you here?'

'I have important information on major crimes committed by a prominent Chinese citizen and a serving officer of the Xi'an police force,' he replied. 'It's urgent that I contact my headquarters immediately.'

'That sounds very serious,' said the Beijing chief.

'It certainly is. And it also has to do with the escaped fugitive from the Daxing women's prison.'

'Then please step into my office.'

Zhao was led upstairs and took a seat, impatient to get the ball rolling. His neck was hurting much worse and his head had

400

started spinning. He felt nauseous. Was it the effect of some drug they'd given him at the hospital? Was he just weak with hunger?

'Now, this information,' said the Beijing chief, sitting expectantly at his desk with a pen poised over a pad. 'Can I start by taking some names from you?'

Zhao opened his mouth to say more, but the only sound that came out was 'I . . . urgh . . . graaaa . . .'

The Beijing chief looked at his colleague a little strangely, then repeated patiently, 'You said you had information on two serious criminals. Their names, Chief Zhao?'

Zhao was suddenly burning up all over. He couldn't speak. The pain coming from that spot on his neck was intensifying more and more, filling every part of him. He tried to loosen his shirt collar to get at it but now he felt he could no longer move his fingers properly.

'Chief Zhao!' said the Beijing chief, rising from his chair in alarm. 'Are you all right?'

Zhao's tongue lolled out as he struggled to utter a few more garbled words. His body went totally rigid.

And then his heart exploded.

AUTHOR'S NOTE

Once again I have to beg pardon for having exercised some artistic licence in writing this novel, notably in my attempt to tackle the task of setting the narrative in China, a land so vast and diverse, so historically and culturally rich, that it's virtually impossible (at least for me) to encompass adequately in a book like this. Those who know China well might be able to spot that I've taken a few liberties with the geographical detail of the country: not having had the privilege of travelling there in person to follow the routes taken by Ben and company in the novel, I was sometimes compelled to resort to my imagination. Some locations featured are real, others are purely fictitious, and others again have been adapted to the purpose of the story. However I hope I was reasonably successful at conveying an authentic enough impression – call it Scott's rendition of China, if not quite the real thing. And I hate to disappoint readers by admitting that the golden library itself doesn't really exist . . . or does it?

What is entirely real, perhaps to the surprise of some readers, is the little-known Eastern martial art of Dim Mak, the infamous 'death touch', as practised by the character of Sifu T'ao on Ben Hope and Chief Zhao (the latter with somewhat more lasting consequences). The idea that a well-placed and initially seemingly harmless touch, inflicted by a highly trained practitioner on a specific part of the body, can trigger off a catastrophic chain of events leading to death, may seem like the stuff of fantasy – and perhaps understandably there is little verifiable information available on this subject – but it appears to be a genuine phenomenon. My own meagre learning of this mysterious craft I owe to my good friend Matt Berry, an expert teacher of the ancient Chinese arts of Tai Chi and Qi Gong, as well as a master of numerous Oriental combat techniques. Matt is based in Pembrokeshire, UK, and runs West Wales Tai Chi, which readers may want to check out. I had the pleasure of inviting Matt to my house to demonstrate the Dim Mak touches used in the book, using his son Cody (himself an accomplished martial artist) as the willing victim. Nobody's heart exploded . . . but all the same I don't recommend trying this at home!

Also real, tragically, is the unspeakable horror of the persecution inflicted by the Chinese authorities – for the sake of diplomacy we should perhaps say elements of the Chinese authorities – against the peaceful followers of the healing discipline of Falun Gong since the end of the twentieth century. If anything, I have understated the appalling atrocities committed against these innocent people, which are well documented but strangely little commented on in the western media, with the notable exception of the international newspaper *The Epoch Times* which has run numerous articles drawing attention to this crime against humanity. For those wishing to learn more about the heartbreaking plight of the Falun Gong followers, the official English version of the short documentary *The Persecution of Falun Gong* can be viewed on YouTube. Beware, as the film does feature a few disturbing images.

I hope that you enjoyed reading THE GOLDEN LIBRARY. Ben Hope will be back . . .

For more unmissable reads,
sign up to the HarperNorth newsletter at
www.harpernorth.co.uk

or find us on Twitter at
@HarperNorthUK

**Harper
North**